Across the Years

DESERT ROSES

Across
THE
Years

TRACIE PETERSON

Across the Years
Copyright © 2003
Tracie Peterson

Cover design by Koechel Peterson & Associates

Published by Bethany House Publishers
A Ministry of Bethany Fellowship International
11400 Hampshire Avenue South
Bloomington, Minnesota 55438
www.bethanyhouse.com

Printed in the United States of America by
Bethany Press International, Bloomington, Minnesota 55438

Library of Congress Cataloging-in-Publication Data

Peterson, Tracie.
    Across the years / by Tracie Peterson.
        p.   cm. — (Desert roses)
    ISBN 0-7642-2518-9
    1. Hotels—Employees—Fiction. 2. Widows—Fiction. 3. Arizona—
Fiction. I. Title.
PS3566.E7717 A66   2003
813'.54—dc21

                                    2002015796

To my dear friend Ramona Kelly
who has been with me across the years—
encouraging, supporting, loving me
through all the good and bad.
You are a blessing to me from God
and I cherish you.

Books by Tracie Peterson

www.traciepeterson.com

Controlling Interests
Entangled • *Framed*
The Long-Awaited Child
A Slender Thread • *Tidings of Peace*

THE BELLS OF LOWELL*
Daughter of the Loom

DESERT ROSES
Shadows of the Canyon
Across the Years

WESTWARD CHRONICLES
A Shelter of Hope • *Hidden in a Whisper*
A Veiled Reflection

RIBBONS OF STEEL†
Distant Dreams • *A Hope Beyond*
A Promise for Tomorrow

RIBBONS WEST†
Westward the Dream • *Separate Roads*
Ties That Bind

SHANNON SAGA‡
City of Angels • *Angels Flight*
Angel of Mercy

YUKON QUEST
Treasures of the North • *Ashes and Ice*
Rivers of Gold

NONFICTION
The Eyes of the Heart

*with Judith Miller   †with Judith Pella   ‡with James Scott Bell

CHAPTER ONE

Winslow, Arizona, September 1929

"Ma'am, my train leaves in less than ten minutes," an irritated passenger complained.

Ashley Reynolds pulled a slip of paper from her apron and handed it to the man. "Sir, there's plenty of time. Here's the check, and I'll have those sandwiches ready for you to take momentarily." She sighed. The life of a Harvey Girl was not all it was cracked up to be. Especially when working the lunchroom counter. Ashley much preferred her regular duties in the dining room. It always seemed the lunchroom counters of Fred Harvey's restaurants were frantic-paced battle-grounds where a girl's only weapons were her charm and quick wit.

In another hour it was all behind her—at least the work was behind her. The worst was yet to come. With feelings of trepidation, Ashley finished straightening her station and headed to the back room.

"Are you going home?" one of her co-workers questioned.

Ashley didn't feel like chatting. "Yes," she answered in a rather curt manner. "See you tomorrow." But even

as she said the words, Ashley realized that wasn't true. She wouldn't be back to work tomorrow or the day after. Maybe never.

Turning in her resignation was the hardest thing Ashley had ever done. After working nearly ten years for the Harvey Company, Ashley was quite comfortable in her routine. Now everything was changing—and not for the better.

A hot desert wind whipped across Ashley's skirt as she made her way home from work. Worn and perspiring from her long hours waiting on customers, the dry breeze created the tiniest sensation of cooling, and Ashley cherished it. A weariness unlike any she'd ever known, however, sapped all remaining strength. How was she ever to find solace when she would soon become the bearer of such bad tidings?

Walking past the construction of the new Harvey hotel resort, Ashley couldn't help wondering if the throngs of tourists would come as they had predicted at the onset of this proposed high-dollar dream. Vast gardens, orchards, and lavish furnishings were to beckon the wealthy to come and take their rest—and spend their money.

Having worked for nine years at the established Harvey House to the west, Ashley thought the new resort a waste of money and time. She found it impossible to believe people would actually spend a small fortune to come and bask in the desert heat. Not that she didn't love Winslow and all it had to offer. This had been, after all, home for the last ten years, and she'd grown rather attached to its idiosyncrasies and lovable characters.

"Mama!"

Ashley glanced up the street. The animated move-
ments of the skipping girl brought a smile to Ashley's
face. Despite the warmth of the day, her daughter fairly
danced along the brick sidewalk.

"What are you doing this afternoon, my little miss?"
Ashley questioned.

"I took over that mending you did for Mrs. Taylor at
the boardinghouse. She said to tell you that you sure do
fine work." Natalie beamed her mother a smile. "She
also gave me a nickel for being such a good delivery
girl."

Ashley couldn't help grinning and shaking her head.
The child positively owned Winslow, Arizona. She was
everybody's darling. Everyone from the train yards to
the downtown businesses knew Natalie Reynolds. Knew
her and loved her.

"Well, that was kind of Mrs. Taylor."

Natalie fished into the pocket of her cotton dress.
"She said to give you this." She handed a dollar bill to
her mother. "She said this was for last week's mending
too."

Ashley tucked the bill into the skirt of her Harvey
apron and pulled out a nickel. "Why don't you go get
an ice-cream cone. I need to talk to Grandpa, and dinner won't be for hours yet. You might well feel done in
before then."

"I already have the nickel Mrs. Taylor gave me."

"Yes, but you may need that later for some other
treasure. This time the treat's on me."

"Thanks, Mama." Natalie took the money. She
leaned up on tiptoe as Ashley bent down, then kissed
her mother soundly on the cheek before making a

beeline for her favorite ice-cream parlor.

Ashley sighed as she watched Natalie's gleeful exit. She was such an easy child to care for, but Ashley worried about her. Being loved by the town regulars, Natalie held a loving attitude toward most everyone she met. With the trains that came and went at a constant pace, there were always strangers in town, yet Natalie knew no stranger. She would just as soon strike up a conversation with someone she'd never met as to talk with a friend. Soon she'd come to an age where that could be misconstrued as flirting—or worse yet, it could become very dangerous.

She's growing up so fast, Ashley thought as she continued her journey home. Had it really been ten years since Natalie had come into the world? Ashley remembered the easy delivery with fondness and regret. She had been alone, except for Grandpa Whitman. Her own parents had exiled her, rejecting her for marrying without their permission. Worse still, she'd married a man of no real means or status, something absolutely vital to her social-climbing mother and father.

Ethan . . . her beloved. The pain that had one time been a stabbing, white-hot torture was now a dull ache. Expecting Natalie had given her a will to go on after receiving notice that her war-hero husband had been killed. Ethan had never even known about the baby they'd created. They'd married in a whirlwind in March of 1918, and before either one knew what had happened, Ethan had gone to war and had given his life for his country. There was no time for letters to tell of the pregnancy. No time for letters telling him how much she loved him. No time for letters saying good-bye.

Ashley paused at the iron gate and stared at the brick house she'd called home. The two-story house was quite simple, but it suited her and Natalie and Grandpa Whitman just fine. They'd had a great life there—just the three of them. Together they never felt isolated. They had each other . . . and loved each other and it was that love that helped them through each difficult event.

But with the doctor's visit at the Harvey House today, Ashley knew all of that was about to change. She'd been serving at the lunch counter when he'd come in and asked to talk to her privately. The news was not good, and now she would have to break it to Grandpa. But how? How could she tell him that he was going to die—and quickly?

Cancer of the liver was the culprit, and like an unseen evil that had crept in while everyone slept, Ashley felt the burden of this horror wrap around her and threaten to squeeze the life out of her.

She pushed open the gate, her legs heavy—weighted, barely moving. She trudged toward the front door and sighed. A person should never have a duty like this befall them, she thought. Ashley had been the one to make her grandfather go to the doctor, and upon completing the exam, Grandpa had flippantly told the doc to just let Ashley know the results of his tests. Grandpa had strolled out of the office as if he owned the world, in spite of the pain he'd been suffering.

Now the tests and examinations were complete, and the doctor felt confident that her grandfather would rather hear the truth from her than from him. He'd offered to accompany Ashley, but she knew her grandfather would resent the intrusion. He hadn't wanted to

go to the doctor in the first place, but the pain had become nearly unbearable, and he could no longer ignore his weakness and loss of weight.

"Grandpa?" Ashley called out as she pulled open the screen door.

"I'm here." His voice lacked its usual firmness.

She entered the room, pausing momentarily to allow her eyes to adjust to the shaded room. Grandpa sat slumped at the dining room table, a newspaper laid out before him.

"We need to talk," Ashley stated matter-of-factly.

Russell Whitman looked up at her, appearing to gauge the importance of the matter without being told. "Sit down and tell me what's wrong."

Ashley pulled out the simple wooden ladder-back chair and sat. It felt so good to be off of her feet. She stretched her legs out under the table before looking up to meet her grandfather's intense stare.

"I talked to the doctor today."

Grandpa nodded, seeming to understand. "It's not good, is it?"

Ashley fought back the urge to cry. "No. It's very bad. You have a cancer in your liver."

"Can anything be done?" the eighty-two-year-old asked as he straightened in the chair.

Ashley longed to give him better news. She wanted so much for the entire matter to be a mistake. She bowed her head. "No. They can't do anything to eliminate it. The doctor did say he could give you morphine for the pain, but otherwise . . . well . . . it's just a matter of time."

"How much time, Ashley?"

His tone was almost childlike, causing Ashley to immediately seek his face. She saw the acceptance in his expression but also something akin to concern, even worry. "The doctor said it could be weeks, maybe even months."

"Not much time, then," he said, growing thoughtful.

Ashley reached out her hand and covered his bony fingers. "Not nearly enough." Again, she forced back the tears. His gruff, weathered face appeared so thin and pale. Just months ago he'd seemed vibrant and alive and now . . .

"Well, we need to make plans." He got to his feet slowly, grimacing in pain. "We have to see to everything right away. I can't be taking medicine like morphine and think clearheaded. I saw what it did to old Jefferson Dawson." He paused and looked at Ashley. "You remember him, don't you? Used to work at odd jobs around town."

"I remember."

"As I recall, he took up with using morphine after he'd had that scaffolding accident. Never was the same after that. I don't need that kind of confusion."

"But you also don't need to live in anguish," Ashley said, getting to her feet and coming to his side. "I don't want you hurting anymore."

He patted her hand. "Sweetheart, soon there will be no more pain. I reckon I can bear up just a little while longer. But the truth is, you and Natalie need for me to make some good choices and decisions now. I don't intend to see you left without provision."

With those words Ashley allowed the tears to come. A sob broke from her throat. Even with this terrible

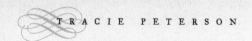

news, the old man was more concerned for her well-being than his own. "I can't lose you."

Grandpa pulled her close and gently patted her shoulder. "There, there. You're not losing me. You know that. I'll go to a better place. A place with no pain or sorrow. Would you deny me that?"

Ashley shook her head. "But I'll still be here with the pain. I know that sounds selfish, and I was really determined to be brave and strong for you. But, Grandpa, what will I do without you?"

"You'll survive. You'll live for Natalie, and you'll work to see her happy and healthy. It's just as it should be. I've lived longer than most. I've had some very good years." He chuckled weakly and added, "And some not so good years. But you'll see. It's all going to work—"

"I know. I know. '. . . together for good to them that love God.' But this is serious."

"So is that. God didn't give us His Word just to have us ignore it or take it lightly. I know you don't hold much stock in such matters. God knows I've tried to help you see the truth of it for yourself, but maybe this is one way you'll finally come to know the truth."

Ashley pulled away. Her grandfather had been after her for over ten years to join him and Natalie at church on Sundays and Wednesdays. But Ashley couldn't understand a god who would let a woman fall in love with the man of her dreams, only to kill him off and leave her alone to raise a child her husband never even knew existed. That wasn't the kind of god she wanted to serve. So she always made sure she had to work whenever church was in session. She also made sure her heart was closed off to any of Grandpa's suggestions regarding God's love.

"Please, let's not make this about me. I want to know how I can best help you. The doctor said you'd need round-the-clock care before long. I've put in for a leave of absence from the Harvey House. I intend to take care of you."

Russell Whitman looked at her with an expression that suggested he just might put forth an argument about her actions, then nodded slowly. "I'd like for you to be with me. It won't seem nearly so tiresome or lonely with you by my side. You've been like a daughter to me."

Ashley hugged him, careful not to hurt his fragile body. "When my world fell apart, you were the one who was there to pick it back up for me. When Mother and Father turned me away . . . when Ethan died . . . when I found out I was expecting Natalie, you were the one who stood by me. Now there will be no one." She pulled away and swiped at her tears with the back of her hand.

"I'm sorry. Here I am a thirty-two-year-old woman, and I'm acting like a ten-year-old. Not even that. I know Natalie will handle this better than I am."

"You mustn't fret. I've got a plan," Russell Whitman said, going to the door. He took up his hat from the peg there and grabbed his cane. "I'm going for a walk just now."

"I'll start supper," Ashley offered.

"Nothing for me," he said as he often did of late. Ashley wondered how he'd managed to stay alive this long with the little he ate.

"I'll just fix something light. You might be hungry when you get back."

He nodded but said nothing more.

Russell Whitman took himself off toward the depot. He liked to sit and think while watching the trains come and go. The rhythmic rumblings as the wheels rolled over the tracks seemed to block out the rest of the world.

Lord, he prayed, *this is a hard one to face.* He continued ambling toward the tracks, mindful of the pain in his right side. *I always knew the day would come when you'd call me home, but there's so much I've left undone—so much I thought I'd have time to see to.*

He lifted his snowy head to the heavens. White wisps of cloud hung like gossamer veils to the west. The land needed rain, but it probably wouldn't come.

"Hey, Russ!" a brakeman called. The man's face bore the same grease and grit that marred his overalls.

Russell waved his cane briefly. His steps slowed to accommodate the lack of support. "How are you doing, Bob?"

The man pulled his billed cap from his head and wiped his forehead. "Doing good. Doing good. The missus told me to invite you over for dinner next time I saw you. Said she'd make your favorite."

Russell smiled and leaned heavily on the cane as he paused beside the boxcar the man had just jumped from. "She makes the best Swedish meatballs I've ever had."

"That's 'cause she *is* Swedish," the man said with a laugh. "God bless Fred Harvey for bringing those girls west. My Inga was the best waitress he ever had and now she's mine."

"She's a keeper, that's for sure," Russell replied.

"You'll come, then?"

Russell thought of his situation and all the work that was yet to be done. Still, it might be one of the last times he'd have the opportunity to share a meal with his friends. "I'll come. Just tell me when."

"How about tomorrow about seven?"

Russell shifted his weight and began walking toward the depot bench. "Tomorrow it is."

He left the man behind and nodded to other workers as he crossed over the tracks. He liked the life here. It was so much more peaceful than Los Angeles, where he'd spent a good deal of his adult life.

He approached the depot and spotted yet another friend of his. Sam Spurgeon got to his feet and waved to the bench he'd just vacated. "I was keepin' it warm for ya."

Russell chuckled and shuffled toward the respite. "Good of you, Sam. Are you heading home?"

"Yup. Been here too long as it is. My daughter's gonna be wonderin' where I got off to." He laughed. "Like she wouldn't know where to find me. I tell her, 'Sissy, I go to watch the trains or to the cemetery to talk with your mother.' Never go anywhere else—no need." He shrugged. "Be seein' ya, Russ."

Russell smiled and took a seat, then sighed in relief. The pain dulled a bit. How long had he ignored it? Two, maybe three months? And now the doctor could only say that it was too late—that there wasn't much time. Maybe he'd known it all along—down deep inside. Maybe that was the reason he'd put off going to the doctor. It wasn't until Ashley had insisted that Russell had finally gone for an examination. Now the truth was known. Cancer.

Russ leaned forward on his cane and sighed again. This time it wasn't from relief. There was a dull ache deep in his heart for Ashley and what she would bear in the days to come. No doubt his care would be extensive.

It's not fair for her to have to care for me. She's had enough to see to. The thought bothered him more than he could say.

She's walled herself up, Lord. She thinks she's safe that way. Safe from the hurt and the people who would rob her of her joy. But we know that's not true. Lord, I worry about her, and the facts are, I don't hardly see how I can come home to you when she's so lost.

A Baldwin 4-6-2 pulling a long line of freight cars signaled down the track. Russell felt the ground quiver under the massive monster's approach. Such power and energy—and all from a man-made machine.

I've seen a lot in my time, Lord. I've seen powerful machines like this. I've watched contraptions take to the skies. I've lived through the War Between the States, the Spanish-American conflict, and the Great War. I've been blessed to not have to take up arms against any man, and for that I am grateful.

The train stopped—not at the depot, but down the line nearer the shops. The ground stilled, but not so Russell's heart.

I've seen a lot, Lord, but I've made a mess of a lot as well. You know the troubles I've caused and been a part of. You know I've not spoken to my own dear daughters in eleven-some years. Not of my choosing, but still it's something I've endured because of my actions.

And there's poor Ashley. Her sorrow has made her heart hard. She's lonely, yet she won't even turn to you for strength.

What do I do, Lord? How can I leave now—just when it appears she needs me most?

———

Ashley climbed the stairs to her bedroom. She longed for a cool bath but knew there wasn't really time. She still needed to work on sewing Natalie's new dress; then there were the new curtains for Mrs. Simpson. Ashley thought of all the bits and pieces of sewing she'd taken on. It gave them a little extra money and that was always nice. They weren't paupers by any means, but they lived cautiously and conservatively. It suited them both after years of wealth and extravagance.

Sponging the heat from her body, Ashley finished by completely dampening her hair. With the short, bobbed cut, she wouldn't have much to worry with. She'd comb it out and maybe later put in a few well-placed bobby pins to add curl. This accomplished, she put her apron to soak and added her uniform to the growing pile of laundry.

"Well, there's going to be more time for the house chores at least," she murmured as she pulled a light-weight cotton dress over her head. "More time to spend with Natalie too." This bonus did nothing to mend her frayed spirit. A weariness and hopelessness—like she'd known the day the news came of Ethan's death—washed over her. Ashley sunk to the floor beside her cedar chest. "What are we going to do?" she whispered. She leaned against the chest for support and buried her face in her hands. Tears came again, but this time they seemed to stretch across the years to that day when hope had died.

She could remember exactly what she'd been

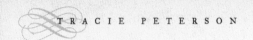

doing—what she'd been wearing when word came of Ethan's sacrifice and bravery. That morning she had donned her two-piece salmon-colored dress—the one she'd worn when they'd married. The skirt fell just about eight inches off the floor, allowing her to show off the sweet little button-up boots Ethan had bought her just before he'd gone off to war. She liked to wear this outfit because it made her feel close to Ethan, and she always dreamed of wearing it when he arrived back home.

But, of course, he hadn't come home.

That August in Baltimore had been very warm, but a cold chill had permeated the house after word of Ethan's death. Only the news that she carried Ethan's unborn child had kept Ashley from throwing herself into the harbor. For days she had refused to see anyone, barely dragging herself from bed each morning.

Her mother, a socialite who valued her position and status more than her daughter, had cut off all communication with Ashley when news had arrived of her marriage to Ethan Reynolds. The man was of no account as far as her mother was concerned. As a student of architectural studies, he could hardly hope to go far; besides, his parents were common factory workers.

After Ethan had joined the army, Leticia Murphy had fought to get her daughter to annul the marriage but without any luck. When this failed, she made one final threat. The words still rang in Ashley's ears.

"Annul this farce of a marriage or you'll never again have anything to do with our family. The choice is yours. It's either him or us."

Ashley hadn't concerned herself overmuch with her

mother's threat. After all, her mother was always creating tirades, storming around for days in order to get her
own way. Ashley had thought of simply going to stay with
Ethan's parents. They lived just outside of Baltimore,
and she knew they'd be delighted to take her in until
their son returned.

Then the influenza epidemics began sweeping the
larger East Coast cities. People were advised to stay
inside, to wear a mask if they went outside—though the
very smell of death necessitated one anyway. This made
Ashley all the more determined to leave town and stay
in the country with her in-laws, but then word came that
both of Ethan's parents had succumbed to the flu themselves. Ashley was devastated. She would have to write
Ethan with the news, and she knew his heart would
break.

But before she could send him word, she was notified of Ethan's death. Shocked beyond words, Ashley
had sat around in a stupor for days afterward. Her entire
world had changed.

Somewhere, someone had told Leticia of Ethan's
death. No doubt she knew full well Ashley couldn't
afford the expenses that would come. Despite her grief,
Ashley had already taken a mental tally of her assets and
knew they were sorely lacking. No doubt her mother
knew this too.

Leticia Murphy came to the little house Ethan and
Ashley had rented and demanded entry. Ashley had no
strength to deal with her mother, but rather than order
her to leave, Ashley waited to hear what her mother had
to say. A thin ribbon of hope still existed that her
mother, seeing Ashley's grief, would find it in her heart

to comfort her daughter. But that wasn't the case at all.

"You look positively ill—you don't have the influenza, do you?" Ashley's mother demanded to know.

"No, Mother. I do not have the influenza." Ashley wasn't sure how to break the news that her look of ill health came from morning sickness rather than the epidemic.

"Good. Look, I've heard of his death." Ashley burned at the thought her mother wouldn't even call Ethan by name. "We can still annul the marriage. You surely can't protest it now. The man is dead and hardly cares what you do. You'll forget about him, and in the meantime, you'll marry that nice Manchester boy your father and I have picked out for you. He's willing to overlook your indiscretion in marrying that Reynolds man."

"Will he also overlook the fact I will never love him?" Ashley threw back, feeling a bit of her determination return.

"Love has very little to do with a lucrative marriage. This is what your father and I want."

"I can't marry Mr. Manchester. Neither can I annul my marriage." Ashley had been about to tell her mother of her pregnancy when the woman began a tirade that didn't end until half an hour later. Ashley had been unable to even offer a word of protest or explanation. When her mother had finished insulting and demeaning Ashley and her choice of husband, Leticia Murphy had picked up her things and headed for the door.

"You are dead to me—just like my father," she decreed like a queen calling down a traitor. She had stormed from the room, but the mention of her father,

Ashley's dear Grandpa Whitman, had given birth to an idea. Her mother had turned away from him, just as she had turned away from Ashley. And all because the man had become religious. He'd sold off a successful business to his partner and settled huge sums of money on his two daughters. But that had only proven to Ashley's mother that her father had lost all sense of reason. She refused to have anything more to do with the man because she believed he was a fool. Never mind that he was trying to put his life in order with his new spiritual beliefs. Never mind that the real estate ventures he'd made a fortune from were underhanded and oftentimes illegal. They'd made money for the family. Money which Grandpa Whitman quite generously lavished upon them all. Now that would stop, and Ashley's mother had been beside herself with the thought of what this would mean.

There had been a trip to Los Angeles for her mother and father. Ashley remembered it well because she'd not yet met Ethan and was still living at home. Her mother had said very little except that she and her sister Lavelle would straighten their father out or have him committed. When her parents had returned from Los Angeles, Ashley had been stunned to hear her mother say that they would no longer have any association with the crazed old man.

Ashley had tried to at least get her father to relay what had happened, but something had changed in him. It was almost as if her father's entire demeanor had taken on a different personality. He was no longer the man she could talk to.

Feeling isolated from her family and tired of dealing with her mother's misery, Ashley had been easily won

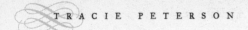

over by Ethan Reynolds's winning charm. Within weeks of meeting, Ashley had married Ethan, furthering the disorder of her mother's once perfectly ordered world. Then Ethan died, and Ashley had wanted to die as well.

Natalie and Grandpa had given her a will to live—they'd made her happy in spite of her loss. And until now, life had been as close to perfect as it could be.

Ashley raised her head and drew a deep breath. She blew it out rather quickly and drew another. The action seemed to calm her a bit.

"Why can't things go on as they always have?" she asked in the silence of her room. "Why must I lose the people I love?"

CHAPTER TWO

A week later Ashley sat across the table from her grandfather. She listened to him read from a list of wishes he had for his funeral. It wasn't at all what she wanted to hear. In fact, Grandpa had been feeling better the last few days, and Ashley liked to believe the doctor was wrong and that he had nothing more terminally wrong than a bout of old age.

"I don't want a lot of fancy flowers," Russell Whitman said firmly. "Never could abide that kind of nonsense. If you want to give me flowers, do it now. That's my motto." He looked up and grinned at Ashley, his gray mustache twitching in boyish charm. "Frankly, I'd rather have candy than flowers any day."

Ashley smiled. He had a way about him that always managed to make her see the hope in every situation. He was just that kind of man. His spiritual walk made him that way, she supposed.

"All right, so when I go shopping, I'll bring you a box of the best chocolates," Ashley finally answered, attempting to change the topic.

"Make sure they have nuts in them," her grandfather said with a wink before turning his attention back to the list. "Now, about the burial."

So much for giving reality the slip.

"I want to be buried next to your grandma back in Los Angeles. The lawyer will have all the information about that and make the arrangements. Don't be thinking you have to have a service here and there. Just have one here, put me in a box on the train, and ship me off."

"I wish you wouldn't talk so casually about such things," Ashley said, feeling a chill run along her spine.

Russell reached out and patted Ashley's folded hands. "But such things only deserve casual reference. I won't be in that box—you know that, don't you, child?"

Ashley knew he'd speak to her again of Jesus and heaven, but for once she didn't mind. Maybe she'd have some peace about her grandfather's dying if only she could make herself believe that God really cared—that He understood her pain. But if He understood, truly knew how she felt and yet did nothing, then that made it even worse.

"I don't know what I believe," she said frankly. "I think it rather cruel of God to give me the man of my dreams—the one great love of my life—and then take him away. Take him before his own child could ever get to know him—before he could get to know her. I think God is merciless at worst, or indifferent at best, to take you away now."

"So God is cruel and awful because He allows for death? Is that it?"

Ashley considered his words for a moment, then met her grandfather's hazel-eyed stare with determination.

"Yes. I suppose that's exactly what I mean."

"But what if one person's death means other people live?" he asked softly. "And what if those who live go on to do profound and wondrous things—things that reach out to the rest of the world and inspire them to do something even better?"

"I've heard all this before," Ashley protested. "I know what's preached—that Jesus died to save us from our sins. One man's sacrifice for the masses. Which just proves my point. God let His own Son die a brutal death."

"I wasn't thinking of Jesus just then," her grandfather said softly. "I was thinking of your Ethan."

Ashley felt the wind go out of her. "Ethan?"

Russell nodded. "Ethan gave his life, throwing himself into the path of certain death, in order to save a unit of men. That much you know. But what you don't know is where it went from there. These things always have a rippling action, like a stone thrown into the water. Ethan saved lives, and perhaps those men in turn went on to save other lives and so on. Perhaps Ethan's sacrifice was the very turning point of the war. You have no way of knowing. Perhaps your daughter is living safe and free from the horrors that we heard about during the war because of Ethan and what he did."

Ashley said nothing. She had always seen her husband as a hero, had taught her daughter the same, but in truth she'd never considered how it might affect anyone else. In her own self-focused pain, she'd never really cared about the benefit to others.

"You're right, child, about Jesus sacrificing His life for the multitudes. But God wasn't cruel in sending His

Son. He was generous and self-sacrificing. We believe God the Father, the Son, and the Holy Spirit are one. God gave of himself—don't you see? Jesus' death and resurrection continue to ripple out amongst the masses and make profound changes in lives everywhere. He came to serve—to be a sin offering in order that those who deserved to die might live. Jesus gave His life, and in turn, I accepted His gift. He saved my life as clearly as Ethan saved those men in the war. Because Jesus saved me, I became a different person, and because of that, I was available to help you when your time of need came. Ripples—don't you see? Jesus gave us a gift of eternal life. Ethan gave a gift of life to his men. Why can you accept one sacrifice and not the other?"

Ashley had no answer. The words pricked her conscience as they never had before. Grandpa had never used Ethan in an illustration about salvation. *It's not the same,* she told herself. *Ethan did his duty. He went where he was sent and followed the orders given him. He had no choice.*

But as soon as the thought came to light, she chided herself, knowing full well that this wasn't true. He had a choice. A choice to stay in his trench or to go after the enemy who was killing his friends and comrades.

"I need to get to work on the laundry," Ashley said, getting to her feet. "You should rest for now."

"I can't rest. The pain is too great," he admitted.

"I have the morphine powder," Ashley offered. "I can mix some up."

"That won't help this pain," her grandfather said, folding his papers. "My pain is over you, and I won't be able to rest until I know you have come to an understanding of the Lord and how much He loves you." He stood, folded the papers into his pocket, then shuffled across the room in a slow, determined manner. "You think on what I've said."

Ashley did think on his words, but if her grandfather had known exactly why she'd chosen to do so, he wouldn't have liked it. Ashley knew Grandpa held great store in his faith and the issues that came out of that faith. He wanted very much for her to believe—to accept the things he'd come to accept.

"Maybe I can do this for his sake," she said softly as she put another dress through the washer wringer. Squeezing the water from the material, Ashley contemplated what she should do.

"Maybe I could just tell him that I've accepted Jesus and repented of my sins and then he'll be happy," she murmured. What could be wrong in that? God would know the truth, so it wouldn't be like she was fooling Him. And Grandpa would die in peace.

Still, lying about something so important to Grandpa didn't seem right. Grandpa had always been able to pretty much read her like a book. Ashley couldn't abide that he was hurting and suffering because of her pride, but should she go to such extremes to make him feel better? Wiping her brow, she sighed. "I just don't know how to deal with this."

———

Natalie fiddled with her food, glancing from time to time down the hall to Grandpa Whitman's closed bedroom door. "He never eats with us anymore," she murmured.

Ashley poured some milk into Natalie's glass and

took a seat opposite her daughter at the small oak table. "I know. He doesn't feel well enough to eat."

"But wouldn't food make him feel stronger? Doesn't he want to get well?"

Ashley knew the time had come to tell her daughter about the illness that would soon take her beloved great-grandfather. "Natalie, you know that Grandpa isn't a young man anymore. The doctor says that this sickness is too strong for an old man to fight. Grandpa probably isn't going to get well." She threw in the word *probably,* hoping to soften the blow.

Natalie put down her fork and stared down the hall. "He's going to die?"

Sorrow gripped Ashley's heart. "Yes."

"When . . . when will he . . . die?" Her voice quivered.

Ashley steadied herself with a deep breath. "Soon. The doctor said it wouldn't be very long."

Natalie's face contorted as she appeared to fight her emotions. "Does it hurt?"

Ashley saw her daughter's eyes dampen with unshed tears. "He's in some pain, but the doctor has given me medicine to help Grandpa. It should help keep the pain down."

"Will it hurt to die?"

Ashley hadn't anticipated the question. "I don't know. I don't think so."

"I wish he didn't have to die." The tears streamed down her cheeks. "I wish the people we loved didn't have to die . . . like Daddy and now Grandpa."

The mention of Ethan only served to multiply Ashley's pain. Why did it still have to hurt so much after all this time? It seemed that Grandpa's dying only served to reopen those old wounds. "We will miss him. Probably more than we realize."

Natalie scooted out of her chair and came to her mother. Ashley hugged her close and then drew Natalie onto her lap. "I wish you didn't have to hurt, sweet pea. I wish neither one of us had to hurt ever again."

"I try to be strong, Mama. I try to remember that God loves all of us and that He knows best. Grandpa said that just last week."

Ashley knew her daughter shared Grandpa Whitman's faith. She'd watched Natalie get baptized in Clear Creek just last year. The child seemed to have a profound grasp of the spiritual and yet, here she was, just a little girl saddened by the events of her life. Ashley wished she could kiss away the hurt and make it better.

Ashley smoothed back her daughter's light brown hair. How baby fine and soft it was, even now after years of rough-and-tumble play. "At least by knowing that Grandpa is going to die, we can say all the things that are really important. Some people never get to do that," Ashley offered.

"Like with you and Daddy?" Natalie questioned, rising up. "You never got to tell him about me."

A tightness formed in Ashley's throat and seemed to settle down over her chest. She strained to breathe and found it nearly painful. "Yes. That's true."

"Then I suppose it's better this way," Natalie said, sounding very adult. She hugged Ashley's neck once more, then hopped up and went back to her chair. The child sat in silence for a few minutes. She dried her eyes

with the linen napkin, then questioned her mother. "Does Grandpa know?"

Ashley nodded. "Yes. He's probably suspected for a lot longer than any of us figured, but he knows the truth of it now."

"Is he afraid?"

"I don't think so, Natalie. I think he trusts that God has it all under control."

"Do you think that's true?" Natalie asked, her dark brown eyes wide with wonder.

Ashley felt trapped. She didn't want to discourage the one thing she knew Natalie would find solace in— her faith. Real or imagined, Ashley wanted her daughter to know the comfort and peace that Grandpa Whitman seemed to have. "Yes, Natalie. I'm sure God has it all under control. We just don't always understand why God does things the way He does." That much was true, Ashley realized. She did think God was in control. She just didn't think He was very fair or kind.

"Will you go to church with me after Grandpa is gone to heaven?" Natalie questioned.

Ashley studied the hopeful look on her daughter's face. It seemed she hung all her hopes on that one question. "I might even go with you before then," Ashley said, making up her mind that she would do whatever was necessary to put both her daughter and grandfather at peace through this dying process.

Natalie smiled. "I know that would make Grandpa feel better. Every Sunday we pray you'll come with us."

The wonder of that statement buried itself deep into Ashley's heart. "You do?"

Natalie nodded and picked up her fork. "Grandpa

said if we prayed long and hard, God would bring it to pass." She looked rather thoughtfully at the food on her plate before raising her gaze again to her mother. "Do you think it's wrong for me to pray that God would send me a daddy?"

The statement completely stunned Ashley, who had never heard her daughter make such a comment. "I . . . well . . . I don't know."

Natalie smiled. "Well, I'm going to pray about it, and I'm going to talk to Grandpa too. He'll know. He might be sick, but he'll know if it's okay to pray about it."

Ashley pushed away from the table. She couldn't take any more of the religious battle that raged inside of her. One minute she was convinced of the validity of such thinking. The next minute she questioned everything she believed. And now Natalie wanted a father. It was all just too much.

"Would you like dessert? I have some fresh berries and cream," Ashley offered.

"Yes, please. Oh, and Mama, can we make a bowl for Grandpa? And can I take them back to his room and eat with him?"

Ashley smiled down at the child. With her hair tied back and a few wispy strands escaping the hold of her ribbon, her face held an elfish charm. Her delicate little upturned nose and finely arched brows made Natalie seem almost doll-like in appearance.

"I'm sure Grandpa would like that. I'll fix the berries."

Ashley produced the bowls of dessert and watched as Natalie carefully balanced them on a tray. She heard Natalie call out, then was glad to see that apparently the

child's request had been met with acceptance. Natalie disappeared inside the room, leaving Ashley to clean the table and contemplate the future.

Russell perked up at the sight of his great-granddaughter. He'd often wondered if there'd been other great-grandchildren. Ashley had three brothers, after all. They had been headstrong businessmen when Ashley had left Baltimore. Family seemed unimportant to them at the time.

"Grandpa, I brought some berries and cream."

Russell scooted up in the bed and swung his legs over the side. "Sounds delicious." It did sound good, even if he had no appetite.

Natalie put the tray down and brought him a bowl and a spoon. "Mama said I could eat my berries back here with you."

He thought she sounded sad. She looked up at him as he took the bowl and added, "Is that okay with you?"

"You know it is." Russell pushed back an errant lock of hair, the same trademark lock his own mother and wife had spent a lifetime pushing back.

Natalie took up her bowl and sat in the chair beside the bed. "I . . . um . . . well, I was hoping we could talk."

"What about?"

She glanced up momentarily, then lowered her gaze to the bowl. "Mama says you're real sick."

Russell heard her voice tremble. Ashley must have told her that he was dying. He'd wondered how long she would wait until telling the child the truth. He'd only mentioned it once before, but Ashley hadn't been ready yet to deal with facing the truth herself, and sharing that knowledge with Natalie seemed impossibly hard.

Russell knew Natalie would need help dealing with this and so he asked, "And you wanted to talk about it?"

"Uh-huh," she said, her crossed legs swinging back and forth as she toyed with the berries.

"I'm sure the news has made you sad," Russell said. He ate a spoonful of the berries and waited for her to respond.

"Grandpa, I don't understand why God would do this." She looked up, and Russell could see the glistening of tears in her dark brown eyes. "We need you here. What will we do when you're gone?"

"Well, child, would it hurt any less if you understood the whys and hows?"

"I don't know. I just don't want you to die." She sniffed back her tears and put aside her bowl.

Russell put his bowl aside as well and opened his arms to her. "Come here, Natalie."

She did so and fell against him, sobbing. The pain in his side ripped through him, but Russell said nothing. He held her close and stroked her head, knowing there were no words that would make her understand or feel better.

After several minutes he said, "You know, God has His own way of doing things, Natalie. We don't always see them as reasonable or understandable. We don't always know what He has in mind, but it's been my experience over the years that God never closes a door without opening a window."

Natalie rose up, wiping at her eyes. "What does that mean?"

"It means that God may be calling me home, but at

the same time He could be sending someone else into your life to help you in my place."

"They could never take your place," Natalie said, her lower lip quivering.

"I didn't say they would. I was merely suggesting they would come to help in place of me. You never know what God has in mind, but it's always better than what we have in mind for ourselves."

"But even if someone else comes, Grandpa, I'll miss you. Who will go for walks with me and tell me stories about the old days?"

Russell laughed. "Child, there's always someone around who will share stories about the old days. Look, we still have a bit of time. Only God knows the hours of man's life. You have to trust that He knows best."

"I do trust Him. I just wish that Mama trusted Him too."

Russell nodded. Nothing would make him happier. "We'll have to keep praying for her, Natalie. We'll have to pray and wait for God to act. Maybe my sickness will make her realize what's missing in her life."

"Like getting married again?"

"Could be," Russell said with a grin. "You just never know what God has in mind."

"I want a new daddy," Natalie said, her tears gone. She went back to her chair and picked up the bowl of dessert. "I'm still praying for one."

Russell picked up his own bowl, not wanting the child to think he didn't appreciate her efforts. He ate some more of the berries and pondered her desires. A father for Natalie and a husband for Ashley did seem like an answer to many problems. Of course, it still wouldn't bring Ashley to an understanding of God. No, that was something God would have to do himself. No human could do it for her.

———————

The food on Ashley's plate served as a reminder that she'd eaten very little at supper. It was hard to think of eating when her world seemed to be falling apart. Ashley scraped the food into the garbage pail, then put the plate in the sink before going back for Natalie's dishes. A knock on the door interrupted her duties, and Ashley glanced at the clock on the mantel. Seven o'clock. Perhaps someone had come to visit.

Exiling the remaining dirty dishes to the kitchen sink, Ashley pulled her apron off and went to see who had come to call. Opening the door, she found Pastor McGuire, her grandfather's minister.

"Good evening, Mrs. Reynolds. I'm wondering if your grandfather is up to receiving a visitor?"

"I'm sure he'd be glad to see you," Ashley said, adding, "Won't you come in?"

The tall redheaded man removed his hat as he stepped through the doorway. His compassionate expression preceded his next question. "And how are you holding up? I know this news can't have been easy on you."

"No, it hasn't been easy," Ashley admitted. She took the man's hat and hung it on a peg by the door, then motioned him toward the small living room. "My daughter is sharing dessert with Grandpa just now. He so seldom eats that I'm hoping her enthusiasm and company will at least get a few spoonfuls down him. If you don't mind waiting just a little while, we can visit here." Ashley led him through an arched opening to the living room. She really had no desire to answer the pastor's questions or, worse still, to be preached to, but she knew she needed to put her own comfort aside and think of Grandpa.

"That would be fine. I so seldom get to share your company." He unbuttoned the lower button on his suit coat and smiled.

"Would you like a cup of coffee?" Ashley offered.

"No, nothing just now. I've just come from our supper table."

He waited for Ashley to lower herself into the rocker before he seated himself in the overstuffed chair. Stroking the patterned red fabric, he sighed. "Ah, this is so comfortable I just might not get back up." He threw her a smile that seemed to light up his entire face.

Ashley nodded. "That's Grandpa's chair. He's always said that a man who works hard all day deserves a good soft chair for the evening."

"And he's so right." McGuire shifted as if to get even more comfortable. Stretching out his legs, he crossed them at the knees and looked quite casual and comfortable.

The action put Ashley at ease for some reason. Maybe it was that he looked less threatening—less likely to start preaching hellfire and brimstone. Looking at her hands, Ashley searched for something to talk about. "So it looks like they're making good progress on the new Harvey resort." That topic seemed harmless enough.

"Yes, I do believe they are. Should be quite the place.

I'm told the food will be even grander, if that's possible. Are you still working at the Harvey House?"

"No, I took a leave so that I could be with Grandpa. The doctor said . . ." She let her words trail off. She really hadn't wanted to get into this conversation, and now that she had, she didn't seem to be able to stop it. "The doctor said his time would be very short. The cancer is quite progressed and very . . . aggressive." Her heart ached to have to acknowledge this truth, yet it was undeniable. She'd watched the old man fail a little more each day.

"It's hard to lose the people we love," the pastor said, nodding. "I'm going to miss your grandfather greatly. Even the promise of heaven isn't much of a comfort at times."

Shocked by his words, Ashley looked at him for a moment and tried to gather her courage to question him. "How can you say that? You're a man . . . of God. You believe that a Christian person goes to heaven."

"True enough, but as you stated, I'm a man first and very human with my feelings. My spirit is at peace because I know Grandpa Whitman is going to heaven. I feel confident of what God has done in his life and what God holds in store for his future—after death. But I'll miss my time with your grandfather. I'll miss our checker games and coffee at the café. I'll miss our talks. I've learned a lot from him."

Ashley felt a warmth in the pastor's loving words. "I'll miss his company for sure. He's so long been a staple in my life. I really have no one else, besides Natalie, of course."

"Well, just know you're welcome at our table

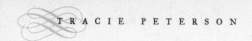

anytime. My wife, Essie, would love to have you and Natalie over for supper sometime. She adores your daughter, and every time we've had her and Grandpa Whitman to our house for lunch after church, Natalie has always been such a help."

"I suppose I didn't realize that they'd ever come to lunch at your place." Ashley felt guilty for admitting that, but it was the truth. "I generally work on Sundays at the Harvey House. People have to eat and travel just the same on Sunday as other days," she added, almost defensively.

"Well, you're always welcome to come to service when you can. I know your work has kept you away." He leaned forward and his expression grew quite serious. "Ashley, I'm not of the mind to make this uncomfortable for you, if that's what you're worried about. People have to make their own decisions and choices. Grandpa's told me some of the issues you've faced. Frankly, given your youth back then and the responsibilities of a new baby, I completely admire your ability to overcome your widowhood. Just know that we care about you, and we'd be glad for you to join us when you can."

There was nothing condemning in his tone. Nothing that suggested he knew Ashley for the heathen she thought herself to be. And yet she didn't doubt that Grandpa had spoken the truth to the man on more than one occasion. No doubt he'd even asked the pastor to pray for Ashley.

About that time Natalie came skipping down the hall carrying two empty dishes. "Look!" she exclaimed. "Grandpa ate his berries and cream."

Ashley saw the look of triumph on her daughter's

face. "Good for you, Natalie. I think that's the first thing he's eaten all day."

"Oh, hello, Pastor McGuire," Natalie said, catching sight of the man. "Are you here to visit Grandpa?"

"I sure am," Pastor McGuire said, getting to his feet. "Would you like to let him know I'm here?"

Ashley got up quickly and took the empty bowls from her daughter's hands. "I'll see to these. You go ahead and take Pastor McGuire on back."

Ashley set the bowls to soak with the other dishes. She still needed to take down the laundry from the line, and it needed to be done before the light was completely gone. The dishes could wait.

Taking up her basket, Ashley slipped out the back door. Her mind reflected back to what the pastor had said. It somehow comforted her to know he'd miss her grandfather nearly as much as she would. She had been so afraid he'd come at her with all sorts of religious nonsense about how much better off Grandpa would be in heaven and how life up there couldn't compare to life down here.

"That may well be true," she muttered, "but it doesn't mean our lives will be better." She knew the sentiment was selfish, but she couldn't help it. She didn't want him to die. She didn't want God taking away yet one more person she loved.

CHAPTER THREE

E. J. Carson studied the blueprints before him as if they were battle plans for an invasion. Helping with the many architectural designs created by Mary Elizabeth Jane Colter, architect and interior designer for the Fred Harvey Company, gave his life purpose and occupied his mind. This project in particular gave E. J. the opportunity to utilize the training and interest he had in Spanish architecture.

Mary Colter worked for the Harvey Company, having been hired at the turn of the century to help invent a personality and vision for the Fred Harvey hotels, restaurants, and tourist attractions. She was a diligent, demanding woman, but she was also brilliant. At least in E. J. Carson's opinion.

Colter's ability to look at the raw bones of a project and breathe life into it amazed E. J. every single time. Too bad she couldn't breathe life into him as well.

He frowned at the thought and forced his attention back to the blueprints. They were building what was to be the cream of Harvey's hotels. A grand resort that would draw in the rich and famous from far and wide.

A resort so magnificent that people would have to book months in advance just to take lodging. The project was ambitious to be sure, but certainly no more so than the dynamite little woman who planned and arranged it all.

Mary Colter was undaunted by the prospects of taking a piece of land where a roundhouse had once existed and turning it into a lush and exotic playground for the wealthy. Considering Mary's vision for landscaping and construction, E. J. had to admit the woman was positively inspired. Her plan was to raise up a resort hotel to look as if it had been there for hundreds of years. She even created her own myths and legends to surround it—giving history to what had just months ago been nothing.

The task wouldn't be easy. It would take more than average attention to detail to build this hacienda-style hotel. It would demand a tremendous amount of work and the highest quality of craftsmanship. It was easy to slap together a square of bricks and windows but something entirely different to fashion a dream.

And it was harder still when your ability to dream had been destroyed in the wake of man's fury.

E. J. pulled his wire-rimmed glasses off and rubbed his closed eyes momentarily. The haunting images of his past were never further away than a thought. The nightmarish vision of men dying was always with him. Blood and decay filled his thoughts as permanent reminders of all that he'd lost. For most Americans, the Great War was over and done with. They seldom gave it consideration. But for E. J., he truly wondered if the war would ever end. Would the ghostly faces of his dying friends ever fade?

He opened his eyes and replaced the glasses once again. *How can I see the vision of a beautiful creation when all of my thoughts are consumed with the ugliness of such an evil?*

For a time after the war he'd immersed himself in studying Spanish architecture and furnishings. He found the dark woods and extensive carving to be a fascination all its own. The buildings, however, were what had truly captured his imagination. Tiled roofs and stucco walls, stone floors and brightly painted tiles—all of it was different and exciting. There was a taste of the exotic in such masterpieces, and it was this interest that eventually brought him to work with Mary Colter.

"Hello."

E. J. looked up to find a sweet-faced little pixie watching as he pored over his drawings. E. J. hadn't expected to find a child on the construction site.

"Hello," he said, trying hard to sound stern. "This isn't really a safe place to play."

"I didn't come to play. I want to build places like this someday. I came to see how it's done."

E. J. smiled. "Oh, you did, now." Her innocent comment pushed away his previous darkness.

The little girl nodded, her two long braids bobbing as she did. "I like to draw. My daddy was an architect. He was going to build all sorts of buildings and now I want to. Do you like to build things too?"

"I do indeed." He rolled up his blueprints and glanced around at the busy construction crew. "Would you like a look around?"

"Oh, very much," the girl answered. She came closer and extended her hand in greeting. "I'm Natalie."

"And I'm E. J. I work with Miss Colter. She's the one who planned all of this." He waved at the framework that would one day become a grand resort. "I would think Miss Colter would very much like to meet you. See, she has been working in this business for many years and can tell you all about how it is for a woman to work in a job that's usually performed by men."

Natalie smiled, but her gaze was fixed on the construction crew. She watched without concern to her own safety as the men moved through the open room carrying impressive loads of mortar, lumber, and tools. As they marched dirty boots across lovely carpets of intricately woven patterns, Natalie looked to E. J. in question.

"Won't they ruin those pretty rugs?"

E. J. laughed. "That's the idea," he said rather conspiratorially. "Miss Colter thought they looked too nice—too new. She's done this before. She likes to have the workers walk on them and make them look old and used."

"But why?" Natalie questioned, scrunching up her face and cocking her head to one side.

The puzzled look on the child's face gave E. J. a feeling of delight he'd not known in years. "It's her way," he answered. "She likes things to look like they've been in a place forever. She says it's a way of making the new look comfortably old and welcoming."

Natalie seemed to consider this for a moment, then took her attention elsewhere. "What are they building back there?" She pointed past E. J.

"That's to be the dining room. Come on, I'll show you around." E. J. picked up his drawings and tucked them under his arm. Natalie quickly followed as he led the way. "See, overhead we have log-beamed ceilings to make it look very Spanish."

"Why?"

"Miss Colter wants the entire place to look like one of the old Spanish haciendas. She wants it to look like it belongs here instead of something that was just picked up elsewhere and plopped down here. Do you understand?"

Natalie nodded. "She doesn't want it to be out of place."

"Right," E. J. replied. "She has a dream to make this a lovely resort where people will come and feel as though they're visiting one of the ancient Spanish ranchos from the early eighteen hundreds."

"Will people like that?" Natalie asked, looking toward the arched windows.

"People are always looking for something different from what they are used to. So I think they'll like it very much. Besides, they already love Fred Harvey's hotels and restaurants."

Natalie smiled. "I know. My mama works at the Harvey House. At least, she did. She's quit for now to take care of my grandpa. He's dying."

E. J. frowned. "I'm sorry to hear that."

"I was too," Natalie said, digging the toe of her leather shoe against the stone floor. "Grandpa's been like my best friend. He's always telling me stories and helping me learn about things."

E. J. had no idea what to say, his own losses fresh in his memory. So many people he'd cared about had died tragically. Friends in the Great War. His parents and wife to influenza. How he missed them all.

"So will they have a lunch counter too?" Natalie suddenly asked, taking E. J. out of his sorrowful memories.

"Yes," he nodded. "It will be over this way." As they walked, E. J. explained, "They plan to use the most beautiful Spanish tile on the counters. It's really going to look impressive."

"My mama doesn't like to work the lunch counter. She says it's a more frantic pace of life than working in the dining room."

E. J. couldn't help smiling at this bit of insight. "I can well imagine that's right. I'm staying over at the present Harvey hotel, and I eat in the restaurant every day. The lunch counter *is* more frantic," he said with a wink.

Natalie grinned. "My mama says people come storming in there shouting their orders, calling out for more attention than the next person. She said it's like they think being louder will make things go faster."

E. J. nodded. "The world is full of those kinds of folks."

They walked around the building site, E. J. pointing out the workers and what they were doing. Finally, they ended up outside.

"What are those people doing?" Natalie questioned.

E. J. looked to where she was focused. "There's going to be a sunken garden over there with all sorts of hidden shrines and fountains. Miss Colter has this wonderful plan, and I know it will be spectacular. Everything she creates is wonderful."

"But why does she worry about the garden part? I thought architects only worried about building things."

E. J. motioned with his arm. "But all of this is just an extension of the building. Don't you see? It's like a giant canvas, and we're the artists who are painting upon it. You wouldn't just paint the building and leave the rest of the canvas blank—now, would you?"

Natalie's face lit up and E. J. was certain she understood. "No," she replied. "You have to make it all work together. Just like Miss Colter wants it to look like it belongs."

"Exactly. We don't want the guests to show up when the building's all done to find that the grounds are still cluttered with building materials and tools. We want to extend the beauty beyond the walls of the hotel. We want it to be a lovely place to come share a quiet moment—a peaceful rest."

"I want to do things like this when I grow up," Natalie announced confidently. "I want to build pretty places where people will be happy. That way my daddy's dreams can come true."

"Your daddy's dreams? What about yours?" E. J. questioned. He found it odd that the little girl should want to fulfill someone else's plan. "Can't your daddy make his own dreams come true?"

"My daddy died in the war. He was an architect like you. He wanted to build wonderful things, and my mama says he was very good." She smiled at E. J., melting his heart. "My daddy was a hero in the war."

"Was he, now?" E. J. found Natalie's adoration of her father quite charming, but talk of the war made him uncomfortable. This little girl had a way about her that took him back to 1918. And it wasn't only the talk of the war. It was also rather disconcerting that the little girl, with her huge brown eyes and dark lashes, made E. J. think of his own beloved wife, now dead and gone. He sighed but tried to maintain his composure. One could never tell when the past would catch up with the present.

Natalie seemed oblivious to his momentary sorrow. "I never got to know my daddy, but everyone has told me what a hero he was. He saved a whole bunch of men in the war. Whenever we have a parade, I get to ride with the veterans in honor of my daddy. I get to help decorate the graves too, and last year a man came from the newspaper in Phoenix and talked to me about my daddy and took my picture with the veterans."

Her expression completely told the story. She practically worshiped the memory of a man she couldn't possibly have known. After all, she was such a little thing, E. J. would never even have imagined she was old enough to have been conceived prior to the Great War.

"How old are you, Natalie?"

She twirled in her yellow cotton sundress and laughed. "I'm ten and I'm going to be eleven next January. How old are you?"

Her question caught him off guard but made him chuckle nevertheless. He stroked his bearded chin as if he had to remember all the years and tally them up. "I'm thirty-two. Kind of old, huh?"

"No," Natalie replied, shaking her head. "That's not old at all. My mama is thirty-two and she's very young, but she works too hard. At least that's what Grandpa says. He says she's trying to keep busy so that she doesn't get too sad."

E. J. had no idea how to respond. The warmth of the afternoon gave him an idea. "Would you like a cold drink? I think we have some lemonade and tea."

"Sure. I like lemonade."

E. J. smiled. "I do too." He was surprised when
Natalie danced off ahead of him. He ambled after her,
realizing suddenly that she was like a balm to his chafed
and wounded spirit. In spite of her comments of the war,
her sweetness and girlish delight in everything she saw
made E. J. most aware of one thing. Life. She was a trib-
ute to the living—joyous, blooming, shining with an
inner light that somehow permeated the darkness of his
soul.

Once inside, E. J. arranged two glasses of lemonade,
then directed Natalie to a reasonably quiet corner of the
area where they'd first met. He offered her a glass, then
sat down opposite her. He'd hoped that Mary would
return before long, which was the real reason, he told
himself, that he delayed Natalie's departure.

"Have you been working here for a long time?"
Natalie asked.

"No, I've only been here this last week," E. J. admitted. "I finished up some final details on a hotel over in
Santa Fe, New Mexico. It's called La Fonda. It's a very
beautiful hotel, but I think this one will be even nicer."

Natalie took a sip of the lemonade and asked, "Did
you build that hotel too?"

"No. The hotel was already there. The railroad
bought it and asked Miss Colter to come in and make
some changes and improvements." Natalie nodded as if
she were a company employee well versed in the routine. E. J. smiled. "You should have seen some of the
things she did."

"Like what?" Natalie appeared to be his captive audi-
ence.

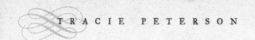

"Well, she designed furniture and special light fixtures. She had murals painted in some of the rooms and redecorated the walls in other parts of the hotel."

"But that's not architect work," Natalie argued.

"She's an interior architect as well as exterior," E. J. explained. "Miss Colter is equally talented in interior decorating as well as creating the actual building and landscape. Remember what I told you about painting the whole canvas? Miss Colter believes that canvas is inside the building as well. Like I said, I think you'd like her a lot."

"So will she make furniture here too?"

"She's hiring it done. She's designed some very nice pieces. There will also be some that are simpler. Miss Colter likes the contrast. She's bringing in beautiful china and copper pots from Europe and Asia. This hotel will even have a patron saint—San Ysidro."

"We don't have any saints at my house. We aren't Catholic," Natalie said, putting her lemonade aside. "We don't pray to saints; we just pray to God directly."

E. J. found himself amazed at her bold yet easy manner in speaking of her faith. "So where do you go to church, Miss Natalie?"

"We go to Faith Mission Church. Would you like to come with us? My mama plans to come to church tomorrow and you could come and meet her. She's real pretty."

E. J. grinned. "If she looks anything like you, I'm sure she's beautiful."

Natalie's brown eyes seemed to flash with an inner light of joy at this comment. "So will you come?"

"I'm afraid I can't. I'm taking the train to Santa Fe

tonight. I won't be back here until next Wednesday. Maybe another time."

Natalie fairly bounced in her seat. "Good. I'll come see you again when you get back. You can tell me about your drawings." She pointed to the papers he'd been carrying around since she'd first shown up.

"I'd be happy to do that, but right now," he said, glancing at his watch, "I have to go. I have a meeting. When you come back, I'll see if I can introduce you to Miss Colter. You'd like her a lot. She sometimes seems mean and gruff, but she's really a very nice lady."

"I'll come after school on Thursday if it's okay with Mama," Natalie promised. "Will you be here?"

E. J. thought about his workweek and nodded. "I should be. Sometimes we have to go scout up workers or supplies, but otherwise, I should be around."

"Then I'll come back. Thanks for the lemonade."

She got up and skipped off, weaving in and out of the construction workers until she'd disappeared. E. J. thought it rather strange and delightful at the same time that a young girl should be so captivated by the architecture and building of this marvelous resort. Some of the local boys stopped by from time to time, but Natalie was the first girl to show interest. He sighed and gathered up his things. The afternoon promised to be long, and then there would be the ride back to Santa Fe. He smiled to himself as he made his way across the lobby floor. Silly as it sounded, he would have much rather spent time talking with the girl than dealing with meetings and contract issues.

———

That night after Natalie and Grandpa had gone to bed, Ashley finished ironing her good dress in preparation for the next morning. She'd promised Natalie she'd go to church, and she intended to see it through. Grandpa had been surprised at the news, and when Ashley had taken some lunch to him he'd told her how much it pleased him.

Ashley remembered the look of delight on his face and knew he really meant it. Grandpa was never a man of false words. At least not since finding Jesus. She thought back to the things he'd told her about his past. Things he was deeply ashamed of. It was the reason he'd left Los Angeles and a lucrative partnership in the land business. Her grandfather had been a great salesman— and con man. He had a knack for convincing people of what they needed and then producing that exact thing. Even in getting Ashley to church, he'd been very persuasive. Had she not been so angry for the past, she might well have gone before now.

A sound from upstairs caught her attention. She strained to hear.

Nothing.

Maybe it was just my imagination. She finished the dress and put the iron aside to cool. Checking to make sure that Grandpa was asleep and didn't need anything, Ashley picked up the dress and made her way upstairs.

Natalie's room was closest to the stairs, and then next there was a small room that doubled as a sewing and guest room. At the end of the hall on the opposite side was Ashley's room and next to it was their bathroom. It was all very compact and neatly ordered. Exactly as Ashley liked it.

Reaching her door, Ashley heard the noise again. She quickly hung her dress in the wardrobe, then made her way back to Natalie's room. Through the closed door, she could hear her child sobbing softly.

Ashley entered the room quietly and went to Natalie's bed. Sinking onto the mattress, she lifted Natalie into her arms and rocked her back and forth. "Did you have a bad dream?" Ashley asked.

"No. I just got sad," Natalie admitted. She pulled away and pushed back her hair.

"Is this about Grandpa?"

Natalie nodded. "I tried to stay quiet."

Ashley shook her head and smoothed back the errant strands of hair that Natalie had missed. The light from the hallway spilled into the room, casting a soft glow across them. "Darling girl, you never have to hide your tears from me. I love you, and what's more, I understand the hurt you're feeling."

"But you grew up with your daddy. My daddy is gone and Grandpa is the only daddy I've ever had. Now he's going away too." Natalie's lower lip quivered as her emotions overtook her once again.

Ashley held her close and kissed the top of her head. "Shh, it's all right. I know how important he is to you, but you mustn't mourn him yet. He's not even gone. Grandpa is still with us. We mustn't make him feel bad these last few days."

Natalie jerked away. "He's going to die in a few days?"

Ashley shook her head. "No one knows when he's going to die, Natalie. I only said that to mean whatever time Grandpa has left should be spent in as much

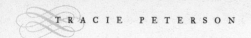

comfort and happiness as we can give him. When he's gone, we can cry all we want, and then it won't hurt him."

"Will he see us from heaven? Won't it hurt him to see us cry then?"

Ashley shrugged. "I don't know if he will be able to see us from heaven. I don't know a lot about heaven, but I remember Grandpa saying there's no pain there. So if that's the case, then maybe he'll only see the good things down here on earth and never be sad again."

Natalie hugged her close. "Will you stay with me till I fall asleep?"

Ashley didn't normally indulge the child, but this time it seemed appropriate. "All right. How about I sit right here beside the bed?" Ashley got up and pulled a chair over to the bedside.

"Would you read to me?"

Ashley smiled and turned on the bedside light. "Just for ten minutes. Then you really need to go to sleep. What do you want me to read?"

"Would you read the Bible?"

Ashley tried to hide her grimace, but apparently she wasn't successful.

"Please, Mama?"

Ashley reached for the black book on Natalie's night-stand. "All right. Where do you want me to read? The beginning?"

"No. Just open at the marker. That's where I was reading earlier."

Ashley opened the Bible and found herself in the Psalms. "Psalm sixty-three?" Natalie nodded and Ashley continued. " 'O God, thou art my God; early will I seek thee: my soul thirsteth for thee, my flesh longeth for thee in a dry and thirsty land, where no water is.' " She smiled. "Sounds like the desert, eh?"

"It's one of Grandpa's favorite chapters. He told me about it," Natalie said, yawning. "He told me there's another verse in the Bible that talks about how God makes rivers in the desert." She snuggled down and closed her eyes. "God can do anything."

Ashley nodded and continued. " 'To see thy power and thy glory, so as I have seen thee in the sanctuary. Because thy lovingkindness is better than life, my lips shall praise thee. Thus will I bless thee while I live.' " Ashley paused, uneasy at the reminder of her grandfather's fleeting days. She looked over the last line. *Thus will I bless thee while I live.* It was such a simple statement. She drew a deep breath and read on. " 'I will lift up my hands in thy name. My soul shall be satisfied as with marrow and fatness; and my mouth shall praise thee with joyful lips: When I remember thee upon my bed, and meditate on thee in the night watches.' "

She glanced over to see that Natalie had fallen back to sleep. Her even breathing left no doubt that she had found her comfort and peace once again. Ashley replaced the marker and closed the Bible. She turned off the lamp and left the Bible on the nightstand before leaving the room. A strange peace was upon her. A peace she hadn't known for some time. Could it really be that simple? she wondered. Could merely reading the Bible—God's Word—give that kind of comfort to her soul?

CHAPTER FOUR

*A*shley sat beside Natalie in church, hoping her nervousness wouldn't show. Grandpa sat on the other side of Natalie, and both were beaming from ear to ear because of her attendance. This only served to make Ashley more edgy. What if she said or did something that embarrassed them—made them sorry she'd come?

They picked up hymnals as directed by Pastor McGuire and turned to the page he directed. Ashley looked at the words to the song while the organ introduced the melody. When the singing began, Ashley followed the words in silence, mesmerized by their powerful effect.

"Oft my heart has bled with sorrow. Not a friend my grief to share." *How very true,* Ashley thought. She listened to her daughter sing the words with great enthusiasm and conviction.

The congregation moved to the second verse. "Once I sighed for peace and pleasure, felt a painful void within." Oh, the words were like affirmation to her soul, and Ashley couldn't help but eagerly seek the

next refrain. "Life was gloomy, death a terror." *Oh yes,* she thought. *Yes. Death is a terror. It threatens to steal away all the joy I've worked so hard to own.*

The chorus interrupted her thoughts. "Is there here a soul in trouble—whosoever needs a friend? Jesus' love your heart will gladden, bless and keep you to the end."

Could it really be that simple? Could turning your heart over to Jesus—accepting His love—really be the key? If so, why didn't everybody do it? Ashley teetered between complete confusion and an intense desire to understand. God had seemed so distant to her when Ethan died. She'd attended church most of her life— her mother had insisted. After all, they'd purchased an entire pew at the front of the grand cathedral and no one was ever allowed there but the Murphy family. It was important to be seen in church. It lent an image of wor-thiness and respectability, her mother had said. This time, however, church seemed different.

The congregation concluded the song and Pastor McGuire began to pray. He prayed for peace for each individual and then prayed for God to speak through his words. Ashley could hardly concentrate. Her thoughts were still lost in the words of the song. Had she missed something all those years ago?

Throughout Pastor McGuire's sermon, Ashley kept coming back to the words of the hymn. *Is there here a soul in trouble—whosoever needs a friend?* That could certainly describe her, but could she accept that the solution was in seeking God? God, who had taken away her husband and turned her parents against her? What kind of friend would that make God?

"Why do we suppose when bad things come that

God is the only one to bring them?"

Ashley heard Pastor McGuire's question and snapped to attention. She looked up to meet the older man's gaze. It was almost as if he'd been waiting for her acknowledgment.

"Sometimes the trials we bear are the consequences of our own actions. We know better than to touch a hot stove. Should we put God to a foolish test and touch it anyway? We know that standing on the railroad tracks in defiance of a speeding locomotive is sure to bring us death. Do we stand there anyway, just to see if God is powerful enough to keep us from harm? Of course not.

"If we put ourselves in harm's way, purposefully seeking our own pleasure and benefit, and then find ourselves in danger, how does this become the fault of our Lord and Savior?" He paused for a moment and studied the faces of his congregation. His expression softened as he continued. "Of course, there are those things that are thrust upon us that are not of our doing." Again he looked directly at Ashley. She warmed under his stare and shifted uncomfortably in her seat. Why had Grandpa and Natalie insisted on sitting so close to the front?

"Sometimes we suffer the consequences of other people's sin. A man is murdered by a thief. He leaves behind a wife and several children. They will bear the consequences of the murderer's actions. Are they to blame? No, of course not, but suffer they will, nevertheless. Does this make God unjust? Does this make God an uncaring bystander who leaves His children to fend for themselves?"

Ashley swallowed hard and leaned forward ever so

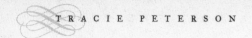

slightly to hear the answer. Surely this man knew her heart—knew the questions and misery that lived there.

"God is not unjust—nor uncaring," Pastor McGuire continued. "He has offered us shelter in His love. The world will do as it will. Sin will abound and the curse of sin will follow from generation to generation. We will neither go untouched nor unscathed. However, we have but to draw nearer to God in order to be healed of the wounds. We have only to rest in Him and find comfort from the pains of this world. Jesus himself said we would have these trials and pains. He said family members would turn against each other because of Him. He said the way would be difficult. . . . However, He promised we would never face it alone."

But I feel alone, Ashley whispered in the depths of her soul. *I feel terribly alone—especially now that Grandpa is dying. How will I make a good home for Natalie once he's gone? How can I be both father and mother to this child?*

She missed the pastor's final comments but stood with the others as they sang another song. This time she paid little attention to the words or music. Ashley knew there was no sense in trying to focus on anything at this point. Her mind was awash in questions without hope of answers.

The days that followed were peaceful ones despite Ashley's worries. Grandpa, although weakened greatly, seemed as alert as ever. The pastor came and played checkers twice, and Natalie read to the older man every evening after supper. The routine seemed comfortable, almost easy.

But by Thursday Grandpa's pain had grown almost unbearable. Ashley offered him the morphine the doctor had given her, but Grandpa was still not yet ready to succumb to the medicated stupor that it promised.

"I need you to go bring my lawyer here. He's been processing some papers for me—some things we have to tend to before I start taking the medicine," Grandpa told her that afternoon.

"I'll go right away," Ashley promised. "Will you be all right alone? I could wait until Natalie comes home from school." It was only after the words were out of her mouth that Ashley remembered Natalie's request to go to the Harvey building site after school.

"No, I'm fine. Just go ahead. I'm going to try to sleep while you're gone," Grandpa replied.

Ashley reached out and gently stroked the old man's snowy white hair. "Grandpa, I love you. I wish I could take this sickness from you."

He smiled up at her, the weariness evident in his expression. "To every man is appointed a time to die."

"I wish it could be otherwise." She took hold of his hand and squeezed it gently. "It's so unfair."

"You're troubled. I can see that," he said, surprising her. "Sit here with me for a minute. The lawyer can wait. Tell me what's on your mind. This is more than just me and my situation."

Ashley carefully sat on the bedside. She knew any movement at all only caused Grandpa greater pain. "I just don't know what to do," she admitted.

"About what?"

She shrugged. "Everything, I guess. I want so much to give Natalie a good home, but I can't be both mother

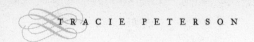

and father to her. I've relied on you for so much over the years, and I don't know how to make it all work."

"You could remarry," Grandpa suggested rather hesitantly.

"That's what Natalie wants," Ashley admitted. "But I could never love another man the way I did Ethan."

"Who's asking you to? Why don't you just love another man for himself?"

"I'm afraid I would always be comparing a new husband to Ethan."

"Child, you only knew Ethan for a short time. Please don't misunderstand me, but can you truly have that much to compare with, or are you living in the memory of what you've created over the long, lonely years?"

Ashley felt as if he'd slapped her. She opened her mouth to speak in anger, then closed it again. Convicted in her own heart, she knew his words held an element of truth. "I suppose there are certain things I've created in my mind. We had so little time together, and I didn't want to lose a single memory. But, Grandpa, he was the love of my life. He made my life seem complete."

"But he's dead and gone. His suffering is over, but yours goes on. Maybe Natalie wants a new father as much for you as for herself. Maybe she realizes how lonely and miserable you are—how much you need a companion."

There was no need to deny it. Ashley knew her grandfather would figure out the truth whether she tried to conceal it or not. "I just don't know if I can open my heart up to someone again. The people I loved so dearly have hurt me so deeply."

"Like your own mother and father?"

"Yes. And my brothers."

"You need to mend that fence."

Ashley jerked upward, bristling at the thought. "Why should I? They care nothing for me. They're the ones who sent me away without another word—without a cent to my name."

"True enough, but they may have had a change of heart. In fact, your brothers and father may never have agreed with your mother's actions at all. You never gave them a chance to voice an opinion. You never let them know where you were, and because you were with me and pleaded for me not to tell them, they don't know how to reach either of us."

"Which is exactly how I want it." Ashley got to her feet. "I can't imagine that they'd care to know where I am—even now."

"But you can't assume that. You need to turn this over to the Lord and work through it, because, frankly, I'd like to see your mama—your aunt Lavelle too before I die."

Ashley had never considered this for even a moment. Up until now, Grandpa had said very little about his daughters. "After the way they treated you, Grandpa, how can you want to see them? They were cruel. They forced you to divide up your property and live without the wealth and possessions you'd collected over the years."

"Those things meant very little to me in light of my children's happiness. I knew the money and things couldn't make them happy," Grandpa admitted, "but I also knew that they would have to come to their own understanding of that. I forgive them for what they said

and did, and I want to put the past to rest."

His expression took on a faraway look, as though he were drawn back in time. "I know there's a possibility they still feel as angry and hateful as they did when I first told them I was leaving the real estate business in Los Angeles. Still, there's the possibility God has done a work in their lives and they've changed." He looked back at Ashley. "I wouldn't want to die and not at least try to make things right. Besides, your mother and father might very well want to be a part of your life— your brothers too. Once I'm gone, you might want them in your life as well. Ashley, at least promise me you'll think about it."

Ashley's breathing quickened with the tightening in her chest. "I'll think about it, but that's all I can promise at this point." But even as she said the words, Ashley knew there wasn't all that much time to think about anything. With the doctor's last visit, she knew there was little time left.

Grandpa smiled. "That's enough. For now."

Ashley thought about his words as she readied herself for town. Running a comb through her bobbed brown hair, she wondered if there was even the slimmest chance that he was right. Maybe her parents had felt bad for the way they'd done things. Perhaps her father, upon hearing what her mother had done, had come to speak with Ashley only to find she'd already gone. It was possible. But did that change things for her? Her mother had still chosen money over love and made it clear that Ashley had no place in her life unless she did likewise. Even if they showed up on the doorstep tomorrow— could she forgive them?

Russell heard the door close and knew Ashley had left the house. He moaned softly as he settled into the mattress.

"Lord, the pain is so great. Please ease it—send me comfort."

He thought of the morphine. It was there for his benefit, and yet he refused to take it. How often in life had there been other things he'd refused—things that might well have made the way easier, less painful?

"I just don't want my head clouded. There's still too much to tend to. I want to see my daughters, Lord. Please bring them to me—please give me time."

Russell had spoken to his lawyer about notifying the women and then stopped short of having the man actually do the deed. Ashley wanted nothing to do with her mother. When he'd moved here to Winslow with Ashley, it had been with the promise that he'd never do anything to give away her whereabouts. Now he needed to ask her to release him from that promise before it was too late.

"She won't like the idea, Lord, but I'm hoping to cushion the blow. Surely once she sees how she doesn't have to worry about where she'll live or the money . . . maybe then she won't mind her mother knowing where she is. Maybe too she'll consider putting the past behind her as I've asked."

"Hello again!" Natalie called to E. J. as she crossed the lobby.

E. J. turned from the older woman and motioned

Natalie to join them. "Natalie, I want you to meet Miss Colter."

Natalie came to a halt in front of the woman and extended her hand. "I'm Natalie, and I want to build things like you do."

Mary Colter nodded and shook Natalie's hand. "It's not an easy job for a woman. Men seldom listen to you, yet they're the ones who generally carry out the actual construction work."

Natalie looked at E. J. and commented, "Mr. Carson says you're the very best. He doesn't mind working for you."

"Yes, well, E. J. is the exception. He seems quite willing to follow instructions."

E. J. laughed. "I wouldn't dare do otherwise. Everyone knows it's better to do what Miss Colter says than to question her. Besides"—he leaned down and whispered conspiratorially—"I think Miss Colter is one terrific lady."

This brought a bit of a chuckle from Mary Colter. "Well, not everyone feels that way, but I'm working on them. Oh, I'll have to talk with you more tomorrow, E. J. I see one of my boys making a mess of the ironwork." She pushed past Natalie without another word.

"Her boys are working here?" Natalie questioned.

E. J. shook his head. "No, she calls all of us 'her boys.' Most of the men hate it, but I find it rather endearing. My own mother is dead and gone, so I don't mind it at all."

"I think she's very nice," Natalie said, watching as Mary Colter waggled her finger at the ironworker.

"Come on, I was just finishing for the day. We can go

look at the garden if you like."

"I really want to get an ice-cream cone. I have enough money to buy you one too," Natalie offered. "Would you like to go with me?"

E. J. considered the matter for a moment. "Wouldn't it seem rather strange for you to go there with a grown man who isn't a member of your family? I wouldn't want your mother to worry."

Natalie whirled around and gazed at the ceiling overhead. "I go have ice creams with lots of grown-ups. People are really nice around here. I don't have to worry 'cause they're all good people. Grandpa says you can always tell good people, and I know you're one of them."

E. J. rubbed his chin. Having had a good portion of his lower face ripped to shreds by the explosion of an enemy potato masher, his jaw periodically ached and caused him pain even after all these years. Today had been one of those days when the dull ache seemed more intense.

"I suppose some ice cream might very well hit the spot," he finally answered. "But it will be my treat."

Natalie shrugged. "If you want to."

They ambled out of the building and headed toward town. "So tell me about your family, Natalie," E. J. said, still not exactly certain that he should be making this trip with the girl.

"My mama and I live here with my grandpa. She moved here before I was even born." Natalie waved to a couple of older men as they ambled along on the opposite side of the street. "Hello, Mr. Braxton, Mr. Lynn." She looked back at E. J. and smiled. "They always walk down to the Harvey House and have supper at exactly five o'clock. My mama says they're always very punctual."

"So you were telling me about your mother. Where did she live before coming here?" E. J. asked innocently.

"Baltimore. She lived there with my daddy before he went to the war. My grandma and grandpa didn't like my daddy, so they were real mean to my mama."

E. J. looked down at the child as if she'd spoken Greek. "Why didn't they like your daddy?"

"He wasn't rich. They wanted Mama to marry a rich man, but Mama said she only loved my daddy and would never love anyone else. And you know what, she never has," Natalie said, looking quite serious. "She says that's what it's like with true love."

E. J. felt his mouth go dry. The child was giving an uncanny account of his own life. How could this be?

"Here's the store I like," Natalie said, rushing into the ice-cream parlor and drugstore without waiting for E. J.

"Hi, Mrs. Nelson," Natalie called as she came to the counter. "I've come for ice cream."

A plump woman stood behind the counter. She put her hands on her hips and smiled. "I suppose you'll be wanting the regular, eh?"

Natalie giggled and nodded. "Chocolate."

The woman then looked to E. J. "Is this man a friend of yours, Natalie?" She eyed him suspiciously.

"Yup. He's working over at the new Harvey House. His name is E. J. Carson and he's an architect like my daddy was. Mr. Carson has been showing me all around the Harvey hotel and he even introduced me to Miss

Colter. She's the one who designed the entire place."

The woman's expression relaxed. She smiled, revealing crooked teeth. "Well, it's a pleasure to meet you, Mr. Carson. Any friend of Natalie's is always welcome here."

"Thank you, ma'am," E. J. replied uncomfortably. He hated to be under anyone's scrutiny, but worse yet, he couldn't stop thinking of what Natalie had shared with him only moments earlier.

E. J.'s mind moved in a hundred different directions. It's just coincidence, he told himself. Just one of those flukes of time and nature. That Natalie's mother should have lived in Baltimore and married against her parents' wishes was just ironic. It wasn't so very extraordinary. E. J. ordered a vanilla cone and paid for the purchase before following Natalie to a small table for two.

"I love to come here. I like to watch the big fans go round and round," she said, pointing overhead. "On a hot day, it's the best place in the world to be."

E. J. nodded and ate absentmindedly. He pulled himself out of his thoughts and looked hard at the child sitting opposite him. Dark brown eyes gazed back at him. Eyes so much like . . .

"My mama likes to come here too, but she's usually too busy," Natalie stated, happily devouring her cone.

"Your mama sounds like a very nice lady," E. J. said, his voice trembling.

"She is. She's the best in the world."

E. J. forced himself to ask the question that wouldn't let him be. "What . . . what is your mother's name?"

"Ashley," Natalie replied. "Ashley Murphy Reynolds."

E. J. stared at the child for a moment, then quickly

got to his feet. "I need to get back. I'm sorry."

"I'll go with you," Natalie said, following him to the door.

"No, that's all right. I forgot something at work."

"There you are!" a familiar voice called out.

E. J. forced himself to look up. It was her. She was alive. His wife was alive.

Ashley moved toward them and smiled. "I figured I'd find you here, Natalie. Who's your friend?"

She didn't recognize him. But why should she? He wore glasses, had a full beard and mustache, and had endured multiple surgeries to set his jaw and lower face in order. There was no reason she should see him for the boyish man who'd gone off to war only a few weeks after their wedding.

"This is Mr. Carson," Natalie told her mother.

"E. J. Carson," he said, extending his hand. He didn't know what else to say. How could he simply introduce himself as her long-dead husband? Furthermore, why did she believe he was dead? Who had told her that? Anger burned inside. Perhaps the same person who had told him she was dead had masterminded a scheme to make her believe he'd perished upon the battlefield.

Ashley's smile was just as he remembered. "It's nice to meet you, Mr. Carson."

"Mr. Carson works building the Harvey hotel," Natalie explained, finishing her ice-cream cone. "He was just going back to work."

"Well, don't let us keep you, Mr. Carson," Ashley said sweetly. "Come along, Natalie, I've been on business for Grandpa and we should get right home. I hate to leave him alone too long."

Natalie nodded and took hold of her mother's hand. "Can Mr. Carson come have dinner with us sometime?"

E. J. cleared his throat uncomfortably. He knew the little minx was playing matchmaker. But he was the only one of the trio who knew there was no need. He was already married to the woman.

Ashley met his gaze and replied, "Of course he can, but not tonight. We have too many things to take care of."

E. J. breathed a sigh of relief. He could barely stand to be this close to her and not pull her into his arms and declare his identity. The only thing that stopped him was the past. A sickening sensation crept over him; the images of his nightmares came to rest on his heart. He was of no good to this woman and her child. *Her child.* Was she also his? His mind reeled. A child? Could he be a father? It was all too much to fathom.

"I really have to go. It was good to meet you, Mrs. Reynolds."

He hurried away, not giving either one of them a chance to reply. With his world crashing down around him, E. J. felt rather like Pandora. He'd opened a box that he'd thought long ago sealed and forever closed to him. His heart begged him to look back over his shoulder—to catch a glimpse of her face once more. But the demons of the past would not let him. How could he saddle a wife and child with the horrors that lived inside him now? He wasn't Ethan Reynolds anymore. In many ways, Ethan Reynolds *had* died on the battlefields of France, just as they presumed he had.

CHAPTER FIVE

E. J. stretched out across his bed and stared up at the ceiling in his hotel room. He'd isolated himself from everyone after learning the truth about Ashley. How could she be alive?

He thought back on every word Natalie had told him. Her grandfather was dying. Would that be Ashley's father? E. J. had never had much to do with the man, but the image of the man's wife, Leticia Murphy, was clearly etched in his memories. As were so many other images.

"She didn't recognize me," he murmured. *But why should she?* He took off his glasses and laid them aside. He looked completely different now. He even shocked himself sometimes when he looked in the mirror. Of course, there was also the fact he'd changed his name. Ashley was introduced to E. J. Carson—not to Ethan Reynolds.

He'd changed his name shortly after learning Ashley was dead. The journalists were hounding him for comments and interviews, for he was heralded as a hero and everyone seemed to want the intimate details of his experiences. When he was stuck in the hospital, there was little he could do to escape the attention. But once he was out, he wanted only to be free from the memories that were stirred every time someone mentioned his deeds. Pity that changing his name hadn't also altered the dark images in his mind.

So he had become E. J. Carson, using the initials of his first and middle names, Ethan James. Carson came compliments of his mother's maiden name. And now he was here in Winslow, where the woman he had long believed to be dead had lived her life for the last decade.

Ashley. He moaned softly and covered his eyes with his hand as if to block out the picture of her standing there in the afternoon sun.

"How can this be happening?" He'd given up hope so long ago. She was dead, they had told him. Dead to influenza. It was reasonable to believe; after all, his own parents had succumbed to the illness, as had vast numbers of other victims. He'd managed to catch it himself after coming home that winter of 1918. Weakened from his injuries, he'd nearly died—so many times he'd wished he had.

He sighed and folded his hands together behind his head and again looked at the ceiling as though it might offer some answers for the questions in his mind.

Ashley's mother must have lied to him. She hated him from the very beginning.

He remembered the night Ashley had first brought him to meet her folks. They were having a celebration of sorts. Ashley's oldest brother had just been made a partner at the bank where he worked. Friends and family had gathered to wish him well and applaud his good fortune. Ashley had insisted on bringing Ethan to the party. Her parents were clearly not pleased, although they had not made a public scene over the matter.

That wasn't true, however, of the next visit he made to their plush Baltimore home. Ashley's mother had made little effort to hide her displeasure. In fact, she'd made more than one comment alluding to Ashley being spoken for—of their plans for her to marry well.

By the time Ashley brought him around for a third visit, Leticia Murphy was willing to speak quite frankly and tell him that he was to leave her daughter alone. When Ashley had gone upstairs to change her clothes, her mother had even offered him money to never see Ashley again. He'd been deeply offended; so much so, in fact, that he'd told Ashley what had happened. Shortly after that incident, Ashley agreed to marry him and on March twentieth they had done exactly that.

Ethan had never known such happiness. He could still see Ashley standing there, her beautiful chocolate brown hair done up in a loose bun. . . .

"She's cut her hair," he murmured, recalling how her hair was bobbed in a fashionable cut. He had never wanted her to cut her hair, but he had to admit the cropping did nothing to take away from her beauty. If anything, it only enhanced her delicate features. No wonder Natalie had appealed to him so much. She looked just like her mother.

Sweat trickled down the side of his face. He wasn't perspiring from the heat, however—it was more a nervous energy that had built inside him since seeing Ashley again. Now, in the quiet of the night, he could scarcely believe the events of the day.

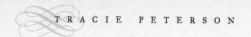
Why hadn't he just told her who he was? Why hadn't he taken her in his arms and . . .

Because you're a coward, that's why, he told himself.

But it wasn't that simple. If it were, that would be easy. Ethan had always found ways to muster up his courage for the moment. No, this was much more difficult and so very complicated.

First there was the obvious problem of letting Ashley know he was alive and well. But then, perhaps she knew that already. Perhaps she had agreed with her parents that Ethan was no good for her and had annulled the marriage. But if that were the case, why had she raised Natalie to believe her father had died in the war?

But was he Natalie's father?

The questions poured in around him like sand through a sieve. What possible good would it do to come back into Ashley's life after all these years? Even if he were Natalie's father, wouldn't it be more harmful than helpful to suddenly make that announcement?

As the night wore on, sleep overcame him and with it came the nightmares that always haunted him. Tossing fitfully, E. J. fought the war all over again. The smell of death permeated the air around him and blended with the heady scent of raw earth. The battle raged and Ethan, with his Springfield rifle, bayonet fixed, waited for the whistle signal that would send him over the top of the trench and into the embrace of eternity.

Suddenly the artillery barrage that had begun at seven that morning stopped. The silence was uncanny, almost deafening. Then without warning, the shrill metallic scream of their advancing signal rent the air. A battle cry rose up from a hundred soon-to-be-dead men as the forces moved up and out of their protective trenches.

Ethan looked to the man on his right—John O'Malley from Boston. They had bonded easily because of an interest they shared in architectural studies. Ethan saw the sheer terror on John's face—and it was as if Ethan stared into a mirror. The man's expression reflected his own heart. They stalked the no-man's-land together, and although hundreds of other uniformed men did likewise, it was almost as if they were alone.

Ethan felt the sweat run down his back and chill him to the bone. The anticipation of enemy fire . . . waiting for the adversary to move from their bunkers to the machine guns . . . waiting for that first spray of deadly rain. It was like a madness—an insanity. How was it that they should find themselves here, like this? How was it that farmers, painters, teachers, and architects were now bearing arms against one another—fighting a war of kings?

Ethan forced himself to keep stride with John and the others as they moved out across the crater-ridden landscape. Someone had mentioned how beautiful the landscape had once been, but Ethan saw only the scars and ugliness. This was the third major battle the area had hosted, and the damage from the artillery had left a desolate and barren land. Even the grass was gone and what trees had existed were now charred, wraithlike figures that rose in ominous fashion—almost as if they were skeletal guards of what had been left behind.

And then the machine guns began their staccato symphony. Bullets zipped past their heads, and the men dove into the nearest crater. All around them soldiers

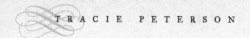
did likewise, some making it without harm, others crying out in pain as the bullets ripped into their flesh.

"For sure it's gonna be a long day," John called over his shoulder. Already he was heading out over the top of the crater. Digging his elbows into the ground, he crawled away from Ethan, pausing only momentarily to raise up his rifle and fire.

Ethan followed, all thoughts of patriotism and bravery faded. All around him men were dying, dropping to the ground with stun-faced expressions. It was almost as if they hadn't expected the possibility of death.

"Help me," one soldier, looking to be only a boy, cried out. He reached out to Ethan in sheer misery. Then his expression changed, the pain vanishing in the noiseless sigh of his last breath. Ethan pushed back the boy's arm and pressed on. The haunting expression stayed with him, however. What had the boy seen on the brink of death? Ethan and his buddies often sat around discussing their lives back home, and every once in a while someone would bring the topic back to the war and the possibility that they would be killed.

John had voiced the question just the night before. "Do you suppose you hear the bullet coming when it's for you?"

Ethan wondered that also as bullets shot past his head.

The danger grew as they closed the gap between their trenches and those of the enemy. The air was thick with smoke and cries of wounded men. With more of the desolate stretch of empty no-man's-land behind them than in front, the men of Ethan's unit and others pushed forward. A charred scarecrow of a tree offered them the tiniest defense. They paused to catch their breath, then saw their comrades moving out.

A sudden *thud* caused the hair on Ethan's neck to rise. He tasted blood and realized he'd bit his own lip. Then, as if time stood still, Ethan froze in place. A potato masher landed only a few feet away. There was no time to yell out a warning. No time to seek cover or turn away. The explosion blasted, sending shrapnel ripping through the lower half of Ethan's face. For a moment there was nothing but the searing heat and sensation of something gone terribly wrong. Then the pain radiated throughout his entire body.

Ethan rolled to his side and touched his face. His hand came away wet with blood. Looking across to his friends, he saw one man's hand torn away. Another man suffered a leg wound. The agony of their pain rose up like a banshee cry on the winds. John was nowhere in sight.

"Oh, God, help us," moaned the man with the leg wound. "Oh, help us, Jesus." The man groped around him for his rifle.

Someone screamed in the distance as another explosion of machine-gun fire cut the air. The scene was unreal; slowed in motion, it seemed to take forever for the unit to move even a few feet.

Ethan struggled to sit up. The rapid-fire barrage of bullets poured over and around him. Across the field, men were struggling to advance, struggling to stay alive. The sight caused something to snap inside him. He was tired of being afraid. Tired of spending his nights in trenches. Tired of this war. Without warning or even stopping to see if he could help his friends, Ethan got to

his feet and stormed across the remaining distance to the machine-gun nest.

He could hardly see out of his right eye; blood and debris barred his sight and made his depth perception questionable at best. But it didn't matter. Staggering as his foot hit a hole, Ethan still refused to stop. Pain shot up his leg and he didn't know if it was from the misstep or a bullet. It didn't matter. Either way, he had a mission to complete.

Pushing past the barrier of sandbags and logs, he fired as he jumped into the enemy trench. The stunned faces of the German soldiers would always haunt him. He shot the gunners first, then bayoneted them even as they cried out in their misery. One man took off down the line and Ethan, in a blood haze that overcame common sense, followed the man.

He couldn't say how many men he killed that day, but he could remember the looks on their faces and the feel of his bayonet stealing the life from them. A dozen or more men dropped their weapons and raised their arms in surrender. Yelling, *"Kamerad! Kamerad!"* But Ethan didn't care that they now wanted to be his friend—that they were willing to give themselves up. He wanted them all dead. He raised his Springfield once again and fired into their pleading expressions.

"Ethan!"

He looked up through the haze and saw John, along with several other men he didn't know. A dizzying sensation overcame him. John and the others pointed their rifles at the enemy just as Ethan felt himself beginning to fall. Helpless, he reached for the open air as if to find something to hold on to, but there was nothing.

E. J. awoke with a start and a cry as he always did. Looking around the darkened room, his mind refused to accept the safety offered there. He got to his feet and turned on a light. The rapid pounding of his heart left him lightheaded and breathless.

"It's all right. It's over," he said aloud.

But would it ever really be over?

He sat down on the edge of the bed, panting for breath. "Oh, God, where are you? Why do you hide yourself from me? Why must this torment go on and on?"

CHAPTER SIX

Ashley sat crocheting a sweater for Natalie, marveling at how much her daughter had grown over the last year. The sweaters she'd made last fall no longer fit and had been given away to friends in the neighborhood. Hooking the red yarn in and out of the loops, Ashley knew in the blink of an eye Natalie would be grown. And then what?

She had tried to save money in order to send Natalie to college, if she desired to go. Right now Natalie wanted very much to train as an architect, but Ashley had no way of knowing if that passion would follow her into adulthood. Natalie would most likely marry, whether or not she went to school. It was just the way of most women. A girl would be frowned upon if she remained single for too long. Even a widow became the object of ridicule if she refused to remarry. Many fellow Harvey workers urged Ashley to consider settling down with one of the railroad men. But Ashley couldn't bring herself to do such a thing. The men, while kind and attentive and often very handsome, were simply not appealing. She'd given her heart to

Ethan, and everyone else paled in comparison.

Still, one day Natalie would make a life for herself. Once Natalie did marry, she would probably move away—maybe far away. She'd have a family of her own.

Ashley shuddered at the thought of being alone. *Maybe I should remarry,* she thought. *I could never love anyone as much as I loved Ethan, but that doesn't mean I couldn't have a good companion. A lot of people marry without love,* she told herself. But what kind of life was that? Would there ever be satisfaction, contentment in such an arrangement?

She was still considering this when the lawyer, Simon Watson, showed up to finalize all of Grandpa's final requests. Ashley put aside her crocheting and opened the door to admit the man.

"Good morning, Mr. Watson," she greeted, reaching out to take his gray fedora.

"Good morning." He smiled ever so slightly and nodded. "Is your grandfather awake?"

"I'm not sure, but I know he'll want to see you. He's weakened considerably since you saw him last week. I'm glad you could make these arrangements quickly because, frankly, he needs the pain medication and he won't take it until his affairs are in order."

The middle-aged lawyer nodded. "He's said as much to me."

Ashley knew there was nothing else to be said. She'd wanted to make certain the lawyer understood Grandpa's plight and apparently he did. "I'll go make sure he's awake," she finally said. "Why don't you have a seat in the living room?"

"Thank you. I'll do just that."

Ashley hurried to Grandpa's room and knocked lightly. "Grandpa? Are you awake?"

"I'm awake. I was just reading." His voice sounded weak and worn.

Ashley came into the room and gave it a cursory examination. Grandpa lay with his Bible in hand. He had asked for several of his favorite books, and they now were stacked beside the iron-framed bed. Beside this, a nightstand of intricately carved oak bore a pitcher of water, a glass, and his pocket watch. Grandpa always liked to keep track of the time.

Ashley went to him and straightened his covers. "Mr. Watson is here to see you."

"Oh, good." Grandpa struggled to sit up.

"Here, let me help you," Ashley said, taking hold of his arm. She carefully helped him to sit, although she could tell his pain was excruciating. Plumping the pillows behind him, she eased him back against them. "How's that?"

"As good as it's going to get," he declared. "Go ahead now and show Simon in."

Ashley fussed with the covers for another moment, then smiled. "Would you like me to bring you something to eat? I could set a tray for you both—a little mid-morning brunch."

"No, nothing. I don't think this will take long. In fact, I need you to stay and hear what Simon has to say."

Ashley had never been included in any of Grandpa's discussions with the lawyer. She nodded slowly. "If that's what you want me to do."

"It is. I have instructions for you, and they need to be carried out immediately."

"Let me go fetch Mr. Watson, then," she said, curious now as to what Grandpa needed her to accomplish.

Ashley bit at her lower lip as she made her way to the living room. The stocky lawyer sat at attention on the sofa. He appeared to be lost in thought momentarily. Ashley stopped and cleared her throat. "Grandpa said he'd see you now. He wants me to come as well."

Watson nodded. "I presumed he would." He picked up his satchel and nodded. "I'll follow you."

Once they were settled back in Grandpa's room, the lawyer turned to open the briefcase he'd brought. "Russell, I believe I've handled everything you asked me to take care of. You'll see that I've sold off the stocks you held and have put the money into a bank account in your granddaughter's name. Here are the figures on these statements." He handed the old man several pieces of paper.

Ashley felt her eyes widen at this news. She had no idea Grandpa even had stocks. She looked to her grandfather for some sign of confirmation, but the old man was intent on studying the papers given him.

"What about the house?" he asked.

Watson nodded. "I've arranged it all. The deed is now in Mrs. Reynolds's name. She owns the house free and clear."

"What's this all about, Grandpa?" Ashley questioned, feeling mild shock at the lawyer's words.

"I've put my affairs in order," Russell Whitman stated simply. He lowered the papers and looked at Ashley with a serious expression. "I paid cash for this house; there are no bank liens on it, so now it's yours without restriction. I don't have long, child. We both know that.

The last thing I want to do is have you fretting and stewing over how you'll manage once I'm gone."

Ashley felt her cheeks grow hot. She had been fretting over that very thing, but not because of the money or her home. She knew she'd get good wages at the Harvey House and besides, she'd already set aside a good portion in savings. She had hoped to make it a college fund for Natalie but knew they could easily use the money to live on if necessary.

"There are conditions, however," Mr. Watson stated in his lawyerly way. He looked to Grandpa to take it from there.

"That's right," Grandpa said. His gaze never left her. "I want to see your mother and her sister Lavelle before I die." Ashley stiffened but said nothing. He continued. "All these years I've abided by your wish that we have no contact with them, but now I need to break that agreement. And I need your help."

Grandpa looked at her with an expression of mixed emotions. "Your job is to contact them both and bring them here. If they need money to make the trip, then tell them it will be provided."

Ashley swallowed hard. The thought of having to deal with her mother at a time like this was more than she wanted to endure. She twisted her hands together. "But what if they don't want to come?"

"That's a chance I must take." Grandpa's voice took on a saddened tone. "I must account for that possibility, but if we don't at least try, we won't know. After all, we've been here for all this time without letting anyone know where we'd disappeared to. Your mother and aunt could be half sick wondering where we are."

Ashley folded her arms against her chest. "Like they would ever care. They didn't care then; why should they care now?"

Grandpa's expression grew pained. Ashley felt terrible for destroying his hopes and immediately tried to turn the tables on her own question. "On the other hand," she hurried to continue, "they could be sorry for the way they acted. They could possibly want to see us both."

The lawyer nodded. "Exactly. There's a good chance that all has been forgiven and forgotten. You must at least give them the chance to refuse."

"I can telegram them at the last known addresses," Ashley added. "Would that be sufficient for a start?"

Grandpa smiled. "I think it would be a good way to begin." He seemed to recover a bit of his positive spirit. "Ashley, I know you have been deeply hurt by your mother and father. I was hurt by them as well. But I want you to know that there is nothing to be gained in holding a grudge. There's also Natalie to consider. Do you want to teach her the same kind of hatred and anger?"

Ashley was rather startled by his words. She'd never wanted Natalie to feel the same hurt and anger she felt. In fact, she'd avoided telling Natalie much of anything about her grandma and grandpa Murphy in order to avoid speaking ill of them. Still, even while she'd tried hard not to show her animosity toward her mother and father, Natalie was no dummy. She knew there were problems, and true to her gentle and compassionate nature, she never pressed Ashley for answers.

"You don't want to teach Natalie to hate her family. If they reject her or cause her grief, then let her decide for herself. Either way, I need to see my daughters—and I need you to help me."

Ashley met his pleading eyes. "All right."

"Good. Now that we have that matter resolved," Mr. Watson interjected, "I want to discuss the sale of your stocks. The result was quite lucrative. I've also been told that there is a buyer for your property east of town. That is, if you are of a mind to sell."

Grandpa looked at Ashley as if for an answer, but she felt she could be of no help. She didn't even realize Grandpa owned stocks, much less property. "What property is Mr. Watson speaking of, Grandpa?"

"Oh, it's just some acreage I picked up a few years past. I was helping out a friend who needed the money," Grandpa replied.

Ashley realized she'd paid very little attention to her grandfather's business dealings over the years. She supposed it shouldn't be that surprising that Grandpa should have found a way to turn a dollar. Everyone was always saying he had a golden touch. Suddenly her curiosity got the better of her.

"Grandpa, what kind of money are we talking about in regard to the sale of these stocks?"

Russell looked to his lawyer for this information. The lawyer looked down at his own copy of notes. "It would appear once funeral expenses and transportation to Los Angeles are subtracted that you would realize the sum of around $82,370 and some odd change. Of course, that doesn't include the sale of the land."

Ashley sat back feeling as though the wind had been knocked out of her. Nearly one hundred thousand dollars! How could this be?

"What's wrong?" Grandpa asked. His tone revealed his concern for her.

"I can't believe . . . well . . . we're rich."

Grandpa winced as he chuckled. "I'm full of surprises. I wanted you and Natalie to be provided for. It was important to me to see that you had what you needed after I was gone."

"But so much? I'm just . . . well . . ." She looked at the lawyer. "I'm shocked."

"Well, I hope it's a pleasant shock. You deserve to be happy, Ashley. You've worked hard all these years to provide for your child. I let you work because it was easier than arguing with you. Besides, in the early days I feared your sorrow would overcome you. You had Natalie, but sometimes I feared she only added to your pain. Then, too, I wanted you to have a sense of self-worth. You know you're capable of doing what needs to be done now. You know that God will provide in any circumstance."

Ashley shook her head. "I suppose if I didn't know that before, I know that now."

Grandpa reached out his hand and Ashley quickly came to his side. Grasping his bony hand, Ashley leaned down to kiss his fingers. The man had once weighed just over two hundred pounds, but the cancer had reduced that number by at least fifty.

All at once, Ashley began to feel very guilty. Did Grandpa feel he had to give her the money and house just to convince her to contact her mother and Lavelle? She felt very ashamed. *I've kept him from his daughters all these years. What if he's right? What if they've changed?*

"I'll do what I can to please you, Grandpa. I'll send the telegrams and encourage Mother and Aunt Lavelle to come, but you don't have to give your money to me. I'd do it anyway—because it's what you want. Besides, if I know Mother, at least, she'll expect the money and house to go to her."

Russell frowned at this. "I gave her an inheritance long ago. Her sister too. They've had what's coming to them. This is for you and Natalie. I took what I had left after settling on them both and came here to start a new life with you. I bought the house free and clear and took the remaining money and invested it. I did so only with the thought that you and Natalie might be provided for. And that's why I've asked Simon to take care of all this business today. There will be no misunderstanding when my time comes. In fact, you needn't even answer any of your mother's or Aunt Lavelle's questions regarding any money. Send them to Simon. There are issues and details that you needn't worry yourself with, that Simon is fully knowledgeable of. He can handle them if they decide to get greedy."

The lawyer nodded. "I've dealt with harder cases than theirs," he said. "You refer them to me if there is any question at all about the settlement of this estate."

"That's the beauty of this arrangement," Grandpa added. "There is no estate. As far as they're to know, the place is yours and everything in it. Because now, thanks to Simon, that's the truth of it. They don't need to know where you came by it or how."

"It means more to me than you'll ever know to have a home for Natalie. She loves it here. And I know the memories of our time here together will keep her from . . . from . . ." Ashley's words halted as she tried to think of a way to say what she needed to without bringing up Grandpa's death.

He smiled as if knowing. "She'll be fine, you know. When I'm gone, she'll be sad for a time, but she'll know where I am and that we'll meet again." He drew a breath that seemed to pain him more than ever.

"You should rest now."

"No, there's one more thing I want to say. Our Natalie wants you to remarry. She's mentioned it in prayer so often that I'm beginning to expect an announcement most every time you come into the room."

Ashley shook her head. "Natalie dreams big."

"You should too. God has a plan for each one of us. You have a child to raise, and I can hardly believe God wants you to do that alone. You need to at least think about remarrying so that Natalie can have a father."

Ashley straightened. She bit back a retort that Natalie *had* a father and although he was dead, he was nevertheless irreplaceable. "I'm thinking on it," was all she could manage to say.

"Well, if there is no further business, I must be getting back to my office," Mr. Watson said, getting to his feet. He tucked his copy of the papers back into the satchel. "I know my way out, Mrs. Reynolds. There's no need for you to accompany me. When you are ready for the details of the bank account and other information, feel free to come see me."

"I will," Ashley replied. "Thank you." She waited until she'd heard the front door close before turning to Grandpa. "I'm going to compose the telegrams for

Mother and Lavelle. Is there anything in particular you want me to say to them?"

Russell Whitman closed his eyes and grimaced. "Tell them to hurry."

CHAPTER SEVEN

*S*o your grandfather has provided for you?" a young blond-haired woman asked, leaning across the Fred Harvey lunch counter.

Ashley nodded to her friend Glenda. "He has and he's done so very generously. I won't even have to come back to work here if I don't want to."

"By the time you're ready to come back to work," Glenda said, straightening up to smooth the white apron of her Harvey uniform, "we'll have moved to the new place." She pushed a piece of pie in front of Ashley and smiled. "The resort is supposed to be the bee's knees. All beautiful blue and yellow tile in the lunch room, and the dining room will be better than ever."

"I've heard all that too," Ashley said, picking up a fork. She cut into the apple pie and took a bite. As always, Harvey food was sheer perfection. She smiled and leaned back to contemplate her future. "The new place sounds really nice. I've been watching them put it up as I walk by to come here. Of course, I don't get out as much as I used to." Ashley continued eating the pie.

"I was going to ask you about that. Is Grandpa Whitman home alone?"

Ashley shook her head and swallowed. "No, I had some things to do, so I asked Mrs. Breck to come over. She lives a few blocks away but always needs to earn an extra dime or two. I feel sorry for her, so when I get extra sewing money, I let her come do a few chores for me."

"You'll be able to hire her full-time now. Goodness, you won't even need to stay in Winslow if you're of a mind to move away," Glenda commented. "You could even get a transfer to one of the Harvey Houses in California. I'd sure love to go to California."

Ashley knew she spoke the truth, but as much as her memories of Los Angeles caused her to want to revisit the sights from time to time, she never really wanted to leave Winslow. "I've no desire to go away from here. I like Arizona, and I like the way the people are here. Besides, Natalie's been here all her life and she's happy here."

"Well, I know that's important, but maybe you'd both be happier in a bigger town." A distant train whistle perked Glenda's attention. "Well, we're bound to get busy now. I'd better stop gabbing. You know how maddening the pace can get at the lunch counter."

Ashley nodded. "I'll finish up here and be on my way. There was trouble with the telegraph lines. They told me to come back later, but I still need to write out what I want to say to my mother and Aunt Lavelle."

"What *are* you going to say?" Glenda asked, her blue eyes seeking Ashley's face for an answer.

Ashley didn't mind her probing question. Glenda

had been as close of a friend as Ashley wanted. They didn't do a lot of running around or going places. Many times Glenda had tried to talk Ashley into side trips on the train or just sightseeing to places like the nearby meteor crater, but Ashley generally declined because of Natalie. She hated leaving Natalie behind for any reason, and a group of single adults really had no use for a child.

Eating the last of her pie, Ashley shrugged and wiped her mouth with a napkin. "Grandpa said to tell them to hurry. Otherwise, I don't know what to say. I mean, how do I just open up the lines of communication after ten years of separation?"

Glenda took up the plate and fork. "I can't imagine not talking to my mama for over ten years."

Ashley felt the cynicism streak up her spine. "If my mother were your mother, you could imagine it well enough."

The rumble of the train drew their attention as the passenger service slowed to a stop outside. "Talk to you later," Ashley said, giving Glenda a little wave. She hurried across the room and out the side door before the crowds could pour in.

She couldn't help smiling at the ruckus behind her. Life in the Harvey House was always exciting. Especially in this town, where the passenger trains came through at regular intervals. Ashley missed the commotion and urgency. She loved being home with Grandpa and Natalie, but Natalie was at school all day and Grandpa slept a good portion of the time. The old man was unable to bear up under the pain, and now that he had finally allowed Ashley to give him doses of the

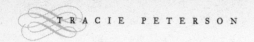

morphine, he slept more than ever. Already she had begun to mourn him—the one thing she'd promised herself she wouldn't do until he was actually gone.

Stepping outside into the comfortable warmth of the late afternoon, Ashley pulled the brim of her straw hat down to avoid freckling from the sun. Consumed with thoughts of the job she had to do, Ashley's steps were slow and methodical.

How do I write to Mother when she swore she'd never speak to me again—never hear a word I had to say? What makes me think she'll even read a telegram that I send? Then it dawned on Ashley that perhaps the best thing to do would be to send the telegram in her grandfather's name. She could send the news that he was gravely ill, not expected to live, and that he desired to see his daughters again. Ashley could even mention that she was now living with Grandpa—Natalie too. But sign the entire message from Russell Whitman instead of Ashley Reynolds.

It seemed reasonable. It also seemed to lessen the feeling that Ashley was betraying herself and Ethan's memory. She had sworn she'd never again talk to her mother or father or have any communication with them as to her whereabouts. Somehow it seemed an honorable thing to do for Ethan.

"Oh, excuse me."

Ashley looked up at the sound of a familiar voice. Strange how thinking of Ethan had caused the stranger's tone to sound so similar. She looked into the face of E. J. Carson and blinked against the glare. "I'm sorry, did I nearly run you over?" she questioned, realizing she hadn't been paying attention to where she was going.

"It's as much my fault," E. J. replied. "I wasn't paying attention either." His voice sounded shaky, almost as if they'd nearly fallen off the edge of a cliff rather than simply bumping into each other on the street.

The silence between them seemed quite awkward, and with nothing else to say, Ashley smiled and excused herself. "Well, I'll be on my way."

E. J. blurted out, "I think you have a very remarkable daughter. She's been here several times to study the architecture of the hotel."

Ashley paused in midstep. "Yes. She loves it. She's quite good at drawing her own designs."

E. J. nodded and a lock of wavy brown hair fell over his forehead, touching his gold-rimmed glasses. Ethan's hair had been wavy and brown as well. He wore it shorter and fashioned just a little different, but nevertheless, Mr. Carson's hair reminded her of her husband. For just a moment, Ashley almost reached up to push it back. She stopped herself just in time and shook her head. "Natalie speaks quite highly of you. I know she enjoys learning about the hotel. It's kind of you to be so patient with her."

He looked at the ground, seeming most uncomfortable. "I enjoy it myself. I haven't had the opportunity to be around many children in my day, but Natalie is so much like a little adult that I scarcely notice the difference."

"She is like that," Ashley admitted. "She is probably far too much like that for her own good." Ashley could clearly see that E. J. wasn't at ease with her. She thought it strange, given the fact he'd started the conversation to begin with, but took that moment to put an end to their talk.

"I must be going. My grandfather is ill and I need to return home."

Mr. Carson nodded. "I am sorry about that. Natalie mentioned her grandfather was ill."

"Actually, it's her great-grandfather, but he's known by most everyone around here as Grandpa Whitman, so she just calls him that too." E. J. looked up and Ashley added, "I hope things go well for you. I'm sure we'll meet again."

"To be sure," Carson replied.

That evening Ashley thought back to her encounter with E. J. Carson while Natalie sat playing jacks on the floor of their living room. He seemed so eager to share his admiration of Natalie, yet so uncomfortable in speaking to Ashley.

Picking up her crochet work, Ashley wondered about Natalie and her artistic talent. She came by it naturally, that was for sure. Ethan had been a master at drawing. He'd won several awards and the esteem of his teachers. Perhaps Glenda's thoughts of their moving away weren't quite so out of line. Maybe Natalie could benefit by moving closer to a school that had classes for architects. It bore some consideration.

Her thoughts quickly moved from Natalie and school, however, to the task of notifying her mother and aunt of Grandpa's illness. The telegraph office had remained closed and it seemed like a respite to Ashley. She supposed it might be prudent to check into telephoning, for her mother and father had put in a telephone in the years prior to Ashley leaving home. But she no longer recalled the number. Maybe they didn't even have the same number, and if that were the case, how would she find out how to reach them?

This is so hard, she thought. *I don't know anything about Mother and Father these days. They could be dead for all I know.* Ashley thought of that for a moment and wondered if it would grieve her to know they'd passed from this life without resolving the differences between them.

Then even as she thought of this, she looked at Natalie and knew how awful it would feel if Natalie rejected her the way Ashley had rejected her mother. *But my mother brought it on herself,* Ashley reminded herself. *I wasn't the one to say I'd never have anything more to do with them, until it was demanded of me that I never return—never write—never contact them at all.*

And for what? Because her mother's pride had been damaged? Because they couldn't seal the deal with their wealthy, politically-minded friends? Because Ashley wouldn't marry into the upper crust of Baltimore society?

She remembered her mother's anger and rage upon learning of Ashley's marriage to Ethan. The conversation had been so ugly and hurtful. Her mother accused Ashley of trying to destroy everything her father had worked for. Leticia Murphy had slapped her daughter hard across the face, telling her that she hoped to "knock some sense" into her wayward child.

Staring down at her crocheting, Ashley realized she'd messed up several stitches and had to pull out the thread and go back. She wished it could be that easy to unravel the mistakes of the past. Maybe her mother was sorry for what had transpired. Maybe she wished over

and over that she'd never acted the way she had.

Ashley looked at her daughter once again. Her mother and father didn't even know about Natalie. Ashley had never been given a chance to explain. They only knew that their daughter had defied them and their wishes for her life. They only knew that their bank accounts would not be quite so large because Ashley had married a lowly architect.

"Are Grandma and Grandpa Murphy going to visit us?" Natalie asked, as if she could read her mother's thoughts.

Ashley continued working, paying closer attention to the stitches. "I don't know, Nat. They might. Grandpa wants them to come, so I hope they will," she said, though she really didn't want them to come. She looked down at Natalie, hoping her daughter would just drop the subject.

"I hope they will too," Natalie said, pushing her jacks aside and stretching out on the floor. She leaned up on one elbow. "Grandpa says he's just holding on for the day he can seek their forgiveness and see the family brought back together. Do you think Grandma Murphy and her sister will forgive Grandpa?"

Probably not, Ashley thought to herself. *Not if my mother is still the self-centered, bitter woman she was when I left.* Ashley shrugged. "You know, I don't see that Grandpa has anything to be forgiven for. Frankly, your grandpa is one of the most giving and loving men I've ever known. If Grandma Murphy and Aunt Lavelle can't understand that, then it's their loss."

"Grandpa hopes they'll come to know Jesus before he dies. He hopes that for you too," Natalie said, smiling. "He says you'll all be much happier if you know the source of life."

Ashley bit her tongue. How dare Grandpa put her in the same category as her mother and aunt? They'd deserted him and done nothing but hurt him. *I'm not like that*, Ashley told herself, feeling a frustration she couldn't begin to explain.

"Look, you need to get ready for bed. Have you put your clothes out for tomorrow?"

Natalie moaned. "Yes, but can't I stay up? It's just eight o'clock."

"If you want to read in your bed for half an hour, then you need to get headed that way. By the time you get your jacks cleaned up, make sure your clothes are ready for tomorrow, brush your teeth, and actually get into bed, it will be eight-thirty. Then if you read for half an hour, it will be nine. So you need to scoot." She smiled at Natalie, trying hard not to take out her frustration on the child.

Natalie yawned and picked up her jacks. "Okay." She pushed the jacks into a little drawstring bag that Ashley had made for her, then came to give her mother a hug and kiss. "I love you, Mama."

"I love you too, Natalie. Always remember that, no matter what happens. We have each other."

"We've got Jesus too," Natalie insisted.

Ashley nodded. "I'm sure we do."

"Mama, what are we going to do after Grandpa is gone?" Natalie asked as she pulled away from the embrace.

"What do you mean?"

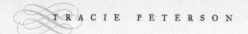

"Well, where are we going to live and who will take care of us?"

"We'll live right here. Grandpa made sure of that. The house is ours. As for who will take care of us—well, I'll take care of us. I have some money and we've always gotten by without any trouble before."

"Sure, but we had Grandpa. When he's gone we won't have a man of the house. That worries Grandpa and it worries me. I think you should get married again."

If a noose had tightened around her neck, it couldn't have caused Ashley more discomfort. The very idea of sharing her life with a stranger was more than she wanted to imagine. She'd given cursory thought to remarrying. She'd acknowledged that she didn't want to be alone for the rest of her life, but marrying again was a fearful thought.

Natalie continued before Ashley could respond. "Mr. Carson is very nice. He's handsome too, don't you think?"

Ashley was even more taken aback by her daughter's reference to E. J. Carson's appearance. "I don't think that's something a little girl should be thinking about."

Natalie shrugged. "His wife died, so he knows how it feels to lose someone you love. He knows a lot about building things too, and he likes the desert. He might like to stay here once the hotel is built, and maybe he'd even like to have a family."

"Where do you get these wild ideas?" Ashley said, shaking her head. "Go on, now, and go to bed. Your imagination will wear you out if you don't."

Natalie turned to go but paused by the arched entry.

"I want a daddy. Someone who will teach me things and who will keep you from being too lonely." She didn't wait for Ashley's reply but instead headed off for her room.

Ashley contemplated her daughter's words and felt tears form in her eyes. "Have I so deprived her by not remarrying? I thought I'd done a good job of raising her. I thought having Grandpa here would make the loss of her father easier—more acceptable," Ashley whispered to the empty room. "Was I blind to her need—to mine?"

———

Russell Whitman stared into the darkness of his bedroom. He'd found it impossible to sleep, although he'd dozed from time to time when the pain hadn't been too much. He wondered if his daughters would come to see him. He wondered, too, if they would be willing to make some sort of peace with him—and with Ashley.

Pastor McGuire had said that God only expected him to do the things that were up to him to do. He couldn't force Lavelle and Leticia to care about him or his beliefs.

"But I want them to love you, Lord," he whispered.

Weary from the battle, Russell drew a ragged breath. "I want them to love me again as well. Is that so wrong?"

He remembered a time when the girls had been very small. They were such giggle boxes, as he affectionately called them. Work kept him away from home much of the time, but when he could, he arranged picnics or outings to show them how much he loved them.

"Ah, Peg, do you remember it?" He spoke to his

dead wife as though she might answer. "You would dress in those lovely silk gowns. You always looked like a billowing cloud. The girls would wear pink ribbons in their hair, and you would don one of those extravagant hats that had become so fashionable."

He smiled at the memory. In his mind he could see his little girls playing ball or hopscotch. Once he had made them a kite and they'd gone to the beach to fly it. It had crashed after only a few short tours in the air, but they'd had a marvelous time.

What had happened to change all of that?

Russell knew he'd taken up with the wrong people and had worried about the wrong things. Money had become increasingly important, and the more he made, the more he needed. It was a vicious circle that robbed him of time and of his children.

I can't change that now, he reasoned, *but if only they'll come and see me, then maybe I can die in peace.*

But there was always the chance they wouldn't come. Streaks of pain shot out across his body, but the pain in his heart was still more intense. If they wouldn't come—wouldn't even acknowledge his need—it would surely kill him quicker than the cancer.

E. J. Carson sat across from Mary Colter at the impeccably dressed dinner table in the Winslow Harvey House. Fine linen tablecloths and napkins lent elegance to the patterned china and silver. The traditional settings of the Fred Harvey table were not to be ignored. Coming into the room, E. J. had immediately been transported from the tiny desert town to one of the better East Coast supper clubs. And that was just as Fred Harvey, the creator of this experience, would have had it. It was good to see that in spite of the man having died over twenty years earlier, his sons were still looking to fulfill and carry out their father's dream.

E. J. glanced to Mary's right, where Earl Altaire, an artist who'd been hired to do paintings on the stucco walls, sat trying to explain a pattern he intended to use. He was sketching on a torn scrap of paper with a piece of charcoal he'd taken from his pocket. Mary nodded and from time to time commented, although E. J. couldn't tell what was being said. To Mary's left was E. V. Birt, master carpenter, who would take Mary's furnishing ideas and recreate an antique look. The man had a true gift for working with his hands, and E. J. had thought to question him about some benches that were being designed for the lobby when the man on his right began to tap on his water glass.

"I'd like to make an introduction."

E. J. recognized the man who spoke. He held some sort of position with the Winslow Chamber of Commerce. However, the man's name totally eluded him.

E. J. paid attention as the older man motioned to a tall, lanky fellow on his right. The man had a good-natured look about him, rather casual and almost out of place at the elegantly set table.

"This man is responsible for designing our airport. Of course, that is but one of his many accomplishments. He was the first to cross the Atlantic, and he sealed Winslow's prosperity when he made her a part of the new Transcontinental Air Transport service. I give you Charles Lindbergh."

E. J. nodded in acknowledgment but said nothing. He didn't really have a chance. Other people began to talk around him, asking Lindbergh questions and listening to the somewhat shy man speak about his exploits.

"What was it like to fly across the Atlantic?" one rather enthusiastic man questioned. E. J. recognized the man as one who assisted Mary in her scheduling.

"It was long," Lindbergh replied with a grin.

The conversation went on, but E. J. found himself bored. Flying was a fascinating thing but much too expensive for the common man to really take note of. There was discussion of how flying would soon put train service out of business, but E. J. found that hard to believe. Trains were more accessible. Trains could be routed via spurs to every city in America—even very small towns could have train service. Planes would never have that kind of accessibility. Besides, he didn't know many people who would trust themselves to such contraptions. Hanging high above the ground was hardly his idea of sensible.

As the conversation at the opposite end of the table continued in the direction of flight, Mary Colter focused on the hotel. "I'm wondering if you found those swatches of material for me to examine, Mr. Birt."

The man perked up at the sound of his name. "I have the silk velour in mulberry, mauve, and plum. Each varies a little from the other, but I think it will give you a nice selection to choose from."

Mary nodded. "I want it for seat padding on the horseshoe chairs," she said, looking to E. J. as if he'd asked a question. "The wood is a lovely walnut, and I believe the cushions will be just as vital as the rest of the chair." She turned to Birt. "I'll see them in the morning."

"I'll have them ready. Also . . ." He hesitated momentarily. "I have some questions regarding the chandeliers you wanted carved. The wood isn't the quality I'd like to see."

They continued to talk about the light fixtures while E. J.'s thoughts wandered back to his own dilemma. Ashley and Natalie were never far from his mind. He toyed with the prime rib he'd ordered for dinner, pushing the pink meat around his plate to give the appearance of actually eating. From time to time he put a piece of the tender beef in his mouth, grateful it wasn't tough like some meat he'd endured. Ever since his jaw had been damaged in the war, his ability to chew had suffered. Funny how something so simple and commonplace could sometimes cause him great pain.

"Mr. Carson, you've not said more than two words this evening. Is there a problem?" Mary Colter demanded.

E. J. smiled. Mary brooked no nonsense from "her boys." "No, ma'am. I'm just reflecting on personal matters."

She nodded, her probing gaze bringing him a moment of discomfort. "Are you able to come with me to that old Mormon fort tomorrow? I want to bring in more of that stone for the west wall. It's perfect for landscaping and giving the grounds an antique appearance. The more we utilize the natural resources at hand, the better off we are."

E. J. had heard it all before. "I can come with you if you need me to. There is still the matter of seeing to that list of issues you had with the west wing."

Mary considered this for a moment then waved her fork at him. "Stay here. I need those things taken care of. I'll take a couple of my boys to help me. If you talk to any of the locals, see if you can round up some old relics that might make pleasant *objets d'art.*" She didn't even wait for E. J.'s reply but turned to the man beside her. "Now, Mr. Altaire, we need to discuss the designs for the hall. I have in mind a vining leaf and flower."

E. J. let his thoughts recede to Ashley and Natalie. It felt strange to realize and truly accept that he had a wife and child to consider. Even if he couldn't be sure Natalie was his child, he knew if he took Ashley back into his life, Natalie would naturally come along too.

Memories of his short whirlwind romance with Ashley Murphy came to mind. He'd first set his gaze upon her in the park. She was there with friends, laughing as she seemed wont to do. She appealed to him because of her vivacious spirit and her simplistic elegance. She'd worn a plain white muslin dress, pleated in the bodice and layered in the skirt. The sunlight gave her face a delightful glow, but her eyes seemed to sparkle with a light all their own. Ethan had been mesmerized.

He'd spied a couple of his college classmates talking with Ashley and her girlfriends. They seemed to be enjoying a leisurely game of croquet and the afternoon air. Ethan knew their social circles separated them, but as a college student he felt he could cross some barriers better than others. He longed to be included in that group, and barrier or no, the next time he saw them gathered, he made certain someone introduced him to the young beauty.

The opportunity came at a war-relief rally. Americans were doing their part to aid their European brothers, and if it presented a reason to have a celebration at the same time, people seemed all in favor of that. Ethan worried that the war would soon spread to engulf the Americans, and he wondered if he would go and fight or avoid taking up arms. He was still contemplating this matter when his classmate introduced him to Ashley Murphy.

He could still picture her warm chocolate brown eyes. She looked at him with such intensity, almost as if he were a piece of art she would study in detail.

"Ethan is an architect," his friend announced.

"Well, at least I'm in training to be one," Ethan corrected. "So far, no one's hired me on."

"It's just a matter of time," his friend interjected. "Ethan is top in the class."

"I'm glad to meet you," Ashley said, reaching out to shake Ethan's hand.

The moment their hands touched, Ethan felt the overwhelming sensation of electricity that moved between them. He wouldn't say it was exactly love at first sight, but it was certainly fascination at first sight.

From that point on, they began a conversation that didn't seem to end until three weeks later, when they agreed on a whim to get married.

E. J. shook the memories from his mind. *I was a different man then. She barely knew me, and what little she knew was completely lost in the trenches of France.*

He nodded as a Harvey waitress in her pristine black and white offered him coffee. The hot liquid helped warm the chill left by the memories of what had been.

Glancing across the room, E. J. noticed a man watching him most intently. The man was just a bit stocky in build, with a head full of curly brown hair. He wasn't at all familiar to E. J., but he stared in his direction as if he knew him. An uneasiness crept along E. J.'s spine. What did the man want? Who was he?

You're just being paranoid, he told himself. He drank from the cup and tried to steady his nerves long enough to take a second glance. The man was still watching.

Then it dawned on E. J. Charles Lindbergh sat at their table. The man was a notable public figure. No doubt the watcher had in mind that he might meet the famous flyer.

E. J. stole another glance and felt his heart pick up its pace. He'd so long hidden himself away from the press and anyone at all who knew him for who he'd been when he called himself Ethan Reynolds. He'd grown weary of his hero status, feeling that people were always trying to claim a piece of him. One woman had even snipped his hair, proclaiming she would have good fortune for the rest of her life because she had a locket of Ethan Reynolds's hair. Now there were Ashley and Natalie to consider, and until he was ready to let them know his identity, he certainly didn't need someone else spilling the news.

E. J. forced himself to go through the motions of drinking his coffee and eating his peach shortcake. It had to be Lindbergh the man was watching. No one knew he was really Ethan Reynolds. Even his wife didn't know, and she'd spoken to him twice now.

He'd convinced himself that his identity was safe, until the man got up from his table and moved across the room. E. J. tensed, fighting the urge to flee. *This is stupid,* he told himself. *It's been ten years. No one knows what I look like or where I've gone.*

"I wonder if I might be so bold as to introduce myself," the man said, standing just to the right of E. J. "I'm Marcus Greeley. I'm a journalist and author by trade. I saw Mr. Lindbergh here and I couldn't help myself."

E. J. breathed a sigh of relief. He didn't even bother to look up as the conversation continued at the other end of the table and introductions were made.

"Miss Colter," E. J. said, putting his fork aside, "I'm afraid a headache is keeping me from being any real use to you. I'm going to make it an early night."

Mary Colter nodded. "I'll speak to you in the morning before I head out. Why don't we meet here and talk over breakfast?"

"I'll be here," E. J. promised.

He moved past Mr. Greeley, only to have the man extend his hand. "The name's Greeley. Marcus Greeley."

E. J. didn't look up but nodded. "E. J. Carson." He shook the man's hand rather abruptly, then turned without another word. The man might think him rude, but he'd never guess his true identity if E. J. had anything to say about it.

The last thing I need, E. J. thought, *is for someone to declare that the famous Hun killer, Ethan Reynolds, is in town.*

CHAPTER EIGHT

I need to send two telegrams," Ashley announced as she approached the telegraph operator's counter. She'd only learned a few minutes ago that the wires were finally up and running. Grandpa was fading fast, and she knew that time was of the essence.

"What do you want to say?" the man asked, taking up a pencil and pad.

Ashley opened the first of the two missives. "This goes to Mrs. Lavelle Guzman. 'Please come to Winslow, Arizona, immediately. I am dying and wish to see you. If money is a concern, please advise. Father.'"

Ashley gave the man the Los Angeles address for her aunt, then folded the piece of paper away and opened the second. "The other telegram is for Mrs. Leticia Murphy." The message read the same, but Ashley added, "'Please be aware I currently reside with Ashley and her daughter.'" She again had him sign the missive, "Father."

"These are urgent," she told the man. "My grandfather hasn't got long to live, and he wants to see his daughters before he dies."

"I'll do what I can from this end," the man assured her. He figured the cost and Ashley paid him before he asked, "If there's a reply, where should it be delivered?"

Ashley hadn't thought of a reply. She wrote her address down for the man and pushed it across the highly polished counter. "Just bring any response here."

She hurried to leave before she could change her mind. She knew the telegrams had to be delivered— knew that Grandpa was only holding on in order to see his daughters again. But Ashley could imagine the conflict ahead and it caused her stomach to ache just thinking about it.

Pushing open the door, she stumbled into the brilliance of the morning sun. Stubbing her toe, she sucked in her breath and fought to keep from crying. Then suddenly it wasn't her toe at all that brought the tears.

"What if Mother refuses to come because of me?" she murmured, wiping her eyes. She tried to straighten and regain her composure. *Then it will be my fault that Grandpa dies without feeling he's made his peace with her. I'll never be able to live with myself if that happens.*

There was a bit of chill to the air. It was well into September and the dry hot days of summer were behind them. Ashley had heard Mrs. Taylor mention the possibility of rain, but the clear skies overhead suggested nothing of the kind. Instead, as the wind whipped up, Ashley tasted the desert grit against her teeth and lips. It only served to make her more uncomfortable.

"Are you all right?"

She looked up into the face of E. J. Carson. Funny how he always seemed to turn up when she least expected it. She drew a deep breath and quickly looked away. "I'm fine." She choked back a sob and shook her head. "No, I'm not fine. I'm sorry."

"Would you like to take a walk, maybe talk it out?" The compassion in his tone became her undoing.

Ashley bit her lower lip as her tears spilled. "I'm afraid I would be a poor conversationalist."

"Never mind talking, then. We can simply walk, and if you feel you can share the burden with me, I'll be here ready and able to listen."

She nodded ever so slightly and allowed E. J. to lead her away from the busyness of town.

E. J. had no idea what had gotten into him. How in the world did he find himself walking along Second Street with his wife? He stared at the ground, trying to think of something to say. A tiny green lizard darted across the tip of his shoe, causing E. J. to make a bit of a side step. Ashley didn't appear to notice, however. Her sorrow, for whatever reason, seemed more than she could bear at the moment.

"Did you have more bad news?" he asked, hoping his tone wasn't too prying.

"No," Ashley replied, using her handkerchief to dab at her eyes. "I just had a difficult job to do."

"I see."

She shook her head. "No, you can't possibly understand. I'm sorry. You really don't have to walk with me." She looked around as if to figure out how she might escape.

E. J. didn't want her to get away just yet. He longed to comfort her, but even more, he longed for her company. He wanted to know the kind of woman she'd become. They'd married so young and so quickly that neither one really knew the other one at all.

He reached out to touch her arm gently, cautiously. "Please tell me what happened."

Ashley looked at the sky and then lowered her gaze to his face. "I had to send a telegram to my mother. She needs to come see my grandfather before he dies. It was very hard to send the message."

"Oh, because she'll be so upset about his situation?"

Ashley laughed bitterly. The sound chilled E. J. to the bone. "Hardly that. She'll be upset because we've dared to disturb her peace. After all, she warned us both."

"What do you mean?"

"She wanted nothing to do with either of us," Ashley explained. "My grandfather took away her financial support when he became a Christian and decided to follow the Bible's teachings. She swore she'd never speak to him again."

"Because he turned to God?" E. J. vaguely remembered something from the past. Hadn't the old man been doing something illegal—but financially beneficial? He rubbed his jaw, trying to remember.

"It's a long story," Ashley said with a sigh in her voice.

"I have the time if you do." He looked at her face and saw the need there. Her dark eyes, still glistening with tears, seemed to consider him momentarily as if to ascertain his worthiness.

"My grandfather was not concerned with business ethics when he was younger. He made a lot of money and in turn he gave generously to his children—my mother and her sister. When his dealings caught up with

him—or rather, when God caught up with him—
Grandpa knew he had to give up his life of crime and
turn over a new leaf."

E. J. nodded and stared ahead at the sandy, rock-
laden landscape. How desolate and lonely it all seemed.
The barren wasteland made him ache to create something beautiful and lovely to put in its empty space. But
wasn't that why he'd come in the first place? He was
here to help with the Harvey resort—beauty amid the
ancient, inhospitable land. And somewhere in the midst
of that aspiration, God had brought him face-to-face
with the past.

Ashley halted rather abruptly, causing E. J. to walk
past her. He stopped and turned to look back at her. She
stared off to the south, past the railroad tracks. He wondered what she saw there.

"I know it sounds completely ridiculous," she began,
"but I'm terrified of my mother coming here." She
glanced at E. J. "I'm afraid of her and what she'll do.
I'm afraid of myself and who I'll become when she's
around."

"What can she possibly do to hurt you?"

Ashley shook her head back and forth slowly. "I'm
not sure, but if there's a way, she'll find it. She doesn't
know I'm here—well, once she gets the telegram she'll
know. But for a very long time, she's had no idea of my
whereabouts. She doesn't even know about Natalie."

"But why?"

A train whistle blew, signaling a Santa Fe freighter
coming in from the east. Ashley watched the train
momentarily, then turned back to E. J. and began walking again.

"My mother is a difficult woman. She wasn't pleased with my choice of husbands. When he was killed in the Great War, I figured she would end her tirade about my choice and leave well enough alone. After all, I was in mourning."

"But she didn't?"

"No. She made matters worse, demanding I annul the marriage, telling me it wouldn't matter to my husband because he was dead."

"Annul the marriage? But if your husband was supposed to be dead . . ."

Ashley seemed to understand his confusion. "She wanted the slate cleaned, as though the marriage had never happened. That's how they do it in high society when they want to pretend things are different than they really are. She wanted me to marry a very wealthy man who could benefit the family name." Ashley's voice lowered to an almost inaudible tone. "But she didn't understand the situation at all."

"You mean Natalie?" E. J. asked, hoping to learn once and for all if the child was his.

"No," Ashley said, leaving him disappointed. "She didn't understand that I could never love another man. I loved my husband and would continue to love him until I was in the grave beside him."

Then, as if realizing she'd become much too personal in her revelations, Ashley stopped again. "Look, I'm sorry. This is too much of a burden to put on anyone, much less a stranger." She gave him a tight smile. "Natalie said you were easy to talk to."

She began to walk back in the direction they'd come, and E. J. had no choice but to accompany her. "So you haven't seen your mother in all this time?" he questioned, hoping she'd not worry about the intimacy of the topic.

"No. I've not seen her or had any form of communication. She wanted it that way and I wanted it that way even more. I figured someone that meanspirited and hateful did not deserve to be a part of my life or that of my child. Now Grandpa wants to see her before he dies, and I find my life turned upside down."

"Will she come here now?"

"I have no idea. I know Grandpa is praying she will, and he seems to have God's ear."

E. J. laughed. "He does, does he?"

Ashley smiled, as if realizing how silly she sounded. "Well, let me put it this way. When Grandpa gets to praying about a matter, things start happening."

"And your grandpa is praying for this reconciliation?" E. J. questioned.

Ashley nodded. "That among other things."

"That's not enough, eh? What else could possibly be as important to him now that he's ready to meet his maker?"

Ashley tucked her handkerchief away. "Grandpa and Natalie want me to remarry." She laughed nervously and shrugged it off. "It's silly, I know. But when those two put their minds to something, well, it's best to get off the track and let the train come on through."

E. J. felt a tightening in his chest. He followed after her, struggling to figure out how to reply. What could he say? He could hardly tell her that she couldn't remarry because she was already married—to him.

"What do *you* want?" he asked instead. They'd come

back to where the new Harvey resort was being built. He stopped and asked again. "What do you want?"

Ashley looked so forlorn and sad. "What I want doesn't matter. I have to think of what Natalie needs."

"And what does she need?" E. J. asked, struggling to know how to deal with the emotions she was evoking.

"She needs a daddy. Someone who can teach her things and keep me from being too lonely," Ashley whispered. Then, drawing a deep breath, she smiled. "At least, that's what Natalie says."

"But what do you say?"

Ashley considered his question for a moment, then came back at him with a question of her own. "Mr. Carson, are you a God-fearing man—are you a Christian?"

He cleared his throat and looked to the ground. "I . . . well . . . yes."

"Why do you hesitate with your answer?"

E. J. looked up and met her curious but beautiful expression. Her dark eyes seemed to study him intently. "I suppose that's a long story on my part. I came to God during the Great War."

"Why?"

He chuckled. "Because I was terrified. Death was all around me and I was all alone."

"Is fear an acceptable reason to take Christ as your eternal savior?"

"Well, I see it as being one way to come to God," E. J. replied. He shoved his hands in his trouser pockets and immediately fisted his hands against his legs.

"Grandpa wants me to come to God," Ashley offered in a surprisingly strong manner. She straightened her shoulders as if she'd suddenly regained her second wind. "But I can't."

"Why?"

"I just don't know that fear is a good enough reason to accept something so serious. You see, it's not that I don't believe in God. I believe in Him quite well, thank you. But I have to question whether He cares about me and what difference it would make whether or not I come to Him. He'll do to me and with me what He wants anyway. It won't much matter that I plead with Him for help."

"I've felt that way too," E. J. admitted. "In the war, things seemed so . . ." He shook away the brutal images. "God seemed so distant, yet at the same time He seemed so close. I wanted to believe that He cared about me there in the trenches. I wanted to believe that He would be with me as we advanced on the enemy."

"And what happened?"

E. J. shuddered. "He allowed the enemy to blow me up."

Ashley's expression went blank and her face paled. "You were . . . were wounded?"

E. J. realized he'd said too much. "Yes, but my point is, I felt betrayed by God. I'd come to Him, pleaded with Him for protection, and then I was suddenly fighting to live. I watched friends die and saw others who wished they had."

"It's just one more thing that makes me question whether God really cares," Ashley interjected, staring past his shoulder. "And why should I put my trust in Him if He doesn't really care? If He's just out there— somewhere—watching and allowing life to go on as it does, why does it even matter to Him if I repent of my sins?"

"Or maybe it matters, but your sins are too great," E. J. murmured.

Ashley frowned. "I'm sorry. I should never have gotten this maudlin. I'm afraid my mother brings out the worst in me. Thank you for the walk."

She turned on her heel, her blue print dress swirling around her knees as she walked away. E. J. watched her for several minutes, completely captivated by the rhythmic way she sauntered up the walkway. *I've driven her away with my talk of war and sins,* he thought. But truth was always painful when it wasn't what you wanted to hear. And his truth—the very essence of who he now was—could never match what she needed him to be. It made his choices and decisions even more difficult.

She doesn't need a wounded war vet who still feels the breath of the enemy on his neck. She doesn't need a man who is afraid of the future and what it might hold.

E. J. looked to the heavens, wishing some great revelation might be revealed. Instead, he felt worse than when he'd set out to walk with his wife. He knew her a little better—that much had been accomplished. But in knowing her better, he also knew without a doubt that he wasn't what she needed. She needed Ethan Reynolds, and that man had died—at least in spirit—on a pockmarked battlefield in France.

CHAPTER NINE

*F*aith Mission Church gave an annual autumn party, and with this excuse the regular members of the congregation and some not-so-regular members had reason to gather that mild October day on the banks of Clear Creek. There was to be plenty of food and games, as well as preaching and baptizing.

Natalie had made certain E. J. received an invitation to the gathering. She'd even gone a step further and showed up at the hotel on Sunday morning to remind him.

"Mr. Carson, are you coming this afternoon?" she'd questioned, nearly breathless from running.

E. J. couldn't turn her down. He felt so captivated by her love of life and the expectancy of her expression that he could only nod.

"Now, don't forget," she told him as she moved toward the door. "We're eating lunch there and then we'll have games. Come to the church by noon and you can drive out with the rest of us. Oh, and don't worry about your tableware. Mama will pack you a plate and silverware."

E. J. had nodded and waved, and two hours later, with some goodies he'd purchased at the Harvey restaurant, he joined the festivities.

Clear Creek ran to the east of town, but the picnic location where they gathered was nearly five miles to the southeast of Winslow proper. E. J. thought it a marvelous respite. After driving out across the sandy red desert dotted only with scrub and cactus, the barren land gave way to natural rock platforms and sandstone outcroppings. Between this framework ran the most beautiful, inviting blue water—Clear Creek. It was easy to see why the location was such a popular gathering place. It was truly an oasis.

E. J. liked it best because it looked nothing like the wartorn lands of his nightmares. Here, in spite of the appearance of being desolate and barren, life sprang up seemingly out of nothing. There were all manner of insects, reptiles, and birds. From time to time a variety of mice, jackrabbits, and even coyotes and mule deer could be seen skittering across the sandy desert floor. In France the only things that had marched on the land were men and death—hand in hand like bizarre players of the same game. The thought chilled E. J. to the bone.

"Why, Mr. Carson, I'm so glad you could come," a matronly woman looking to have enjoyed quite a few picnics commented. "Do you know my husband, Mr. Willis?"

"He's on the town council, is he not?"

"But of course he is," the older woman stated as if to suggest otherwise was simply ludicrous. "I'll have to make sure you're better acquainted. My husband is quite knowledgeable about Winslow and has played a prominent role in seeing that the Harvey Company chose our town for their new resort. He promises it will bring in millions."

"Let's hope he's right," E. J. replied.

"But of course he is," the woman said, looking down her nose at him. "My husband is never wrong. Why, he predicted the strength of our economy years ago. Put Hoover in the office of president, he said, and we'll see nothing but prosperity. Of course, we could hardly elect that Catholic Mr. Smith or the Indian Charles Curtis. What tragedy would have befallen this great nation then," she declared, as though she were making a speech for some great occasion.

Ethan longed to get away from the woman, but instead he found himself hopelessly entangled as she continued. "So, Mr. Carson, tell me what the railroad is doing to entice tourists to the new resort. I do hope we'll get good, solid citizens to come. I've nothing against the flamboyant celebrities of the movie industry, but Mr. Willis says there's really no future there. And, of course, we don't want to see nothing but consumptive patients. My word, but we've had our share of people coming to this great state to take the cure for their disease-filled lungs."

Ethan struggled to figure out what he could say in regard to her question, then just as quickly realized that she'd probably never give him a chance to reply.

"Mr. Carson!" He looked behind him to find Natalie skipping up the trail with her mother at her side. How wonderful Ashley looked. Her soft pink suit seemed just casual enough for a picnic, while at the same time it gave her a clearly feminine, almost elegant appearance. With her face raised to the sun, he thought her radiant.

"Hello, Natalie," he called out, waving at the child. He cast a quick glance back to Mrs. Willis, who by this time was frowning. "Natalie invited me here today," he said as if the woman had questioned him.

"Poor child. Her mother's a heathen, don't you know." The woman leaned toward E. J. to whisper this, but her voice somehow carried on the breeze. E. J. tried to keep the shock from his face but wasn't very good with the cover-up. "Oh, it's true," Mrs. Willis said, leaning in closer. "Why, the woman has only been attending church services the past few Sundays. I think her grandfather's impending death has given her reason to consider the status of her soul."

"Mr. Carson, do you remember my mama?" Natalie asked as they approached.

E. J. didn't know whether to acknowledge Mrs. Willis's comments or the child's. Finally he dismissed himself from the older woman's company, much to her dismay. "If you'll excuse me."

Mrs. Willis *harrumphed* and marched away, as if he'd verbalized that he didn't mind the company of heathens. He couldn't help but smile at the thought of what she'd tell her friends.

"I remember your mama," E. J. said as Natalie grinned up at him. "My, but don't you ladies look nice."

"Mama's wearing a new hat, but the dress is just an old one."

"Natalie!" Ashley's embarrassment was apparent.

E. J. laughed to lighten the moment. "I think both pieces of apparel are quite fetching. But I must say, Miss Natalie, your dress is even nicer." The child, clutching a small basket to her chest, whirled to make the skirt of the lemon-colored dress swirl out around her tiny legs. How very small and delicate she looked.

"Mama made it. She's a good sewer. That's something a wife should know how to do, don't you think?"

E. J. looked past the girl to find Ashley gazing at the skies. "I'll bet she's a great cook too," he said, noting the picnic basket in Ashley's hands.

"She is a good cook. She makes the best fried chicken and—"

"Natalie, that's enough. Why don't you take our basket and set out the things we've brought to share?"

"I could help," E. J. offered. "I just delivered some Harvey pies to the dessert table. I managed to sneak a peak at the main table and it looks quite promising."

Natalie put her own basket down in order to take up her mother's. "I'll leave the dishes here," she announced, and Ashley nodded.

Natalie took hold of the handles on her mother's basket, but E. J. could see she struggled with the weight of it. "Why don't I carry it and you can lead the way? It's just over there," he said, pointing.

Natalie nodded and let him carry the basket. "I can show you what Mama made and you can decide for yourself if she's a good enough cook."

Ashley opened her mouth as if to chide her daughter again, then closed it rather quickly. She offered E. J. an apologetic smile and turned to gaze at the crystal clear water.

E. J. would much rather have stayed with his wife, but instead he followed after Natalie, weaving in and out of congregation members, trying to tip his hat as he returned their greetings.

"I'm so glad you came today," Natalie said as they reached the table. She took hold of the basket and pulled it away from E. J. Settling it on the ground, Natalie quickly opened the latch and pulled out a platter. Removing the dish towel that covered it, she held it up and smiled. "Fried chicken."

"It certainly looks delicious."

"It is," she said confidently.

E. J. helped her find a place on the sagging makeshift table. Natalie took out several smaller containers, one of creamed peas and potatoes and one of a delicious-looking squash. He helped her arrange the food, then followed her back through the crowd to where they'd left Ashley.

"Mama wasn't going to come, but I told her we had to. I told her I'd invited you and that there wouldn't be any food for you if she didn't make some and come too."

E. J. knew from the sight of the luncheon tables that this would never have been the case, but he only smiled and nodded. The child was clearly enjoying her role as matchmaker. The thought amused E. J., and yet at the same time it seemed quite strange to be thrust into a situation where he was being set up to court his own wife.

By the time they rejoined Ashley, she had settled herself on a blanket on a flat, rocky outcropping beside the water. When she saw they'd returned, she issued a warning to her daughter. "Be careful for snakes and such." She looked at E. J. and added, "There are quite a few poisonous critters that live in the area. Rattlesnakes, scorpions, and so many other things. If you haven't been advised of this, it's a good time to take note. They like to hide in the rocks, and if you disturb them, they'll retaliate."

He looked around them, feeling a strange sense of protectiveness. "I'll keep that in mind."

"Why, Mrs. Reynolds. You're a sight for sore eyes." A stocky man strode up to share their company. He settled alongside E. J. and held out his hand. "Todd Morgan."

"Mr. Morgan," E. J. acknowledged, shaking his hand. "I'm E. J. Carson."

"You're new in town, aren't you?" He let his gaze travel up and down E. J. as if assessing him as an opponent.

"I'm here with the Harvey hotel."

"Mr. Carson is an architect," Natalie offered.

"That's nice, kiddo," Morgan answered, quickly ignoring the child. "It's good to see you, Ashley. I haven't seen you at the Harvey House lately."

E. J. bristled at the usage of his wife's first name. Who was this man to treat her so casually?

Natalie reached out and took hold of E. J.'s hand. "I want to show you my favorite place. It's over by the bridge."

E. J. looked at Natalie and then Ashley. "If it's all right with your mama."

"Can I show him around, Mama?" Natalie begged.

"Of course. Just be careful and mind your step."

E. J. hated to leave her there with the personable Mr. Morgan, but he felt he could hardly act the part of jealous husband—even if that was what he was.

Natalie pulled him along to the bridge, where she threw stones into the water below. "Isn't this the best place in the whole world?"

E. J. looked down the long meandering stream and had to admit it was truly an oasis. "It is wonderful. I can see why you like it so much."

"I'd like to build my mama a house right over there." Natalie pointed to a rise of red rock. "That way she could always see the creek and be happy."

"Why do you suppose that would make her happy?" E. J. asked, needing to know about the woman he'd married and who she'd become in the last decade.

To his surprise, Natalie shrugged. "I don't know. I just think she'd like it. My daddy was going to build her a really wonderful house, but then he died."

E. J. felt a quickening in his soul. He easily remembered the two-story house he'd designed, patterned after the early classical revival style so popular in the early eighteen hundreds. Ashley had told him of her passion for the style, pointing out several houses in the Baltimore area.

E. J. had taken the things she liked most, the portico with its lower and upper levels supported by slender Doric pillars. The second-story porch would be accessible to them through artistically carved French doors in the master bedroom. E. J. could see it all as if it were yesterday. He had sketched the house while Ashley detailed it, and before he'd left for the war, he'd given her the drawing, reminding her that when he returned they would build their home together.

Only he hadn't come home. At least not when she'd expected him to.

". . . but she really wants me to go to college first."

E. J. shook away his thoughts. "What did you say?" He looked at Natalie, who was still staring off toward the red rocks.

"I want to build my mama her house and make it just like my daddy planned it out, but she wants me to go to college first."

"Well, that's not a bad idea," E. J. replied. "After all, you'll need training to be an architect."

"I know, but I don't want to leave Mama alone. She's been so brave and strong all these years, but she's had Grandpa to help her. She's going to need someone to be with her if I go away."

E. J. glanced back to where Ashley sat. Todd Morgan had squatted down to talk with her and still remained. It looked to E. J. as though he were trying to convince Ashley of something as he waved his hands throughout the conversation.

"I think maybe we'd better head back. It won't be long till they say the blessing, and I don't want to miss a chance at your mother's fried chicken."

They walked back in companionable silence. Natalie seemed content in her efforts to walk up and down various rocks, balancing like a ballerina on tiptoes as she jumped from one boulder to another.

"We're back, Mama," Natalie announced, jumping down to land between Todd and her mother.

"Natalie, be careful," Ashley warned.

Todd rose to stand beside E. J., but his gaze was still fixed on Ashley. "So will you come with me?"

Ashley looked most uncomfortable but finally replied, "It's difficult to leave my grandfather. Besides,

with his impending death, I'm really in no mood for excursions. I'm sure you understand."

Morgan looked none too happy with her reply but tipped his hat. "Well, I suppose if that's the way it is."

E. J. watched the man walk away, feeling delighted that Ashley had rejected his advances. The mood surprised him. Todd Morgan had no way of knowing he'd just propositioned E. J.'s wife. Ashley, herself, had no idea she was anything but the widow she believed herself to be. What a tangled web they'd all woven for themselves.

Plopping down on the rock across from her, E. J. smiled. "I hope we weren't gone too long."

"No, you came back just in time."

Ashley removed her brimmed straw hat and let the breeze blow through her dark hair for a few minutes. With her face raised to the clear blue skies and the wind gently rippling her hair, E. J. felt himself falling in love with her all over again. For just a moment he was twenty-one and innocent of war.

"Let's gather for the blessing, folks," Pastor McGuire declared.

E. J. jumped up and extended his hand to Ashley. She paused momentarily to replace her hat. Fixing it with her long hatpin, she smiled up at E. J. and allowed his help.

"Thank you," she murmured, not seeming to mind that E. J. still held her hand.

Natalie took hold of her mother's other hand and pulled. "Come on, Mr. Carson wants to be sure to get some of your fried chicken."

Ashley beamed him a smile. "If you miss out here,

I'll fry up another batch just for you."

E. J. found himself almost praying the china platter would be empty when they reached the table. He wouldn't mind at all lingering over a private dinner of fried chicken with his beloved wife.

Pastor McGuire offered the blessing, and soon the crowds were divided into two lines, passing down both sides of the table. By the time E. J. reached Ashley's platter, all but the tiniest chicken wing had been claimed.

"Look, Mama, it's all gone," Natalie declared. "Now you'll have to fry up some more chicken for Mr. Carson."

E. J. met Ashley's face. "You don't have to, but . . ." He grinned and let his expression speak for him.

"But if I don't, I'll never hear the end of it from my daughter," Ashley replied. "I'll be happy to fix some for you—in fact, Natalie could bring it over when she visits you at work."

"No, Mama, let him come to dinner tomorrow night," Natalie demanded, pushing matters right along. "Please?"

Ashley looked from her daughter to E. J. "That's fine with me."

E. J. nodded, finding it impossible to speak. Never in his life had he ever wanted anything more.

Later that afternoon, as the sun began to set, Pastor McGuire concluded the party with a final sermon. E. J. felt sated and happy, and for the first time since the war, he found himself looking forward to the next day.

"We've had a good day here," Pastor McGuire announced. "Now the chill of evening is upon us and we need to make our way back while there's still light to see. But before we go, I just want to say something that's been burdening my heart. I feel as if the Lord is telling me that someone here needs to hear this message."

E. J. shifted and stretched his legs out in front of him. Seated there on the banks of Clear Creek, he waited for the pastor to continue.

"We often do things in life because they are thrust upon us to do," the pastor continued. "We find ourselves feeling compromised in our beliefs and dreams. Sometimes this comes when we least expect it. Maybe through the death of someone we love. Maybe through an event that changes our lives forever.

"In times like these, God seems so distant and far removed. We convince ourselves that He's gone away because of something we've done or said. I just want you to know today that God doesn't leave. He's not the leaving kind. He's steadfast. The Word tells us that God is faithful, and because He's faithful, we can rest assured that He will never leave us."

E. J. found himself longing to hear more. The words burned in his heart like a tiny spark of hope.

"Now, that isn't to say that we won't walk away or choose to ignore God. It isn't saying that circumstances won't come up to deceive us and make us believe God has turned from us, that He doesn't care. But God's love and forgiveness are real and permanent. If you seek Him, He will be found.

"You might say, 'But, Pastor McGuire, I've done things in the past. Things that weren't pleasing to God.' And I'm here to tell you that I've been guilty of the same. Many of you have heard about my younger, wilder days. I'm not proud of the man I was back then, but with

God's help, I've become a new creation."

E. J.'s discomfort grew. The pastor's words dug in deep. Still, E. J. couldn't imagine that Pastor McGuire had all that much to be ashamed of in his past. Maybe he'd been given to drink or to gambling. Maybe he was a womanizer or a con man; either way, it couldn't be as bad as what E. J. had done. He could see the faces of the men he'd killed. The looks of shock, the stunned disbelief that they were dying.

Reliving the nightmare, E. J. tried to draw a good breath but found it almost impossible. The shadows of evening began to play tricks with his mind as he looked out across the desert.

"God knows your heart and He understands your pain. He's offering you forgiveness today. But you have to be willing to take it. Don't let the hurts of the past keep you from coming into right accord with the Almighty. If you've put up a fence between you and God, now's the time to take it down. Now's the time to reach out and accept forgiveness."

Someone began singing in a clear baritone voice, and soon the entire gathering joined in—except for E. J. and Ashley. E. J. looked at Ashley, wondering if the words had disturbed her as much as they had him. Her face was a mask of indifference, however. There was no reading the emotion there, because there frankly didn't appear to be even the tiniest thread of feeling.

It dawned on E. J. then that this was how she had survived the years since his disappearance. She had carefully put aside her feelings, hidden them away so that she wouldn't have to deal with even the smallest, most insignificant emotion. She was like a beautiful china

doll. Cold and hard and forever fixed in time with a painted smile and empty heart.

When he'd seen her on the street crying, that had been the exception. Her feelings had caught up with her, overwhelming her and demanding attention. She probably would never have allowed anyone to see her like that if she'd had a choice.

Still, he reminded himself, there was Natalie. Natalie meant the world to her mother and he could easily see this. But even there, it seemed that Ashley held back a part of herself. Almost suggesting that if Ashley loved Natalie too completely, she might also lose her—as she had lost her beloved Ethan.

Even thinking of his name caused E. J. pain. A part of him wanted to be Ethan Reynolds again. Ethan—the man Ashley loved. Ethan—father to Natalie. Ethan—the promising young architect who would change the world with the beauty he'd design.

But with that name and that man, he also had to remember he was Ethan—war hero. Ethan—the killer of young men who had thrown down their weapons and begged for life.

How in the world could there be forgiveness for that?

CHAPTER TEN

Ashley rose that Monday morning with a great deal on her mind. After seeing Natalie off to school, she bathed Grandpa and tried to encourage him to eat a bit of hot cereal.

"You have to eat," she said, doing up the buttons of his sweater. During the day he liked to wear his regular clothes, even though he seldom left his bed.

"I have no appetite, child," he said softly.

"I know, but you're wasting away. You need the nourishment." She picked up the cereal from the tray and extended it toward him. "It's really quite good, and I've put a dollop of brown sugar on it, just the way you like."

"I'm sure it's delicious, but there's no stopping this kind of wasting," Grandpa replied. "What I would like, however, is another pillow. Have you one?"

"Of course. I'll . . ." A knock at the front door interrupted her, and Ashley put aside the bowl of cereal. "I can't imagine who that might be." She grabbed a pillow from the closet and worked to position Grandpa comfortably before going to see who had come to call.

To her surprise she found a young Mexican man on her doorstep. "I have a telegram for Mr. Whitman."

Ashley gasped and nodded. "I'll take it." She grasped the envelope, then started to close the door. "Oh, wait." She went to the living room and found her pocketbook. Taking a dime from it, she rushed back to the door. "Here. Take this."

The young man's eyes lit up at the extravagant tip. *"Muchas gracias."* He tipped his cap to her and pocketed the coin as if it were a great treasure.

Ashley quickly forgot the man and closed the door to read the telegram. It was from her aunt Lavelle.

FATHER STOP COMING IMMEDIATELY STOP CAN'T WAIT TO SEE YOU STOP LOVE LAVELLE

The notification was so very brief, but even so, Ashley felt encouraged by the words. Her aunt Lavelle was coming and she loved her father. Surely those were good signs.

Ashley returned to the bedroom. "Grandpa, it's a telegram from Aunt Lavelle."

The old man perked up a bit at this. "What does she say?"

"She's coming," Ashley replied. "She's coming right away and she says she can't wait to see you." She handed him the telegram, not entirely sure he could read it. "She signed it, 'Love Lavelle.'"

He clutched the paper to his chest. A tear escaped his eye, trickling down his cheek and onto the pillow. "Thank you, Lord," he whispered. "Thank you."

"I thought it very good news," Ashley said, trying hard not to grow weepy herself.

"Yes, indeed. She was no doubt stunned to hear from us after all this time," Russell said, looking again to the telegram.

Ashley felt a wave of guilt wash over her. "I'm sorry that I made you promise not to let them know where we were. It was wrong of me, but I was so hurt."

"I know that," he answered. "It's behind us now."

For several moments neither one spoke; then he turned to Ashley. "And what of your mother? Has she sent word?"

Ashley stiffened. "No. There's been no word from her." She was afraid he might see her relief in that fact, so she turned and busied herself by straightening his bedcovers. He would never understand how much she dreaded seeing her mother.

"She'll come. I know she will."

"Please don't get your hopes up, Grandpa. She had little use for either one of us."

"But neither did Lavelle," Grandpa replied. "And now she's coming."

Ashley nodded and picked up the tray with the bowl of cereal. "I know, Grandpa. I know. We have to have hope that Mother will understand the importance and put aside her differences from the past." *But can I put aside our differences? Can I welcome her here after all this time?*

Mrs. Breck came around noon to sit with Grandpa while Ashley went to shop for that evening's supper. She needed to buy another chicken to fry, and as a last thought, she decided to also make a cobbler.

In spite of her nerves about having E. J. Carson to

dinner, Ashley actually found herself looking forward to the evening. E. J. had been very kind to her that day when she'd cried. He didn't make her feel as though she were silly for her tears. She remembered a time long ago when one of the neighbor men had caught her crying as she tended her garden. He had chided her to buck up and be strong, telling her that only silly females were given to fits of tears. Ashley had never forgotten the rebuke. She had worked hard to keep her emotions under control, and that day with E. J. Carson had been the first public display of emotion since being taken to task. E. J. had been compassionate and kind, listening as well as speaking. He didn't seem to mind her crying, and when they'd parted company he hadn't left her with quaint platitudes. That meant a lot to Ashley.

E. J. Carson would be a good change of pace. Grandpa had been a poor conversationalist of late. He wanted only to talk of his will and death. Ashley couldn't abide either one, so she always sought to change the topic. Then Grandpa would find a way back to it, or he'd bring up her mother and Aunt Lavelle, and that was even worse than talking of his impending departure. Ashley had come to realize at the picnic how much she longed for adult conversation. She'd not seen how she'd filled her loneliness by talking to customers at the Harvey House. Those conversations had been light-hearted and, in many ways, of no consequence. Now, however, she could see that they filled a need in her life.

The customers there kept her apprised of the world outside of Winslow. Passing salesmen would tell her of scandals in big cities far away, while well-dressed women accompanying equally stylish men would offer her some insight into the world of fashion. Sometimes the people didn't really talk to her as much as to each other, but Ashley took part as a listening bystander. How strange that it should have meant so much to her, and she'd never even known until now.

Of course, it wasn't Grandpa's fault, but Ashley could already tell his death was going to leave her more lonely than she'd ever imagined. The old man had been her mainstay—her focus along with Natalie. Those two people meant more to her than anyone else in the world, and now she was losing one of them.

"But I'll lose Natalie one day too," she murmured as she walked to the store. She felt a band tighten around her heart. The world seemed to be closing in on her. Maybe it was better not to love so deeply, she thought. Maybe it was better to cut those feelings off before you lost them to other things. Grandpa would die and his love would be taken from her, but maybe it would hurt less if Ashley buffeted her heart against the loss. Maybe she should reinforce her heart with stronger stuff than the love she felt for Grandpa. But what was stronger than love?

Moving up and down the aisles of the small grocery store, Ashley was amazed at the number of people who stopped to ask her about Grandpa.

"How is Russell?" one old woman questioned.

"He's very weak," Ashley told her, then smiled and added, "but very stubborn. He still insists on playing his weekly checkers with Pastor McGuire."

The old woman smiled. "Your grandfather is a good man. It'll be hard to see him go, but then again, I don't suppose I shall be here all that much longer myself."

Ashley didn't know what to say. The woman's casual reference to her own passing made Ashley uneasy.

She picked up the things she needed, sharing snippets of conversation with each one who engaged her. Always they asked about Grandpa. They knew him well and loved him. It gradually began to dawn on Ashley, however, that she had never really bothered to formulate any relationships with these folks. She knew the people around her from having seen them on nearly a daily basis. Some had come to the Harvey House where she worked, while others were the storeowners she did business with. Still, beyond knowing their names and occupations, Ashley really didn't know these people at all.

Somehow she had lived her life disjointed from her surroundings. Somehow she had isolated herself in the midst of her community. Like most small towns, there were some people who were only too happy to give detailed accounts of everyone and everything, but Ashley had always turned these people away. Now she almost wished she hadn't.

In the past, Grandpa always told me about people, she mused. *I didn't have to get to know them for myself.* She knew about Mr. and Mrs. Willis's business problems and their son who was training to be a doctor. She had heard accounts of Mrs. Moore's arthritis and Mrs. Morgan's bouts with various blood disorders. Why, Ashley even knew about building projects and plans for the town's expansion because of the things Grandpa had shared.

When he's gone, she thought, *I'll have to make the effort to get to know people better.*

It wouldn't just be an issue of loneliness that she could fill through her job at the Harvey House. And it wouldn't be just a matter of knowing what was going on in the community and in the lives of those whom she'd known for so many years.

I won't be able to rely on Grandpa to help me fit in—to have a place in this town. I won't be able to live vicariously through him anymore. This thought, coupled with her earlier musings of how she could keep from being lonely, made Ashley feel tired and discouraged. *How could I have lived to this age and not even realize that I'm not really living at all, but merely existing?*

Struggling with the grocery sack as she made her way home, Ashley pushed the thoughts aside and tried to regain a more positive spirit. She thought of her aunt's impending arrival. She hoped the things she'd picked up for meals would be pleasing to the woman. Ashley had become a pretty fair cook over the years, but that didn't mean it would satisfy her aunt's particular tastes. Whatever those tastes might be.

Ashley had only seen her aunt once, at least once that she could remember. It had been the summer Ashley was thirteen. Lavelle and her husband had come from California on the train. The trip had been grueling and had stripped them of all energy. Ashley remembered her aunt and uncle being tired the entire time of their visit. She also remembered Lavelle's beautiful clothes. Dresses with beautiful colors and evening gowns that shimmered in the light.

In spite of their exhaustion, the Guzmans had accompanied Ashley's parents out every evening, and Ashley remembered how magical it all seemed. Her mother's own fashion sense was keen, but where her choices were more matronly, Lavelle appeared youthful and exciting. Ashley remembered pining over one particularly lovely green gown.

Best of all, Lavelle surprised everyone by announcing that she'd brought Ashley a present. It turned out to be the most remarkable leather suitcase. The hand etchings had been painted to create a riot of colorful flowers along the upper edge of the case. Her aunt said Mexicans had created the design and that they were very good with leather crafts. Ashley saw this for herself in Winslow. Across the tracks in one of the clusters of Mexican homes, Ashley had witnessed many varying accomplishments among the workers there. The Harvey Company had even allowed the people to come and sell some of their wares to the train passengers. Everything from purses, to saddlebags, to saddles and belts had been offered to the public.

Ashley had to smile, however, as her memories took her back to Aunt Lavelle and the suitcase. The case had been most beloved to Ashley. In fact, she still had it tucked under her bed upstairs at home. It was full of Natalie's baby things now—things Ashley hoped to one day give to Natalie for her own children.

Maybe her aunt would still be kind and sweet. Maybe her attitude and reactions toward Grandpa all those years ago had been a one-time occurrence, brought on by the worry of losing the things that were important to her. Of course, there was no way to know until she actually arrived, and by then it would be too late.

Back at home, Ashley began preparing the dinner. She wanted things to be special for Mr. Carson, but at the same time she found herself growing nervous about having a stranger to dinner.

We really know nothing about him, she thought. Glancing at the clock on the wall, she realized time was getting away from her. Where was Natalie? Why hadn't she come directly home from school?

Ashley wasn't really worried, but she couldn't help wondering, since Natalie had been nearly beside herself at the thought of Mr. Carson coming to dinner. Ashley was going to have to find time to talk to the child before Mr. Carson arrived.

As if drawn there by her mother's thoughts, Natalie came bounding in through the back screen door.

"Mama, I got an A on my report about the Great War. I told them all about Daddy and all the things he did. Nobody else had any stories like it. Teacher said my stories were special because Daddy was a hero."

Ashley smiled at her daughter. Pigtails danced down her back as Natalie flitted about the room in unconfined energy. "I stopped and talked to Mr. Carson. I told him about my A too. He was really happy for me."

"I'm sure he was. You should have come straight home, however. Look at the time. We still have to set the table and get things ready for supper. He'll be here in half an hour."

"I know, that's why I hurried home," Natalie said, her eyes lighting up. She washed her hands and dried them on a dish towel before reaching up into the cupboard for the plates. "Can we use Grandma Whitman's good china?" she asked, even as she reached for the delicate white plates trimmed with posies and gold. "It's really important that things look nice."

"Natalie, about Mr. Carson. You really shouldn't try to . . . well . . . what I mean to say is, you shouldn't play

matchmaker. Mr. Carson and I aren't interested in each other that way."

"But you might be," Natalie said, looking rather perplexed.

Ashley felt sorry for her child. "Natalie, it's just not right to try to meddle in people's lives. I'm just suggesting you leave well enough alone. The man probably has no interest in being in the middle of your schemes."

"Well, I don't think he minds at all," Natalie said, balancing the plates as she headed to the table. "He told me he thinks you're beautiful."

The words made Ashley's cheeks grow hot. It also left her speechless. What could she say to make her daughter understand?

Giving up for the moment, Ashley focused her attention on the chicken, sprinkling in just a touch of paprika and cayenne pepper to the flour and salt mixture. She liked the flavor the spices added and hoped Mr. Carson would like them as well. She'd learned the trick from Mrs. Breck, who told her that often the blandest foods could become a feast with a little seasoning.

"Mama, do you think Mr. Carson would like to sit in Grandpa's chair?"

Ashley gave it little thought. "I'm sure that would be a good place for him to sit. Grandpa's chair is bigger and very sturdy." She plopped a plump chicken breast into the heated lard and watched it sizzle and pop. Putting the rest of the chicken into the cast-iron skillet, Ashley glanced again at the clock. It was time to take out the cobbler.

Reaching for the potholders, Ashley found her hands trembling. Why was she so nervous? This was just a friendly gesture—nothing more. It wasn't like Todd Morgan, who had asked her out to the picture show. His intention clearly ran along the lines of serious commitment. He'd told her more than once that he was looking for a wife.

The cobbler's crust was golden brown with blackberry juice oozing out from the sides. Ashley placed it in the warming box and leaned forward for a sniff. Natalie came alongside and did likewise.

"That smells really good. I bet Mr. Carson will like it."

Ashley nodded and deposited the pan on the cooking rack at the back of the stovetop, then turned to slice a few tomatoes for the table. After this, it was time to turn the chicken, and before she knew it, it was time for E. J. Carson to arrive.

Right on schedule, E. J. knocked on the door.

"I'll get it!" Natalie declared.

Ashley went to check on Grandpa while Natalie went to the door. The old man slept soundly, the covers pulled up under his chin. Ashley backed out of the room so as not to disturb him. She headed back to the kitchen, pulling off her apron as she went.

"Mama, look what Mr. Carson brought us," Natalie declared.

Ashley looked up to find Natalie holding a bouquet of daisies. "Oh, they're very pretty," she said, patting Natalie on the head. "Why don't you give them to me and I'll find a vase." Natalie quickly complied and turned her attention back to Mr. Carson.

Ashley met E. J.'s steady gaze and smiled. "Thank you."

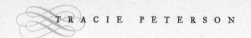

He nodded, but Natalie's animated chatter captured his attention.

"You get to sit in Grandpa's chair since he's too sick to join us," Natalie announced. "It's a nice chair. Good and strong for grown men. I used to like to sit in it when I was a little girl and pretend that I was all grown-up."

Ashley caught the conversation from just inside the kitchen door, smiling to herself, for she still considered Natalie a "little girl."

Ashley reentered the room with the vase of daisies in one hand and a platter of chicken in the other. "Natalie, we need to get the rest of the food on the table."

"May I help you?" E. J. questioned.

Ashley noted that his brown hair was still damp from washing up. Obviously he'd wanted to make a good impression. His eyes watched her every move from behind gold-rimmed glasses. She thought him a handsome man in spite of his beard and mustache. She'd never really cared for facial hair, but Mr. Carson wore it well.

"No, Natalie and I can finish up. You go ahead and have a seat. Would you like coffee to drink?" She positioned the daisies in the middle of the table, then stood back to wait for E. J.'s answer.

"Yes, thank you, that would be fine."

Ashley went back into the kitchen and poured coffee into two china cups. The china had belonged to her grandmother, and it was one of the only things Grandpa had held on to, refusing to let his daughters strip it away from him. He had told Ashley on more than one occasion that he would always remember his beloved wife sharing a cup of tea or coffee with him as they sat together over a candlelight dinner. The china was his link to her and to happier days.

They all sat down to the meal and Natalie prayed, asking God to bless the food and to let them enjoy each other's company. She prayed God would be merciful to Grandpa and not allow him to be in pain, and she prayed that her grandma Murphy and aunt Lavelle would come quickly to see him before he died. After concluding her prayer, she turned to E. J. and extended a bowl of black beans and squash.

E. J. took helpings from each of the dishes and mar-veled at the flavors as he sampled everything. "You were right, Natalie. Your mother is a good cook."

"I know. She makes wonderful food. She learned about cooking from Mrs. Breck and at the Harvey House. She said when she was first married she couldn't cook at all. She even had trouble making tea. She said they might have starved to death but for the fact that my daddy could boil water."

E. J. smiled and threw Ashley a glance that made her cheeks grow warm. It was almost as if he knew this to be true for himself.

"I'm sure there is something else we can talk about," Ashley encouraged. But to her surprise Natalie said very little. She wolfed down her food as if she were starving, then asked if she could take some of the black beans and squash to Grandpa.

"This is his favorite," she explained to E. J.

Ashley wanted to call her daughter back, but it seemed she could hardly do so without explaining to E. J. Carson that she was suddenly uncomfortable with the idea of being left alone to make conversation with him.

With Natalie gone, the room seemed smaller, and Ashley wondered how she would make it through the rest of the meal without making Mr. Carson bear the brunt of her discomfort.

"So will you return to work at the Harvey House once your grandfather is gone?" E. J. asked, surprising her.

Ashley picked at her chicken and nodded. "I like the work. The new resort promises to be even better. I suppose I'll work there at least during school days. I'd like to be home for Natalie, since Grandpa won't be there to keep an eye on her."

E. J. nodded. "She's a special girl."

Ashley nodded, knowing that she had to speak her mind or go on feeling completely out of sorts. "Look," she said, putting down her fork, "Natalie has it in her mind to play matchmaker with us. I don't know why, but she's now focused on finding herself a father."

"And that makes it difficult for you, doesn't it?"

Ashley straightened and looked E. J. in the eye. "Why would you say that?"

"Well, it's obvious that you are uncomfortable with the idea."

Ashley folded her hands together. "Mr. Carson . . ."

"Please call me E. J.," he interrupted softly. "Mr. Carson is much too formal."

But formal was how Ashley wished to keep things. Wasn't it? "E. J., my daughter doesn't understand how love works. My heart is forever taken. I loved my husband and will love no other. It would hardly be fair to put that off on another man. Although, I must admit, I have considered it. I know I'll be lonely when Grandpa is gone. I know Natalie needs a father. All of these things rush through my mind but refuse to be settled." She couldn't believe she was telling him all of this. She calmly picked up her fork and began eating again, hoping he'd put the topic behind them.

"It's all right. I'm not looking for another wife."

She looked up to see the sorrow in his expression. "Natalie said your wife died in the influenza epidemic. I'm very sorry."

"I wasn't with her when it happened. I'd been severely wounded in battle and by the time I made it back to the United States, the war was over and so many people at home and abroad were dead from the influenza. I caught it myself and lingered in a horrible state for weeks, but I guess I'm too tough to kill off. Just rest assured that, like you, I have no mind to marry again. I loved my wife completely and seek no other."

His tone sounded so sad to Ashley that she immediately thought to change the subject. "Are you ready for the blackberry cobbler?"

"Sounds good."

Ashley quickly put aside her fork and napkin and went to retrieve the cobbler. She felt a trembling inside at the turn of events this evening. Who would have ever thought she'd have the boldness to clearly state her position to E. J. Carson? Moreover, she was amazed to realize her heart in the matter of remarriage. For once she saw clearly that she could never marry another man. He would forever live in Ethan's shadow. Even Natalie would constantly compare the two, although she might not understand that now. It would be hard to explain to the child, and Ashley felt guilty for putting her own needs ahead of Natalie's. *She'll understand one day,* Ashley thought. *When she falls in love and marries, she'll understand why I can't have another man taking hold of my heart.*

E. J. waited in silence while Ashley moved about in the kitchen. He thought of her openness with him and how her love for her husband warmed him through and through. *She still loves me,* he thought. But then he chided himself. *No, she loves Ethan Reynolds, the happy-go-lucky architectural student who was set to change the world with his passion for building great beauty. She loves Ethan Reynolds, the man who took her away from her unfeeling mother and preoccupied father. I'm not that man anymore, and I can't pretend that I can go back to being him.*

"Here we are," Ashley said, putting a bowl heaping with blackberry cobbler and cream in front of E. J. "I hope you like it."

"I'm sure I will. It smells wonderful."

Ashley took a smaller portion with her and sat opposite E. J. once again. "I do appreciate the kindness you've extended Natalie. She's quite enthusiastic about the new Harvey resort."

"Yes, I can see that. She studies it with an architect's eye." E. J. tasted the dessert and knew he'd never had anything so wonderful. Natalie's comments about Ashley's inability to cook in her early days of marriage were true. Ashley had been a pampered child, the youngest of four, if Ethan remembered correctly. She'd lived with cooks and maids prior to their marriage, never needing to arrange meals for herself. Her early kitchen concoctions had nearly killed them. She'd even gone through several kettles, burning them one after another when she'd forget them on the stove and go off to do something else. The thought made him grin, and he quickly ducked his head so that Ashley wouldn't question him on it.

"This is really very good," he murmured. "As for Natalie, I'm sure she'll one day be a great architect herself. If that's her dream, she strikes me as the kind of person who will make it happen."

"She takes that from her father," Ashley admitted.

"She must have been very small when he died."

Ashley shook her head. "She wasn't even born. Ethan never knew about her. He was killed before I could get word to him. That hurt almost as much as losing him. I wanted very much for him to know about the baby. I know it sounds silly, but I suppose that was the romantic girl in me."

E. J. felt the cobbler stick in his throat. So Natalie was his daughter. But then, hadn't he known it all along? The ease with which they communicated, their passion for building and design, her natural talent with drawing—it all made perfect sense.

He swallowed hard and lifted the coffee cup to his mouth, hoping to push the cobbler on down.

"Natalie adores her father," Ashley continued. "I've tried to keep his memory alive, but it hasn't been easy. Ethan and I had so little time prior to his going off to war. Natalie knows he was a great hero. You might even have heard about him—he saved an entire unit of men by sacrificing himself. I don't know a lot about what happened. I tried to find out, but no one talks much to young widows." She bowed her head and picked at the cobbler with her spoon.

E. J. grew uneasy. To sit there and say nothing about the truth of who he was made him the worst sort of cad. Yet he couldn't bring himself to speak. Just as Ashley had confessed her inability to love another man, E. J. knew confidently that he couldn't impose the man he'd become on this sweet woman and her child. He struggled with his emotions for several moments. Finally the urge to tell her the truth was overcome once and for all with the fear of what the truth might mean to them both.

"I'm afraid I'm going to have to go," he said, pushing the cobbler back. "This meal has been most delightful, and the food has been incredible. I thank you for having me."

Ashley seemed relieved more than upset. She got to her feet even as he did. "I'm glad we could share our meal with you."

He looked into her eyes, knowing the mistake in doing so. He wanted to lose himself in their depths but knew he had no right.

She walked behind him to the door. He could hear her light steps clicking on the hardwood floor and then silenced as she joined him on the entryway rug.

"Thank you again. I'm sure I've never had anything quite so delicious. Will you tell Natalie good-bye for me?"

He barely waited for her assuring response before opening the door. With long-legged strides, he hurried from the house and the memory of what he'd left behind. Ashley's soft voice echoed in his mind. *"I loved my husband and will love no other."*

The words were an embrace, a kiss, and a curse—all at the same time.

CHAPTER ELEVEN

*W*ith Natalie in school and Mrs. Breck sitting with Grandpa, Ashley stood on the depot platform waiting for the Santa Fe eastbound passengers to disembark. Her aunt Lavelle was to be among the travelers, as stated in her last telegram. Ashley looked at the message one final time to make sure this was the right train.

When Lavelle Guzman stepped from the train, Ashley had little doubt as to her identity. Although it had been half a lifetime since Ashley had seen her, Lavelle looked strikingly similar to Ashley's mother. There was a difference, however. Lavelle smiled in greeting. Ashley couldn't remember the last time she'd seen her mother smile—if ever.

"Aunt Lavelle?" she questioned, skipping to greet the dark-haired woman. Moving closer, Ashley could see a shock of silver-streaked hair peeking out from her cloche brim.

"Ashley!" the woman gasped her name, reaching out to embrace her tightly. "I can't believe it's you." She held Ashley at arm's length. "Let me look at you."

Ashley endured her study momentarily. "I hope you had a good trip."

"It was a wonderful trip. I only wish I could have come the very moment you sent the telegram. I pray I'm not too late." She frowned and added, "Is Father . . ."

Ashley nodded. "He's still alive. Grandpa is in great pain and he's slipping away fast. I wish I could say that he was better. He takes very little of his morphine because he longs to see you and to have his head clear. He longs to renew the relationship between you."

"Oh, my poor father. How he must have suffered these long years." Lavelle looked at the ground. "I feel so awful for the past."

Ashley felt uncomfortable with the topic and looked down the track to where they were unloading the baggage. "I've arranged for a friend, Pastor McGuire, to pick up your luggage. He's going to drive us home. Usually I just walk, but I didn't want you to have to do that."

Lavelle reached out again and touched Ashley's shoulder. "Have you heard from your mother?"

Ashley shook her head. "Not a word."

Lavelle's expression hardened. "Leticia is a difficult woman. She's very opinionated and harsh. I know what she did to you. Mind you, I didn't know about it until years after the fact. She never wrote me with much of any detail. When Father disappeared from Los Angeles, I'm sorry to say I was caught up in my own problems. I never even tried to see him—and all because your mother convinced me it was for the best."

Ashley wanted nothing to do with talking about her mother, but her aunt was insistent on bringing the past to light. "Mother always seemed to believe she knew what was for the best. Frankly, I try to put it from my mind. Grandpa has been good to me, and we've had a wonderful life here."

"He's a good man," Lavelle replied. "I wish I'd seen that sooner. It might have saved me years of pain."

Ashley was surprised at her aunt's words. "I thought you hated him, as Mother did."

Lavelle's eyes narrowed. "I suppose I did at first. Leticia convinced me to do so."

The passengers around them cleared out, some heading to the Harvey restaurant to partake of lunch, while others were eager to reach their destinations.

"There's Pastor McGuire," Ashley said, spotting the man as he worked his way through the crowd. "We can continue our conversation at home where you can relax, and I'll fix us some tea or coffee."

———————

With Lavelle's suitcases put in the spare bedroom, Ashley bid the pastor and Mrs. Breck good-bye, then set out some refreshments for her aunt. Grandpa was in a deep sleep, so Lavelle and Ashley both thought it best to let him rest. Ashley wondered if she would find it difficult to communicate with her aunt. The woman seemed nothing like Ashley's mother and yet she, too, had just as easily turned her back on her father.

"This is such a sweet little house," Lavelle said, coming into the kitchen where Ashley worked. "I love this flowered wallpaper. I'd like to have something like this in my kitchen. It makes everything so bright."

"It does at that. I used to have it painted a light yellow and that was nice, too, but I found this paper and

thought it rather charming," Ashley admitted, studying the delicate rosebud print. She drew her thoughts back to the task at hand and smiled. "I've made some tea and have some cookies, if you'd like."

"The tea alone is fine, my dear." Lavelle smiled. "I just can't believe this is you all grown-up. What have you done with yourself all these years?"

Ashley brought the cups of tea and motioned to the dining room. "We can either sit at the table or we can go to the living room."

"Wherever you're most comfortable."

Ashley led the way to the living room, knowing she could pick up her crocheting between sips of tea. Once they were settled, Ashley answered Lavelle's question. "You wanted to know what I've done with myself. Well, I have a daughter."

"You do? Why, that's marvelous. I didn't even know you'd married. Well, I mean, I knew about the man your mother hated."

"Yes, Ethan. He's my daughter's father. He didn't know I was expecting when he went to war. He never knew."

Lavelle's expression changed to one of genuine sorrow. "Oh, my child, how awful for you."

"Mother wanted nothing to do with me, since I wouldn't cooperate with her plans. I never even had a chance to tell her about Natalie. I contacted Grandpa, knowing that you and mother had rejected him, and figured we'd make each other good company."

"So you came to Los Angeles?"

Ashley nodded. "He was just finishing the last of his business dealings. I told him my situation, and he took me under his wing. We came here to Winslow because he'd heard the climate was very good and the life-style simple. He bought this house and let me furnish it the way I wanted to. It's been a good life these eleven years."

"I can tell. You're beautiful and gracious." Lavelle sipped her tea for a moment, then asked, "Would you tell me about him?"

"Grandpa?" Ashley grinned. "I've never known anyone with a more pleasant and contented disposition. Grandpa says that becoming a Christian changed his entire outlook and that the things that seemed important to him so long ago were no longer as valuable to him."

"I know what he means."

Ashley looked at her aunt oddly. "You do? You're a believer?"

Lavelle nodded. "You see, not long after your mother forced me to break ties with our father, my husband became ill. It was only after he died that I learned he'd squandered a good portion of my inheritance. He owned several businesses, none of which was all that profitable. I sold those off. Sold the lavish home we'd built and managed to put aside what money I made in those sales. I dismissed all my servants, with exception to one dear sweet old woman, Eva, who had been with me since I'd married Bryce."

"I'm so sorry about Uncle Bryce. I had no idea he was gone."

Lavelle opened her mouth to speak, then closed it again. Ashley couldn't imagine what had stopped her from speaking her mind, but she let it go.

"I hope you don't mind if I work on this while we

visit," Ashley said, picking up her crocheting. She gazed at her aunt, who looked ever so elegant and refined in her camel-colored traveling dress. Her hair, now free of the hat, was shaped in soft waves of brown with silver highlights.

"I don't mind at all," she said, offering Ashley a weary smile. She took up the tea again and grew very thoughtful. "My housemaid, Eva, led me to an understanding of what my father had found. She shared the Bible with me, and it changed my life."

Ashley nodded, not wanting her to give any detail to the matter. She was already feeling conviction enough from Natalie and Grandpa. "Grandpa will be glad to hear that. He puts great store in his faith. All of Winslow esteems him for his generosity and kindness. He's a great man—they'll be sad to see him go."

"I could have guessed that. My father was always a charismatic soul. He could have made friends with the enemy in any war," Lavelle said, laughing. Then she sobered rather suddenly. "I would give any amount of money to turn back the hands of time so that I could spend more days with him. I hope that while I'm here you'll allow me to take over his care—or at least help."

Ashley smiled and worked at the stitches of the sweater's collar. "I'm glad for the help. Frankly, it's been hard to watch him deteriorate. Some days he seems to rally a bit. He'll get out of bed and sometimes even join us for a brief time in the living room, but most of the time he stays in bed, weakened by the cancer."

"I want to spend whatever time we have together. I want to talk to him and have him talk to me. I hope your mother will feel the same way."

"Don't count on that." Ashley's snide tone drew her aunt's stare. "As I mentioned, I haven't had a response from the telegram I sent her. I sent it at the same time I sent yours."

"Well, I'll see to that. I'll send her one myself and get her to at least explain why she isn't here."

Ashley put down the crochet hook. "Have you been in touch with my mother over these years?"

Lavelle looked away as if uncomfortable with the question. "I have had some contact. Your mother and I are hardly close anymore. She doesn't share my feelings about faith or God."

"I could have guessed that," Ashley said, still unwilling to admit she didn't share them either. Tucking her hair behind her ear, Ashley picked up her cup.

"We've exchanged a few letters—a very few. Your mother seems to think that unless a person can profit her in some way, they are useless."

Ashley nodded. "I know that well enough. It's the reason I came here. But I'm not sorry I came. I've had a good life here. I've worked as a Harvey Girl at the station for most of those years. I'm the top waitress now, although I've taken a leave of absence to be here for Grandpa."

"Will you go back to it now that I'm here?" Lavelle asked.

Ashley finished her tea before answering. "I might. It couldn't hurt to have the income." She didn't want to let even her aunt know about the bank account the lawyer had set up.

"I intend to earn my keep while I'm here," Lavelle stated. "I will buy groceries as well. I'm not wealthy by my previous standards, but I'm certainly not destitute. You needn't worry about the extra mouths to feed."

"I wasn't," Ashley quickly said. "We're quite comfortable here, as I've already told you. I have preserves put up, and I know how to stretch a meal if need be. I came here hardly knowing how to boil water, but over the years I've learned to fend for myself quite nicely. We'll be just fine." A train whistle blew in the distance, and Ashley looked at her watch. "Natalie will be coming home from school soon." She looked at the sweater and picked up her hook one more time. "Before she gets here, I wonder if you would mind my asking you something."

Lavelle put down her cup and nodded. "Please do."

Ashley met her aunt's curious expression. "Why did Grandpa's choice make Mother so mad?"

"Well, that's an easy question. He threatened her comfort."

"But my father was a wealthy man. He was from old New England money."

"Yes," Lavelle admitted, "but while the prestige was there, the pocketbook didn't always match the expense ledger. Our father was a generous man who lavished us with large sums of money for no reason at all. He spoiled us terribly. As a young woman, I remember only having to ask for some bauble or trinket and Father would see to it that I had it. We wore Worth gowns and ate off of Crown Derby china. We had wonderful collections of jewels and our own carriages and teams of horses.

"Of course, we were his only family. And Father simply knew how to make money. He was quite gifted. After

Mother died, he poured himself into his work even more than he had before. The only way he could feel our approval or love was to bestow his wealth upon us, and he did so with great flourish." She paused and grew misty eyed. She twisted her hands together and sighed.

"One day Father wrote us a letter. He told us he'd been in an accident. A car accident."

"Yes, I know about that—he told me. He'd broken his back and nearly died."

Lavelle drew a deep breath. "It was during that time someone shared the Gospel with him. He didn't know if he'd live or die at that point."

"I remember he said the hospital chaplain came to see him. He asked Grandpa if he were to meet God that night, would it be a good thing or a bad thing?"

"Exactly," Lavelle said and continued. "He tried hard to share with us how he felt about learning of God's love, but your mother was focused on the other parts of that letter. Father told us he'd put an end to his business dealings with his partner, Jerreth Sanders. He'd sold out his holdings and had used part of the money to try to make things right with people he'd swindled. Your mother went completely out of her mind. She said he was setting himself up to be sued or worse."

"I can't imagine her caring about that," Ashley said without thinking.

"Oh, she didn't care about Father's well-being; she only cared that the funds would be completely drained in a legal battle. I feared it, too, for your mother and I discussed our own situations and knew we needed Father's continued support. We were used to spending well beyond what our husbands gave us, and frankly, our husbands were used to the extra money as well."

"What did you do?" Ashley questioned, knowing the ultimate outcome but not understanding how they arrived at it.

"Your mother and father came to Los Angeles. It would have been that trip they made the winter before you married."

"I remember. All I knew was that they were very upset with Grandpa."

Lavelle sighed. "Yes, well, upset hardly says it all. They arrived and your mother took me aside first and discussed the situation in detail. Then our husbands joined us and finally we went as a force to meet with Father. It was ugly. We were ugly." Tears streamed down Lavelle's cheeks. "We said things that should never have been spoken."

Ashley felt sorry for the woman. She was so clearly contrite for what she'd done, and it made Ashley feel some small amount of hope that perhaps her mother had changed as well.

"Before the day was over, Father had agreed to divide his remaining estate and settle it upon Leticia and me. It was no small pittance, and he agreed he'd rather we have the benefit of his money than to see it go to some lawyer and settlement. But with that agreement, he tried to tell us of God and how much we needed to know the truth. I listened but saw the anger in Leticia and figured it couldn't be something good for either of us. I rejected his thoughts and listened to her. She said he was crazy—that he should be put away. She actually talked of locating a sanitarium where he could get help. My husband wanted no part of that. He had friends in

Los Angeles who could very well make or break him. To have a crazy relative—especially a father-in-law—was hardly a glamorous calling card.

"Finally, your mother agreed we'd let it drop. Father was so hurt by us and how we acted. By then I think he was glad to see us go."

"I had no idea. He's never spoken out against either of you, even once," Ashley said, saddened by the scene she envisioned.

"Somehow that doesn't surprise me," Lavelle said, dabbing a handkerchief at her eyes. "Years later, when Father had vanished and no one seemed to know where he'd gone, I found out that Bryce had lost most of my inheritance. He suffered a heart attack and lingered for days, then finally died. Like I said, I sold off most everything and now have enough to live on until I die. Perhaps if I'd had children as your mother did, I wouldn't have done things that way. But I'm not sorry for it. I don't miss the house and the trappings. I don't miss the servants whispering behind my back. And I certainly don't miss the worry that accompanied owning more than I could ever hope to use."

The ringing of a bell brought Ashley's attention. "Grandpa's awake." She smiled. "He'll be so happy to see you."

"I hope so," Lavelle replied. "I want very much for this to be a good reunion."

Ashley got to her feet. "This is a dream come true for him, Aunt Lavelle. To find that you share his faith and have come to see him again are the only things he's longed for."

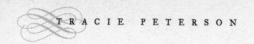

Her aunt sniffed back tears. "Thank you so much for sending me the telegram."

Ashley shook her head. "Come to think of it, I'm not even sure how it found its way to you, given the fact I sent it to the last address Grandpa had for you. That must have been the house you sold."

Lavelle smiled. "God always finds a way, even when there seems to be no chance at finding one. This is His doing, Ashley. Pure and simple."

The idea bothered Ashley in a way she couldn't understand. Trembling at the thought of God's divine intervention in matters of her life, Ashley pushed the idea aside. God didn't care about the details. He didn't care about her.

Or did He?

CHAPTER TWELVE

*R*ussell looked up to see the face of his younger daughter. Oh, how much she favored her mother. For a moment, all he wanted to do was memorize the way she looked. It was almost like having Peg with him again.

"Papa?"

His heart swelled with pride. "Come here, child. I've so looked forward to this moment."

Lavelle left Ashley at the door and took the chair beside the bed. She reached out to grasp Russell's hands. "I can't believe it's been so long."

"I need to pick up more medicine from the doctor, so I'll leave you two to talk," Ashley said, closing the door quietly.

Lavelle looked to her father, as if awaiting some instruction on how she should comport herself. Russell felt sorry for her and immediately set out to soothe her conscience. "I've asked you here to seek your forgiveness."

"What?" Lavelle questioned, shaking her head. "You can't be serious. I'm the one who's come seeking forgiveness. You've done nothing wrong." She began to weep softly, pulling a handkerchief from her sleeve. "Oh, Papa, I can't believe it's come to this."

Russell squeezed her hand. "I'm so glad you came. I was worried that you wouldn't."

"And you had good reason, given our last encounter. Oh, I can't tell you how ashamed I am of the way I acted. I was so influenced by Leticia and Bryce, but even then, I cannot blame them for the path I chose. I could have taken a stand and told them I didn't agree with the way they wanted things to be. But I was weak and silly. Bryce had me convinced that this was the only way to ensure our survival—and he had a good reason to feel that way."

She dabbed at her eyes before continuing. "Oh, there aren't even words for all the things I want to say. That day . . . that day when you divided the money, I thought I understood life so well. I thought money was the way to be happy. Bryce certainly thought so—Leticia too. I figured if I just went along with everything, I would find that same happiness."

Russell saw the weariness in his daughter's face. She'd aged so much since he'd seen her last. Perhaps that was why she reminded him so much of her mother. "Lavelle, my sweet Lavelle. You always were such a gentle soul."

"But I wasn't then," she said, pulling back as if her presence might pain him.

"But the past is in the past. That's why I wanted you here today." Pain tore through Russell as he struggled to sit up.

"Here, let me help," Lavelle said, getting to her feet. She gently supported his shoulders as Russell pushed up with his feet. The movement cost him all pretense of strength. He fell back against the pillows and closed his eyes, willing the pain to diminish. He knew he needed another dose of morphine, but he had no desire to spend his last days on earth in such a drugged stupor.

"I want the past to be behind us," he finally whispered. "I want your forgiveness for anything you might believe me guilty of. I know I was given over to making money—any way I could. I know I was often away from the family, and I know you probably suffered for it."

"Papa, I forgive you if it sets your mind at ease, but believe me, I feel there's nothing you need to be forgiven of. I'm the one who wronged you. I need your forgiveness. I've prayed over these last few years that if I ever had the opportunity to see you again, I wouldn't rest until I set this right between us."

Russell opened his eyes. "So you've made your peace with God?" He smiled and closed his eyes. "That's what I've always prayed for."

He breathed just a little easier, knowing that his hopes had been realized. His child had come to God. He thought of his long-departed wife and how she had pushed for the family to attend church. It was the acceptable thing to do, to be sure, but at the same time, Russell found no purpose in going other than the possible financial benefits. Many had been the time he'd made a good deal in the vestibule of the church. Never mind that he'd joined the den of thieves who robbed the focus from God and put it on money.

"I kept remembering things that you said to us that day," Lavelle began. "Things about how we wouldn't find our stability in money or possessions. Then one day

Bryce took sick and died. It wasn't long after our fight."

Russell opened his eyes and looked at her sad expression. "I'm sorry, child. I had no idea."

"But of course you didn't." She shook her head. "Bryce was no good with money or numbers. He had a weakness for gambling and his gambles never paid off. When he died and I finally knew exactly where we stood, I was shocked. Most of my inheritance was gone. I had a palatial estate to show for it and a handful of other properties, but nothing like I thought I had."

"What did you do?" Russell asked.

"I sold off most everything—the house, the jewelry, the businesses, even some of the furniture. It was then that I came to realize who my true friends were. Good friends—or at least those I thought were good friends—turned away from me when my social and financial status began to drop. The more I rid myself of the trappings of wealth, the less interest I held for those in my old circle.

"Little by little I dismissed all of the servants except one. I kept my maid Eva. I don't know if you remember her or not; she was an older woman with a sweetness about her that made my days brighter. She was also a godly woman. She began sharing her Bible readings with me and eventually we started going to church together. I came to realize that the things I valued in life were not the things that would matter in death—nor in the afterlife."

Russell nodded. He could almost hear his sweet wife say the same thing. If only Leticia and Ashley would speak likewise, he could die a happy man. He bolstered his hope. He'd thought Lavelle lost too, and God obviously took care of that matter. God was big enough to see to Leticia and Ashley. But as usual, it would have to come in His timing and not Russell's.

––––––––

Ashley hurried from the doctor's office, hoping to get home before Lavelle or Grandpa should need her. She knew Grandpa would be overjoyed to learn that Lavelle's heart had been softened over the years. He would rest easier and that made Ashley happy. She knew the morphine powder now secure in her purse would also make him rest easier. The doctor had increased the dosage, suggesting that Ashley not pay attention to her grandfather's request to keep the doses light.

"He needs this medicine," the doctor had told her. "He's a stubborn man, and oftentimes that means the rest of us must intercede to make choices for his good."

Ashley had agreed, but even now she wondered if she could go forward with the plan to give Grandpa a stronger dosage.

"Mama!" Natalie called, running up the street at a rapid pace. With school out, she appeared to have one purpose and goal.

"Natalie, people must think you run positively wild," Ashley said, laughing. Her daughter's wool skirt flew up in an unladylike fashion, revealing her bare knees, but Natalie didn't care. She barreled into Ashley, using her mother's body weight as a stopping block for her momentum.

"Mama, can we invite Mr. Carson to dinner again? I want to go see what they're doing with the building

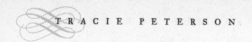

today, and I thought it would be fun to have him come to dinner."

"Natalie, your aunt Lavelle is here from Los Angeles. We already have one dinner guest."

"So it wouldn't be any trouble to have two—right?"

Ashley shook her head. "Natalie, you need to have some consideration for your great-aunt. She's probably not interested in meeting anyone new tonight. The train ride was very long and no doubt tiring."

"Please, Mama! He's all alone."

Natalie's pleading expression was Ashley's undoing. It wasn't as though Mr. Carson was poor company. And she had set him straight on how she felt about Natalie's matchmaking plans.

"All right, I suppose you may invite him. We'll eat around seven-thirty."

"Thanks, Mama!" Natalie called over her shoulder as she skipped away. "I'll tell him to come over at seven so I can show him my pony."

Ashley rolled her eyes heavenward, then started to head for home when she thought to tell Natalie that she might let Mr. Carson know what they were having for dinner. She spied Natalie turning the corner for Second Street, but she also saw something else as well. A man appeared to be following her daughter.

Concerned with this, Ashley carefully picked up the trail herself. She watched as the man followed Natalie at an even distance. He watched Natalie cross Second Street and waited until she closed the distance to the construction site before he did likewise.

To Ashley's relief, Natalie spotted E. J. early on. He was outside directing some work on one of the windows.

Ashley held back and watched the man as he walked past them, then disappeared into the shadows.

Maybe I'm just imagining this, she thought. *Maybe it was just coincidence.* She shook her head. *No, the man had clearly been watching Natalie.* Ashley hadn't recognized the man. He seemed well enough dressed, but a long coat could hide a poor wardrobe. His coat and hat had shrouded his face and physique. Ashley had no idea what he really looked like.

She swallowed hard, feeling the uneasiness drench her in a cold sweat. *Maybe the man is a transient, one of the railroad bums. Maybe he's just trying to get back to the tracks without anyone recognizing him.*

Ashley breathed a little easier. *Yes, that's probably what it is.* From time to time the less fortunate hitched rides on the boxcars. Still, he didn't look to be that type of man. Perhaps he was a train passenger. He might have been visiting someone in town, or maybe he didn't like the crowds at the Harvey House. The man had probably come into town to get something to eat and was now headed back to catch his train. She waited a moment more, and when Natalie raced off for home and no one followed her, Ashley smiled and continued her own journey.

I'm just being silly, she thought. *Grandpa's sickness has wearied me and given rise to my imagination.*

She reached the iron gate of their yard and smiled. Natalie had forgotten to close it again. In her hurry to get changed out of her school clothes and get to her pony, she often forgot to take care of little things like open gates. Pulling the gate shut, Ashley made her way inside. She hoped her aunt had enjoyed a pleasant visit with Grandpa.

"Ashley, is that you?" Lavelle questioned, coming down the hall with a worried expression.

"Father is in a great deal of pain. Can we give him something to help?"

Ashley pulled the medicine from her purse. "I'll mix him something right now. I didn't intend to be gone so long, but I ran into Natalie."

Lavelle smiled. "I heard the door open and someone run upstairs. I thought it might be her."

"She likes to groom her pony or go for a ride on nice evenings. I'd imagine she's changing her clothes to do just that. I'll make her stop long enough for an intro-duction."

Ashley moved toward the kitchen. "If you want to join me, I'll show you how this is done. Then, if I'm not around, you can feel free to give him the medicine when he needs it most."

"I'd like that. I'd like to assist with Father's care. I feel it will give me the precious time I might otherwise not have had."

Ashley wasn't sure how to feel. On one hand, she had hoped to have that time for herself. On the other, she knew that Lavelle needed to have time to say good-bye to her father. Smiling, Ashley reached out and embraced her aunt. "The help will be greatly appreci-ated. We can relieve each other, and that way Grandpa will always be with family. The doctor said we're getting to a point where we might want to keep someone in the room with him at all times."

Lavelle nodded. "It's good he has such a nice large room on the first floor."

"It used to be his study," Ashley said. "About six years ago his knees and hips started hurting him something fierce. I suggested we convert the room at least enough to put a daybed there for him. That way on nights when he didn't feel like climbing the stairs, he'd have some place to rest." Ashley put water on the stove to heat. "The daybed gave way to a regular bed, and he's been there ever since. Oh"—she motioned to the teapot—"he likes to take the morphine in hot sweetened tea. It seems to help cut the bitterness."

Lavelle nodded. "That makes sense."

"Mama, I'm going out to brush Penny," Natalie called from the hall. "Mama, where are you?"

"I'm in the kitchen, Nat. You needn't yell," Ashley replied, shaking her head at Lavelle's grin. "Come meet your great-aunt."

Natalie came into the room, her braids and jean-clad legs bouncing to the same rhythm. Ashley had found the pair of boy's pants at the secondhand store and on a whim had bought them and altered them for her daughter. No one seemed to mind, given Natalie's status of town darling.

"Hello," Natalie said, beaming Lavelle a smile.

"You must be Natalie," Lavelle said, reaching out to touch the little girl's face. "My, but you're a pretty little thing."

"Thank you, ma'am," Natalie replied.

"Natalie, this is my aunt Lavelle. She's your great-aunt."

Natalie nodded. "Mama said you would come today.

I'm glad you're here. I always wanted to meet you. Grandpa told me stories about when you and my grandma were little girls."

Ashley started at this. She hadn't realized that Grandpa had told Natalie much of anything about the family.

"Grandpa said you and Grandma got in lots of trouble one time when you decided to pick all of the neighbor's flowers for a bouquet for your mama."

"I remember that well," Lavelle said, laughing. "I was all of six or seven, but I remember to this day having to go and apologize for my wrongdoing."

"No doubt Mother put you up to it," Ashley said rather bitterly. Turning away, she tried to focus on the tea. She didn't even want to consider that her mother might have been innocent.

"Grandpa's told me lots of stories," Natalie continued. "I like hearing them. It's almost like I know you."

Lavelle chuckled. "I should like very much for us to know each other better, Miss Natalie."

"Me too. But right now I need to go take care of Penny. She's my pony. Would you like to see her?"

"We need to get Grandpa his medicine," Ashley told her daughter. "Maybe Aunt Lavelle could see Penny later."

"Yes, I'd like that, Natalie. Would you be willing to show me your pony later tonight?"

"Sure." She snagged a cookie from a plate on the counter, then hurried to the back door. "Oh, Mama, Mr. Carson said he'd be pleased to come to dinner."

With that she was gone and Ashley was left to explain to her aunt. "Mr. Carson is a man Natalie met over at the new Harvey hotel building site. She's fascinated with him because he's an architect. She's also trying to make a match, so be forewarned. She seems to be convinced that I need someone in my life."

Lavelle smiled. "She's absolutely delightful, Ashley. A sweet and loving child to be sure. How much she must love you to worry about your having someone in your life."

"It's for herself as much as me," Ashley replied, beginning to feel a bit desperate to change the conversation. But instead of bringing up something else, Ashley chose to focus on the work at hand.

They worked together in a companionable silence for several minutes. Ashley hoped she hadn't offended her aunt by suddenly going silent. It wasn't that she wanted to hide their life away from Lavelle; rather, she didn't know how much to share. Some families were very close, but obviously this one wasn't.

Finally the silence seemed stifling. Ashley strained to think of what she might talk to her aunt about. Then it came to her. "Did you have a nice talk with Grandpa?" Ashley asked, trying to sound nonchalant and hoping she wasn't being impolite. She arranged a napkin and small bowl of cottage cheese on a tray. She hoped she might get Grandpa to eat just a bite or two.

"It was wonderful," Lavelle admitted. "I'm afraid I cried a good deal." She smiled, then looked away. "We made our peace with each other, and that's what counts."

Ashley nodded. "I'm sure Grandpa was pleased."

"I know it put my heart at rest. I don't want to see him go, Ashley, but I couldn't have made it through if

I'd never had the chance to seek his forgiveness. Thank you for that—for sending the telegram. I couldn't leave things as they were. The ugly memories of how I acted are not what I want him to remember of me."

Ashley put a spoon atop the napkin. "I'm sure he won't remember those things at all. He'll probably see you as a little girl in frilly calico and muslin. He'll remember the good things—he's like that."

Lavelle grasped Ashley's hand. "I pray that's the way it is. It's all I could ever really want for him."

Ashley nodded and pulled away just as the kettle began to whistle. She poured the water and said, "I just make half a cup; that way he doesn't have so much to drink. Just stir in the morphine powder while it's still hot and then add the honey." She mixed the concoction, then turned to her aunt. "Do you want to take it to him?"

Lavelle took hold of the tray. "Please."

"He may not want anything to eat, but I always try. I know if I have it with me and he asks, then he'll eat it. If I don't bring something, he won't allow me to go after it."

"I'll keep that in mind."

Lavelle went off into the dining room and down the hall. Ashley followed, watching her manage the bedroom door with ease. She felt a bit empty—almost useless—but realized it was for the best. Ashley had had the old man to herself for the last eleven years, with exception to Natalie. It was time to share him with those who also loved him.

Frowning, she couldn't help thinking of her mother. Would she be one of those who cared? Would her mother show up as Lavelle had, all sweetness and gentleness? Somehow Ashley couldn't imagine that happening.

"And even if it does, that doesn't mean I have to accept her back in my life," Ashley whispered. "Grandpa might want me to make peace, but there's a difference between that and allowing her a place in my heart."

CHAPTER THIRTEEN

E.J. approached Ashley's house with a sense of fatal fascination. He knew he should have told Natalie no when she'd invited him to supper that afternoon, but he couldn't. Truth was, he was only too happy to share the company of Natalie and her mother.

Lately, Ashley and Natalie had filled his thoughts. Especially Ashley. He'd thought about their days together—about their wedding and their wedding night. He couldn't help feeling a sense of elation at knowing she was still alive, but at the same time the feelings were mingled with regret of the deepest kind.

And the confusion that came from those feelings was maddening.

One minute E. J. was absolutely confident that he needed to explain his identity to Ashley. The next minute he was just as convinced that such a thing would be sheer insanity.

Now, pausing to knock at Ashley's front door, E. J. knew he'd remain silent. *Test the waters,* he thought. *See what might or might not be best. It's the reasonable thing to do.* It didn't make him a coward—it merely made him

prudent.

He knocked, then felt his heart begin to race. He twisted his hands together, then pulled them apart and plunged them into his coat pockets. Would she open the door? What would she be wearing? How would she look?

But it wasn't Ashley who greeted him, it was Natalie. She smiled up at him with her endearing expression—her brown eyes huge with wonder.

"You're here!" she declared. "Come on in. We can go through the house and out the back door and I can show you my pony." She reached for his hand and pulled him along.

"Good evening to you too, Miss Natalie," E. J. said, laughing. She had such a way about her. It completely disarmed him and took away all fear of the evening.

"Mama said I should show you the pony first and give you plenty of time to clean up. But Penny's not a dirty pony. I keep her real clean. I comb her every day."

"You sound very devoted," E. J. replied.

"Mr. Carson," Ashley said as she came into the hallway. "We're glad you could make it on such short notice."

E. J. looked up and felt his breath catch in his throat. She was a vision in the butterscotch-colored gown. The most feminine of lace collars trimmed the neckline of her dress, giving her a dainty appearance in spite of the rather shapeless straight lines of her outfit. The dress was a bit longer than most fashions these days, but E. J. liked it very much.

"I appreciate the invitation. The food was so delicious last time that I felt I had to try it again."

"I hope you'll enjoy our southwest flavoring tonight.

I've put together a few Mexican dishes."

"They're my favorite," Natalie chimed in.

"I'm sure to love them, then," E. J. responded.

"Mama, I'm going to show Mr. Carson my pony. Is that all right?"

Ashley smiled. "Of course." She looked at E. J. and added, "I'll introduce you to my aunt when you come back. She's with my grandfather right now."

E. J. nodded. "I'll look forward to it."

E. J. followed Natalie outside to the backyard. Living on the east edge of town had afforded them a bit more space than some. The yard was large, with an area that had been cultivated for flowers and maybe even vegetables. A small lean-to served as Natalie's stable, and around this someone had built a circular wooden fence. Inside that fence was the object of Natalie's affection.

"Penny's really friendly." Natalie whistled for the pony and sure enough, she came trotting to the gate, kicking up dust all the way.

"She's very pretty," E. J. offered as he inspected the pinto. He'd picked up a bit of horse knowledge when he'd worked for a time on a horse farm in Kentucky. The brown-, black-, and white-spotted pony seemed a perfect fit for Natalie.

"I've only had her a year," Natalie told him. "Grandpa got her for me for Christmas, and then he got me a saddle for her on my birthday."

E. J. smiled. "Seems like a very fitting present for you."

Natalie grinned up at him. "I'm going to see if my mom will get me a dog this year."

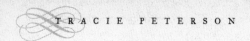
He laughed. "Are you trying to build your own farm here?"

"Nah, I just don't want Penny to be lonely. Besides," she said soberly, "after Grandpa's gone, it might be nice to have a watchdog."

E. J. didn't want her to dwell on the sadness in her life. "Well, she's a perfect horse for you. I don't think I've ever seen one prettier."

"She can go pretty fast too, but Mama doesn't like me to ride her that way."

"Your mother sounds wise. A lot of things can happen when you ride too fast." He hated the very thought of his daughter meeting injury for any reason. He stroked the pony's velvet nose, while Natalie stroked her mane.

"I called her Penny 'cause I used to have a doll named that, but I lost her," Natalie said as though he'd asked the question. "When I get a dog, I'm going to call him Duke 'cause my daddy had a dog named that when he was a boy."

E. J. drew his breath in sharply. He hadn't thought about that dog in years. "A black Lab," he murmured.

"How did you know?" Natalie asked, her eyes wide in amazement.

E. J. realized his mistake. He quickly worked to cover his tracks. "That just seems like the kind of name you'd give to a dog like a black Labrador."

Natalie nodded. "My daddy was really smart." She smiled in her girlish self-confident manner and went back to stroking the pony's neck. "If you were a daddy, what would you name a dog?"

The words rang in his ears and echoed in his heart.

"If you were a daddy . . ." But I am your daddy and I want to be your daddy. E. J.'s stomach knotted and he forced the thoughts away. "I don't know. I guess I like Duke well enough."

"Natalie, it's time to wash up for supper," Ashley called from the house.

E. J. rubbed his stomach. "Good thing too. I'm starved."

Natalie giggled. "Mama made lots of good food. You won't be starving for long." She took hold of his hand once again. The action caused a lump to rise up in E. J.'s throat. For a moment he actually felt tears sting his eyes. This was his daughter, a child he scarcely knew. How could it be that she so easily reached out to him when she didn't know him at all? How was it that they had found each other across the years and miles that had separated them?

The question haunted E. J. all through supper. The food proved to be as delectable as Natalie had promised. He'd had three helpings of the enchilada pie before realizing he'd made such a pig of himself.

"I'll have to be the one to furnish dinner next time," he said apologetically.

"Nonsense," Ashley replied, offering him more spicy rice. "I made plenty."

The real surprise of the evening was that Grandpa had asked to join them for dessert and coffee. Ashley had already enlisted E. J. to help get the old man to the table. When E. J. waved off the rice, that seemed a signal to the group. Ashley gathered up several of the empty dishes while her aunt took up the serving dishes. Natalie collected silverware and the salt and pepper.

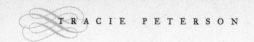

"Maybe you could see if Grandpa is ready to join us," Ashley told E. J. as she returned from the kitchen. "Natalie can show you the way."

He pushed back from the table and placed his napkin beside the plate. "I'd be glad to." Ashley reached for his dishes and met his gaze. The warmth there in her eyes might have given him reason to believe she held an interest in him, but E. J. knew better. That was merely a look of gratitude for his kindness to her grandfather. It was nothing more.

Natalie hurried off down the hall. "Grandpa!" she called. "Grandpa, it's time for dessert."

E. J. followed at a slower pace to give the man time to compose himself after Natalie's invasion. E. J. wondered if Russell Whitman would be angered at his appearance; after all, the man didn't know E. J. at all. They'd never met—not even in those earlier years when life seemed so charmed.

E. J. entered the dimly lit bedroom and smiled. The room was warm and inviting—a man's domain to be sure. A bookshelf with numerous volumes sat in one corner, while additional books were stacked beside the old man's bed.

Overhead, a Mexican-styled iron fixture offered light, giving the room a decidedly regional flavor. He'd seen Mary Colter use similar pieces. He turned to the old man, who was even now watching him, while Natalie fussed with finding her great-grandfather's slippers. "I'm E. J. Carson. I'm here to help you."

Russell Whitman eyed him seriously for a moment, then smiled. "Glad to know you, E. J. I'm Russell, but most folks your age call me Grandpa. You might as well."

His voice held none of the strength he must have once known, but E. J. immediately liked the old man. "I'd be honored to call you Grandpa. I've never known my own. Both my grandfathers died before I was very old."

"My grandpa is the best in the world," Natalie offered. "He's got enough love to share, so he can be your grandpa too." She put the slippers on her grandfather's feet, then stepped back.

E. J. was touched by her words. "I'd like that," he said softly, realizing how dearly he missed a sense of family. He'd been very close to his mother and father, perhaps because his younger siblings had died as toddlers or at birth. There had been a sister and two brothers, but polio had taken one brother, meningitis another, and his sister had been stillborn. It gave his parents great reason to cling to him, and because he was older and knew the pain of losing part of his family, it caused E. J. to feel the same way. Perhaps that was why it hurt so much to return home from the war only to find his parents gone.

The short walk down the hall was a strenuous effort for the old man. As they neared the table, E. J. nearly carried him in full. Helping Grandpa to take a chair, E. J. couldn't help noticing the laborious way the man strained to draw a breath. He looked at Ashley, meeting her worried expression. Grandpa's time was certainly running out. Her expression acknowledged this fact with a sorrow that seemed to permeate her entire being.

"I've made Grandpa's favorite chocolate cake,"

Ashley announced, appearing to recover from her sadness. E. J. watched as she put her defenses back in place, her expression masking the pain he'd seen there only moments before.

The old man looked up with a hint of gratitude. E. J. thought his eyes looked rather cloudy. Probably the medication, he reasoned. "Thank you, young man," Grandpa murmured.

E. J. took his seat and nodded. "Glad to help. I've heard so many wonderful things about you, I knew I had to meet you for myself."

Soon they were served with large pieces of what E. J. clearly knew was the best chocolate cake he'd ever tasted.

"I remember Mama made a cake similar to this," Lavelle said, sampling her dessert.

"It's the same recipe," Ashley replied, forking into her own piece.

"How in the world did you get it?" Lavelle questioned.

"Grandpa gave me a book of recipes that had belonged to Grandma. They were among the things he managed to save when . . ." Ashley's voice trailed off. Her expression was clearly one of embarrassment.

"When we forced him to divide up the household?"

Ashley looked away, and E. J. felt most uncomfortable in this sudden baring of dirty family linen.

"I'm so sorry, Aunt Lavelle. I didn't mean to say anything hurtful."

"Nonsense, Ashley. I've caused my own hurt." Lavelle reached over and patted Ashley's hand. "Don't give it a second thought. You could, however, copy the recipes down for me." She smiled lovingly.

E. J. thought the matter closed until Grandpa spoke up. "Lavelle, I hope you and Leticia understand that I've left my remaining possessions to Ashley. There isn't much—your mother's china, some odd pieces of furniture, and a couple of photo albums."

"The things we didn't pillage in our war with you, don't you mean?" Lavelle asked softly. "Oh, Father, I'm so sorry for the past. Of course I don't mind those things going to Ashley. Who better to care for them and pass them down through the generations?"

"Mother won't like it," Ashley declared, surprising E. J.

"Have you even heard from her?" Lavelle questioned.

"No, but that doesn't mean she won't make her presence known when it comes to possessions and what she believes she has coming to her."

Lavelle reached out again to Ashley. "Darling, you have no idea how she might react. Let's give her a chance. Tomorrow I'll do what I can to locate her. I have friends in Baltimore who can help."

Ashley bowed her head, and E. J. longed to put his arm around her and offer whatever comfort he might.

"I don't care if she comes at all, except that I know it means a great deal to Grandpa."

"It does mean a lot," Grandpa managed to say. This brought Ashley's immediate attention. "It means even more to know that you'll try to put an end to this bitterness and let the past die."

Ashley nodded. "For you, I would do that."

"I hope you'll do it for yourself and for Natalie too."

The little girl smiled and leaned over to touch her head to the old man's shoulder. "Grandpa's been praying for us, Mama. It's bound to work out. And Grandpa said we don't have to be afraid, because perfect love casts out fear. That's in the Bible."

Ashley nodded. "But the only perfect love I knew was with your daddy, and he's gone."

E. J. felt as if he'd been punched in the gut. The chocolate cake, as light and succulent as any he'd ever known, suddenly felt like a lead weight in his stomach.

"Perfect love is God's love, Mama. People can't love perfectly, but God can. And He doesn't want us to be afraid. So when we love Him, we don't have to be afraid of what will happen or what other people will do."

"You should listen to the child," Grandpa said, breathing heavily. "She knows what she's talking about."

Later that night E. J. continued to think on Grandpa's and Natalie's words. Reluctantly, he took out a Bible Natalie had brought him. She had lent it to him when E. J. admitted he didn't have one of his own.

Now, turning the book over and over in his hands, E. J. felt almost afraid to open it. What if he read something there that caused him even more pain?

"But how can I not seek God's direction?" he whispered aloud. "I've long put off paying attention to what God wants in my life. I've tried to deal with the past in my own way, but still it haunts me." He ran his hands through his hair and shook his head. "Nothing is working. I still have nightmares. I still struggle with my guilt, and now I have this revelation that my wife is alive and I have a daughter. I have to at least try to figure this out—with His help."

For so long he'd held God at arm's length. He didn't feel as Ashley did, that God didn't care, but rather it was more a situation of God putting more on him than E. J. could bear. God seemed a harsh taskmaster, pushing E. J. to limits that were far beyond his ability—then standing back to laugh cruelly at his plight.

But the God Natalie described—the loving Father Pastor McGuire preached of—didn't seem the kind to laugh at his children's sorrows. *Perhaps I've missed something*, E. J. thought. If his little daughter could hold God in such esteem and trust the future to His care, then what was it that kept E. J. hesitant?

E. J. opened to the Psalms, remembering they offered comfort and wisdom. His gaze fell to the page where the thirty-second chapter declared, *"Blessed is he whose transgression is forgiven, whose sin is covered. Blessed is the man unto whom the Lord imputeth not iniquity, and in whose spirit there is no guile."*

E. J. read on, a prayer in his heart that the words would somehow give him strength and encouragement. Several verses later he came to a passage he could not ignore.

"I acknowledged my sin unto thee, and mine iniquity have I not hid. I said, I will confess my transgressions unto the Lord; and thou forgavest the iniquity of my sin."

E. J. took off his glasses and rubbed his eyes. "Oh, God, can you forgive me? The wrong I've done is so hideous—so destructive. I've killed men. I've watched them die, even as they pled with me for life. How can you forgive that?"

The silence did nothing to reassure him, but a quickening in his heart ignited a spark of hope. God was in the business of forgiving grave sins. He recalled a story his friend John had told him about a man in the Bible, King David. The man had been a chosen king of God—a man after God's own heart. Yet David had sinned greatly in the eyes of the Lord. He had committed adultery with another man's wife, then arranged for that man to be killed on the battlefield. David had murdered the man as sure as if he had wielded the weapon himself.

And God forgave David.

The spark ignited and his heart warmed.

"You can forgive me. If I choose to repent . . . if I give this to you and seek your forgiveness . . . if I let the past be put to rest . . . then I can have peace and maybe even be a husband and father in action as well as deed."

E. J. knew he'd never wanted anything more in his life. These past weeks of getting to know Natalie and Ashley had greatly blessed him. Even Mary had noticed the change in his attitude and temperament. Natalie and Ashley were good for him. Was it too much to ask God that he might be good for them in return?

CHAPTER FOURTEEN

*T*he next few weeks were spent in a routine that Ashley found much to her liking. Lavelle sat with Grandpa in the morning while Ashley took care of the house chores and sent Natalie off to school. Then around noon Ashley would relieve her aunt, and Lavelle would take care of her own needs. Near to the time when Natalie was due home from school, Lavelle would take over Grandpa's care again, freeing Ashley to be there for Natalie. By evening Grandpa was usually fast asleep, completely worn-out from his efforts of trying to stay awake and communicate through the day. It was only at suppertime that he'd allow Ashley to give him a large dose of morphine, pleading with both her and Lavelle to understand that he needed to be cognizant for as long as he could stand the pain.

Near the end of the month, however, Ashley felt her neatly ordered world once again shift. A telegram arrived from her mother. After weeks abroad, her mother had finally returned to Baltimore to receive word that her father was dying. Lavelle received this information from friends who lived nearby and knew

Ashley's mother.

Ashley felt the wind go out of her at the words on the telegram. WILL ARRIVE ON THE TWENTY-EIGHTH TO OVERSEE THIS MATTER.

The words pierced her heart. Her mother was making it clear she intended to take control of the situation.

"Well, we won't allow it," Lavelle said, trying to encourage Ashley. "Your mother will find us both much stronger than when she last saw us."

"Have you not had contact with Mother these last eleven years?"

Lavelle brushed lint from her already immaculate navy blue dress. "There have been letters, but I only saw your mother once in that time. It was about four years ago. She and your father came to Los Angeles on business. She was greatly disappointed in the way in which I lived. I have only a modest home, not even as big as this one. I live very comfortably, but your mother was completely put off by it. She had hoped to step into Los Angeles society through my introduction. When she found that was not to be the case, she found other ways, of course."

"Of course," Ashley said.

"She did ask me whether or not I knew where Father had gone. Of course, I didn't know. I think she might have even hired someone to find where he'd gone, but she never found out. I'm sure she went home from that trip very disappointed in me. It didn't help matters at all that I'd become a Christian."

I should become a Christian to spite Mother, if for no other reason, Ashley thought. But immediately she knew that would never work. She might lie to the world, but she couldn't very well lie to God.

"Your mother said I was weak, just like Father. I'm sure that's why she feels she must come and oversee matters now. But, Ashley, she has no power here except that which you give her. The house is yours. Father told me all about giving it over to you, and I'm quite pleased he did. I'm glad he left you the entirety of his estate, and I will support you in this one hundred percent."

"I appreciate that, Aunt Lavelle, but . . ."

Lavelle took hold of Ashley's hand. "Look, I know you've not yet put your trust in God. Father told me of his concern for you. I don't know what keeps you from doing so or why you distance yourself from God—but no matter what, He is here and wants only the best for you. It might not always come in a comfortable, easy manner. Growing is sometimes very uncomfortable—think of when you carried Natalie. I've heard many a pregnant woman complain of the discomfort."

"But don't you feel that God . . . well . . . doesn't it seem sometimes that He's forgotten you—that He doesn't care?"

Lavelle hugged her close. "Ashley, we all go through moments of time when we feel confused by the things that happen in our lives. We wonder where God is and why He allows such tragedy. There are times when we feel completely deserted. Even Jesus bore that feeling."

"He did? When?" Ashley's voice belied her disbelief.

"On the cross, dear. He said, 'My God, my God, why hast thou forsaken me?' "

The words went through Ashley's heart like a white-hot coal. They seared her mind and burned deep into her lost memories and dreams. The words of Christ were her very own.

Lavelle seemed to understand the impact. "Ashley, God might seem silent for a season, but be assured, He is never absent. He won't leave you to bear things alone unless that's the way you choose to bear them. He leaves it up to you."

———

The next few days seemed to drag by in some ways and fly by in others. Ashley furiously cleaned the house, certain her mother's biggest criticism would be in how they lived. She beat the rugs and took down all the curtains to wash and iron. The hardwood floors were scrubbed and polished and the furniture carefully dusted and wiped. Lavelle tried to assure her the place was already spotless, but Ashley continued to find fault.

"If only I'd thought to paint the living room," Ashley reflected. She was on her knees scrubbing the baseboard when this idea came to her. She looked up at the walls, wondering if there still might be time.

Finally, Lavelle brought Ashley her sweater and demanded she go for a walk. "You haven't been out of the house since that telegram arrived. Now go."

Ashley looked up in complete surprise. "But I haven't scrubbed out the fireplace yet."

"Ashley! Your mother's arrival isn't worth this grief. We know her to be a critical woman. Do you really suppose that your efforts will matter? If she's still of the same meanspirited temperament, she won't appreciate the effort. And if she's had a change of heart, then none of this will matter."

The words made sense. Ashley slowly got up from her aching knees. "I suppose you're right. I just wanted to . . ."

Lavelle touched her face tenderly. "I know, sweetheart. I know."

Ashley put aside her sponge and bucket. "I suppose I should go to the market and pick up a few things."

"Or at least take a walk and enjoy the sunshine."

Ashley nodded and took up the sweater. Pulling it around her shoulders, she sighed. "I'd like to believe she's changed, but I have no faith in that. Not given the telegram."

"I know. But God is sufficient even in this. He'll see us through—you simply have to trust Him, Ashley."

Trust. That was the real crux of the matter.

How could she trust God when she wasn't even sure who He was?

She didn't like that her mother's impending arrival was giving her cause to act so completely out of character. She couldn't help questioning herself. *I've not cared what that woman thought in eleven years. Why is it so important that she approve now?* Just as her aunt had told her, if Leticia was the same woman whom Ashley had parted company with all those years ago, nothing Ashley did now would meet with her approval.

Walking to town, Ashley couldn't help sidetracking in order to see the Harvey hotel's progress. She hadn't talked to E. J. Carson since that night at dinner weeks ago. Natalie had asked several times to have him over, but Ashley had always refused for one reason or another. There was something there that made her uncomfortable—almost uneasy. Maybe it was the easygoing manner in which she shared E. J.'s company. Maybe it was the way he seemed to know things about her.

His tenderness toward Grandpa had nearly been her undoing that night. He was so gentle with the old man— so careful of his frail, pain-filled body. She could easily remember his expression, so concerned, so compassionate. Something in his manner reminded her of Ethan; at least she was fairly confident that the memory was true. As the years went by she had to admit that it was harder and harder to remember his mannerisms, his voice. It grieved her, but as Grandpa had suggested, it was very possible that she was also assigning things to the past that had no bearing in truth. She and Ethan had shared only a matter of weeks together. It was hardly enough to build a lifetime on. But then again, it had given her Natalie.

Natalie adored E. J. Carson. There was no doubt about that. She talked about the man from morning until night. But now that her mother was coming, she'd have ample excuses to delay his visits when Natalie insisted.

Ashley wouldn't impose her mother upon anyone. Especially if she were to have the same nature as before. No, their house and dinner table would be full. Ashley would give up her bedroom to her mother and share Natalie's bed, and while she knew the arrangement would be adequate for most anyone else in the world, Ashley was confident it wouldn't meet with her mother's approval.

"Mrs. Reynolds!"

E. J. Carson called to her from beyond a newly constructed portion of stone fence. Ashley felt her stomach flutter. Suddenly she was aware that she was quite happy he'd sought her out. *Why should this man have the power to make me feel this way?* Guilt immediately washed over her. What of Ethan?

"Hello, Mr. Carson."

He tipped his hat and smiled. "I was hoping to see you today. In fact, I had thought to come by. I have a question for you. Remember? I promised you dinner sometime."

"Yes, but that's hardly necessary," Ashley argued. The last thing in the world she wanted was to be asked out on a date with this man or any other.

"Well, I've been talking with several of the workers," he continued. "I was wondering if you've ever been to the meteor crater west of here?"

Ashley shook her head. "No. Grandpa and I talked about going, and Natalie has nagged us both about it ever since hearing about it in school, but we've never managed to make arrangements. We have no car, you see."

"Well, I do. I've just acquired the use of a vehicle, and I'd like very much to propose a picnic tomorrow. I figured since it's Saturday and I have the day off and Natalie will be out of school, we could take all day. It's about twenty-one miles to drive there, so we'd have plenty of time to explore."

The thought of spending all day in the company of this gentle-spirited man held both appeal and terror at the same time.

"I know it's short notice, but I would bring a picnic from the Harvey House," he said, his voice almost pleading.

Ashley knew Natalie would be beside herself if Ashley were to say no. How many times had she begged her mother to ask Pastor McGuire for the loan of his car for just such an adventure? The only problem was, Ashley didn't drive.

"I'm sure Natalie would enjoy the trip," Ashley began, almost confident that she would turn down E. J. Carson's offer for herself. But when it came time to speak the words, she found herself agreeing instead. "I'll need to make sure Aunt Lavelle doesn't mind taking care of Grandpa all day. Still, I wouldn't want to leave her alone for too long. We'd have to be back by dark."

E. J. smiled. "I can arrange that; just leave it to me. I'll pick you both up about nine in the morning. We'll get there in an hour or less, and that should leave us plenty of time." He tipped his hat again, then sauntered off as if he'd single-handedly won the World Series.

Ashley had to smile, until she heard him start to whistle. The tune left her cold. She could hear Ethan whistling the same song. It was his favorite ragtime melody. He'd whistled it incessantly while they'd courted.

E. J. disappeared into the construction site, but Ashley felt fixed to the spot where she stood. All at once she exhaled, not even realizing she'd been holding her breath. *Oh, Ethan, why should you be gone while E. J. Carson is here? It's not at all how I saw life when you married me.*

Her heart ached within her and the memory was more than she wanted to deal with. *How am I to spend the day with this man and not die from loneliness?*

———

E. J. felt a sense of renewal in his spirit. He had actually taken time since last seeing Ashley to pray and seek God—and it felt marvelous. Though he still suffered the terrors of his war memories as he slept each night, the dreams seemed shorter and less violent. Perhaps true healing had begun.

Now he waited for his wife and daughter to join him on an outing to the meteor crater, and an overwhelming giddiness engulfed him. He wanted this freedom of spirit. He wanted to look forward to the day and to know that it would come around right in the evening. He wanted for once not to dread the nightfall.

Natalie came bouncing out the door as she so often did. She wore her dark hair pulled back into a high ponytail, which swung back and forth as she came down the path to the borrowed car. Her skirt jogged up and down, revealing rolled-up pants beneath.

E. J. reached out and opened the door for her. "I see you wore jeans under your dress. You must be planning for quite an adventure."

Natalie jumped up on the Packard's running board. "Mama said I had to wear the dress over them," she replied, wrinkling up her nose in distaste. "She doesn't understand that sometimes I like to climb and not worry about dresses."

Natalie climbed into the backseat and plopped down dead center. "I get all this room to myself?"

E. J. laughed. "Well, so long as you mind the picnic lunch I've put down on the floor behind my seat."

"Is this your car?" she questioned, running her hand over the seat. "This is the nicest car I've ever been in."

"This is one of the Harvey company cars. They gave

it to Miss Colter to use, but since she's out of town, she told me I could borrow it for our trip."

About that time Ashley came from the house. Her face glowed from beneath a wide-brimmed straw hat. She caught him watching her and smiled hesitantly, her gaze curious, almost as if she were trying to figure out a puzzle. E. J. felt a wave of guilt for keeping his identity from her. He knew she deserved to know and make the choice for herself as to whether they'd continue their marriage or end it.

"I hope I've dressed all right," she said, breaking his thoughts. "I thought a simple skirt and blouse would be easiest."

He nodded and noticed she'd put on very sturdy walking shoes. "You look perfect. Natalie too."

"I've brought some sweaters, although I doubt we'll need them as the day seems so fair. Oh, and I've brought a couple of blankets for the ground. I didn't know whether or not you'd think to bring something to sit on."

"No, I totally forgot about that. Glad you considered the matter for me." He smiled and took the blankets from her while she handed the sweaters back to Natalie. E. J. held the door for Ashley as she stepped up on the running board and got in. He watched her gracefully arrange herself on the seat before nodding to him.

Soon they were on the road, driving west with the sun at their back, the world stretched out before them in a raw and rugged landscape that begged exploration. Cactus, scrub, and a variety of nondescript brush dotted the red, sandy soil. The dusty desert road offered nothing in the way of shade or real diversion, but E. J. hardly cared about that. He'd made up his mind. He was going to tell Ashley the truth. Once they were at the crater site and Natalie was preoccupied with her exploration, he would break the news to Ashley as gently as possible.

The anticipation of that moment was enough to keep E. J. focused and energized on the journey west. For over an hour he contemplated what he would say.

Ashley, there was a mistake about your husband dying in the war.

Ashley, I didn't know until I saw you that you were still alive.

Ashley, the government makes mistakes, and I'm not dead like you thought.

Nothing sounded exactly right, but he was certain the words would come when the time was right.

Upon finally arriving without mishap, Natalie's chatter caught up with his thoughts. "I've wanted to come here forever. We learned all about this place in school. Did you know they were trying to mine the crater for iron ore? They stopped because they couldn't find very much and they just kept striking water or having other problems. They just stopped work this year."

E. J. smiled as he parked the car. There were only two other cars at the location, probably belonging to whoever might remain on-site to answer questions, he figured.

"My teacher said the meteorite probably weighed three hundred thousand tons but that it probably broke apart and smashed into little dust pieces when it came to earth. Isn't that hard to imagine?"

"Indeed it is," E. J. replied.

"This is all she has been able to talk about since yesterday," Ashley told him.

"It's just that it's the most amazing thing in the world, and it's not very far from home. People are going to start coming here more and more to see it, and that's going to make this area very popular."

E. J. laughed and opened the car door. "And that's important to you?"

"Sure," Natalie said, jumping from the car. "The more people who come and want to live here, the more they're going to need architects to draw the plans for houses and businesses. That will give me a job."

E. J. shook his head. She certainly had it in mind to stick to her guns regarding her dream.

The meteor crater proved to be fascinating, but E. J.'s mind couldn't completely appreciate the phenomenon. He wandered around for a time with Natalie and Ashley, listening to his daughter marvel at the impact indentation nearly a mile across in size. All the while the words of his explanation to Ashley ran through his mind.

"See down there?" Natalie questioned E. J., pointing to the floor of the crater. "My teacher said that some of those rocks that just look like little stones to us from here are actually boulders. Isn't that amazing?"

"Indeed it is." He found great delight in her reactions. "Say, are you ready to eat yet?" he asked Natalie. "I'm starving."

"You and Mama can go ahead and eat, but I just want to explore. Please?" She looked at her mother first and then E. J.

"I think that's perfectly acceptable," E. J. said, then

looked at Ashley and added, "If it's all right with your mother."

Ashley nodded and Natalie took off without another word.

"Her energy level is daunting," E. J. said, still watching Natalie skitter over the rocks.

"She never wears out. She's on the go constantly." Ashley looked up at him, her face shaded by the brim of her hat. She seemed to study him, especially his eyes. Could it be she already suspected the truth?

They walked back to the picnic basket and blankets. Ashley had placed the covers atop the basket, but before E. J. could take hold of it, she grabbed it. "We'll need to shake these out just in case something has crawled in."

E. J. took up the other blanket and followed her example, snapping it open. Once assured they were safe, they spread them on the ground. As they sat down, E. J. decided to get his confession out of the way. There was simply no telling when Natalie would return.

"Ashley, there's something I need to talk to you about."

She looked up, rather startled. Cocking her head to one side, she seemed to contemplate his expression and waited for him to speak—seeking understanding in the silence.

"Well, that is . . ." Why did this have to be so hard? She was his wife—she needed to know the truth. "Something happened a long time ago," he began again. "Something that forever changed my life."

"Ashley! Hey, Ashley!"

E. J. looked up to find a tall, slender blond woman

waving. At her side, a beefy-looking man studied him with an arched brow.

"Glenda, hello!" Ashley called back and waved.

E. J. held his breath, hoping—even praying—that this would be the end of the matter. The woman moved forward, however, dashing his hopes.

"I thought that was you. How are you? Where's Natalie?"

Ashley put her hand to the brim of her hat as if to further shield the sun. "She's exploring. There she is, over there." She pointed to the north and the couple turned in unison.

"Oh, sure. I see her. Goodness, but that girl can climb like a mountain goat."

Ashley smiled and nodded. "Glenda, this is E. J. Carson. He's actually become a good friend of Natalie's and thus mine. He's working with the new Harvey House construction." She turned back to E. J. "This is Glenda and her fiancé, Marvin."

"Nice to meet you both," E. J. said, not really meaning it. It wasn't that he minded meeting Ashley's friends, but now wasn't the time.

"I see you're having a picnic. We brought some food too," Glenda said, motioning to Marvin and the basket he held.

E. J. held his breath. *Please don't ask them to join us,* he thought over and over. *I need the time to tell you the truth, Ashley.*

"Why don't you join us?" Ashley moved closer to E. J. "There's plenty of room."

"Are you sure?" Glenda asked, then looked at Marvin. "Would you like to join them?"

"You bet," he said, pushing back a rowdy shock of red hair. "I'll go anywhere you go."

Glenda laughed. "You'd better."

They joined E. J. and Ashley, laughing and talking about people they knew at the Harvey restaurant or on the railroad. Glenda asked about Grandpa Whitman, and Ashley made comments about how quickly he was fading. She also mentioned that her mother was due in town on Tuesday.

By the time Natalie was completely satisfied with her rock expedition, it was time to go. In frustrated silence, E. J. drove back to Winslow. Natalie dozed in the backseat, completely spent from her day of running and climbing. Ashley stared absentmindedly out her window, then suddenly turned to him.

"You were going to say something to me back there. You'd started to tell me something about the past."

He considered for a moment that he might break the news to her before Natalie woke up, then decided against it. There was always a chance she might awaken in the middle of his explanation. No, he'd just have to wait until another day.

She'd gone eleven years without knowing the truth. He supposed she could wait another day or two.

"It wasn't important. We'll save it for another time," he replied good-naturedly. But inside, E. J. knew a building frustration that refused to be ignored. He had to tell her—and it needed to be soon.

CHAPTER FIFTEEN

*M*onday. That dreaded day.

Ashley looked out her bedroom window, then turned to face the room itself. She'd tried to arrange it perfectly, but no doubt her mother would take displeasure with something. How was it that a person could live thousands of miles away and still heavily influence the heart and mind of another?

Ashley smoothed the chenille spread on the bed. The white ridges were dotted with tiny pink flowers and green leaves. Her mother would probably say it was too feminine or too childish. The pillows would probably be too flat and the temperature of the room too cool at night.

Checking the freshly washed and ironed curtains, Ashley inspected the material for any holes or snags. She just wanted to give her mother as little reason for criticism as possible.

Sighing, Ashley took a handful of her clothes and moved them to Natalie's closet. Hanging her dresses on the bar beside her daughter's, Ashley bit her lip to keep it from trembling.

"I'm absolutely terrified of her coming here."

Once the words were spoken, it was almost a relief. It was as if by speaking them, Ashley could finally accept them.

"She will criticize and cause me grief. Of that I can be sure."

And that was perhaps more troubling than anything else. If her mother were the same woman she'd been eleven years earlier, Ashley knew there wouldn't be a moment's peace. And that was what this house had always represented to her. Peace.

This house—this home—had been a respite and a comfort. She'd sought sanctuary here and felt warm and loved within these walls. Now her mother would come and all that would change. The house would become a battleground—no different from the other places Leticia Murphy had stormed.

"I have to get ahold of myself," Ashley said, speaking into the mirror over her daughter's desk. She saw her expression in the reflection there and it only served to further discourage her. She looked scared, and her mother would feed upon that like vultures to carrion.

————

"I know she's afraid," Russell told his daughter. "She believes her mother will come here and wreak havoc on her life. And she may have a point."

Lavelle nodded. "If Letty is the same woman she used to be, then Ashley has good reason to believe that."

Russell fought against the waves of nausea and pain. "I know, but I want her to have hope. Ashley can't change her mother, but she can change herself." His words were barely audible, but Lavelle apparently heard, for she nodded as she got to her feet.

"Papa, if I find Leticia to be as she's been in the past, I'll speak to her sternly before we arrive. She must understand that she cannot come in here and turn everything upside down. She may not like it, but she will hear me out."

Russell nodded. "I'm glad you're going for her and not Ashley."

Lavelle glanced at her watch. "The pastor will be here momentarily to escort me."

"You go ahead. I'll be praying," Russell said, shifting only the tiniest bit to see if the pain decreased. It didn't.

Lavelle had only been gone a few moments before a knock sounded on his open bedroom door. Glancing up, Russell smiled weakly and motioned Pastor McGuire to come in.

"I see you're still taking life easy," the pastor teased. "How are things today?"

"Difficult."

"A lot of pain?" Pastor questioned.

"Yes. And I find myself just wishing to slip from this body into heaven."

McGuire reached over and touched Russell's shoulder. "The time will come, my friend, soon enough. I don't desire you to live out your days in pain, but I do cherish your existence. You'll be sorely missed when you're gone."

"You're one of only a few folks I know who can talk so openly about my dying. It's a relief, you know, to be able to say the words out loud. It's not as if it is a secret."

McGuire nodded. "I know. My mom and dad both

said the same thing when they were dying. People avoid speaking of it when they're with you because they're afraid of causing you more grief. Yet what they don't realize is that some things need to be said."

"Exactly."

Russell looked up to find Ashley standing in the doorway. He figured she'd heard their discussion, and he quite frankly hoped it might make a difference. Ashley was one of those people who avoided speaking the truth—as if in keeping silent, she might stave off death. It only got worse the closer he came to actually dying.

"Ashley, come on in, child."

Pastor McGuire looked over his shoulder and nodded. "Yes, do. We aren't speaking of anything that you can't be a part of."

Ashley looked most uncomfortable. "I . . . uh . . . just wanted to let you know that Aunt Lavelle is ready to go. The train is due ten minutes from now."

"Well, I suppose we should head out, then," Pastor McGuire said. He offered a quick prayer of hope and comfort, then headed to the door. "Ashley, we've certainly enjoyed having you in church when you're able to be there. I hope you know that."

Ashley smiled tentatively. "I've . . . well . . . I've enjoyed it too."

Smiling, the tall pastor nodded. "That's music to a minister's ears. I'll look forward to seeing you Sunday."

Russell could see his granddaughter's uneasiness. It was something akin to embarrassment. "Ashley, would you sit with me for a moment?"

"Sure, Grandpa." She came to his bedside and pulled a chair close.

"I wanted to talk to you before your mother got here." He bit back a cry as his side exploded in pain. The shock of it left him gasping for breath.

"Are you all right, Grandpa?"

He opened his eyes and noted her concern. "It's just this momentary trouble. Soon I'll be right as rain."

Ashley frowned. "I heard what Pastor McGuire said. I didn't know that you needed to talk about dying."

"It's not so much the actual dying, but there are things I want to say before I slip away. It's one of the reasons I don't want to take the medicine." She nodded and he continued. "You're afraid . . . aren't you?"

Ashley laughed bitterly. "I'm terrified. Of so many things."

"Tell me."

She looked toward the wall, avoiding his eyes. "I'm just not that confident of being able to handle things once you're gone. I'm afraid Mother will come in here and make a mess of everything and demand her way, and I won't have the strength to stand up to her."

"I know those things worry you, but God is with you. You've only got to reach out to Him."

"Will God keep my mother under control?" Ashley asked seriously. "If so, why didn't God do that for you all those years ago?"

Russell knew she desperately needed answers, but he had none. "God is not in the habit of explaining himself to me." He smiled and it took all his energy. "You've got to have trust, Ashley. You can trust Him to be faithful. Let your Mother rant and rave if that's why she's come. Let her talk of what money she expects to get after I'm dead. She can only hurt you if you let her. Her words may be caustic, her temperament harsh. But she cannot change the fact that this house is yours and the bank account is yours. She can't reach into your soul and separate you from what's most important—God."

"No, I suppose I've done a decent job of that myself," Ashley admitted. "Grandpa, I've been thinking of all the things you've told me. I've been listening to Pastor McGuire as well. I wish I could say I have the faith to believe it's all true, but right now I just don't."

Her lost expression and the pain in her eyes made Russell wish he could give her his own precious salvation, just in order to see her at peace—happy.

"It's all God's timing," he said, more to remind himself than her.

"I know, Grandpa. I just want you to know that I'm trying to understand it all. I want to understand. I can even honestly say that I want to trust God again."

He nodded, closing his eyes. "That's enough for a start. Just give Him a chance, Ashley. He's more than happy to prove himself to you."

"God? Prove himself to me?" Ashley asked in surprise. "But I thought it was the other way around—I thought I was supposed to prove myself to Him by trusting and believing and doing all that other stuff."

"The Bible says that we should 'Taste and see that the Lord is good: blessed is the man that trusteth in him.' See, first it says, 'Taste and see.' In other words, give God a try and see if He doesn't prove to be exactly what He said He'd be. Faith and trust don't come overnight, Ashley. They grow, and just as people need time to get to know one another, so it takes time to get to know God and grow in trusting Him. But blessed are you when you come to that place." He closed his eyes, exhaustion claiming the last bit of his strength.

He felt Ashley kiss his forehead. "You rest now, Grandpa, and I'll be thinking on what you said. I promise."

He drew a ragged breath but said nothing. *Lord, please don't let this time go wasted. Let her hear your words and take courage. Let her come to you and heal her wounded heart. I cannot rest until I know she is safe.*

Lavelle stood on the platform waiting for her sister. She squared her shoulders and prepared for the battle to come, believing in her heart that Leticia would come off the train with guns blazing.

She's always been like that, Lavelle reasoned. *She's always been the kind to act first and think later. She never cares who she hurts or how difficult she makes life for someone else. Those things are immaterial.*

Lavelle had never really stood up to her older sister. Leticia had ruled their nursery with an iron will to match that of any adult. Lavelle had just calmly gone along with most any plan Leticia thought up. *But I can't be like that anymore. I need to be strong for Ashley, and I need to stand firm in my faith. Letty won't like it, but that's the way it will be.*

Now Lavelle fretted over the fact that she'd never found an opportunity to tell Ashley that her father had passed away some years earlier. When Lavelle had first arrived, she'd felt certain she'd have to explain it, because Ashley kept talking about her parents and wondering if Lavelle had had contact with them. But there never seemed to be the right opportunity to speak to the matter of Marcus Murphy's death, and so Lavelle had left it unsaid. Now she regretted it, knowing that Leticia would be the one to break the news. And no doubt she'd not do the telling in a gentle manner.

Lavelle knew that Leticia blamed Ashley for her father's passing. Marcus had fretted and worried over Ashley's disappearance—that much Leticia had shared with Lavelle. Letty felt he had worried himself into the grave over Ashley, and she probably held Ashley accountable for the matter. Regret washed over Lavelle. "I should have told her," she whispered.

The westbound Santa Fe passenger train blew its whistle from down the track and Lavelle held her breath. She walked out a pace from the depot and exhaled softly. *Lord, give me strength to deal with my sister. Give me love to shower upon her, even though I don't feel very loving.*

The train pulled in and groaned and ground to a halt. Porters and other railroad men moved into position to make the detrainment as simple and orderly as possible.

And then before Lavelle knew it, Leticia was stepping from the train. She looked for all the world as though she owned not only the train she'd just come from but the land upon which she'd just stepped. Overdressed in an elegant three-tiered bolero coat and dress by Chanel, Leticia demanded attention. The dark red color made Lavelle immediately think of blood, and she couldn't help wondering how her sister would stage the first lethal blow.

"Leticia," Lavelle said, going to her sister. "I'm so glad you've come."

"Is he dead yet?"

The opening thrust of the sword.

Lavelle startled at the question. "No. Our father is still alive. I think perhaps he's been holding on to see you again."

She made a huffing noise and turned to look past Lavelle. "Where is she?"

"Who?" Lavelle questioned, completely taken aback by her sister.

"You know perfectly well. Ashley. Where is she? I suppose she doesn't have the good manners to be here."

Blow number two.

"She stayed home with our father," Lavelle explained. "Someone needed to be there, and I told her I thought it best if she stayed and I came."

"I see. Well, let's not dillydally at the station," Leticia said. "I've come this far; I might as well finish it. I'm sure there's much to be done. I certainly can't count on anyone else to have managed Father's affairs. The incompetence in this family speaks for itself."

The third in what was to become a long line of plunging attacks cut Lavelle to the quick.

"Leticia, before we go, I want to say something." Lavelle lifted her chin and straightened her shoulders. "You were not asked here in order to create a scene. Our father is dying, and I do not wish to see him in any more pain than he's already enduring."

"I don't know what you're talking about." Leticia shifted her matching handbag and stared at her younger sister.

"I'm talking about you. It is my fondest hope that you will be peaceable with Father and with Ashley. They are both suffering in this, and I don't want to see them hurting more than they already are."

"Might I remind you, you are my younger sister. I did not seek your advice. Furthermore, I do not intend to stand here and be dressed down by anyone—but especially not you."

Lavelle bolstered her courage. "Leticia, you're a headstrong and often cruel woman. I won't stand for it this time. You'll either conduct yourself civilly or—"

"Or what?" Leticia laughed haughtily. "You have no power over me. You're as destitute as most of these people." She waved her arm to the departing crowd. "I have enough money to buy and sell you many times over. I'll hire a lawyer if need be, but you won't stand here and threaten me." The woman's dark eyes seemed to blaze with fire.

Lavelle remained calm. "I'm not trying to threaten you. I'm merely stating that our . . ." She paused. She'd started to reference the house as belonging to their father, but that would never do. Better to set the stage early. "Ashley's house is a peaceful one at this point. Father is much beloved in this community, and it would grieve those around him to know his own daughter cared nothing more about him than to cause him even more pain. I want to see him die in peace."

Leticia pushed past her sister. "And I'm just ready for him to die."

———

E. J. was relieved to have the workday behind him.

He had thought to go to check up on Ashley and her grandfather but remembered that her mother was coming to town today. Her mother was the one person who very well might remember him. He couldn't risk running into her—not just yet.

He whistled and made his way to his room at the Harvey House. He hoped to simply spend the night reading his Bible and praying. There was still the matter of telling Ashley the truth, and he hoped he could keep his courage to do so by drawing closer to God.

"Mr. Carson, wait up!"

He turned to find Natalie running after him. "I drew you a picture at school today." She waved the folded paper as she approached.

"Why, that was very kind. What is it? The meteorite crater?"

"Nope. This is the house I'm gonna build my mama someday."

She came to a halt in front of him, her pigtails resting down her back. He took the paper from her and opened it. There, in a very detailed manner, was the house he'd once designed for his wife. Of course, it was an amateur attempt, but he easily recognized it.

"Do you like it?"

E. J. nodded. "I like it very much, Natalie. Thank you."

"Sure," she grinned. "I think my mama likes you."

E. J. was taken aback. "Why do you say that?"

"Well, she sure never took trips with anyone else. I think she only let you take us to the meteor crater because she likes you."

"I think she likes you," E. J. teased. "I think that's

the reason she allowed the trip."

"Well, she liked me before and we never let Mr. Morgan take us to the meteor crater." With that, she turned to go. "I have to get home. My grandma is coming today. I've never met her, but I sure hope she's nice."

E. J. waved good-bye. "I hope she is too, Natalie." It was a sincere wish, but remembering Leticia Murphy, E. J. wasn't at all encouraged to believe Natalie's hopes would come true.

He took the picture with him and made his way to his hotel room. He couldn't imagine what Ashley must be enduring, seeing her mother for the first time in so very long. He wished he could be there for her—to offer support and to stand ready to defend her against her mother's meanspirited blows.

"God, you're the only one who can intercede in this. Please don't leave Ashley alone."

He smoothed out the drawing on his desk and traced the lines with his index finger. Memories flooded his mind, and before he knew it, E. J. had taken up his own sketch pad. Within a few moments, he'd drawn a rough outline of the house. Standing there, hunched over the picture, E. J. realized how very much he'd missed creating beautiful things. He felt his demons leave him—at least momentarily—as he sketched out more and more detail. Perhaps this had been the answer all along. Maybe in his creativity—his passion for beauty—he could find a way to dispel the darkness in his life.

"A little light can make itself quite evident in the blackest night," he murmured.

CHAPTER SIXTEEN

*A*shley watched her mother scrutinize the house as Pastor McGuire carried her luggage upstairs.

"It's rather what I expected," her mother said, sounding very bored.

Without elaborating on her comment, Leticia turned her sights on Ashley. "I see you haven't changed much. I understand you have a child. Is she legitimate? Who's her father?"

Ashley raged inside at the question of her daughter's legitimacy. "She's Ethan's daughter, of course. I've never remarried."

"I don't recall you mentioning that you were with child when I last saw you in Baltimore."

Ashley barely held on to her anger. "I don't recall being given a chance. You were, as I recall, far more focused on getting my marriage annulled than knowing the truth of the situation."

"Well, it's of no matter. No decent man would have you now—especially with a brat." Leticia lifted her chin and looked left and then right. "This is an awfully small house. I understand from Lavelle that you're the

owner?"

Ashley looked at Lavelle and then back at her mother. "That's right."

"Humph."

"Natalie should be home any minute. I do hope you'll be kind to her," Ashley said, trying hard to stand firm without resorting to her mother's nasty tactics.

"She's a darling child, Leticia," Lavelle interjected. "You'll be pleased to have her as a granddaughter." She stood close to Ashley.

Ashley narrowed her eyes, watching her mother's every change of expression. It was rather like watching a rattlesnake prepare to strike. What would the woman do next? Where would she attack?

"Where is my father?" Leticia asked, surprising Ashley.

"His room is at the end of the hall. But before you visit him, I want you to understand something." Ashley bolstered her courage. "Grandpa has advanced liver cancer. He's in a tremendous amount of pain. You were notified to come at his request." She hoped her mother understood the implication that she had not been brought here because of Ashley's desire. "He cannot be up and about. He doesn't eat, and he has been given pain medication, though he often refuses to take it because he desires to think in a clearheaded manner.

"It's Grandpa's desire to put the past behind us. I'm willing to at least give pretense to that, for his sake," Ashley said, her voice unemotional. "I would like to know your intentions toward that matter."

Leticia looked at her daughter as if she'd suddenly grown horns. "I don't think that merits an answer. You are my child. I do not answer to you."

Ashley stepped between her mother and the hall leading to her grandfather's room. "Until I understand if you mean to cause him more pain and suffering than he's already enduring, you are not going to be allowed to visit with him."

"Of all the stupid, disrespectful—"

"I agree with her, Letty," Lavelle said. "Father is in no condition for one of your scenes. He has no money— no possessions—nothing monetary to advance your position whatsoever. If you're here for that, you might as well turn around and head back to Baltimore."

Ashley watched her mother's face contort. Her eyes blazed with anger and hatred. "Do not make me seek help from other sources in dealing with you two. As I told Lavelle, I have more money and power than either of you could ever hope to know. I will do what I have to in order to ensure that things are properly handled."

"Grandpa has already turned matters over to his lawyer, Simon Watson. If you have questions regarding the business of Grandfather's estate, then you will talk to him and not to Grandpa. That is how it will be," Ashley replied sternly. "Otherwise, I'll have you removed from this house—my house."

The battle lines were drawn.

"Mama, I'm home!" Natalie declared, coming through the front door.

Leticia turned, apparently startled at the sound of the child's voice. Ashley watched as she studied Natalie's pixielike face. She was such a delicate and tiny child, and for a moment Ashley wanted to rush between her mother and Natalie to protect her from whatever vile

things Leticia Murphy might say.

"She looks just like you," Leticia commented, appearing not to realize her own words.

"Are you my grandma Murphy?" Natalie questioned.

Ashley didn't wait for her mother to comment. "Yes, Natalie. This is my mother—your grandmother."

Natalie smiled sweetly. "I'm sure glad you came to visit us, Grandma."

Leticia eyed her suspiciously, then lifted her chin. "Call me Grandmother."

Natalie frowned but only momentarily. "All right. Grandmother."

"I suppose you've had your head filled with all manner of evil when it comes to me and the rest of the family."

Natalie's expression changed to complete confusion. She looked to Ashley as if for an answer. Ashley's heart swelled with pride for her child. She went to stand beside Natalie and gently embraced her.

"I've always stood by the conviction that if you couldn't say something nice about someone, don't say anything at all. I've actually told Natalie very little about my family." Ashley knew she shouldn't speak thusly in front of Natalie, but her feelings were still smarting from the earlier exchange of words.

"She's terribly small," Leticia said, returning her attention to Natalie. "Is she sickly?"

"Not at all," Ashley said.

Lavelle laughed at this and agreed. "She has the energy of ten children her age. I've never seen anyone so in love with life."

Natalie beamed a smile in Lavelle's direction, then

turned her attention back to her grandmother. "I have a pony. Her name is Penny. Would you like to meet her?"

Leticia looked rather horrified. "I should say not. I've no time for ponies."

"Your grandmother needs to be with Great-Grandpa," Ashley said, squeezing her daughter's shoulders. "Remember, I told you she would probably have very little time for us. Grandpa hasn't long, and we want her to spend as much time with him as possible."

Natalie nodded somberly. "I remember."

"Why don't you go change your clothes and then take care of Penny? Maybe later at dinner, you and Grandmother can talk some more."

"Sure, Mama." Natalie darted off for the stairs without another word.

Ashley waited for her mother's painful comments. She didn't have long to wait.

"She doesn't look old enough to be the child of that Reynolds man."

"Well, she is," Ashley stated flatly. "I left Baltimore and went to live with Grandpa in Los Angeles and moved here shortly before Natalie was born. We've had a good life here, and the folks who know us love and adore Natalie. I don't intend to see you hurt her." Ashley hadn't meant to let the latter statement slip out, but now that it had, she intended to stand her ground.

"I'm going to check on Father," Lavelle said, looking as if she wanted Ashley and her mother to have a moment alone. She hurried down the hall.

"I know you don't want to be here. Just as I don't want you here," Ashley said flatly. Honesty, blatant and brutal, seemed to be the only way to deal with her mother. "I had hoped your attitude would have changed, but I realized even in your telegram that you had your own ideas to come here and take over. That's not at all how things will be. Grandpa, Natalie, and I have lived very comfortably these last years. I won't allow you to turn our order into chaos. Do you understand me?"

Leticia seemed taken aback but not enough to keep from commenting. "You are still the same stubborn, headstrong child you've always been. You dug your own grave eleven years ago, but you'll not dig one for my father as well. I will take charge of his estate."

"No, you won't."

Leticia's eyes narrowed. "You can't hope to win against me."

Ashley thought of something Grandpa had once told her. Something about all things being possible with God. Was that true? Could she count on God to help her if she called upon Him? *God, if you're listening, I guess I need help now.*

"I don't intend to stand by," her mother continued, "and see you take from me that which is rightfully mine."

Ashley shook her head. "There is nothing here that belongs to you. The house and its contents are mine. Grandpa settled his affairs some time back. He's arranged his own funeral here, with his body afterward being shipped for burial beside Grandma in Los Angeles. His lawyer has the details of his will. His pastor has a finalized eulogy. You may discuss this with either of them, but I will not argue it with you any further."

Ashley turned to go, but her mother seemed determined to have the last word. "You might notice," her mother began, "that your father is not here. That's because he's dead."

Ashley turned back around and drew her hands together. "I'm sorry to hear that." The statement shocked her, but she'd not allow her mother to see her weakened or made vulnerable by this news.

"You should be. You're the one who killed him. He never got over what you did. He died three years ago, his heart still broken at your disappearance."

Ashley saw her mother's face. She seemed delighted—almost expectant. It was almost as if she thrived on the telling of bad news. Shaking her head, Ashley replied, "I won't accept any blame in his death, Mother. If there is someone to blame, you might consider yourself. Your negative temperament and bitterness would be enough to kill anyone living close to you."

With that, Ashley went quickly to the kitchen and out the back door. She heard her mother's gasp of surprise but didn't care. The news of her father's death had been a shock, but nothing that she couldn't bear. Everyone died, she reminded herself. Ethan, Grandpa, and now her father. Everyone died.

That evening, after a most uncomfortable dinner, Ashley took up her week's worth of mending and sat down to relax in the living room. She'd laid logs in the fireplace earlier and now a fire roared in welcome from the hearth. She loved quiet evenings like this, and usually Grandpa was with her. Now there'd never be any more nights with Grandpa telling stories from his boyhood. There'd never be moments of Natalie stretched out before the fire, watching as Grandpa spoke in his animated way, her eyes wide with the wonder of his memories.

Even her mother's animosity couldn't ruin the memories of those times for Ashley. She smiled and picked up her needle and thread. With Natalie and Lavelle taking an evening stroll and her mother visiting with Grandpa, Ashley had a few moments alone to contemplate the day's events.

Her mother hadn't changed, nor had Ashley expected she would have. Ashley wanted very much to ask about her brothers and if they'd married or had families, but she couldn't yet bring herself to even attempt the questions. Somehow, she knew her mother would use it against her. She could detect weakness in Ashley through her curiosity . . . and even her caring.

Ashley loved her brothers and had always wished to have maintained communication with them. She'd been their darling little sister, much as Natalie was a darling to the people of Winslow. They had doted on her and given her much attention. No doubt her mother had corrupted their feelings toward her. They probably blamed her for their father's death as well.

Sighing, Ashley picked up one of Natalie's blouses and began to mend a tear in the sleeve. The child was always getting a tear here or there. Humming one of the hymns they'd sung at church on Sunday, Ashley felt a bit of contentment wash over her. What were the words to that song? She remembered at least the first line—it was the same as the Scripture quoted by the pastor. "Let not your weary hearts be troubled."

Her heart was weary. So weary of the load she'd had to bear alone all these years. It was hard to deal with the way her family had turned away from her . . . to bear Ethan's death . . . to raise Natalie alone.

But you were never alone, she chided herself. *Grandpa has been here all along. How very ungrateful I am acting. Yes, I wish Ethan would have been here, but he wasn't and Grandpa was, and I cannot discredit the love of that old man.*

God had made provision. The thought startled her. Grandpa was always telling her this. Always commenting that God had never left her to bear the past or the future alone. Could God truly buffer her from her mother's harsh and bitter ways?

Grandpa said the key was in forgiving. Forgiving people even when they didn't deserve to be forgiven. "It releases you," he had told her. "It sets you on a journey of freedom, and whether the other person involved desires that same freedom or not, forgiveness has a way of lifting you above the mire that weighs you down on the road of life. If the other person wants to stay back in the mud—you can't very well force them to leave it."

She thought on those words while moving the needle in and out of the blouse. She'd learned so many skills over the last decade. She was nothing like the scared girl she'd been. Was it possible that God truly had been there all along, helping her each step of the way, giving her exactly what she needed—when she needed it? Was this the next thing she needed? Forgiveness?

"You need to forgive your mother and father," Grandpa had told her. "They were wrong in the way they treated you, but you were wrong too. You went against them and dishonored them by refusing to obey. True, you were an adult, but you were still under your father's authority, and you should have sought a different way of resolution."

Ashley knew it was true. She'd married Ethan in such a whirlwind—as much from a wish to defy her parents' plans as from her own emotions and desires. She had taken great pride in putting her parents in their place and asserting her own authority. That attitude had been wrong. She knew that now.

"He's asleep," her mother stated matter-of-factly.

Ashley had been so deep in thought that she'd not even heard the woman come into the room.

"Yes, I would imagine so. It's been a big day for him," Ashley said softly. "I'm sure it pleased him greatly to have you come." *I can do this,* she thought. *I can be kind and gentle tempered. I can forgive her for Grandpa's sake.*

"He said little. He was in a drugged stupor most of the time."

"The pain is so great," Ashley said, looking at her mother's expression to gauge whether she was really listening. "He doesn't want to take the morphine, but he needs it. It clouds his thinking, however, and leaves him unable to communicate as he would like. You'll have a better time of it in the morning."

Her mother crossed the room and looked out the front window. "It's really of no matter. It's obvious the old man is not in his right mind and probably hasn't been for some time. He mentioned giving you this house. Is that true?"

Ashley straightened uncomfortably. "Yes. It's true."

"Well, that won't do. We'll sell it once he's gone. The

money will be divided between Lavelle and myself." She turned to Ashley. "The same goes for the household goods. I know you had no money when you came here. You may have purchased things over the years with your waitressing salary, but you could never have afforded to do so had he not provided room and board. Therefore, everything will be sold."

"No, Mother, it won't be," Ashley said flatly. She looked at her mother, challenging her to contradict her statement.

"My lawyer will see to it. You'll have no say in the matter."

Ashley went back to her sewing as if to prove to her mother that she was unconcerned. "I'll leave it in the hands of Mr. Watson, our lawyer. He warned us you might try something like this and he's already pre-pared."

"Warned you, eh? Probably because he knew of the lack of legal standing."

"Mother, you live in wealth and plenty. You have nothing to gain by spending any of your money on this matter. This house wouldn't bring even a pittance of the price it will cost you to battle for it. As for the furnishings ... again, they are mostly secondhand or inexpensive pieces we've acquired over the years."

"I don't care. I want what is mine."

Ashley was quickly losing the ability to control her temper. "You got what was yours and then some many years ago. Grandpa told me all about it." She looked up to catch her mother's face contort in anger. "He said emphatically you were to have nothing else."

"The nerve of you both! You've done nothing but

cause me pain and suffering. I received only what I deserved when that old man decided to sell out to religion. He owed me every cent he gave me.''

"You had already married and married well, I might add. Grandpa owed you nothing. He wasn't in this world to cover the cost of your life-style. How can you be so cold and calculating in this? Your father is dying. His last wish was to have you and Aunt Lavelle come and see him, and all you can think about is whether there is some trinket or bauble you might sell. What a sad thing. What a very sad person you've become.''

"I demand you be silent! You have no right to speak to me like this. You're a hateful woman, just as you were eleven years ago. I'm glad I took matters into my own hands when the truth came out.''

Ashley looked at her mother's reddened face and the ugly scowl fixed on her expression. "What are you talking about?''

"Your husband.''

Ashley felt her heart skip a beat. For a moment she wasn't sure she could draw enough breath to reply. "What about him?''

"He's alive. At least he was in the summer of 1919.'' Her mother smiled smugly. "But I told him you were dead. Told him you'd died in the epidemic.''

Ashley gasped for air. "I don't believe you.''

"Oh, you should. He showed up all scarred and ugly from war. He was never much to look at before, but now he was less to look at. Apparently he'd had a good portion of his face blown away.''

Her mother shook her head and smiled. "I couldn't see you wanting him after that. Besides, as far as I was concerned, you were dead to me."

Ashley felt the truth of it sink in. Her mother wasn't lying—she was taking far too much satisfaction from this for it to be a lie. "He's alive?"

"I'm sure I cannot say. I certainly did nothing to keep tabs on him. I sent him packing, as you should have done in the beginning."

Ashley carefully gathered up her things and systematically put them into her sewing box. Getting to her feet, she stood trembling. "I was trying hard to do what Grandpa had suggested and forgive you for your cruelty and vicious nature." She stared at her mother's self-satisfied expression and wanted nothing more than to banish her from the house, but for Grandpa's sake she would let her stay. "But I'll never forgive you for this."

She walked to the arched doorway and turned.

"So long as you do nothing to cause harm to Natalie or Grandpa, you may stay here. But—"she paused to draw a deep breath—"do even one thing—one thing, Mother—to hurt either of them as you've hurt me, and you will rue the day you came to Winslow."

Ashley walked to the stairs in a methodical, mechanical manner. She climbed and with each step the words reverberated in her brain.

Ethan's alive.

CHAPTER SEVENTEEN

*N*ews of the stock market crash in New York trickled in with the passing of each new train. E. J. listened to the comments of railroad officials as they spoke with Mary Colter about their thoughts on the matter.

"This is a passing problem," one man assured Mary as they moved out to the depot platform, where everyone but E. J. expected to catch the awaiting westbound train.

"The railroad is secure. We'll weather the storm," another man added. "We made some very good business decisions months ago, and it leaves us in good stead, unlike some of the other lines. We'll ride out this problem as we have every other storm."

"So you do not see this creating a problem for the hotel we're building?" Miss Colter questioned.

Her gaze scrutinized each man at length. E. J. almost believed the woman to be capable of reading minds for the truth. The thought made him smile, but he quickly lowered his face so that no one would believe him less than serious about the situation.

"No, I don't think there is anything to worry about.

We've invested heavily in this hotel. Plans are even set in motion to move the present Harvey House next door. It will have to be plastered and covered in stucco to match the décor, of course. McKee Construction Company assures me that this can be done with relative ease. Not only that, Miss Colter, they assure me the hotel will be completed on schedule. They still give December 15 as the completion date, despite this stock market nonsense."

"Good," Mary said, then turned to E. J. "I want you to make sure those northern balconies are properly fitted with the wrought-iron rails. Remember the problems we had on the west side? See that we aren't repeating history."

E. J. nodded. "I'll see to it."

The conductor called for final boarding, and E. J. bid the trio good-bye. He turned to go back to work, relieved to be left behind. The business dealings were of very little interest to him. In fact, since sitting down to sketch out the house he'd promised to build Ashley, E. J. knew his desire lay in creating. He wanted to become more heavily involved in design work—in the actual laying out of plans. That wasn't something he was likely to get a hand at working with Miss Mary Elizabeth Jane Colter. Miss Colter let no one come between her and her creations. The intelligence, creativity, and drive of the woman was positively daunting, but she operated much like a one-man band. Oh, she had workers and assistants. She had "her boys," but she was the queen of her kingdom and that left little room for E. J.'s own creativity. Perhaps this would be the last time he worked for Mary Colter—perhaps he'd remain in Winslow and develop his own company, a company he could pass on to his daughter.

E. J. had nearly reached the Harvey hotel building site when he heard Natalie calling his name. She crossed Second Street with only the briefest pause, then hurried to where he stood. Across the street, a man rather stocky in build paused for a moment, as if watching Natalie and E. J. There was something familiar about the man, but his hat was pulled low and it was impossible to see his face. E. J. wondered what the man wanted and thought to hail him over, but as if realizing he was being watched, the man darted away, leaving E. J. feeling rather uncomfortable.

"I'm glad you stopped by. I have something for you," E. J. told Natalie. He reached into his pocket and pulled out the rolled-up drawing. "I did this from the drawing you gave me."

Natalie put her book satchel down on a nearby rock and took the drawing from E. J. She unrolled it carefully, as though she'd been given a great treasure map. "Oh, it's wonderful. It's even better than the one my mama has."

E. J. smiled. He'd embellished a few things here and there. Things he thought might work better than the original plan. Things he and Ashley had considered changing after the original drawing was made. "Do you like it?"

"I do, very much," Natalie admitted. "I'm going to keep this in a special place."

"I don't think you should show your mama just yet. Since your daddy drew the last picture, we wouldn't want to make her sad."

Natalie nodded in complete agreement. "Grandmother is making her sad enough. I wouldn't want to make Mama cry again."

"Your grandma made your mama cry?" E. J. felt a tightening in his gut. He knew how very destructive Leticia Murphy could be. After all, she was the one who had told him Ashley was dead to begin with.

"My grandmother isn't being very nice," Natalie said, frowning. "I don't know why. She talks real mean sometimes and it hurts my mama's feelings. Mama's sharing my room 'cause she gave her room to Grandmother. Mama doesn't know I heard her crying last night. She thought I was asleep. I heard her say something about never forgiving Grandmother for what she'd done. I don't know what Grandmother did, 'cause Aunt Lavelle and I took a walk, and I think whatever she did happened while we were gone."

E. J. chilled in the afternoon air. What had Leticia done to Ashley? Had she confessed the fact that she'd lied when Ashley's husband came home from the war? The thought left him cold through and through. He had to find a way to let Ashley know the truth. This had gone on entirely too long, and if Leticia was the one to break the news, it would make Ashley believe he no longer loved her—that he hadn't even cared to look for her. But maybe if Leticia had told Ashley of his showing up that day in 1919, she would also confess to telling him that Ashley was dead.

"I have to get home. Mama wants me to help her with supper. I sure wish I could invite you to come, but Mama said it was best not to have extra guests right now."

"And she's absolutely right," E. J. said. "Your mother has a great deal on her mind and an entire household of people to care for. I'm sure we'll have time to share supper in the future."

Natalie tucked the drawing into her skirt pocket and skipped away. "I'll see you tomorrow," she called over her shoulder.

She was gone from sight before E. J. realized her books still sat on the rock at his feet. He picked the satchel up and quickly crossed the street and headed down the sidewalk in the direction of Natalie's house when he noted the same stocky man from before—only this time he appeared to be slinking along in the shadows. E. J. couldn't tell if the man was watching Natalie or himself. He thought to call to the man, but just then Natalie came running from the opposite direction. When she saw E. J. she called out.

"I forgot my books!"

He smiled nervously and held up the satchel. "I know. I thought I'd bring it to you."

When he glanced over his shoulder to see if the stranger was still there, he found only an empty place in the doorway where the man had hidden himself only moments before. E. J. felt a sickening dread in the pit of his belly. It was like being stalked by the enemy, only this was an enemy he didn't know or recognize.

Worse still, what if the man had no interest in E. J. at all but rather was stalking Natalie?

"Natalie, it might not be a good idea to come by the hotel tomorrow. In fact, you might give it a few days before you do. There are some difficult jobs to be done and you might get hurt."

She looked hurt—disappointed in his obvious rejection. "You don't want to see me?"

"It isn't that, sweetheart," he said, hoping she wouldn't take his words so personally. "It's just that some dangerous things will be going on. It would just about break my heart if you were to get hurt."

She shrugged. "Okay. I'll wait until Saturday and come with my mama."

He nodded. "That would be just fine."

She took off again, while E. J. studied every doorway and shadowed corner. The man was nowhere to be found. He struggled to think who the man might be. There was something familiar about him, but E. J. hadn't been able to get a good look.

"God, please protect her," he prayed aloud. "Don't let harm come to my child or my wife."

————

Russell had refused to take any medicine that morning. The pain was excruciating but no more so than the burden he had for his eldest child. "Letty, I'm glad you came to see me. There are some things we need to set straight between us."

"Oh, I certainly agree. This whole nonsense of having given Ashley the house and furnishings is ridiculous. I'll have my lawyer on the case before—"

"Letty, my lawyer has already seen to the transfer. There is nothing for you here." He spoke with a deep pleading in his tone. "Please don't make yourself any more unwelcome than you already are."

"What's that supposed to mean?"

Russell reached out to take hold of her hand, but

Leticia pulled away. "Letty, you've made yourself unwelcome in the way you treat people. All your life you've hurt folks and made them feel unimportant. That's not the way you should treat people—especially family. Especially your own child."

Leticia scowled. "You are a foolish man, and I have no intention of letting you ruin my life the way you've ruined your own. This has nothing to do with Ashley. It's only sensible and reasonable that you should settle your estate on your children."

"Which I did nearly twelve years ago. I told you then that I would yield and give you what you demanded." He paused and gasped for breath against the pain. His tone took on a gravelly sound as he continued. "You never could see that the most important, most valued thing I had to give you was my love and the knowledge of what God had done in my life."

"Nonsense!" Her eyes narrowed, and the hateful look on her face made Russell actually cringe. "Love doesn't put food on the table or furniture in the parlor. It doesn't buy the pleasures of life or pay for the problems of it. You may believe whatever you choose, but when your beliefs infringe upon my comfort, then it's time for me to look out for myself. You made choices that changed my life. That was unfair."

"Letty, you were a grown woman with a husband. A wealthy husband, I might point out. I was under no obligation to continue supporting your expensive dreams."

"Humph, and you talk of love. Wouldn't a loving parent desire for his child to have a better life than he had? Wouldn't a parent want to see his child content, comfortable, and well cared for?"

"I might ask you the same thing in regard to Ashley. She's happy here. This has been her home since before she gave birth to Natalie. Now you suggest I take that away from her. Is that love? Or is that simply your way of making clear what everyone knows—that you don't love your own daughter?"

"My daughter stopped loving me the day she went behind my back and married that no-account art student."

"He was an architectural student—soon to be employed by a well-known firm, as I recall Ashley telling me."

Leticia lifted her chin, a habit of defiance Russell had dealt with since she was an infant. "That doesn't make what she did right."

"No. No, it doesn't and I've even told Ashley that. She should have found a better way to deal with you and the problems she felt she had at home."

Leticia looked at her father in disbelief, then quickly masked her surprise. "Well, it's of little matter now. As far as I'm concerned, she made her bed and I owe her nothing."

"Just as I feel you've made your bed, Letty. You insisted on your inheritance long ago, and you received it. I owe you nothing. Fight me if you must, but you won't win. Ashley is well-known and loved in this town—Natalie too. If you bring in your lawyers and fuss about, you'll only cause yourself grief."

"People are always causing me grief. I must fight for what is mine, although I don't expect you to understand. Yes, I have wealth, but I learned a long time ago the only way to keep that wealth growing is to amass more. I've grown wiser through the years."

"I don't see greed and wisdom as the same thing," Russell replied.

Letty's eyes seemed to blaze with a fire all their own. "Call me what you will. Call me greedy—I don't care. The one thing I've learned, the wisdom that has kept me stable when others around me were floundering, is that I must put myself first. I can be of no use to my children or anyone else if I don't take care of myself."

"And has taking care of yourself in turn caused you to be more generous with your children?"

Leticia squared her shoulders. "I've taught them to be self-sufficient."

Russell shook his head. "Something I should have taught you a long time ago. Letty, I've tried to teach you the important things of life, but they've eluded you. You are selfish and greedy. I honestly thought that your reaction all those years ago was due to fear—fear of the money you would lose—fear that you might have to change your life-style." He gasped for air and closed his eyes momentarily. *God, give me strength. I have to try to make her see.* He opened his eyes slowly.

"Letty, the people in your life are far more important. You can always make more money. Even if you lose it all, you can find a way to make more."

"It didn't work that way for you. You live in poverty here," Leticia replied snidely.

"I made as much as I wanted to make," Russell replied. "We didn't need a great deal of money to be happy. We had one another."

Leticia's expression fell momentarily and she looked away. Russell felt sorry for her and tried to reach out to her. She would have no part of that, though, and crossed her arms tight against her chest.

"Happiness, Letty . . . true happiness isn't found on the pages of a bank ledger or in the number of jewels you can call your own. Possessions are temporary and never last."

"You don't know what you're talking about, old man." She eyed him with contempt. "You're only saying this hoping that I'll change my mind. Well, I won't. I intend to have what belongs to me."

Russell gave up. "You may not recall it, but you and your husband both signed certain legal documents when I gave you your inheritance."

Leticia frowned. "What documents? I don't remember any such thing."

Russell eyed her seriously. "I had papers drawn up that you signed in order to receive your bank drafts. You agreed to take your inheritance at that time and seek no further compensation from me."

"I recall nothing of the kind."

"Go see my lawyer, then. He has a copy of the agreement you signed, as well as a copy of your sister's. You should also reread the clause that states that should you seek to benefit from any additional part of my future estate, you will forfeit the original agreement—and all monies and articles given to you as inheritance, which are also listed there, will be returned within thirty days of the condition being broken."

Leticia gasped. "I . . . I would never have signed such an agreement."

Russell knew she would take such an attitude. He had expected it twelve years earlier and he expected it now. "You did sign it. In fact, you had your lawyer go over the paper and agree to the terms. Letty, it's finished. You need to let go of this madness that you can somehow milk another dime or dollar from me. What I have accumulated since then has gone to Ashley and Natalie. Try to take it from them, and my lawyer will see you fulfill the requirements of a forfeited contract."

"You conniving old man! I . . . well . . . I will see to it . . ." Her words trailed off in sputters and gasps as if she were a fish out of water.

"Letty, there is one thing I want to share with you." His voice sounded firm and clear. Russell silently thanked God for strength and now prayed for the words to share his heart.

She perked up at this and leaned forward. "What is it?"

"Jesus."

She rolled her eyes and shifted in her chair. "Do not start that drivel with me. I've lived quite well without any religious nonsense touching me. I see no need for a religious crutch to support me."

"Letty, money isn't everything. I know from experience. It can buy you some good times and some comfort—for a while. But after that, it can also be a noose around your neck, a burden. What happens when it's no longer there—when you have nothing else to turn to?"

"That isn't going to happen," she said in a smug, self-confident tone.

"Letty, I want to tell you a story. There was this man, see. He was a wealthy man and he had just about everything a guy could want. His house was full of things and his fields were full of crops. In fact, his harvest was so

great that he couldn't begin to get everything in the many barns he had for storage. So instead of sharing his good fortune and blessing others with what he'd been given, he chose instead to build a bigger barn."

"That's only prudent. A wise man, indeed," Leticia responded.

Russell shook his head and tears came to his eyes. "No, Letty. He was greedy and selfish. He didn't care that he could help anyone else. He thought only of himself and how he could continue to prosper."

"Again, he was only being smart," Leticia said. "He was storing up the things he would need for his comfort later."

"Letty, that night the man's soul was required of him. He died." She looked taken aback but said nothing. "His money and stored goods could not keep him from facing the eventuality that we all have to face sooner or later—death. Letty, what will you do when that happens to you? What good will your wealth do you when you are the person lying on the sickbed, waiting to die?"

"My money will buy me a decent doctor and hospital, for one."

Russell shook his head. "Letty, everyone has to die. It's appointed to man to die once. But if you die without Jesus as your Savior, you'll die a second death."

"Listen to yourself. How ridiculous you sound. Second death. Yes, I realize everyone dies sooner or later." She got to her feet. "I never said I would live forever."

"But you can," Russell said softly, his strength giving out. "With Jesus you can live forever."

"I didn't buy into this nonsense twelve years ago, and

I'm certainly not buying into it now."

Just then Russell's door flew open. Ashley stood there, looking rather stunned. "I just heard some news. Apparently something terrible has happened in New York with the stock market. Some people have lost everything, and rumor has it several banks have collapsed. There are even reports that grown men threw themselves from the windows of their buildings and killed themselves."

Russell watched the color drain from his daughter's face. "Where's the telegraph office?" she demanded. "Where's a telephone? I have to talk to your brother."

Ashley stood back as her mother rushed through the door. Russell thought Ashley looked quite alarmed. "Child, this isn't that worrisome for us. We sold our stock, remember? We'll be just fine."

Ashley came to him and offered him a drink. "I know, but I just feel this sense of dread. Like the world has come to an end."

"For some folks, it has," he said softly. "But for others, it might just be the new beginning they've been waiting for."

"What if Mother has lost all her money?"

Russell smiled. "Then maybe there will be hope for her too."

CHAPTER EIGHTEEN

*T*hree days later, Ashley stood with Natalie at her side while Leticia read the results of the stock market crash on her holdings.

"The news is more devastating than I could have imagined. Mathias says that we might well be ruined." She looked up in disbelief. Her hand shook, causing the telegram to flutter.

Ashley thought of her brother Mathias and his work with the banks. What would this mean for him? "Does he say how this will affect his job?"

Her mother looked at her rather dumbly, then frowned. "I have no idea, and frankly, I don't care. This isn't about Mathias; it's about the family fortune. We stand to lose everything."

"I'm sure this will come around right," Lavelle said, reaching out to gently touch her sister's arm.

Leticia jerked away. "This is not going to come around right. The other telegrams from Mathias are just as bad. There were even runs on some banks. This is terrible. We must go to the bank and see what funds we can pull out."

"Perhaps it wouldn't be such a good idea to panic," Lavelle stated. "After all, the crash happened several days ago."

"Stupid hick town. If I'd stayed in Baltimore, I would have known about this. I might have been able to save my stocks, and then I wouldn't be facing ruin. Mathias probably tried to reach me prior to this but simply couldn't locate me."

Ashley had no idea what to say. She couldn't muster up a single ounce of sympathy for her mother. Over and over, the only words she could hear in her mind were the ones that spoke to Ethan being alive. Ashley still hadn't figured out what she was going to do about that situation. She needed to talk to someone—to be counseled on how to go about searching for her husband.

Her mother's ranting grew to a louder volume still. "None of you understand because you had nothing to begin with!"

Ashley thought of the money her grandfather had the lawyer deposit into the bank for her and Natalie. Were the funds still safe? She supposed she should talk to the lawyer. But on the other hand, her mother was partly right—they'd never had that much to begin with. If suddenly her money were all gone, Ashley knew she'd simply go back to work and continue to support them as best she could.

"Letty, you must calm down," Lavelle insisted. "This isn't going to do you any good."

"I can't calm down." Leticia used the telegram like a fan. "This is the worst thing that has ever happened to me."

The worst thing that ever happened to me was losing my

husband, Ashley thought. But immediately that idea was canceled out. *No, it is worse knowing that he is alive and thinks I am dead.*

"Grandmother . . ." Natalie left Ashley's side and went to Leticia. "We just need to pray. God will take care of us."

Without warning the old woman slapped Natalie full across the face. The child instantly began to cry and ran to Ashley's arms. Ashley was stupefied. "How dare you? She's just a little girl."

"Oh, Leticia, you shouldn't have done that. She's only trying to help," Lavelle declared. "She's right. We must pray and trust God to take care of us."

"You and your stupid God nonsense. This is ridiculous. First Father and now all of you. God couldn't care less about me. He's proven that on more than one occasion."

Ashley cringed and pulled her sobbing child closer. The words could have been her own, and they left a bitter taste in her mouth. Stroking Natalie's head, she felt a deep offense and sense of protectiveness toward her child.

"I think you'd be wise to pack your things and move into a hotel," Ashley said. Her tone caused both her mother and aunt to look at her. She pulled Natalie with her toward the stairs. "You are unwelcome here, Mother. Aunt Lavelle, please help Mother make other arrangements. You may visit Grandfather but only with my approval."

Natalie cried all the way to her room, and it wasn't until they were safely behind the closed doors of her daughter's bedroom that Ashley, too, broke into tears.

"I'm so sorry, baby. She should never have done that." Ashley felt the pain of a lifetime wash over her.

"Why is she so mean and angry?" Natalie asked, sobering at her mother's tears.

"I don't know," Ashley said as she sat down on the bed. She opened her arms to Natalie, who quickly fell into her mother's lap. Ashley saw the angry red welt on her daughter's cheek, the outline of her mother's hand-print. She longed to go downstairs and pay her mother back in kind. Why should a little child have to suffer?

Natalie hugged her mother close. "I'm glad you're sending her away. She isn't nice and she makes Grandpa sad." She straightened up and looked Ashley full in the face. "Everything has been hard since she came here. Maybe you and Grandmother are right. Maybe God doesn't care."

The words pierced Ashley's heart. "No!" she exclaimed, not meaning to startle her child. "Your grandmother is wrong. God does care."

"Do you really believe that, Mama?" Natalie searched her mother's face. "I mean, God is letting Grandpa die and Grandmother's lost all her money. Nothing good is happening to us . . . just bad stuff."

Ashley thought of the news that her husband, Natalie's father, was alive. He was out there somewhere living his life without them. Maybe he'd even remarried. After all, it'd been eleven years. The idea that Ethan might have a life without her hurt Ashley so badly she couldn't even speak the words. So while it was good news, it was bad as well. Ashley certainly couldn't tell Natalie about it and give her false hope, but there had to be something positive she could tell the child.

"Natalie, I don't think our life is just bad stuff. Grandpa has given us this house and—" she looked toward the door and lowered her voice—"and a great deal of money. We will be just fine."

"But if Grandmother lost all her money, couldn't we lose all of ours?"

"I don't know, but even if we do," Ashley assured her, "God will take care of us." For once, Ashley actually believed it. She felt a quickening in her spirit that gave her a lightness she'd not felt in years. "God gave you to me in the darkest hour of my life, Natalie." She gently touched her daughter's cheek. "I know God cares for us, or He would never have done such a wonderful thing."

Natalie wrapped her arms around Ashley's neck. "I'm so glad you think God cares for us. I think He does too. I guess I was just scared, but I know God is good."

"Then don't let your grandmother's ugliness take away your hope and faith in Him. Grandmother's acting out of fear. She doesn't know how to trust God."

Natalie pulled away and looked up with an expression of expectation. "Do you know how to trust God, Mama?"

Ashley smiled and nodded. "I think I'm learning."

––––––––

With her mother and Lavelle out of the house, Ashley went to sit with her grandfather. The old man slept fitfully, finally waking just a few minutes after Ashley took a seat beside him. The past few days had taken their toll on him, and Ashley knew it wouldn't be long before he gave up the fight. His labored breathing seemed to echo throughout the room. Ashley found herself trying

to breathe with him—for him.

"Ashley," he murmured. Gone was any pretense of strength.

"Grandpa, I know the time is short," she said, remembering what Pastor McGuire had said about needing to be open and honest with a dying person. "Grandpa, I love you. I love you so much. I don't know what I'll do without you."

"God—Ashley. God will be everything you need."

"Grandpa, I want to believe that. I think God has been working on me." Ashley thought she noted a hint of a smile on Grandpa's lips as she continued. "Grandpa, Mother told me something very painful. She lied to Ethan and it set into motion an entire lifetime of sorrows. Ethan's alive, but I don't know where. He came home from the war—apparently there had been a mistake and he hadn't died on the battlefield."

"But that's . . . good," Grandpa gasped.

"Yes and no. Mother told Ethan I was dead. She told him I'd died in the influenza epidemic. He probably thought it made sense. After all, my letters stopped because I thought he was dead."

"Oh, Ashley."

"Grandpa, I want to forgive her, but she's forever altered my life. I could have had a life with Ethan. He could have been there for Natalie—for me. I know it would have been difficult to find me here with you, but she could have at least told him I was alive." She began to cry. "I can't believe he's out there somewhere. I can't believe he's alive but not a part of our lives here. How could she be so cruel? I hate her for what she's done.

"And not only this thing with Ethan, but she slapped

Natalie. She's been vicious and cruel, seeking only her own benefit. She never shows concern for anyone but herself. I look at her and see such hardness—such ill will."

"Give . . . to . . . God."

Ashley nodded. "I want to, Grandpa. I want to give it all to God. I want to do the right thing and know Him for myself."

This time Grandpa did smile. He closed his eyes, his breath rattling in his chest. "It's . . . easy. Just . . . ask."

"I remember what you told me before. Ask for forgiveness and ask Jesus to take over my life. I did that before I came in here, Grandpa. But even if I allow God to help me forgive Mother, how can I ever forget what she's done? I might never find Ethan again."

"God . . . has . . . a . . . plan."

A shadow passed across the window. Ashley straightened. Perhaps her mother and aunt were returning. She wanted to bar the door and never let her mother back in the house, but she knew she had to allow it—at least until Grandpa was gone.

"You will pray for me, won't you, Grandpa?" Ashley whispered as she looked back to where he lay.

Grandpa said nothing. His breathing slowed, his chest barely moving with each strained gasp. Ashley knew he was fading away—leaving her behind and going to his heavenly mansion, as one of those lovely church hymns spoke of.

Stroking his hand, she began to sing, remembering the words of that hymn. " 'My heavenly home is bright and fair; no pain nor death can enter there. Its glittering towers the sun outshine; that heavenly mansion shall be

mine.' " Tears streamed down her cheeks, and her voice caught as she sang the chorus and Grandpa drew his final breath.

" 'I'm going home, I'm going home, I'm going home to die no more; to die no more, to die no more, I'm going home . . . to die no more.' "

She kissed his weathered cheek. "It's all right, Grandpa. You go on home."

CHAPTER NINETEEN

*A*shley was relieved to find it was not her mother who had returned to the house but rather Natalie.

"Sweetie, I have something to tell you," Ashley said as she met her daughter in the hallway.

"Is it about Grandpa?" Natalie asked, seeming to know.

"Yes. He's gone."

Natalie's lower lip quivered. "I know it's a good thing because Grandpa suffered so much, but it feels so bad here inside."

Ashley pulled her into her arms and held her tight. "I know. It hurts me too. But you know what? Grandpa died a happy man. I told him that I'd turned to God and that made him very happy."

Natalie nodded as she looked up. Tears glistened in her eyes. "That's the best news Grandpa could have had. He just wanted to be sure he'd see you again."

"I know. Look, I need a big favor from you."

"What?"

Ashley gently held her daughter's chin. "I need you to run and fetch Mr. Watson. We'll need him here when Grandmother Murphy gets back. You tell him about Grandpa. He'll also know to get the funeral home to come."

"Sure, Mama," Natalie said, straightening. "That's an important job."

"It sure is and one that only you can do for me. I can't leave and do it myself because Aunt Lavelle and Grandmother Murphy might come back and I'll have to tell them about Grandpa."

Natalie nodded somberly, the weight of responsibility combined with great pride. "It's Saturday. Will he be at his office or should I go to his house?"

"Hmm . . . start at the office, since it's so close. Then go to his house if he's not there. I think you should ride Penny," her mother encouraged. "Mr. Watson's house is clear on the other side of town, just off of Douglas."

"I remember," Natalie said. "I'll come right back so you don't have to be alone." She embraced her mother once again, then ran through the house and out the back door.

Ashley fretted that her mother and aunt would return before Mr. Watson had a chance to come and offer his support. She found herself uneasily praying.

"I know I just started turning to you, Lord. And I know I've brought more than my share to you already, but please just get Mr. Watson here before Mother and Lavelle return. I can't bear to face them alone."

With each passing moment, Ashley jumped at every sound. She set out to straighten the living room, knowing that as soon as word got out about Grandpa, people would start showing up to bring food and offer comfort to the family.

When a knock sounded at the front door, Ashley nearly came undone. She hurried to see who had come and found a stranger. The stocky man lifted his hat in greeting. There was something vaguely familiar about him, but Ashley was uncertain where she might have seen him.

"May I help you?"

"I hope so. You are Mrs. Reynolds, are you not?"

Ashley felt an uneasiness come over her. "Yes."

"And you have a little girl. I believe her name is Natalie."

It was then that Ashley remembered the man. He'd been following Natalie on the street. "Who are you and what do you want?"

"I'd just like to talk to you about your husband, Ethan Reynolds—about his war efforts and his death. See, I'm putting together a book . . ."

"I have no time for this," Ashley declared. "We've just had a loss in the family. I'm going to have to ask you to leave." She started to close the door, then pulled it back open. "Oh, and leave my child alone. I've seen you following her and if I see you again, I'll contact the police."

She closed the door and leaned against it momentarily. How could she tell this man anything about Ethan? She didn't know anything. Didn't know where he was or why he was alive instead of dead as the army had told her. Tears streamed down her face. "I can't help you, mister. I can't even help myself."

Half an hour passed and Ashley slowly recomposed herself. She heard a car pull up and stop in front of the house. Looking out the window, Ashley saw a black sedan, and behind it, another car also came to rest. Ashley recognized it as belonging to Pastor McGuire, and in the front seat Natalie sat all prim and proper. Penny was tied to the back. The scene brought a smile to Ashley's face. Natalie seemed to take life and death in stride. She didn't seem to bear any long-lasting grudge against her grandmother, and neither did she seem destined to despair over her great-grandfather's passing. Perhaps she would handle the news of her father's surviving the war as well.

Natalie jumped out and saw to Penny, while Pastor McGuire and Mr. Watson made their way past the wrought-iron gate and up the walkway. Ashley met them at the door. They took off their hats as they walked into the house.

"I'm so glad you're both here."

"Has your mother returned?" Watson asked, peering past Ashley toward the living room. Apparently Natalie had told him of the urgency involved.

"No," Ashley said, taking the men's hats. "I thought for sure she would be back by now. She and Lavelle have gone to the bank, forgetting that it's Saturday. I suppose they've tried to locate the bank president and see what can be done about all this business of last week. I've asked my mother to move out of the house. She struck Natalie, and I have no intention of letting it happen again."

"Struck her?" Watson questioned.

Ashley nodded. "Mother was upset by the telegram my brother sent. It had to do with the stock market troubles."

"Ah, I see." Watson nodded thoughtfully.

"Anyway, Natalie suggested we needed to pray about the matter, and my mother let her nerves get the best of her and she slapped Natalie. I told her to pack and get out. Perhaps that's where they are now. Maybe my aunt is helping Mother arrange to move into the Harvey House."

The men nodded. "We will just wait with you, then," Simon Watson stated matter-of-factly.

Pastor McGuire gently touched her arm. "I know Grandpa's passing is both a relief and a grief."

"Yes, to be sure," Ashley said, drawing a deep breath. "Would you like to see him?"

"Yes. Yes, I would," McGuire responded. "Simon?"

"You go ahead. I'll pay my respects later."

Ashley led Pastor McGuire back to Grandpa's room and closed the door quietly once they'd entered. "I need to tell you something," she said softly, almost reverently, as if God's spirit had settled over the room.

Pastor McGuire looked at her rather oddly. "Oh?"

"I . . . well . . . I prayed." Ashley knew it sounded silly, but she felt completely flustered. "I've taken Jesus as my Savior."

Pastor McGuire grinned. "No wonder Grandpa felt he could finally go. What a blessing that must have been to him—he did know, didn't he?"

"Yes, he knew." Ashley had a great sense of peace about being able to honestly come to God before Grandpa died. "I had thought of just telling him what he wanted to hear. After all, God would know the difference."

"So would Russell Whitman. The man was no fool."

"I'm sure you're right. Like I said, I toyed with the

idea, but I could never bring myself to do it. Then I thought of coming to God merely because my mother so thoroughly rejects Him. That hardly seemed right either."

Pastor McGuire's smile broadened. "No, it would never do to come to God in order to spite someone else. It wouldn't be genuine."

"I know. It just seemed that the more trouble came, the less confidence I had in myself or anything else. It hurt to deal with the past and the present, and the future just seemed like a nightmare waiting to happen. I wanted nothing more than peace of mind and heart, but it eluded me at every turn."

"And do you know that peace now, Ashley?"

She looked into his compassionate face and smiled. "I do." She looked back to where she'd left Grandpa. She'd neatly combed his hair and pulled up the blanket to his chest. She'd carefully brought his arms together, and it looked as though he were simply taking his afternoon nap. "I can't imagine life without him."

"Nor can I," the pastor replied. "Good men like Russell are hard to find. We need to cherish them when we come across them."

For some reason Ashley thought of E. J. Carson. He seemed to be such a kind and considerate soul. Always so gentle and loving with Natalie. Perhaps that alone should have endeared him to Ashley. But then there was the issue of Ethan. Somehow she had to know the truth about him.

"Pastor McGuire, there's something else." Ashley swallowed her pride and self-reliance and explained the situation regarding Ethan. She noted the man's expression as it changed from sympathetic to intense concern. "I don't know," Ashley continued, "how to go about finding him. He may be remarried, and how awful that would be, because we're still married—I'm not dead." She knew she stated the obvious, but she needed to hear the words aloud.

Pastor McGuire put his arm around her shoulder. "I'll do what I can to help you. There are records the army keeps and people who can help in this. Don't worry. But tell me, does Natalie know?"

Ashley shook her head. "I don't want to tell her until I'm certain he's still alive. She positively worships his memory. It would be so hard for her to think he'd come back to her, only to lose him again."

"I understand, and I think you're wise. We'll take care of matters with Grandpa, and then we'll get right on this other."

The unmistakable sound of voices in the hall confirmed that her mother and Lavelle had returned. She heard her mother saying something about taking over the matter of her father's burial just before she opened the bedroom door and pushed past Ashley to Grandpa's bedside.

"So he's finally gone," she stated, then looked to Ashley and the pastor as though she'd posed a question.

The pastor maintained his hold on Ashley, and she wondered if he did so out of fear of what she might do to her mother. He gave her a gentle squeeze of support before speaking. "Your father is in a better place now. He's finally out of pain."

"Be that as it may," Leticia said, looking to them again and then to her sister and the lawyer, who had now joined them. "There are matters to be taken care of."

"All the arrangements were made by your father," Simon Watson stated.

Leticia's expression changed to one of smug assurance. "But I am here now and have my own ideas of how things will be handled."

"I'm sorry you feel that way, Mrs. Murphy. Your father stated specifically that I was not to allow you to make any changes in the arrangements. You are, of course, free to return home and not participate in the plans he made. However, there will be no changes."

"I am quite sure—"

"No changes, Mother," Ashley stated, pulling away from the pastor.

"You are in no position to dictate to me." Leticia arched her brow and squared her shoulders. She held the look of a tyrannical queen.

Ashley thought to demand that she leave, but instead she stayed her anger. She didn't know how she was supposed to act or respond as a Christian—not really, but she did know what Grandpa would want her to say, and he was a Christian. She could almost hear him saying, "Be a peacemaker, Ashley."

"Mother, you need to respect Grandpa's wishes. I think you should sit down with Mr. Watson and Pastor McGuire and listen to what they have to say. You too, Aunt Lavelle."

Lavelle nodded and agreed. "I think we should, Letty. Why don't we go out into the living room and talk about this." Lavelle led her sister toward the door.

To her great surprise, Ashley watched as her mother

allowed Lavelle to direct her down the hall. Simon Watson followed, with Pastor McGuire bringing up the rear. Ashley glanced back at Grandpa's still figure.

"I wish you were still here to advise me," she murmured.

———

Ashley listened to the lawyer quietly explain the situation surrounding Russell Whitman's last requests and arrangements. Her mother often interrupted to dispute issues, but Simon Watson was no small-town lawyer to be bullied. The man had come to practice in Winslow after a long career in Chicago. Had his wife not needed the dry climate, he might be there still, he'd told Ashley previously.

Tiring of the details she already knew by heart, Ashley dismissed herself to make some refreshments for the group.

"Mama?" Natalie questioned quietly. "Oh, here you are. I thought you'd be out there with Mr. Watson."

"I'm fixing a plate of cookies for our guests. Do you want to carry it out to them and then come back and have a couple for yourself?"

"Sure. Can Penny have something too?"

Ashley took an apple and cut it into four pieces. "You may give this to Penny when you get back."

Natalie picked up the plate of cookies and started to leave. She paused, however, and turned back to Ashley. "We will be all right, won't we?" She dragged the toe of her shoe across the tiled floor.

Ashley saw the apprehension and uncertainty in her daughter's face. The moment reflected the questions in her own heart. "Grandpa said we would be just fine. He said God would take care of us. You believe that, don't you?"

Natalie looked at the floor. "I want to believe, and sometimes I feel really strong. But sometimes, like now, I just don't know. Will God be mad at me?"

Ashley had no idea what to say, but her heart was overwhelmed with love for her child. She reasoned the matter quickly. "Natalie, sometimes bad things happen, right?" Her daughter nodded. "And we don't always understand and sometimes they scare us."

"Like when you found out about Daddy dying?"

Ashley stiffened. "Well . . . yes. When bad things happen, it's easy to forget that God is there. That's what happened to me all those years. I didn't think God cared about me anymore. But I know now that I was wrong. God does care." She felt strength mixed with turmoil. There was no easy answer to give her child, but she wanted very much for Natalie to be at peace. "Some of this is just as hard for me as for you. I wish I'd listened to Grandpa a long time ago. I wish I'd read my Bible and gone to church, and I wish I knew better what to expect from God. The truth is, I don't know what will happen in the future, but Grandpa told me that God has a plan for us."

"He told me that too," Natalie said. "And Grandpa never lied."

Ashley smiled. "And God doesn't lie either. That much I'm confident of."

Natalie's expression changed to one of relief. "That's true—and Grandpa said that Jesus promised to be with us always. So we'll be okay."

Ashley could see that Natalie now had great satisfaction in this solution. Somehow her daughter's confidence gave Ashley strength. "Exactly. So you deliver the cookies, and then you can take the apple out to Penny."

Natalie disappeared and in a few moments she was back collecting her own cookies and Penny's apple. Ashley figured she'd dart right outside, but instead, Natalie posed another difficult question.

"Mama, is Grandma ... I mean Grandmother ... going back home now?"

"I suppose after Grandpa's funeral she will. She has no reason to stay here."

"She doesn't love us, does she?"

Ashley stopped fussing with the coffeepot and looked at her daughter's curious expression. What could she say? There was no way to lie to the child. She already knew the truth of it. Kneeling down, Ashley toyed with her daughter's braid. "Some people don't know how to love, Natalie. I think Grandmother is one of those people. I don't think she does it because she wants to be mean or hurt people. I just think she's got a lot of anger and bitterness inside and there's no room for love."

Natalie's eyes widened. "Just like there's no room for Jesus. Grandpa told me that God is love. He showed me a verse in the Bible that says that. If Grandmother doesn't have any love inside, it's probably because she doesn't have God inside either."

"I suppose that could very well be true," Ashley said, amazed at how insightful her daughter could be.

"Mama, after I give Penny her apple, can I go let Mr. Carson know about Grandpa?"

"Sure. Just be careful."

"Oh, I will. Today was the day we were supposed to go see him anyway. He didn't want me to come by last week because they were doing dangerous things and he didn't want me to get hurt. But when I told him I'd come today and bring you, he said that was okay."

"I can't go with you," Ashley said, almost wishing she could go along. "But you tell Mr. Carson we'll have him to dinner once Grandmother goes back to Baltimore."

"I know he'll like that," Natalie said, grinning. She gave Ashley a kiss, then burst out the back door as if the house were on fire.

Ashley laughed and went back to work on the coffee. That girl never slowed down for more than a second. She put her grandmother's posy-patterned cups and saucers on a tray, then added the sugar bowl and creamer, some napkins and spoons, and finally a china coffee server. She filled the china pot with coffee, then hoisted the heavy tray and made her way to the living room.

Seeing that Simon Watson had the situation clearly under control, Ashley felt a sense of relief. She wondered if she should begin to pour the coffee and glanced at her aunt. Lavelle waved her off and reached for the pot instead.

Sensing that the trio had her mother fairly well managed, Ashley backed out of the room. There was no point in remaining, especially when there was so much work to be done.

Thinking that she should probably get their Sunday clothes ready for the following day, Ashley went upstairs to Natalie's bedroom. She chose her plum-colored dress, knowing that it had been Grandpa's favorite. She wasn't going to wear black to church. She might very well don it for the funeral but not for church.

The thought of a black dress made her smile. *I could always wear my Harvey uniform,* she thought. *Minus the apron, of course.* And then it came to mind that she was now free to go back to work. Free to work for the Harvey Company while she tried to figure out what was to be done about Ethan. She made a mental note to contact her supervisor on Monday.

She rummaged through Natalie's dresses and found a dark green one that seemed serviceable. Ashley hoped to avoid any last-minute ironing and quickly inspected the dress for wrinkles. It appeared quite passable.

She put the dresses aside and went to make sure Natalie had clean socks to wear. Sliding open the top drawer of Natalie's dresser, Ashley noted at least three pairs. She also noted a rolled-up piece of paper. She smiled. No doubt Natalie had been drawing again.

Unrolling the paper, Ashley couldn't help but gasp aloud. There in charcoal, just as it had first been sketched, was the house she had dreamed of building with her husband. Surely Natalie hadn't drawn it. The lines were too perfect—too certain. From the columns to the French doors to the . . .

A strange feeling washed over her as her gaze caught sight of the initials in the right-hand corner. EJC.

Her breath caught in the back of her throat, then released as a low moan. Hurrying from her daughter's room, Ashley threw open the door to her own bedroom. Under the bed was the suitcase her aunt Lavelle had given her so long ago. Ashley knelt down and pulled the case out. Opening it, she searched for what she knew she'd find.

Along with Natalie's baby clothes and other cherished memorabilia was the drawing Ethan had sketched for her so very long ago. She tenderly unfolded the paper and placed it atop the bed. She pushed the suitcase back and got to her feet.

Picking up the drawing, she walked back to Natalie's room and placed the drawings side by side. She already knew they'd be nearly identical. The way the house sat amidst the imagined landscape. The same light fixtures in the portico. Only here and there did Ashley find any real differences, and even then they only served as more conclusive evidence. They were changes she and Ethan had discussed.

Closing her eyes and drawing a deep breath, Ashley prayed, "Oh, God, I'm not very good at this, but please hear me. I . . . what's happening? What does this mean?"

But even as she asked the question, she knew what it meant. She opened her eyes and looked at the initials in the corner of Natalie's drawing. Then she looked at the corner of her own drawing. EJR. Same style of writing with the "R" being the only change.

Without thinking another single thought, Ashley took up both pictures and darted from the room. She raced out of the house so fast she gave no one any indication of where she was going. The sun was setting in the southwest, the blue sky mottled with orange, pink, and yellow. It was a cold sky nevertheless. Or maybe it was just that the world seemed suddenly cold.

Ashley went to the new Harvey resort and marched into the building without slowing. She looked from side to side, seeking E. J. Carson. She found him in the dining room. Holding the drawings behind her back, she fought to steady her voice.

"I need to speak to you . . . in private."

E. J. nodded. "Is something wrong?"

Apparently Natalie hadn't caught up with him yet. Ashley nodded. "Yes. I need to talk to you."

He appeared to catch on to the urgency, for he moved across the room quickly and didn't even stop to talk to a worker who was signaling him. "Come this way. Is Natalie all right?"

"She's fine," Ashley said, the words sticking in her throat. "For now."

He looked at her oddly, but Ashley dropped her gaze. How could this be? How could this man have eaten at her table—walked beside her—and she still not know who he really was?

E. J. led her to a private office. "This is where I usually work. Now tell me what's wrong." He stood directly in front of her.

Ashley raised her head, praying for strength. She held up Natalie's picture. "I found this."

E. J. looked away. "I drew it for her from a drawing she'd given me."

Ashley held up the original. "She sketched hers from this. The drawing my husband did for me eleven years ago." She saw it then. Saw the familiarity behind the glass and wire of his spectacles. She remembered his whistling the same ragtime tune Ethan had loved.

"I don't understand," she said, her voice breaking. "I don't know how it can be that you're my husband and I didn't even recognize you."

"He's not my daddy!" Natalie cried from behind her. "He's Mr. Carson. My daddy died."

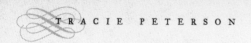

Ashley whirled around and saw the look of disbelief on her daughter's face. "Natalie, I . . ."

"No!" Natalie screamed, then ran from the room.

Ashley started to go after her but stopped. If she left now, she'd still have no answers for the child. Her heart pounded as she turned to face the truth. Leaning heavily against the open door, Ashley braced herself.

"Ethan," she breathed his name. "Please tell me how this can possibly be."

CHAPTER TWENTY

E. J. wanted nothing more than to go to his wife and embrace her. He wanted to tenderly hold her, to kiss her and breathe the scent of her hair. Instead, he calmly went to the door and gently took hold of her hand and led her to a chair. He returned to the door and closed it before pulling up a chair in front of her.

"I've only known a short time myself," he said, his voice hoarse with emotion. "Your mother told me you were dead."

"I know."

She spoke the words so softly he wasn't sure if he'd heard them or imagined them. E. J. drew a deep breath. "I was nearly killed in France. An explosion left my face hopelessly mangled, and I suffered several other injuries. They took me to the nearest hospital, where I lost consciousness. When I awoke, my face was completely bandaged, even my eyes. I was terrified. I thought I'd died and this was some sort of eternal holding place. I thought maybe all that stuff I'd been told about God was wrong. See, I'd learned to pray and to trust God during the war, but now I wasn't so sure."

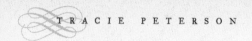

Ashley said nothing. She stared at him as though he were a ghost. Her pale face only served to remind him that while he'd known for some time that she was his wife, Ashley was just now coming to understand that her husband was alive. After eleven years, it had to be more than she'd ever imagined having to deal with.

E. J. leaned forward. "I had to endure several surgeries; that's why I don't look very much like the man you knew me to be. The ordeal left me badly scarred, but at least I could grow a beard to hide most of it.

"After the surgeries, I fought infections. They thought for sure I'd die, but I kept thinking of how I would come home and find you waiting and everything would be all right. I learned the war had ended, but I was still so sick. They nursed me back to reasonable health, then shipped me back to Baltimore. I hadn't been back in the country long before I came down with influenza. Men throughout my ward died, but I kept fighting it—thinking of you—knowing I had to recover. I tried to get in touch with you. I had a couple of different people offer to take you a message, but they were unable to locate you. I figured you'd moved. I thought maybe you'd even gone back to your mother and father's house, but I couldn't really believe that you would."

"I'd moved to Los Angeles and then to Winslow, with Grandpa," Ashley explained. "I'd received word that you were dead." Her eyes filled with tears. "They told me you were dead. The army said you died in battle— that you were a hero."

She sounded desperate, almost as if she needed him to believe her. He did.

E. J. nodded. "I know. I figured that part out."

"I was going to have a baby and my mother was try-ing to force me to remarry. She didn't know about Natalie—just as you didn't know."

"No, I didn't," he admitted. "When I finally recov-ered and was released from the hospital, I went to your parents' house."

"Yes, I know." She seemed to regain a bit of strength. "Mother blurted out a confession the other night. See, I hadn't seen or talked to her since leaving Baltimore. She'd disowned me—told me to never try to communi-cate with her or Father. She came here for Grandpa—he wanted to see her again. Then in the middle of one of her tirades, she just spilled out the truth. She told me she had seen you after the war, that you were alive." Tears flooded Ashley's eyes. "I wanted to die and shout for joy all at the same time."

E. J. knew exactly how she felt. "When I first met you on the street, that day Natalie introduced us, I was sure there had to be some mistake. But there you were, look-ing so much like you did all those years ago."

"Why didn't you say something then?"

"I couldn't. I . . . well . . . you have to understand, Ashley, I'm not the same man you married."

"What do you mean? You're Ethan Reynolds, aren't you?"

"Yes. I changed my name to avoid dealing with the hero status they were awarding me. People were hound-ing me. Veterans' groups wanted to hear me speak of defeating the Germans. Ladies' clubs wanted to have me as the guest of honor at their teas. I couldn't handle it. I felt so ashamed of who I'd become in the war. You have no idea of the things I did." He fell silent and looked at the floor as if for answers. "I killed men—boys, really. I killed them even when I didn't have to."

"You were a soldier. You did your duty." Her words were calm and gentle.

"Yes, maybe," he said, still unable to look her in the eye. "But I did it too well."

"I still don't understand why that would delay you in telling me who you were."

E. J. looked up. "Ashley, up until a short time ago, I could hardly stand admitting to myself what the past had done to me—what I'd done to myself. Every night I still have nightmares. The torment and demonic visions that come to me in my dreams are more than I could ever subject anyone to—much less you."

"But that choice should be mine," she said, meeting his gaze. She searched his face, as if to find some scrap of evidence that he was who she knew him to be.

Finally she asked, "How did you come to be in Winslow?"

"After your mother told me you were dead, I didn't care what happened to me. I drifted for a time. I had no desire to live. My parents had died from the influenza as well and I had no home—no one."

"I'm so sorry. If I'd only stayed in Baltimore," Ashley said, looking past him to the wall. "But it was so awful. I was so alone. Mother had disowned me and I was going to have a baby."

"No, don't blame yourself. You did the right thing," E. J. said, reaching forward to take hold of her hand. "You had to think of yourself and Natalie. You thought

I was dead. There was no reason to stay in Baltimore and wait around."

"I know, but I just keep thinking of all those wasted years. It was so hard." She didn't seem to notice that he continued to hold her hand. Instead she appeared lost in her memory. "I wanted to die. I wanted to join you wherever you were. I couldn't bear the idea of your being dead. Natalie was the only one to give me a reason to go on. Grandpa tried, but he just couldn't understand. Natalie was a part of you, and in a way, I guess that's why she strengthened me and gave me hope."

Ashley returned her gaze to E. J. "She's everything to me, and now with Grandpa gone . . ."

"Grandpa died?"

She nodded. "Just this afternoon. That's why Natalie was coming here. She wanted to tell you about him. But I found the picture and knew . . . the truth. I didn't even consider that she might overhear us talking."

E. J. squeezed her hand. "I had planned to tell you the day we went to the meteorite crater. I had a speech all prepared, and then your friends joined us and I couldn't tell you. I even thought about telling you on the drive home, but I worried that Natalie might wake up and overhear us."

Ashley shook her head. "I've spent the last few days since Mother told me about you wondering how in the world I'd ever find you again. I worried that you would have remarried and that in finding you I would completely ruin your life. I didn't tell Natalie because I was even afraid you might have died sometime after Mother saw you. I didn't want Natalie to lose her father all over again. She adores you."

"She adores Ethan Reynolds."

"But you are Ethan Reynolds," Ashley said firmly. "No matter what you did in the war and no matter what has happened since, you're Ethan Reynolds . . . my husband." She pulled away from him and put her hands to her cheeks and exhaled loudly. "What do we do now?"

The question rang over and over through Ashley's mind. *What do we do now?* Her thoughts were so jumbled—so disjointed. *Ethan is alive, but Ethan is E. J. Carson. My husband is alive, but he's not really my husband at all. We knew each other only a brief time and then he was gone. We have a child. Oh, Natalie, where have you gone off to?*

"I have to find Natalie." Ashley jumped up. "I have to try to explain this to her."

E. J. got to his feet as well. "I'll come with you."

"No, she's too upset. I need to talk to her alone—to try to explain."

But how could she rationally explain any of this to a ten-year-old girl when she could hardly begin to comprehend it herself?

"I want to help," E. J. said. "Is there anything I can do?"

Ashley shook her head. "I can't think of anything—though of course you could pray."

He looked at her with such a mix of compassion and sorrow. Ashley regretted leaving him alone just now, but she couldn't subject Natalie to even more pain. It was clear the shock had been too much for her to handle.

"I'll let you know . . . we can . . ." She fell silent. "I'll talk to you later."

Ashley hurried from the room and made her way outside. It was already growing dark and the chill of the night was upon them. The desert could get so cold at night—so very cold. Ashley felt the urge to run all the way home but fought it. She needed the time to pray and collect her thoughts. What was she going to say to her child? How was she ever going to make Natalie understand?

Making her way inside the house, Ashley found it strangely quiet. A note had been left by Lavelle. Picking it up from the dining room table, Ashley read, *We've gone with the pastor to the funeral home.*

Ashley breathed a sigh of relief. At least it would give her time to deal with Natalie alone. "Natalie!" she called as she went upstairs. She fully expected to find her daughter stretched out across her bed, crying her heart out.

"Natalie, hon," Ashley said, turning on the light. She wasn't there. The bed was still made and the green- and plum-colored dresses were laid across the end just as Ashley had left them.

She searched the rest of the upstairs, but Natalie was nowhere to be found. Flying down the stairs, Ashley searched through the rest of the house. She went to Grandpa's room first, thinking that Natalie might have found it comforting. The sight of the empty bed only served to make Ashley feel alone.

"Oh, Grandpa. If only you were still here."

Ashley thought of Penny and how much Natalie loved the pony. That had to be the answer. Natalie was

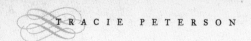

with Penny. Ashley hurried through the house and out the back door. The screen slammed hard behind her as Ashley called out in the growing darkness.

"Natalie! Natalie, where are you?"

She went to Penny's little corral, but the pony was gone. Searching the stall, Ashley realized the saddle and bridle were also missing. Natalie had taken Penny and ridden off. But to where?

Ashley's heart filled with dread. She thought of all of Natalie's favorite places. Where would she go to hide out and deal with this news? She had her friends and might have gone to see one of them, Ashley thought, but even as the idea came, Ashley dismissed it. Natalie would want to be completely alone.

Surely she wouldn't head out away from town. Ashley looked past the yard off toward the open desert. Night was upon them and the desert was no place to play. Would Natalie be so foolish as to venture beyond the safety of town?

"Oh, God, help me. I don't know where she's gone. I don't know how to find her." Ashley blinked back tears. "She's everything to me, Father. Please don't take her too."

Ashley went back into the house. She had to get help, and Ethan was the only logical one to ask. How could she possibly explain the situation to anyone else? She pulled her sweater out of the closet and was just putting it on when her mother and Lavelle came through the door.

"Where are you off to at a time like this? In fact, where did you disappear to earlier?" her mother questioned.

"I have to find Natalie. She's taken the pony, and I don't know where she's gone," Ashley said, picking her words carefully. She wasn't about to tell her mother about the encounter with Ethan. At least not yet.

"That child runs positively wild. I would give her a sound spanking when she gets home," Leticia said sternly. "You've obviously raised her with little or no discipline."

"Letty, that isn't kind," Lavelle scolded. "Today has been very hard on Ashley and Natalie. No doubt Natalie has been saddened by her grandfather's death and has gone off to grieve." Lavelle looked to Ashley as if for confirmation.

"Yes," Ashley said. "She was very upset." That much was true.

"She is an inconsiderate, undisciplined child to put us through such a scene," Ashley's mother said, refusing to back down.

Ashley thought of reminding her mother that she was no longer welcome here, but she bit back the retort and instead moved to the door. "If Natalie comes home, please tell her I'll be right back."

"You should just wait here. She'll get tired of being alone and return. Then you can punish her properly. It might not yet be too late to instill some discipline. I'm sure my father spoiled her beyond belief, and with you off working at that Harvey place . . . well, the child has no doubt had to raise herself."

Ashley opened the door, forcing herself to remain silent. It would serve no purpose to explain herself or her life. Natalie was out there somewhere and the night was coming.

Lavelle turned to her sister. "You shouldn't be so critical of Ashley. She's done a wonderful job raising Natalie. The child is positively perfect."

"A perfect child wouldn't run about without consideration for her elders," Leticia replied.

Lavelle shook her head. "Letty, you have a beautiful daughter and an equally beautiful grandchild. You've pushed them away most of your life. If you aren't careful, you'll lose all opportunity to draw them close again. Because sooner or later, you're going to push hard enough that they won't come back."

Leticia's expression softened more than Lavelle had expected. "That happened a decade ago. Ashley will never forgive me."

It was the first time Lavelle had ever heard Leticia speak of needing her daughter's forgiveness. "Perhaps if she knew you desired to be forgiven, it might change things." Lavelle smiled ever so slightly. "Perhaps if you each knew how sorry you were for the lost years—for the mistakes."

Leticia shook her head and gathered up her things. "I won't make myself vulnerable in that fashion. Apologies are for weaklings." She stormed off for the stairs, not waiting for Lavelle's reply.

Lavelle watched until her sister had disappeared. She heard the bedroom door close upstairs and sighed. The day had been a defeating blow for Letty. Lavelle felt sorry for her. She had learned her fortune was in jeopardy—their father had died—and the lawyer had reminded them both in no uncertain terms that the estate of their father was forever set. Lavelle felt a bitter-sweet relief, whereas she knew Letty felt only fear.

"God, please help her," Lavelle prayed. "She's so very lost and alone."

CHAPTER TWENTY-ONE

E. J. could barely gather up the strength to go back to his hotel room. The work was finished; they were right on schedule and so far the problems had all been minimal—at least all his work problems had been minimal. E. J. sat at his desk, cradling his bearded chin, gazing at the chair in the same room where his wife had recently sat. How strange life had twisted this time. Up until a few weeks ago he'd thought his life would be spent alone with his images from the past. He hadn't believed it possible to get past the war and what he'd done, but now he felt God had helped him to renew his hope. Even Ashley didn't condemn him for what he'd done.

"Can I really let go, Lord? Can I let go of the past and be a better man?" he whispered. E. J. wanted desperately to believe he could. He loved Ashley—he'd never stopped. If it wouldn't have been inappropriate, he would have swept her off her feet and kissed her soundly. *But she doesn't know me,* E. J. realized. *She knows only the young man I was before I went away to war.*

He shook his head. "I don't know what to do, Lord.

I don't know how to help. Natalie brought my attention back to you, but for what? How do I make this right? How can we be a family? How do I go back to being Ethan Reynolds?"

Without warning, the door flew open, slamming against the wall with a reverberating crash. Ashley came into the room like a speeding freight train. "She's gone."

"What?" He got to his feet. "Who's gone?"

"Natalie. She's gone." The look on Ashley's face was one of pure panic.

E. J. didn't think the situation so distressful. "She's probably just thinking things over. You know, just walking around town."

Ashley looked at him as though he hadn't a clue of the seriousness of the matter. And the truth was, he didn't—and it made him feel foolish for his comment.

"She's ten years old, Ethan. She has no business wandering around town or elsewhere at this hour," Ashley replied indignantly. "Besides, her pony's gone, and that can only mean that Natalie's on horseback trying to get away from all of this. That means she's planned more than just a short walk around town. We have to find her, Ethan." She burst into tears. "You have to help me."

He reached out and pulled her into his arms. It felt like the most natural thing in the world. In a rush of memories he was just twenty-one and she was his first and only love. "Of course I'll help you. She's my daughter too." He stroked her hair and tried to think about what should be done.

"I saw a couple of our friends on the way over here," Ashley said, pulling back just enough to see his face. "I told them to keep their eyes open for her—to ask around. I asked them to check around town, but Ethan, I'm sure she's not there. I just have this very bad feeling. Call it a mother's intuition."

"Does she have a good friend she might have gone to see? Someone in whom she'd confide all of this?"

"She has friends, but I don't think she would be inclined to go share this. She's hurting and scared. Her whole world has been turned upside down today. First Grandpa and now this. Oh, Ethan, what are we going to do?"

"Excuse me," a man called from the doorway.

E. J. looked up to find Marcus Greeley, the journalist who had introduced himself at the dinner with Lindbergh. "Ethan Reynolds?"

"You!" Ashley declared. She looked back at Ethan. "This man came to my door asking to talk to us. I think he's the same one who was following Natalie." She looked back at Greeley.

"You were following my daughter," Ashley said. "I know it was you. I saw you hiding and following her."

"Actually, ma'am, I was following the both of you, but your daughter just seemed to come to see Mr. Reynolds more often than not, so I found it more productive to follow her."

"Do you know where she is now?" Ashley asked, stepping away from Ethan.

"No, I can't say that I do, but I heard from some of the railroad men that she was missing. I want to help with the search."

"I don't understand why you were following

Natalie," E. J. stated. "Or why you would follow either of them."

"Because unless I've missed my guess, you're Ethan Reynolds."

E. J. knew there was no sense in lying. "I am Ethan Reynolds, but I still don't understand. If you were looking for me, why bother them?"

"It's kind of a long story, but since time is of the essence here, I'll try to shorten it a bit." Marcus twisted his fedora and shrugged. "I've been looking for you since you were sent home after the Great War. See, I was on that battlefield when your act of courage saved hundreds of men. I wasn't in your company, but my company was in your division, and we were pinned down by the same machine gunner that got some of your friends. I was wounded early on and losing blood fast. There wasn't much hope of getting me out, and then you went charging through the bullets as though they were nothing more than horseflies. You saved my life."

Ethan stiffened. "I just did what had to be done."

"Yes, but no one else had been able to do that, and if you hadn't acted when you did, I wouldn't have lasted another hour. Your act of heroism allowed my buddies to get me out and back to a field hospital."

"That doesn't explain why you're here now," E. J. said, eager to get the man's focus away from battle.

"At first I just wanted to find you and thank you. I started this back in 1920," he said, laughing. "I wanted to meet you and give you a smoked ham from my folks. Sounds silly now, but it was important then. After a time when I kept running out of places to look, I thought to check with the army and see if they had any record of you.

"The army could only tell me that you had a wife, Ashley Reynolds, and where she lived. I went there, but of course she was gone. I kind of gave up the search for a while. I needed to settle on my writing. I put together a collection of stories on the war and found it well received. I wrote for several newspapers, and then one day the same publisher who'd contracted my book of stories came to me and asked me to write another book. A book about the war and the men who'd fought and where they were now that the war was ten years behind them. I immediately thought of you and what you'd done. I knew I had to try again to find you."

Ethan shook his head. "I can't imagine it being that important."

Marcus rubbed his bare chin. "Well, it was to me. My big break came one day when a friend who knew what I was trying to do with the book sent me a newspaper clipping from Winslow. It showed your daughter in a parade with some veterans. The article had stories about each of the men. He actually thought I'd want the information on the other men, but what I really found of value was the information about your daughter. I knew from reading the article that her mother's name was Ashley Reynolds—and that it had to be the same woman. I was stumped by the fact that your little girl was quoted as having lost you in the war before she was even born. I knew you were alive.

"Anyway, to make a long story short, I came here to see if I could talk to your wife and daughter and figure out why they thought you were dead. I thought maybe they were trying to hide something or maybe the newspaper writer had tried to make the story more of a heartgripper than the truth would allow. So I decided not to approach Mrs. Reynolds and Natalie right off the bat. Instead I nosed around and asked questions here and there. Surprisingly enough, Natalie led me to you. Now I want to help find Natalie."

Ethan's mind was still reeling from the story, but he knew there'd be time to sort out the details later. "I'd appreciate the help." He turned to Ashley. "Where should we look? I really don't know the area."

Ashley shook her head. "She has several favorite places, but she isn't thinking rationally. She could have taken off to Clear Creek—she loves it there. Or she could have gone up toward the river. There are . . . some places along the . . ." Ashley broke down, burying her face in her hands.

Ethan again pulled her close, but he looked over her shoulder to Marcus Greeley. "Do you have a car?"

"No, but I'd be willing to bet money we can get one. I'll start asking around," Greeley said and quickly exited the room.

"Ashley, listen to me. You have to be strong for Natalie. You have to think clearly and help me here. I can't do this alone."

She looked into his eyes. "You aren't alone." She sniffed back her tears and regained her composure. "I'm here with you."

He nodded. "Come on. Let's see what's to be done about transportation."

They stepped from the office and into the lobby hallway to find a growing collection of people.

"We're here to help," said one man, his overalls grease-smeared along with his face.

"It's too dark to see," someone else commented. "We can look around town, but going out much farther will have to wait for first light."

"That's true," yet another person called. "Too many dangers."

Ashley grabbed E. J.'s arm. "She can't be out there all night. It's already chilly and it will get much colder. There are dangers for her as well."

E. J. looked at the men who surrounded them. "Is there no way to go searching—even with a car?"

"You can drive the roads in the dark, but you won't be able to get off across country. If she's riding that pony like she's done in the past, she ain't sticking to the roads," a balding man threw back.

E. J. looked at Ashley. "If we can get a couple of cars, we'll at least drive around and call for her. We might actually spot her. You just never know."

Ashley nodded. "I'll go find Pastor McGuire. He has a car."

"I'll run for him," the man who'd first spoken up offered. He took off before anyone could acknowledge him.

E. J. stood feeling rather helpless while several of the local men organized the collection of people into a search party. He listened to the chatter around him. People presumed Natalie was just upset because of her grandfather's death. They were sympathetic and hopeful that she'd come home before much longer, but they were also happy to look for her. Their obvious affection for his daughter warmed him through and through.

Within the hour Ethan and Ashley joined Pastor McGuire in his car, while Marcus Greeley and several other townsmen piled into an assortment of cars and flatbed trucks. They'd all agreed to meet back in one hour at the Harvey hotel. Ethan had never known when he'd been more frightened. With Ashley clinging to his hand, he knew his worry over their child was worse than anything he'd faced on the battlefield.

Lord, he prayed, *please keep her safe. Please don't allow any harm to come to her.* The prayer seemed so little—so ineffectual. Surely he could do more than pray and drive around in the dark.

But there was nothing else to be done. Just as he feared, the car lights were no real benefit against the blackness of the empty desert. After the allotted time, they turned around and headed back to town. Ashley began to sob softly against E. J.'s shoulder.

"It's going to be all right," he whispered. "We have to have faith. God wouldn't bring us all together like this just to see us separated again."

Pastor McGuire spoke up just then. "I'm having a hard time understanding what's happening here. I heard Ashley call you Ethan earlier."

Ethan drew a deep breath. "Yes. I'm her husband."

"But you were believed to have died in France."

"I know. I was pretty close to dead, but apparently the army made a mess of things and sent her the wrong letter. We've only just learned the truth for ourselves."

"And is this the real reason for Natalie's disappearance?" McGuire asked as they pulled up in front of the Harvey hotel. He stopped the car and waited for Ethan's answer.

"She overheard her mother confront me. It's a long story, but yes, this is the reason Natalie is gone. This is why we weren't inclined to believe she'd just come back home before long. This is why we're both so scared."

The pastor shut off the engine and smiled. "Well, I'm happy to say that I know for a fact God still answers prayer. Natalie's fondest wish and deepest heartfelt prayer was for God to send her a daddy. I know because she got me in on it as well." He laughed. "Once she thinks this through, she's going to be delighted. In the meantime, we'll just pray for her safety and that she'll see the reason in coming home quickly."

E. J. nodded. He wanted to believe the pastor's words. He wanted very much to have hope so that Ashley could take courage from him. Suddenly it was very important that she see him as the man she needed him to be.

Dismissing the searchers for the night was the hardest thing E. J. ever had to do. He watched the men leave in the same spirit of dejection he felt gripping his heart. Fear was a powerful opponent, and right now it seemed to be an unbeatable one.

"Why don't you go home and get some sleep?" Pastor McGuire suggested to Ashley. "Besides, Natalie might have already returned."

"My mother and aunt Lavelle are there," Ashley said softly. "I should go check and see if they've heard anything, but I couldn't sleep. Not in a million years."

"I'll go with you," E. J. said. He extended his hand to the pastor. "Thank you. Thank you for helping us tonight and for the prayers."

"I'll be back in the morning. I'll bring some saddle

horses. We'll have a better time of it if we look for her on horseback."

E. J. nodded. "Thanks. I'll be here."

He pressed his hand against the small of Ashley's back. "Come on. Let's see if she's gone home."

They walked in silence along the city streets. Ashley didn't seem to mind that E. J. had taken hold of her hand. He wasn't entirely sure why he'd done it. They'd only just come back together, but it seemed so very right.

Ashley opened the front door and was immediately greeted by her aunt. "Have you found her?" Lavelle questioned.

Ashley looked at E. J. and bit her lower lip.

"No," E. J. replied. "We'd hoped you might have heard something."

Lavelle shook her head. Worry etched her face. "I've put on a pot of coffee." She looked at Ashley, her expression suggesting dread. "Your mother went to bed. She was quite worn-out."

"You needn't make excuses for her," Ashley replied. "She doesn't care about Natalie."

"I think she does . . . in her own way," Lavelle reasoned. "I just think she's taken this whole news of Father and the stock market quite hard. I think it's catching up with her, and Natalie was just the final straw. This very well may be a turning point in her life, Ashley. We must pray for her."

"Well, frankly, I hope she stays up there. No, actually, I wish she weren't here at all. After what she did to Natalie . . ." Ashley's words were hard and cold. "I don't need her making this worse."

"There weren't any hotel rooms available for tonight," Lavelle explained. "They've reserved her something for tomorrow. I took it upon myself to tell her to plan on staying here tonight."

"I suppose I have no choice," Ashley replied bitterly. "After all, it would hardly be the Christian thing to do. Oh, but I don't feel like being very Christian when it comes to that woman."

Her aunt patted her on the arm and turned to E. J. "Mr. Carson, isn't it?"

E. J. straightened and looked to Ashley. "I . . . uh . . ."

"Aunt Lavelle, I think we should sit down to coffee and then continue this conversation. There's something you need to know." Ashley motioned E. J. to the living room. "Just take a seat and I'll get the cups."

She and Lavelle disappeared momentarily, and when they returned she carried a tray and three cups, along with a plate of cookies. "I thought you might be hungry," she told Ethan. "Neither of us had supper."

"I could make some sandwiches," Lavelle offered, still looking curiously at the two of them. When Ashley took a seat close to E. J. on the sofa, Lavelle raised her brows in question.

Ashley poured the coffee and began the long explanation. E. J. sat in silence, knowing that it was probably better to let Ashley vent her emotions and thoughts.

"He seemed so familiar," she continued to explain, glancing at E. J. "He walked the same way Ethan walked. He even liked to whistle Ethan's favorite ragtime tune. It seemed like a silly coincidence, and in fact, I thought I was just making it up in my head. You know, because I wanted so much to remember Ethan."

"Well, this certainly is stunning news," Lavelle said. She took a long sip from her coffee, then looked E. J. in the eye. "So what happens now?"

"Now we find Natalie," E. J. replied. "Nothing else matters until we know she's safe and sound."

"I agree," Lavelle said, nodding, "but you have to be prepared for her questions. And knowing my great-niece, one of the first questions on her mind will be whether you intend to stay here in Winslow and be a father to her."

E. J. cleared his throat nervously. "I love Ashley as though the lost years between us had never happened. She's easy to love, but of course, you know that. I don't know that I'd be much good anymore as a husband or a father, but . . ." He fell silent and looked at Ashley. "I'd like a chance to try."

And in that moment, he knew it was true. Despite the past, he wanted his future. And he wanted that future to be with Ashley and Natalie—but not as E. J. Carson. He wanted his life as Ethan Reynolds back. Ethan was the man Ashley had fallen in love with, and from that love, Ethan was the man who helped create Natalie. "Ashley, I want to be Ethan again—the man you once loved and married."

The house was silent a moment before Lavelle coughed quietly and then bid them good-night. Ethan noted the time was nearing eleven. "I should go," he said softly.

Ashley had said very little since giving her explanation of who he was. She'd sat beside him on the sofa staring pensively into the fireplace.

"It's so hard to be here all safe and warm," she said as though she hadn't heard him speak, "and know that she's out there alone."

"I know," Ethan said, reaching out to take hold of her hand.

To his surprise, Ashley leaned against his shoulder. "This is like a dream and a nightmare all wrapped into one. You're here—and that's all my dreams come true. But Natalie's lost and that's all the horror a mother's heart could ever imagine."

"She's a smart girl. She's going to be all right."

"Do you really believe that?" Ashley asked, barely suppressing a yawn.

Ethan squeezed her hand. "I do. I've just spent the last few weeks in her company. She's told me stories about her life here—about her dreams. She thinks things through, and even though she acted out of emotion tonight, she'll think things through and come home."

"But what if she's not able to come home?"

"Ashley, we can't think like that. It wouldn't serve any good purpose. We have to believe that God is in control and that He's heard our prayers and will protect her."

"For so many years, I didn't believe God cared. Maybe He's punishing me."

Ethan's heart nearly broke. "No," he whispered. "God doesn't work that way. I don't know a whole lot about the Bible, but I do know that God wouldn't purposefully bring harm to an innocent child."

"But someone else might," Ashley whispered.

"God will see us through this, Ashley. I promise you,

He will. She's going to be all right."

They sat in silence watching the fire, and it wasn't long before he realized that Ashley had fallen asleep. Her rhythmic breathing comforted him. Ethan eased Ashley into his arms and leaned back against the sofa and closed his eyes. It felt so right for her to be here with him.

———————

He hadn't intended to sleep, but when Ethan woke up just before dawn, he realized what had happened and smiled. For the first time since the war, he hadn't been riddled with battlefield nightmares. In fact, he couldn't remember a single image haunting his sleep. Ashley had made that possible—he was certain of it. It was almost as if God had given him a sign he so desperately needed. A sign of peace and tranquility. A sign that with Ashley at his side, he could leave the past behind.

"Ashley," he whispered against her ear.

"Mmm."

"Ashley, love, wake up. It's almost light. We need to prepare for our search."

Ashley woke up slowly. She looked up into his face, her dark eyes searching his as if in a dream. "Ethan . . . you're here," she said. Apparently sleep still kept her mind from remembering the night before.

"Yes, I'm here, but we need to go look for Natalie."

She came awake instantly at the mention of their daughter's name.

"She hasn't come home."

It was a statement, not a question, but Ethan felt he needed to respond nevertheless. "No, but she will. I promise you—she will."

CHAPTER TWENTY-TWO

*E*than and Ashley prepared some supplies and headed back to the Harvey hotel. The sun was barely on the horizon when to their surprise a group of men, mounted on horseback, arrived. Soon others joined them, both on horseback and in cars. True to his word, Pastor McGuire was there and with him Marcus Greeley, who looked rather uncomfortable atop the bay mount the pastor had lent him.

"I've put Brother Roberts in charge of the church and told him I needed to pastor this search." Pastor McGuire motioned to the extra horse and handed down the reins to Ethan and said, "I've brought you a good mount. Now, where do we start?"

Ethan took hold of the horse. "I think if we form a circle around the outside edge of town and keep working our way out, we'll cover more territory."

"I think that's wise," said the town marshal. "Some of my men and I will lead the teams going north and west. The rest of my men can stay here and run messages to us if needed and keep things under control. If you men will take the east and south, we'll have a good chance of covering just about everything in a ten-mile radius. I can't see her getting any farther away than that."

Ethan had no idea who had thought to let the man know of their predicament, but he was grateful for the help. In fact, he was deeply touched by the way the community had turned out to help look for his daughter.

"You stay here in case she comes home," Ethan told Ashley as he mounted the black gelding Pastor McGuire had given him.

"But I want to come and look for her too. I can't just do nothing," Ashley protested.

"But she may slip through our lines and come home. Or she may have been hiding here in town all along. We'll need to know that as soon as possible."

"But . . ."

"Mrs. Reynolds, he's right," the marshal stated rather sternly. "You need to stay here and let us do the hard work."

Ethan longed to lean down and kiss her good-bye, but instead he took the canteen she offered. "She'll be all right. Just keep praying."

"I want to believe, but my faith is weak."

Pastor McGuire overheard this and smiled. "When we're weak, then God is strong. We know for sure then that we're not operating in our own strength—but in His."

Ashley nodded and handed Ethan his pack. "Be careful."

He smiled, feeling the warmth of her concern. "I will."

Emptiness washed over Ashley as she watched the men ride away. She'd heard one of the railroad men say that the night had been warmer than usual. She prayed it was true. She had no way of knowing if Natalie had thought to take warm clothes or food.

I should have inventoried things, she thought. *That would have given me a better idea of what she might have with her.* But even as Ashley thought this, she knew it would also give her a good idea of what Natalie hadn't taken, and then she would have worried all the more.

Ashley searched around town, checking Natalie's favorite spots and talking to friends as they prepared for church. No one had seen the girl, but they assured Ashley that they were keeping an eye open for her. Ashley thanked each person for his concern, then continued her own search.

She walked down Third Street to Berry and up to Oak, then back east toward home. With every step her heart grew heavier and hope seemed out of reach. By the time she came to the wrought-iron gate of her own home, Ashley longed to break down and cry. She looked at the little two-story brick house and felt her heart overflow with grief. This used to be a home. She and Natalie had been very happy here. Would they ever be happy again?

Ashley pushed back the gate and made her way to the house. Despite her mother's claims to repossess her home and Grandpa's savings, Ashley knew she'd never give up their home—not so long as there was breath in her body. This was where she had raised Natalie. This was Natalie's home.

But what if something happened to Natalie? What if she's gotten herself killed?

The question came against her will. Ashley wiped at the tears that followed. *She can't be dead. She must be all right. Please, God, let her be all right.*

The house was quiet when Ashley entered. She checked the clock and saw that it was only nine-thirty.

"Any word?" Lavelle questioned, coming from the kitchen wearing Ashley's apron and carrying a cup of coffee.

"No. The men have formed a search party and have taken off on horseback to search the open ground."

Lavelle placed the cup and saucer on the table and pulled out a chair. "Here, sit down and have some coffee. I'll bring you some breakfast in just a minute."

"I'm not hungry," Ashley said, taking the offered seat. "The coffee sounds good, though. Thank you."

Lavelle nodded and sat down beside her. "This is the hardest part. Waiting."

Ashley took a long drink. The hot liquid warmed her chilled body. She couldn't tell if she'd grown cold because of the temperature or her own fears.

"Well, has she been found?" Ashley's mother questioned as she entered the room.

Ashley was in no mood to deal with her mother's haughty temperament, but she swallowed another sip of the coffee and shook her head. "They're still searching."

"This is certainly a fine mess. You should have been less lenient with the child. Giving her a pony was sure to lead to disaster. Why, people are killed from being thrown off of horses, and a foolish child racing out in the dead of night is sure to meet with a terrible fate."

"Mother, stop!" Ashley cried.

"Yes, please, Leticia. Try to be more encouraging."

Ashley's mother drew her chin up in defiance. "I will not be hushed or dictated to. I have a right to my opinion, and that opinion is that you've done a poor job of raising your daughter."

"Well, if I have, it's because I had a poor example to follow," Ashley retorted, her anger growing. All the frustration and fear of Natalie's disappearance quickly reordered itself into rage. "You've always concerned yourself with things that held importance only to you. You hardly gave me the time of day, much less the time I needed. Had you been able to share your time and heart as freely as you spent Grandpa's money, I might have desired to maintain a relationship with you."

"You are a vicious and cruel woman," her mother countered, "just as you were an inattentive and inconsiderate child. You never cared about the things that were important to me."

The gauntlet had been thrown down, and Ashley picked it up with great relish. "I might have cared if those things so near and dear to your heart would have included me."

"Always you. Always. You were never happy unless you were the center of attention. Your brothers doted on you. Your father doted on you. But that wasn't enough. You needed to be the center of my world as well," Leticia stated angrily. "Well, I hardly had time for spoiled little girls. There were important people to deal with, and as you grew you could have been an asset—could have helped me—but you were too self-absorbed."

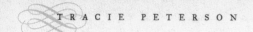

Ashley opened her mouth in disbelief. "That isn't true. You had my life planned out for me, and when I refused to follow your guidelines, you dismissed me like a servant you'd caught stealing."

"You might as well have stolen from us. You took everything we offered without worrying about where it came from or how expensive it might have been."

Ashley pounded her fists on the table. "Because money never meant anything to me. I saw it only as something that occupied my father's time and consumed my mother." She got to her feet and stared her mother hard in the eye. "I have no understanding of your philosophy, because I've lived another kind of life since leaving Baltimore.

"I'll give you this much, Mother. I was selfish and inconsiderate as a child and young woman. I was . . . because I was taught to be such. I was taught that when things or people didn't meet your satisfaction, you sent them away. I was taught the price of everything and the value of nothing. It wasn't until Ethan came into my life that I understood there was something more."

"Always that man. That man coming between my plans for you—that man taking what was never his to own in the first place. I say good riddance to him. Wherever he may be, you may be sure he's amounted to nothing."

"He's out searching for our daughter," Ashley said, enjoying the look of surprise in her mother's expression. "That's right. He's here in Winslow. What you thought to destroy, God saw fit to reunite. Ethan is here, Mother, and once he finds our daughter, he's going to come home . . . and he'll deal with you."

Leticia actually paled. She gripped the back of the chair. "How can he be here? You didn't even know he was alive until I told you."

Lavelle stepped toward her sister. "God has a way of working these things out, Letty. I think you should both calm down and realize that Natalie is still out there somewhere. We should be praying and keeping our focus on her. The rest of this is just anger speaking out."

"I hate you for what you've done to us," Ashley said to her mother, her voice deadly calm. "I hate you for robbing us of eleven years of happiness. I'm glad you've lost your fortune. I hope you suffer, and suffer dearly. Furthermore, I'm glad you disdain God, because I certainly don't want to have to share eternity with the likes of you."

Ashley suddenly looked away, despising herself for her angry words. She pushed Lavelle aside and headed down the hall to Grandpa's old room and locked herself inside. Throwing herself across the bed, Ashley began to cry a torrent of tears.

Why can't I be forgiving like you wanted, Grandpa? Why can't I let go of what she did so long ago? She hurt you, too, but you loved her to the end. Why can't I just love her and forget the pain she's caused?

And then her words turned to prayer. "Oh, God, why does this have to hurt so much? Why, when Ethan has come home and hope is restored and there is a road toward a real future together in sight, does my mother have to make my life so miserable? I was happy until she came. I was happy until I learned that Grandpa was dying."

But was she? Ashley was immediately struck with her

own bitterness. With an honesty that tore at her heart, she could only remember her anger and unhappiness. Loneliness and bitter regret had hardened her heart years ago. She had blamed God for taking Ethan away from her in the first place, and she had blamed her mother for trying to force her plans upon Ashley. And now she blamed her mother for keeping Ethan away for so many years.

"Being a Christian is too hard, Lord. I can't do this. I can't forgive her. She doesn't deserve to be forgiven."

"Nobody deserves forgiveness." Grandpa's words settled on her heart. *"God offered us what we didn't deserve, in order to save us from what we did deserve."*

Ashley remained very still, trying hard to remember the details of their conversation. He had been speaking to her about coming to God—about seeking forgiveness for her own sins. Her sins were just as unforgivable as her mother's.

"But that can't be," she murmured. "I've never been like her. I've never lied like that or stolen someone's life away from them. She might as well have killed me."

Ethan's words from the night before came to her. *"I killed men—boys, really. I killed them even when I didn't have to."*

She could readily forgive what he'd done in the line of duty, even when he proclaimed himself to have acted outside of duty. Ethan's wrongs scarcely even bothered her. Why could she forgive him that and not forgive her mother?

"Because she doesn't want to be forgiven," Ashley said, sitting up. "She doesn't think she's done anything wrong. She hurts people and causes deep pain, but she doesn't care because she has no standard by which to gauge it."

Ashley considered the situation in the depth of her soul. "If she doesn't want forgiveness because she doesn't believe she's done anything wrong, then why should I forgive her? Why does it matter what I think or feel toward her when she's perfectly content to believe herself absolutely right in these matters?"

Forgive her for your own sake. Forgive her for the freedom that comes in letting go of the past. Forgive her because I've forgiven you.

The words seemed to come from somewhere deep within. The quickening in her spirit left Ashley no doubt where the inspiration had come from. Ashley looked to the Bible on Grandpa's nightstand. Picking it up, she hugged it close.

"I don't know if I can do this," she whispered. "God, I'm only human, and I don't know how to forgive her for this. Grandpa would tell me that I should lean on you, and so that's all I have—that's all I can do. You'll have to show me how to forgive her. How to stop hating her. Please, God. Please show me."

CHAPTER TWENTY-THREE

*S*preading out across the windblown desert, the searchers looked for any sign that might give them hope that Natalie had passed that way. Ethan found himself praying continuously. Suddenly nothing in life was more important than finding that little girl.

"Lord, I know I've asked for her safety over and over during this ordeal, but I just can't keep from asking again. Help us to find her—help me to find her. I want so much just to hold her and know that she's going to be all right."

Ethan watched as the distance between himself and the other riders grew. They were like the spokes of a wheel heading out from their hub—Winslow. It seemed a responsible way to search, but the slow, methodic manner in which they conducted themselves did little to ease his concerns.

He studied the horizon with a burning desire to kick the horse into a full gallop. He wanted to reach whatever destination would prove to him that Natalie was safe and sound. He didn't even care if she was mindless of the suffering she'd caused. He didn't care

if she was still as mad as a wet hornet. He just wanted to find her and bring her back safely to Ashley.

Ashley.

Even thinking of her now warmed his heart. He knew just by looking in her eyes that they had a future. She didn't care about the past. She didn't care that he'd killed men and still had nightmares. Ashley would open her home and her arms to him if that was what he wanted.

He looked at the ground for any sign Natalie might have left behind, then scanned the horizon once again. The turmoil in his heart got the better of him and a tightness rose up in his throat. *I know I'm not perfect, but I can try to be a good husband and father. I would like to try. I want to do the right thing in spite of the years that have gone by.*

Ethan looked at Pastor McGuire, who was riding toward a large collection of sandstone rocks. The reddish boulders would create the perfect hiding place.

"I'm going to check out these rocks!" McGuire called out. Ethan slowed his horse and held his breath, waiting for some sign. The pastor picked his way around the rocks, disappearing momentarily from Ethan's sight, then coming around in view again.

"She's not been here!" McGuire called out. "I don't see any tracks at all to suggest otherwise."

"Okay!" Ethan replied and waved. Disappointment welled up inside. She seemed to have vanished from the face of the earth.

Ethan studied the ground for hoof tracks that might prove the pony had passed this way, but the wind whipped up the sand and dirt, blowing it first one direction and then another. A dust devil blew up not ten feet in front of him, spooking the mount. The horse reared up a bit and the action caused Ethan to nearly lose his seat. He wasn't much of a horseman, and this added intrigue was almost more than he could handle. The gelding danced around for a moment as Ethan fought to regain control.

"Easy, fellow," he called soothingly. "Whoa, now."

The horse calmed as the windy formation spent itself and the sand fell back to earth in a new location. The animal proceeded in a cautious fashion, ears slightly back, alert to the ever-present danger that another whirlwind might threaten them. Ethan tired of the slow walk and urged the gelding forward, picking up the pace to a trot. Surely he could spot something just as easily at this speed.

After a time, Ethan could see the rock formations that edged Clear Creek. How pleasant their picnic had been here on that Sunday so long ago. He looked off in the distance. Wasn't that the direction in which Natalie planned to build her mother a house? He slowed the horse and patrolled the rock-lined creek, seeking some clue that his daughter was here and safe. He was just about to call out to Pastor McGuire when the man motioned and called to Ethan. "Look over there!"

Ethan followed the direction indicated and caught sight of Penny, Natalie's pony. His heart sank. The pony was saddled but without a rider. Ethan pressed his horse into a full gallop, but as he neared, the pony spooked and pranced away nervously. Ethan pulled back the reins and brought the gelding to a stop. "Easy, boy," he called and patted his horse's neck.

By this time Pastor McGuire and Marcus Greeley had joined him. The men had served as Ethan's right and left flank. Dismounting, he tossed his reins to McGuire and went in pursuit of Penny.

"Come on, Penny-girl." He clucked softly as he'd heard Natalie do, then reached into his pocket for the apple Ashley had given him shortly before they'd left the house. "Look what I have for you." He held up the apple and walked ever so slowly toward the spooked horse.

Penny seemed to remember him and started a slow, plodding walk toward him. Ethan took out his knife and cut a hunk of the apple and held it out. Penny picked up her pace and came to a stop only a few feet from Ethan. She eyed the offering for a moment, then apparently judged him to be a safe risk. Moving forward, she took the apple, even as Ethan took up her reins.

"Good job, Ethan," Greeley called out. "The west will make a cowboy of you yet."

Ethan smiled. "I don't recall wanting the job." He stroked Penny's nose. "I sure wish you could talk. I wish you could take me to Natalie."

"At least we know she's somewhere here in the area. The pony's not lathered or worked up." Pastor McGuire dismounted and walked to where Penny stood enjoying Ethan's attention. He forced his fingers between her saddle blanket and back. "She doesn't feel the slightest bit damp. I'd say she hasn't had this saddle on long at all. Maybe Natalie rested here for the night and when she went to saddle Penny, she got away from her."

"That could be," Ethan said, trying not to worry. "Maybe Natalie is really close," he added. "Here. I'm going on foot." He handed Penny over to McGuire. Setting off across the ground to the rocks, Ethan began calling. "Natalie! Natalie, where are you?"

Greeley did likewise, heading downstream.

Ethan felt his heart pounding at a pace he couldn't hope to calm. He scrambled onto the rock that edged the creek. The wind spit sand against his face momentarily, but once he started climbing down the creek bank, Ethan found himself more sheltered from the wind. "Natalie! Natalie, if you can hear me—answer me!"

"I'm here." Her voice sounded perturbed.

Ethan strained to listen. "Natalie, where are you?"

"I'm over here." Exasperation rang clear.

He followed the sound and spied something red sticking out just over the next ridge of rock. Scrambling over the barrier, Ethan came face-to-face with his daughter. She wore a red oblong cap that tied under her chin and a dark brown jacket that had what appeared to be a fresh tear on the sleeve. A cut on her forehead and some scratches on her face and hands were the worst of her injuries—as far as Ethan could tell. She looked otherwise unharmed but very annoyed.

Sitting there, elbows on her knees, face in her hands, as if contemplating what was to be done, Natalie looked like someone who'd rather be left alone. Ethan didn't care. He was so happy to see her safe that he acted without thinking. Picking her up, he hugged her close.

"Oh, Natalie, I thought we'd lost you for good. We found Penny, but we had no idea if you were hurt or worse." He couldn't even bring himself to suggest that she could have died.

"Penny lost her footing on the edge. It wasn't her fault. I was too close. I fell off and Penny ran away," Natalie said matter-of-factly. "Please put me down."

Ethan did as she asked. "We've been looking all over for you," he said, continuing his mental inventory. She didn't appear to have any broken bones, but the bump on her head was bleeding. "Your mother is sick with worry." Ethan reached out to touch her, but Natalie withdrew and crossed her arms.

"Is she all right?" Pastor McGuire called from where he stood with the horses.

Ethan called back, "She's fine. Would you please leave Penny and the mount you lent me and go notify the others that she's all right and that we're heading home?"

"Of course," Pastor McGuire replied. "Natalie, I'm so relieved to see you're all right. We've sure been praying for you."

"Oh, Pastor McGuire, would you also let Ashley know we're coming home?"

The man grinned down at them. "I'd be delighted."

Ethan looked down at his daughter. "You ready to head back?"

Natalie only shrugged and stared at the creek. Once the pastor and Greeley had taken off to alert the others, Natalie sat down again. The anger in her voice was apparent. "Why didn't you tell me the truth? I'm not a baby, you know." She looked at him, her brows knitted together. "I thought we were friends."

"We are friends, Natalie." Ethan sat down on the rock opposite her. "I didn't know the truth at first. You told me your father died in the war and I presumed he had. I sure didn't expect to find out that I was really your father. In fact, I didn't know the truth of it until I came face-to-face with your mother that day you introduced us outside the ice-cream store."

"You could have said something then." She looked back at the water instead of him.

"I thought it would be unfair to your mother. I figured I should tell her in private."

"But you didn't. You had lots of time to do it, but you didn't tell her. Why? Are you ashamed of us? Were you just going to leave without telling us?"

Ethan thought his heart might break at this statement. "Of course not. It had nothing to do with you and your mother. It had everything to do with me—with who I was inside."

"That doesn't make sense," Natalie said, getting to her feet. "You lied to me."

Ethan shook his head. "I didn't lie to you. You never asked me if I was your father. You made it clear you wanted a new father—a husband for your mother—but you didn't ask me if I was Ethan Reynolds." He spoke softly, trying to be honest yet careful. He wanted to calm her down, but her growing anger was apparent. "Natalie, I didn't say anything because I didn't want you to be hurt."

"Well, I am hurt, and I'm mad too." She stomped across the rocks to where the pastor had left Penny and the black mount.

Ethan followed quickly, not willing to let her get away from him again. He helped her up onto Penny, then noticing the lump on her forehead, thought better of it. "Maybe you should ride with me. You've hit your head

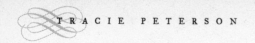

pretty hard, and I don't want you passing out."

"I'm not going to pass out." She tossed her pigtails over her shoulder and tried hard to look older than she was. "I told you, I'm not a baby."

Ethan's heart went out to her. He stood beside Penny, holding the pony in place. "Natalie, I don't blame you for being mad at me, but please listen. I didn't mean for you to be hurt in this. I wanted to talk to your mother first—to see if there was some way we could work everything out."

"Where were you all those years? Mama said you were dead. Did she lie to me too?"

Ethan felt panicked at the question. How could he explain? He certainly couldn't tell her that her grandmother had lied to him—not without making a bad situation worse. "No. Your mother had no idea until you heard her talking to me. The army had told her I was dead. She really thought I was. And remember, I thought she was dead because someone told me she'd died from the influenza. We had no idea either one was still alive, or we would have been together.

"Furthermore, I didn't know about you at all. Your mama had never told me she was going to have a baby. You know that's true—your mama told you that much." Natalie nodded but only slightly. He continued. "When I heard you talking about your father and how he died a hero in the war, and then later when you told me what your mother's name was—I couldn't believe it. It was so shocking to me that I was almost sick from it. I couldn't believe I'd lost all those years and that I had a daughter."

"But how could Mama not know it was you?"

"I don't look like I did when we married. I have glasses and a beard now. I've had a lot of surgery on my face too. Your mama might have had suspicions about me, but she didn't know until yesterday. She saw the picture I'd sketched for you. That's why I'd asked you to keep it out of sight. I knew if she saw it, she would probably know the truth, and I hadn't had a chance to talk to her yet."

"Were you really going to talk to her?" Natalie asked. She looked down at him with an expression that betrayed all of her mistrust. "Or were you going to just leave us when you were done building the hotel?"

"Natalie, I always planned to tell your mama. That day we went to the meteorite crater, I wanted to have a long talk and tell her the truth. I knew you'd be busy, with the way you like to hike around and explore. I thought while you were playing, I could tell her who I was and see what she wanted to do about it. I thought by telling her there, she couldn't run away from me and not listen. Like you did."

Natalie's frown deepened. "Then why didn't you tell her?"

"Her friends interrupted my discussion with her and I couldn't. I really wanted her to know the truth. I wanted you to know the truth too."

"It's not fair. I wanted you for my new daddy. I don't want you to be my old daddy."

"But, Natalie, I'm the same man." And in that moment, Ethan knew the truth for himself. He was the same man. The war hadn't robbed him of everything. "Natalie, I want very much for us to be a family. I want to love you and be there for you. I want to teach you about drawing and architecture. I can't turn back the hands of time, but we can make a good try at the future."

"But it changes everything," Natalie said, her voice quivering with emotion.

"Yes. Yes, it really does. You've been living a certain way all these years, and now it will change. But I'd like to think that it will be a good change."

Natalie said nothing, and Ethan could clearly see the confusion on her face. She was wrestling with this new status—with the truth of who he was. She looked at him oddly for a moment, scrutinizing him as if seeing him for the first time.

"You aren't the way I thought you'd be. My mama told me stories about you and her. You aren't like she described."

"No, I don't imagine so. I look different . . . and I'm a different person inside," Ethan admitted.

"Now I won't get to have my picture taken with the veterans," she said, looking away.

Ethan thought he saw tears in her eyes but decided not to make any comment about them. "Natalie, you're still one very important little girl. Your mother loves you and so do I."

"But people are going to treat me different. With you alive, it changes everything."

Ethan wasn't sure he understood her comment, but he did realize the change in her life was more than a little upsetting. Natalie desperately needed to figure out how to make sense of this situation. She needed to know how she would fit in once everything was out in the open.

She looked at him, and this time he could see the tears. "People won't care about me anymore. They only loved me 'cause my daddy was a war hero."

"I seriously doubt that, Natalie." Ethan reached up to touch her cheek. "I think they love you because you're you—a sweet, wonderful little girl. Don't think them so shallow to only care about you because of what I did in the war."

"Can we go home?" she asked, wiping her nose with the back of her hand.

Ethan nodded. "Sure."

He took up the reins and mounted his horse. They rode toward Winslow in silence. How, he wondered, could he make this better for her? Should he try harder to explain? Should he stay out of the picture until Natalie and Ashley had a chance to work through the situation for themselves?

"I don't feel good," Natalie said, breaking the silence.

Ethan pulled up alongside Natalie. She looked pale. "Give me Penny's reins."

He wrapped the reins around the saddle horn, then reached out to take hold of Natalie. "I'll hold you in front of me, and then if you feel sick you won't fall off."

She nodded and willingly went to him. Ethan pulled her close and wrapped his arms around her. Every protective instinct in him took over. He wanted to shelter her from all the hurts in the world. He wanted to snap his fingers and make her feel better.

"You won't let Penny get away, will you?" she asked, leaning her head against his chest.

"Nope . . . and I won't let you get away either."

CHAPTER TWENTY-FOUR

*A*shley moved through the day in a leaden manner. Food had no taste; the air felt stale and lifeless. She could focus on nothing but Natalie. But already it was nearly three and still no word.

Lavelle had taken herself off to church after Ashley's outbursts earlier. She told Ashley she hoped to answer any questions that friends of Grandpa Whitman might have regarding the funeral and also stave off the curiosity of those who wondered why Natalie ran away.

Ashley's mother had locked herself upstairs and hadn't bothered to reappear until around noon, when she descended the stairs and partook of a cup of coffee. Her demeanor had changed. Surprisingly, she was very quiet. She asked about Natalie, then had the good graces to say nothing more when Ashley had replied that her daughter was still missing. After that, Leticia had taken herself back upstairs. Ashley had been delighted not to have to deal with her.

Lavelle checked in shortly after Leticia's appearance, then announced she was going to walk around the town and see if she could learn anything about

Natalie. Ashley felt completely abandoned, yet at the same time, she knew she could bear the hours better on her own than in trying to make senseless conversation while her heart and mind were elsewhere.

Working in the kitchen, Ashley decided to bake a batch of Natalie's favorite sugar cookies. The deed made her feel more confident that Natalie would be found safe and returned home before she spent another night in the desert.

Ashley was just retrieving the first batch when her mother reappeared in the kitchen. She was dressed in her going-out suit, a dress and jacket of dark purple, trimmed in black braid. Her hat was perched to one side, her gloves were in her hands, and her pocketbook hung from her left arm.

"Are you going somewhere?" Ashley questioned, knowing it was too late for church.

"I'm moving into the Harvey House. I've arranged for them to pick up my things later this afternoon."

Ashley stared openmouthed at her mother. She couldn't help it. To hear her mother's declaration without snide comment or cruel remark was totally out of character.

"I know you're surprised," Leticia said, looking at her daughter with an expression that seemed to suggest regret. "I don't wish to further grieve you."

"Why this sudden change of heart?" Ashley asked. She went back to the task at hand and began removing the cookies from the pan. She could scarcely believe her mother's civility.

"You did make the request and it is your home," she said rather sternly. "Besides, I plan to leave immediately following Father's funeral on Wednesday. I might as well be near the train station."

Ashley couldn't stand it. She had to know why her mother was suddenly acting so genteel. She put the pan down and turned around. "Mother, why? This isn't your style. I don't understand. You had plans to fight me for this house and to change Grandpa's funeral and make a big issue out of the settlement of his estate. Now you sound as though you have accepted it all."

"I have accepted it," Leticia replied. "I know when to leave a thing alone. Father made certain provisions, and those provisions, if altered, will bring about consequences that I'm not willing to pay. Not that I'd have it to pay—not now."

Ashley still didn't know what to make of her mother's new attitude. "You aren't usually given to walking away from a fight. Why this time? Why now?"

Her mother's expression grew harsh. "It's really none of your concern what I do. You made that choice long ago."

All of Ashley's defenses rose to the occasion. "No, you made it for me," she replied. "I wasn't of a mind to never see you again. You're the one who told me to never come back—that I was dead to you. You turned your back on me when I needed you most."

"You ruined the plans your father and I had. Plans that we needed for the benefit of the family."

Ashley had never truly understood this. "Why?"

Her mother looked uncomfortable. "It's water under the bridge now and none of your business."

"It is my business," Ashley insisted. "It forever

changed my life and that of my child. I feel I'm entitled to know."

Leticia looked away and cleared her throat. "We needed your marriage to the Manchester family. We had arranged it in a somewhat tentative agreement; then you up and married Ethan Reynolds." She looked back at Ashley. "Your father suffered a tremendous financial setback because of that. I had to cancel our European plans and fire two housemaids in order to trim our budget."

"I had no idea." Ashley hadn't realized her actions had made any real impact on the family.

"Your father had to sell some investments in order to keep your brothers in college. Of course, Mathias had landed a solid job with the bank, but the other two would need help in setting up their livelihoods once they finished their degrees. It wasn't an easy time, but your father forbade me to say anything to you about it." She lifted her chin defiantly. "I thought when your husband died that this was a reprieve for us. I began to immediately set plans in motion to revive the original agreement. It might have worked too, but you refused to even consider it."

"I was carrying Ethan's baby. What man of social standing was going to overlook that little bit of information?" Ashley asked matter-of-factly. Some of the bitterness faded from her heart.

"I didn't know about that. You only mentioned being unable to love again. That was nonsense in my book. Many women marry without benefit of love. I did. I saw no reason for you not to do the same."

"But had I known you were motivated out of need, rather than mere greed—"

"You would have acted no differently," her mother interrupted. "You and I both know that. You were lost in your grief and pain, and you cared nothing for mine."

Ashley knew it was true. It pricked at her conscience. *Forgive her,* that still, small voice whispered deep from within.

"I'm sorry, Mother. I truly am. You're absolutely right. I was very self-absorbed those days. When you told me you wanted nothing more to do with me, I convinced myself that I wanted nothing more to do with you as well. Grandpa always wanted me to contact you and let you know our whereabouts, but I wouldn't do it, nor would I let him. He'd told me how you'd treated him— how you'd demanded your inheritance and how he gave up trying to reason with you. I've never understood how you could have done that."

Her mother twisted her gloves. "I have no need to justify myself to you. There were reasons for my decisions. Reasons that I never expected you, a mere child, to understand."

"Maybe I'd understand them now."

"Be that as it may, I've no desire to discuss it."

Ashley shrugged. "No, I don't suppose you do." She felt her own anger stirred. *How can I forgive her when she acts like this? She doesn't feel she's done anything wrong. She just goes on and on about how things were ruined for her— never mind how she ruined things for other people.* "You've never felt you needed to explain anything you said or did. Grandpa didn't understand it, and neither did I. So we did as you demanded and took ourselves out of your life. You made your choice and it was my choice to see that you lived up to the full impact of that decision."

Leticia stiffened. "You needn't sound so smug. Your father died a broken man because of those choices."

Ashley hadn't really considered how her father might have dealt with her disappearance. She didn't like to think of him pining for her.

"He hired detectives, but the trail went cold around St. Louis."

Ashley remembered there had been some problems with her train in St. Louis. She had to change three times before she was finally sent on to Kansas City. There again, she changed trains and was given the wrong reservation for a different Mrs. Reynolds. She had ended up in Dallas, Texas, instead of Los Angeles. It hadn't been an easy trip for an expectant mother.

"You made me believe he was of the same heart and mind as you were. It was never my desire that Father should suffer."

"But it was your desire that I should suffer?" her mother questioned.

Ashley knew there was no sense in lying. "Yes. Just as it was your intention to make me suffer when you told Ethan I was dead."

Leticia nodded. "I suppose, then, we're somewhat even."

Now Ashley felt nothing but regret. Her heart ached at the thought of all those lost years. And now her daughter might be lost to her as well.

"I don't care about being even. I care about . . ." Ashley fell silent. What did she care about? Her daughter and Ethan, of course. But what else? Did she want to mend this fence between herself and her mother? Did she care whether her mother walked out the door to go stay at the Harvey House?

With a deep sigh, Ashley shook her head. "It isn't important." She turned back to the bowl of cookie dough. *Forgive her. Let the past go.* God nudged her conscience again. Sighing, Ashley knew what she had to do. For a moment she wrestled with the idea, then finally spoke before she could change her mind.

"You may stay here until you leave. If you want to."

Her mother said nothing for a few minutes, and Ashley refused to turn around. *That's the best I can do, God. It's the only step I can make right now. I'm trying to forgive her—I'm really trying.*

Her mother's silence was unnerving, but instead of forcing the issue, Ashley spooned the dough onto the pan and waited for some sort of response. She was ready to put the cookies in the oven before her mother finally replied.

"I'll stay here, then. Lavelle and I can visit some more, and we can be here when Natalie returns."

Ashley turned at this. She looked at her mother's expression. She had masked all emotion, lest she be too vulnerable—Ashley knew that trick very well. She tried to think of a proper response, but a knock on the front door drew her attention instead.

"Natalie!"

Ashley ran through the house and threw open the door. Pastor McGuire stood there, hat in hand. The grin on his face instantly dispelled her first fears. "Ethan has found her. She's safe and should arrive shortly. I can't stay, as I'm getting the word out to the marshal and his men."

Ashley hugged the surprised man and tears poured from her face as she stepped back. "Where was she?"

"Clear Creek, just like you suspected. You know her very well." He tipped his hat and hurried back down the sidewalk. "Ethan's bringing her home. They shouldn't be far behind."

Ashley clutched her hands together. *Natalie is safe. She will be home soon.* Putting her hand to her forehead, Ashley looked first down the street in one direction and then the other. Nothing. Just Pastor McGuire making his way at a rapid pace to the east.

Remembering her baking and fearing that it might already be burning, Ashley moved back to the kitchen. She was surprised to find her mother pulling the pan of golden sugar cookies from the oven.

"Thank you," she stated, not at all sure how to deal with her mother. Anger had been the officiator at every adult conversation up until now. The art of forgiving was an unknown factor between them.

"I couldn't see letting the house fill with smoke." Her mother's barriers were all back in place. Ashley would have smiled if not for the fact she knew it would annoy her mother. For all her life, Ashley had never seen the woman do anything this domestic.

"That was Pastor McGuire. He said that Ethan found Natalie and that she's all right. They should be here soon."

"I'm glad, Ashley," her mother said. Then after depositing the cookies, she put the potholders aside.

"Ashley!" Lavelle called. She rushed through the

house to the kitchen and took hold of Ashley's arm. "I just heard that they've found Natalie."

Ashley smiled. "Yes. Yes, they did and she's safe."

"Oh, that is good news," Lavelle replied. "Is it not, sister?"

Leticia eyed Ashley and Lavelle with a blank expression. "I've already told her I was glad. Now I wish to go rest."

"Rest? But you look as if you're ready to go out," Lavelle commented.

"Nevertheless, I'm going to go rest."

Leticia pushed past them without another word. Ashley shook her head. "I've just had the strangest conversation with her. She was actually quite open for a few moments. Now she appears just as she always has. Hard and unreachable."

Lavelle patted her arm. "Give her time, Ashley. This transition will not be easy for her, and she may even decide not to make it at all."

"I just don't understand why she is suddenly willing to even consider it."

Lavelle shrugged. "It's hard to tell, and with Letty, I'm sure we won't receive an explanation. Perhaps upon losing Father, she's come to realize life is too short to act in such a cruel manner. Maybe her conscience is getting the better of her. We've prayed she might come to understand the truth—perhaps in time she will."

Ashley stared past Lavelle and through the dining area. "Even this morning, when I said what I did about her disdaining God . . . I'm ashamed to admit it but I meant the words, Lavelle. Isn't that awful? How could I

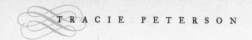

say something so hideous and still expect God to love me?"

Lavelle reached out and hugged Ashley close. "Child, we all do awful things. We fail to care when we should and we worry too much when we oughtn't. Don't forget to forgive yourself as you work on learning to forgive her."

Ashley pulled away. "I'll try to remember that."

A noise at the front of the house caught her attention, and Ashley rushed to the front door and found Ethan dismounting a tall black horse. He wrapped the reins around her fence post, then took Natalie—their precious daughter—in his arms and carried her up the walkway.

"Oh, Natalie!" Ashley cried as she crossed the distance to greet them. She sobbed as she reached out to touch her daughter's face. Immediately she spied the lump on her forehead and the cuts. "Oh, you're hurt." Ashley's tears flowed in torrents.

"I'm sorry, Mama. I didn't mean to make you cry." Natalie looked as if she might burst into tears herself. "Please don't cry."

"Oh, sweetie, I can't help it. I'm so happy to have you home. Ethan, I'll take her. Would you see to Penny and send for the doctor?"

"Doctor's already on his way," Ethan replied. "I'll carry Natalie up to her bed and then tend to the horses."

Ashley nodded and opened the door for them. Ethan took the stairs quickly with Ashley right on his heels. Lavelle only smiled at them as they passed by.

Ethan gently placed Natalie on the bed and turned

to leave the room. Ashley was standing only inches behind him, however, and the movement caused him to reach out to her in order to balance himself. Ashley felt an electrical charge surge through her body at his touch, but she tried to appear calm and collected.

"Sorry," he murmured.

"Don't be," Ashley said, looking deep into his eyes. "Thank you, Ethan. Thank you for finding her." She reached her arms around his neck and hugged him close. At first Ethan stood like a statue, refusing to hold her, but after she held on to him for several moments, he finally returned her embrace.

She finally let him go, but not without placing a kiss upon his bearded face. *Who was this man—her husband? Would they have a future? Could they remake their life together?* The questions overwhelmed her, threatening to steal her focus from what she needed to do for the moment.

"Let me get a basin of water and we'll clean you up," Ashley said, looking back to where her daughter lay. Natalie watched her with a worried frown, but Ashley ignored it and went quickly to work.

Returning with the basin and a washcloth and towel, Ashley began stripping away the grime and dust from her daughter's face and arms.

"I was so afraid," she said, her voice full of emotion. "I thought I might have lost you forever. I couldn't believe you were gone."

"I'm sorry. I was afraid too," Natalie admitted.

Ashley tenderly washed her daughter's cuts and scratches. "What happened to get you this lump?"

"I fell off of Penny." She came quickly to the pony's defense. "It wasn't her fault. I was riding her too close to the rocks. She misstepped and I fell and hit my head."

Ashley nodded. "I'm sure Penny was upset by the situation just as you were."

"Mama, did you know that Mr. Carson was really my daddy? I mean before you went to talk to him yesterday?"

Ashley straightened. "No, Natalie. I honestly didn't. There were things about him that reminded me of your daddy, but I thought he was forever lost to us—after all, the government said he was dead. I didn't figure they made mistakes. I never gave it a single thought that he might be alive."

Natalie bit at her lip, then questioned, "So are we going to be a family now?"

Ashley had no idea what to say, but she longed to know her daughter's heart. "What would you like?"

"I don't know." Natalie's voice sounded so frightened and lost.

Ashley hugged her daughter close. "Don't worry. You don't have to know. We'll pray and ask God to show us the right way."

"But I did pray, see," Natalie said, pulling away. "I prayed for God to send me a daddy just like my old one. Only instead of one like my old daddy . . ."

"He sent your real daddy—alive and well," Ashley filled in.

Natalie nodded. "And that changes everything."

Ashley gently laid her daughter back on the bed. "Why? Why does it change everything?" She needed desperately to understand her daughter's fears.

"Because it's not the same. I won't be the same

person. Everybody's so nice to me because my daddy was a war hero."

"He's still a war hero, Natalie."

"Yes, but they thought he was dead."

Ashley shrugged. "We all did. Why does that change anything?"

Natalie shook her head. "I don't know." Exasperation filled her voice. "It's just different. I don't know what's going to happen."

Ashley was rather surprised by her daughter's reaction. "I suppose what will happen is that we'll all talk together and figure out what God has planned for us. Seems like God wouldn't have brought us all together if He hadn't meant for us to stay that way, though."

"Will they still let me decorate the graves of the veterans? Will I get to ride in the parades on Decoration Day?"

Ashley suddenly realized the heart of the situation. Her daughter's identity was at stake. "I'm sure they will, Natalie. As I said, you're still the daughter of a great war hero. Your daddy saved the lives of hundreds of men by risking his own life. But you know what?"

Natalie shook her head.

"I imagine," Ashley continued, "that the men who went out to look for you today—all those veterans who think so highly of you and took their Sunday to go out across the desert as part of the search party—won't care if your daddy is alive or not. They just love you because of who you are. They love you just for being Natalie Reynolds."

"That's what Mr. Car . . ." She frowned and drew a deep breath. "That's what Daddy said."

Ashley smiled. "He was always a very smart man."

Natalie seemed to ponder her words for a moment before adding, "He's a nice man too."

"Yes, he is. He's very nice."

The doctor came and pronounced Natalie no worse for the wear. He admonished her for giving the town a fright and suggested she just might have to share her sugar cookies with him. She in turn told her mother to be sure to share her cookies with the doctor. Which Ashley did quite happily.

The doctor had gone and Ashley was tucking Natalie into bed when her mother came into the room unannounced.

"So what did the doctor say?" her mother asked rather gruffly.

Natalie eyed her grandmother with a worrisome frown while Ashley took up the plate of cookie crumbs. "He said she's fine, but she should rest."

"I see." Leticia looked as if she might like to say something more, then turned to go. Stopping just outside the door, she turned back around. "I'm glad you're all right, Natalie." She exited then as quickly as she'd come.

Ashley looked at her daughter and smiled. "I think that was Grandmother's way of saying she loves you. But don't tell her you know," she said in a whisper. "She'd rather people think her strong and capable of doing everything without having to love anybody at all." Natalie giggled and Ashley thought she'd never heard a more pleasant sound in all her life.

CHAPTER TWENTY-FIVE

*W*ednesday afternoon the friends and family of Russell Whitman filed into Faith Mission Church to pay their last respects. Ashley was pleased to see such a large turnout. She'd known her grandfather was well loved, but it warmed her heart to see the proof. Grandpa wouldn't have wanted them to be maudlin and downcast, but rather he would have wanted a sense of celebration. He had gone to a better place, and therefore his last wishes had been that there would be laughter and positive stories about his life.

Ashley couldn't help getting a little teary at times, however. Pastor McGuire did a wonderful job of speaking on Grandpa's life. Several times he mentioned Grandpa's generosity to the townspeople, and Ashley glanced back slightly to see nods of affirmation.

Over and over she looked at the shiny pine casket where Grandpa's body lay. The casket remained closed, as was Grandpa's wish, but Ashley's mother and aunt had paid for a huge spray of white carnations and red roses to be placed upon it. Ashley had remembered Grandpa's wish for no flowers, so she had talked to

Natalie, and they'd agreed they would purchase a plant instead and keep it alive in memory of Grandpa. Natalie asked if she could keep the plant in her room, and Ashley had agreed.

Oh, Grandpa, you'll be so missed, Ashley thought. *So many times I think of things I'd like to say to you. I'd like to have your advice about Ethan and about Mother. . . . You would be so good with explaining about forgiveness and how to keep from being bitter about the past. And you'd keep me from losing my temper with Mother. I know I can pray now and talk to God, but having you here was much more comforting.*

He's only gone from earth, Ashley reminded herself. *He's in heaven, healthy and well, with a new body.* It pained her to think of how the sickness had ravaged him. He'd wasted away to nothing, and Ashley knew he didn't want to be remembered that way. She found herself fighting to block those images. It had been hard to lose Grandpa, but it would have been harder still to see him linger with the cancer.

Ashley reached out and squeezed her daughter's hand. *Thank you, Lord, that she's here and safe. Thank you that we're not having two funerals.* The thought caused Ashley to shudder. How tragic it could have all been. She knew God had looked out for her child, but still the memories caused her grief. *But what if there's a next time?* Ashley knew they were in for a long journey together before they'd ever feel like a true family. What if Natalie could never accept Ethan as her father? What if she ran away again?

Oh, Lord, help us. It's so hard for Natalie to understand what's happened. It's hard for me to understand as well. I'm so new to this whole thing of faith. Do you love me less if I find it hard to trust you? For so many years, I'd convinced myself you didn't care. I feel like a scared child, wanting to trust and believe that it will all be well . . . but knowing from experience that bad things could still come my way.

Ashley looked past Natalie to Ethan. She wondered if he struggled with the future as much as she did. They were married. They would celebrate their twelfth anniversary in the spring. Twelve years of marriage . . . and only a few months of actually being together.

Folks probably wondered why he had joined them in the family pew. Then again, gossip had no trouble making the rounds in Winslow. By now there were bound to be many folks who knew the truth and just as many who'd embellished the truth. Sooner or later they'd know for sure what had happened. Especially if Marcus Greeley had anything to do about it. He still planned to write his book, and now more than ever, he had plans for devoting a thick chapter to Ethan and all that had happened.

Ethan. Ashley still couldn't believe Ethan was truly here. It all seemed so much like a dream. Sometimes she was completely convinced she would wake up at home and find Grandpa still alive and well and that the events of the past few months had been nothing more than her imagination working overtime.

"Russell Whitman will be sorely missed," Pastor McGuire said. His words pulled Ashley's attention away from her worries. He continued. "I myself will miss our games of checkers and chess, our walks and discussions, and the humorous way Russell had of looking at life. But most of all, I'll miss his faith. Grandpa Whitman was a man of such deep conviction and faith that he put most of us to shame."

Ashley noticed her mother shift in her seat, as if the words were entirely too much to bear. Lavelle sat beside her and reached over to pat her sister's hand as if understanding her discomfort.

"Whenever I had a problem and needed counsel, I went to Russell. One of the first things I could expect him to ask me was this: 'Sean, do you believe God can take care of this problem?' "

Ashley heard a few chuckles. No doubt more than one person had been faced with this same question. She herself had been asked that by Grandpa. Most of the time she *didn't* think God would take care of the problem. It wasn't a matter of whether or not He *could* take care of it—she just didn't believe that He would.

I'm sorry, God. I wish I'd come to know you sooner. I wish I'd listened more to Grandpa. Ashley felt tears come to her eyes and wiped at them with the hanky she'd remembered to tuck into her sleeve.

"Sometimes I told Russell I knew God *could* take care of the problem. I just didn't know if He *would*."

Ashley startled at the pastor's words. Sean McGuire looked at her and smiled, as if knowing her thoughts. Ashley felt her face grow flushed and lowered her gaze to her gloved hands.

"Russell would just laugh and tell me I wasn't being honest with him. He'd say, 'Sean, I know you believe He will resolve the problem—you're worried, however, that He might not solve it your way.' "

Most everyone laughed, and even Ashley had to smile. Pastor McGuire continued, his voice taking on a great deal of emotion. "Russell Whitman knew the right thing to say to get my eyes off myself and back on God. I think that's what he'd also ask of us today. He'd not want our focus to be on him and all that he'd done for us. Russell would want our focus on the Lord and what He did for us. Russell would want us to remember that it was only because of God that he was the man he was."

Ashley knew it was true. She listened to Pastor Mc-Guire conclude the service and felt at peace. Grandpa was in a better place and happier than he could have ever been here on earth. She needed to remember that. She also needed to remember that Grandpa's illness and Ethan's appearance in Winslow had not taken God by surprise. God knew the way things would play out.

They were escorted from the front pews, with two elders from the church offering their support to Lavelle and Leticia. To her surprise, Ashley watched her mother dab tears from her eyes before accepting the man's offer. Maybe a little of the ice had thawed.

That day in the kitchen had been so strange to Ashley. She had never seen her mother act in such a way. At one moment she wanted to open her heart, and in the next breath she'd be angry and hostile. Still, Ashley knew her mother a little better for the telling of her tale. It didn't make things right between them, but it was a start. Perhaps it would take months or even years for her mother to figure out the truth for herself. Maybe she would never be warm and affectionate, but at least she could learn that Ashley and Natalie and even Ethan weren't the enemies in her life.

Ethan took hold of her arm and guided Ashley out to follow her mother and aunt. Natalie had stepped aside to bring up the rear and walked beside Pastor McGuire. The sunlight seemed rather diffused in the November setting. Soon Thanksgiving and Christmas would be upon them, and sometime between those two events, the Harvey hotel construction was to be completed. Ashley wondered what it would mean for Ethan and his job duties.

He'd implied that he intended to be there for them—that he wanted to be a family again. But once Mary Colter took her entourage and moved on to the next Harvey job, would Ethan feel the tug to move along as well? By his own admission, he'd never settled into one place for long since coming back from the war.

She looked up and found Ethan watching her. She fixed her gaze on him, trying to will unspoken answers from his heart. He nodded and looked away as if telling her he had no answers to give. It made her feel even more doubtful of what would happen next.

The ladies of the church had set up a meal for Ashley and her family at the house. Pastor McGuire offered to drive them home while Grandpa's coffin was being loaded in the hearse and taken to the train station. Lavelle would catch the afternoon westbound train and escort her father's body back to Los Angeles. Ashley frowned at the thought. *He'll be so far away. Why couldn't we just bury him here? At least then I could visit his grave and put flowers on the stone.*

But it was Grandpa's last wish, she chided herself, knowing she sounded more like her mother than she wanted to admit. It was Grandpa's desires—not her own or her mother's—they needed to honor. After all, he would be buried next to Grandma, and Ashley knew that was only fitting.

They crowded into the car, Ashley's mother taking a place up front with the pastor and his wife, while Ethan, Ashley, and Lavelle rode in back. Natalie sat on Ethan's lap, as it seemed the only alternative. She didn't seem bothered by the arrangement; in fact, Ashley thought Natalie looked rather content.

Ashley smiled at her daughter. Her bruised forehead wasn't quite so visible after they'd restyled her hair to give her bangs. And Natalie seemed at ease with Ethan, but there was still a hesitation in the way she interacted with him.

Time. Ashley knew it would take time. Time for Natalie to adjust her thinking and accept Ethan as her father rather than Mr. Carson the architect. Time for them to become a family.

And what about the time you need? she asked herself. *Ethan has changed. He told you so and now you've seen it for yourself.* The idea of being a wife again was both terrifying and thrilling. She could easily find herself quite content to keep house for this man—her husband.

"Do you need me to come drive you to the station this afternoon?" Pastor McGuire questioned Lavelle as they climbed out of the car a few minutes later.

"No, Ethan has offered to walk over and borrow one of the Harvey cars. He's going to drive me."

Pastor McGuire smiled. "It's been a real pleasure to get to know you, Mrs. Guzman. I hope you have a safe journey back to Los Angeles."

"Thank you, Pastor. You did a wonderful job on the eulogy. I know my father would have approved."

"Yes," Ashley added, "Grandpa would have said you did it just right." She reached out her hand. Pastor McGuire shook it vigorously.

"See you in church on Sunday?"

"Absolutely," Ashley replied. She put her arm around Natalie's shoulders and led her to the house.

"Hmmm, it smells good in here," Natalie declared, immediately going to investigate the meal.

Ethan and Ashley followed at a slowed pace while Lavelle and Ashley's mother walked behind them. Ashley wondered if her mother would comment on the service. So far she'd said very little, and Ashley couldn't help wondering if the words had made any sort of impact in her mother's heart.

The ladies from the church finished putting the food on the table just as they entered the dining room. "Look, Mama. Fried chicken," Natalie said, coming to her mother. She looked up at her mother and then at Ethan. "My mama loves fried chicken."

Ethan nodded, as if this bit of news was an important fact to remember. Ashley smiled. "I certainly do."

They took their seats and as the food was passed around, Natalie again interjected a comment. "Don't give the lima beans to Mama. She hates those." She stated this again for Ethan's benefit.

Ashley quickly realized her daughter was trying to help Ethan get to know who Ashley was. It seemed rather funny that after having Natalie play matchmaker, now she would act as guide and interpreter to help Ethan better know his own wife. Maybe in doing this little deed Natalie was also better able to adjust to the situation herself. Ashley wouldn't have put it past the child to fully comprehend what she was doing and to meticulously plan it out for everyone's benefit.

The meal soon passed and it was time to take Lavelle to the station. Ethan had gone to borrow Mary Colter's car and had just pulled up in front of the house when Lavelle came downstairs with Leticia close behind.

"Sister is going to accompany me," Lavelle told Ashley. She'd already mentioned to Ashley that she'd like to have some privacy with her sister. Ashley had agreed she'd remain behind when the time came to go to the train station.

"Oh, I'm glad. I wasn't going to be able to get away," Ashley said. "I've some things I'd like to take care of. I hope you don't mind if I stay here."

"Not at all," Lavelle replied and hugged Ashley close. "Thank you," she whispered in her niece's ear.

Ashley kissed her aunt on the cheek and bid her farewell. Natalie did likewise, then announced that she was going to go tend to Penny. Leticia, in her dark purple suit, looked at Ashley for a moment, then returned her concentration to the front door. Ashley wasn't sure if her mother had intended to say something about the pony or Natalie or if she'd wanted to comment on another matter altogether. Whatever it had been, she said nothing instead.

"Are you ready to go?" Ethan questioned as he came through the door and spied Lavelle.

"I am. If you would be so kind as to retrieve my trunk, I'd be most grateful."

Ethan nodded and bounded up the stairs, taking them two at a time. Within a moment he was heading back down, the black trunk on his shoulder. He headed

out the door and Lavelle turned again to Ashley.

"I promise to visit you in the spring, and you remember your promise to come see me in the summer. Natalie will love the ocean."

Ashley could well imagine her daughter wanting to remain in Los Angeles for that feature, if nothing else.

"I won't forget," Ashley replied. And if Ethan had no objections, Ashley fully intended to see her promise through.

––––––

Ethan was glad to see that Lavelle had worked out getting Ashley and Natalie to stay home. He had plans for talking to Leticia in private and hadn't been at all sure how to go about it. He drove the two ladies to the station, listening to them comment on the future. The uncertainty of the financial world was still of grave concern to Leticia Murphy. She had little understanding of exactly how bad things might be once she returned home. He hated to see anyone suffer, but his heart was rather scarred where this woman was concerned. He didn't want to hold a grudge or treat her with indifference, but she needed to understand his position and that he would no longer allow her to interfere in his life or Ashley's and Natalie's.

They arrived at the station and Ethan made arrangements for Lavelle's luggage while Leticia bid her goodbye. Returning to where the two older women stood waiting, Ethan said, "I'm glad for the opportunity to have gotten to know you, Mrs. Guzman."

"As am I. You are a miracle. Without a doubt. I know this is all going to work out." She smiled and reached up to pat Ethan's cheek with her gloved hand. "Just give God time."

"That's the trick, isn't it?" he commented.

"To be sure."

Ethan glanced at the steam engine down the track. Wisps of steam escaped here and there, and the heady scent of oil, grease, and creosote filled the air. These were the smells of the railroad—an odor he'd gotten quite used to in his work with Mary Colter. Would he now leave that world and remain in Winslow to settle down and piece his family back together? Would they pick up and go elsewhere with him if that were the direction God led?

"I think I'll just wait in the car, Mrs. Murphy. That way you two can have some privacy," Ethan offered, knowing that the questions in his head would not be easily resolved standing there on the platform of the Winslow depot.

Leticia said nothing. Her façade of strength and fierceness held everyone at bay. Ethan didn't really care. He didn't need or desire a relationship with his mother-in-law, but he was bound and determined to have one with her daughter.

Walking back to the car, Ethan forced his thoughts to come into order. He replayed the speech he intended to make to Leticia. *If I don't make it clear now,* he reasoned, *she'll try to walk all over both of us.*

He waited nearly twenty minutes before Leticia returned. Without giving her a choice, Ethan went around to the front passenger door and opened it for her. Leticia didn't so much as glance at him. She stepped into the car and continued to stare straight ahead.

They were soon on their way, but when Ethan should have turned for home, instead he began to talk. "I have something to say to you," he began. "You may not be inclined to listen otherwise, so I'm making it so that you'll have to listen." He drove out of town and headed east.

"Where do you mean to take me?" Leticia questioned, her voice betraying fear.

"I only mean to drive out far enough that you can't just walk back, and then I mean to talk to you about Ashley and me."

Leticia looked at him for a moment. "I really have no desire . . ."

"I don't care. This is how it will be."

Ethan drove for nearly fifteen minutes before he felt comfortable pulling off to the side of the road. Once he was satisfied with their safety and the ability to see traffic coming from either direction, Ethan turned to Leticia.

"I don't trust you," he said firmly. "You lied and made Ashley and me most miserable." Leticia said nothing but continued to gaze out the windshield, as if there might be something of great interest outside.

"Your selfishness denied my wife and child a better life. Your lie left me grief stricken and hopeless for years on end. At one point, because I'd drawn away from God so completely, I even contemplated taking my life. Had you even bothered to consider that you might have contributed to the death of another human being?"

He didn't want to deal with her in anger, but her cold reserve chiseled away at his self-control.

"I won't let you cause this family any more harm," he finally said. This seemed to get her attention.

"Oh, and what will you do? Kill me here and now?"

Ethan shook his head. "No. I'm not going to cause you harm simply because that's *your* method. But I will do whatever it takes to protect my family. I have friends in high places now. Friends with money and power, just as you have. Both sets may be a little worse for wear given the crash, but I'll use whatever means I need to keep Ashley and Natalie safe."

"And you think you need to protect them from me?" she asked in disbelief.

"Absolutely. You were at the very heart of their pain. You told me Ashley was dead. And you allowed Ashley to go on believing I was dead."

"I had no way of finding her. Her own father had tried to locate her," Leticia said in her defense. "I couldn't have told her the truth even if I'd wanted to."

"But that's my point. You didn't want to. You wanted to keep us separated because you never thought I was good enough for your daughter. I'm just making sure this matter is clear once and for all. You will not inter-fere in our lives anymore."

"I'm Ashley's mother and I have a right to see her."

"A right you gave up a long time ago when you sent her away without a penny." He stared hard at the older woman and hoped her fidgeting was a sign of discomfort under his scrutiny. "Besides, until this moment, I've not heard you even mention wanting another chance to see her. You came to Winslow with an entirely different motive."

Leticia's shoulders rolled forward slightly. "What is it

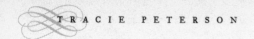

you want from me, Mr. Reynolds?"

"An understanding," Ethan said, trying to steady his temper. "I want you to be a part of Ashley and Natalie's life if that's what they desire. However, I want it on their terms." He paused and added, "And my terms." He let the words sink in for a few moments before continuing.

"If you want to spend time with them, you'll leave your fury over our marriage in the past. You'll not malign my good name, and you'll not force your opinions on my wife and child. Also, you're never to raise a hand to my child again. Do you understand?"

Leticia looked at him for a moment, her piercing eyes never so much as blinking. Then her expression seemed to soften. "I understand."

"And do you agree to those terms?"

"I suppose I must."

Ethan shook his head. "No one is forcing anything on you, Leticia. You choose to come willingly into my family or not at all. I want no moping or grudge holding. I want no false tears of martyrdom. You are the only living grandparent Natalie has. I don't know if you have other granddaughters, but she's a pretty special girl. She needs someone to look up to. What she doesn't need is someone or something else to regret."

"I understand," Leticia stated, then returned her gaze to the windshield. "I want only what I deserve."

Ethan shook his head. "No. No, you don't. Because if you were to get what you deserve, it certainly wouldn't have anything to do with Ashley and Natalie. Ashley and I were wrong to marry in the fashion we did."

This caused Leticia to turn back to him. Eyeing him with a look of disbelief, she waited for him to continue.

"I know that now," he said. "I didn't then. I was young and idealistic and foolish. The war was on and it seemed that there might not be a tomorrow. I didn't think about the consequences of anything. I fell in love with Ashley and married her—and never gave a single thought to respecting your wishes. For that I'm sorry, and I do apologize. I hope that somehow you can find it in your heart to forgive me—to forgive Ashley too."

"Well . . . I . . ." Leticia shook her head. "I find this highly unexpected."

"I don't need answers today, Mrs. Murphy. I just want you to consider everything I've said, including the fact that I want your forgiveness. I brought you out here because I wasn't sure we'd have another chance to talk alone before you headed home this evening. Just think on my words, and when you feel confident of an answer from your heart, then let me know."

He maneuvered the car back onto the road, not even waiting for the older woman to answer him. He thought long and hard about the way their conversation had gone. He'd done his best, and even though there was some anger in his words, over all, Ethan felt he'd managed the situation quite well. He could only pray that Leticia would come around to seeing things their way.

———

Later that evening, Ethan, Ashley, and Natalie stood on the depot platform bidding Leticia good-bye. It was a stilted and awkward moment for all three. Natalie was still very apprehensive of her grandmother, and Ashley had no idea what to make of her mother's attitude. Ever since that day in the kitchen, she seemed less harsh but

more reserved. Maybe God was truly doing a work in her heart. Ashley could only pray that it was true.

"Please let my brothers know where I am," she told her mother as the conductor called the final board. She was relieved to have finally learned that her brothers had all married and were raising families. Mathias had two boys, Richard had three boys and a girl, and Parker had two girls and his wife was expecting. There was an entire family out there that Ashley had no knowledge of.

"I will," her mother promised. "I'm sure they'll be pleased to know. They've never understood what happened."

"Perhaps it's time to tell them," Ashley replied.

"Perhaps." Her mother's words were thoughtful. She looked at the train car and drew a deep breath. "Mr. Reynolds, Natalie, I am glad for the opportunity to have met you both. In future visits, I shall look forward to getting to know you better." She met Ethan's gaze, and Ashley thought that something unspoken was exchanged between them.

Ashley lowered her face and smiled. It wasn't much in the realm of an apology or pledge of love, but for her mother, Ashley knew it was the best she could offer. And because of how God had dealt with her own heart of late, Ashley knew that for now, it was enough.

Leticia moved toward the train, and Ashley followed her while Ethan and Natalie remained behind.

"Mother, I'm glad you came to be with Grandpa. I know it meant the world to him."

"He would have liked it better had I told him everything he wanted to hear," Leticia replied. "But I've never been given over to religious nonsense, and I'm still not convinced it has any place in my life."

Ashley nodded. "I know. But I also know how Grandpa was about planting seeds." She smiled. "After all, he found a way to cultivate a little hope in my heart. I'm sure he was able to manage at least that much with you."

Leticia lifted her chin and looked down her nose at Ashley. It was a look Ashley would always remember her mother for, as long as they lived. "Perhaps." Then quickly changing the subject, Leticia added, "I will see you in the spring. Perhaps for your new resort opening."

Ashley nodded. "It's scheduled for May, which around here is already summer, but you're more than welcome to come. Just let us know."

"Of course, it will depend on the financial status of the country and of my own personal estate. But if things do come together in proper order, maybe your brothers and their families will accompany me."

Ashley smiled. "I'd like that. I'd like that very much."

Leticia said nothing more. She allowed the porter to assist her onto the train, then stood at the top and turned only momentarily. She exchanged a glance with Ashley, offered the tiniest of waves, then disappeared into the interior.

Ashley thought of how different this departure had been from Aunt Lavelle's. Lavelle had hugged and kissed Ashley with great affection. Leticia hadn't offered a single touch. Ashley felt sad for her mother's isolation. It was the first time she'd had that feeling rather than a

sense of her mother getting what she deserved. Smiling to herself, she pulled her jacket close and turned back to her family. The healing had truly begun.

"Let's go home," she said softly.

CHAPTER TWENTY-SIX

*A*fter sharing a sumptuous Thanksgiving meal with Pastor McGuire and his wife, Ashley and Ethan settled down in front of the fireplace, determined to talk about their future. Natalie stretched out on the floor at their feet and worked on a small weaving loom, making potholders for her mother.

Ethan had been waiting for this moment ever since Ashley suggested it. Thanksgiving seemed a good time to share their hopes for the future, and while Ethan was still uncertain as to what Ashley and Natalie wanted from him, he knew very well what he hoped for.

Clearing his throat nervously, Ethan picked lint off his navy blue suit coat, then looked down at his daughter. She was staring up at him—watching, waiting. She knew he wanted to talk to them, but Ethan wasn't at all sure what her response would be. He'd tried hard to get her to talk to him prior to this, but she wouldn't. She'd even stopped coming to the hotel where he was working.

"I suppose," he began rather awkwardly, "that you both know how important this is to me. How important

you are to me."

Neither one said a word, making it all that much harder for Ethan. "I know we're strangers in many ways. We've spent some time together and . . . well . . . we know each other a little better than when we first met." He was making a mess of things. There just didn't seem to be words for what he wanted to convey.

How did he tell his wife and daughter that he loved them, despite the years that had separated them? How did he explain that his life would be very empty if he had to go back to living without them?

"When is the hotel scheduled to be completed?" Ashley asked.

Her soft words brought Ethan out of his thoughts. "December fifteenth is when the exterior and structure should be finished. Then we're faced with a great deal of interior work. They plan to open in May, as scheduled, in spite of the stock market problems and issues of money loss. The railroad isn't doing too badly, and they believe the money they're still putting into this creation is money and time well spent," Ethan replied.

"So what are your plans? Do you intend to see it through?"

"I'd like to," Ethan replied. "I've enjoyed working for the Harvey Company."

"As have I," Ashley stated. "In fact, I intend to start back to work as soon as possible. The Christmas season is always busy, what with folks traveling all over the countryside to be with loved ones. They'll need my help."

"But you don't have to work. I'll help with the expenses and—"

Ashley held up her hand. "No. I have plenty of money. At least for now. I plan to go to work because I like it, and I don't like sitting around here with nothing but my memories. Natalie will be in school all day, and that's when I shall work. They'll allow that schedule because I'm one of their best Harvey Girls," she said, smiling.

"Mama really is," Natalie added, as if Ethan needed convincing.

Ethan nodded. "I'm quite sure she puts them all to shame."

Natalie smiled and went back to her weaving. Ethan looked at Ashley and tried to regain control of what he had planned to say. There seemed no other way to open the discussion but to simply put his thoughts out there for everyone's scrutiny.

"I'd like for us to be a family."

Natalie and Ashley both looked at him. They seemed quite content to await his explanation on the matter. Ethan felt as if the tie around his neck were tightening. *Lord, don't let me make a mess of this.*

"I know we have a ways to go in getting to know each other, but I already love you both," Ethan said, feeling embarrassed by the words. He'd never been given over to his emotions—at least not like this. But then again, he'd never had so much at stake.

"The years that separated us weren't of our own doing—not entirely. We can't change what happened back then, but we can change what happens from this point on."

"I think we all want the same thing," Ashley said, smiling.

Ethan saw the love in her eyes and knew deep within his heart that she did indeed desire the same thing he did. Glancing at Natalie, he saw her expression was pretty much unreadable.

"I'd like to set up a design firm here in Winslow if you're both of a mind to go on living here. If not, we can easily move elsewhere. I like it here, though. The people are pleasant and good-natured, and the desert is beautiful in its own way. Still, I'll happily go to the ends of the earth if it means we can be a family."

He didn't see any change in his daughter's face. He'd so hoped she'd at least smile or give him some sign that his words met with her approval. "I'd like to teach you everything I know about drawing and design," he said to Natalie. "You are very talented and I see great promise. I believe with dedication to your dream of becoming an architect, you and I could one day have the best father-daughter team around."

Natalie perked up at this and sat up. "Would we have an office and everything? Would I have my own drawing table?"

Ethan chuckled. "Absolutely. You'd have whatever you needed to make you the very best architect."

"That would be the bee's knees," Natalie declared.

"Natalie, where in the world did you pick up that expression?" Ashley questioned.

Natalie laughed. "Jane says it all the time and so do my other friends." She glanced at the clock and gathered up her things. "I need to go give Penny her treat."

"Don't be long," Ashley said. "We've still got a lot to talk about."

Natalie nodded and slipped away, humming. Ashley

turned to Ethan, her eyes wide with question. He wanted to lose himself in her dark-eyed gaze.

"Ashley, I know I'm not the same man you married. I don't even look like that man," Ethan said, stroking his well-trimmed beard. "I'm still going to struggle from time to time with nightmares from the war—and while my walk with God is growing stronger, it's still very young."

"As is mine," Ashley said, reaching out to take hold of his hand. "But at least we can share that walk."

Ethan turned toward her and gripped her hand tightly. "Ashley, I want a new life for us. I want to court you again—this time without the desperation of war looming over us, making us act irresponsibly and hastily."

"Do you regret our haste?" she asked, frowning.

"No, of course not. I wouldn't trade the time we had together for all the architectural jobs in the world. I loved you dearly, as I do now. That will only grow stronger with time."

"I love you as well," she whispered. "I never stopped. People thought me troubled because I refused to remarry or consider anyone else. But there was a part of me that couldn't let go of you—even across the years."

He nodded knowingly. "It was the same for me. I knew I couldn't bring you back from the dead, and yet you were all I wanted."

"I felt the same way," Ashley assured him.

"I want us to remarry," he said, surprising himself. "But only after we have time to get to know each other again and to help Natalie adjust. There's no need to rush this time. There's no war—no family working against us."

"I'd like that very much," Ashley said, leaning closer. She reached up and gently touched his bearded cheek. "I've dreamed of this moment for so many years. I'd cry for joy because you had come back to me. Then I'd wake up and cry in sorrow because I saw the truth of it in the morning light."

Ethan pressed her hand against his face and held it there. "You were all that kept me alive on the battlefield. I would think of you and know that I had to go on—that I had to come back. Then when I was wounded, I held on to your image and my faith that God would bring us back together."

His chest tightened and he reached out and pulled Ashley into his arms. "I cannot tell you, nor do I need to, how much it hurt to think you dead."

"I know. I know exactly."

Their faces were only inches apart, and Ethan knew he would kiss her. He only hoped that she desired it as much as he did. He leaned closer.

"Ashley?" He spoke her name as a question. He wanted permission to kiss her.

She closed the distance between them and for the first time in eleven years, they shared a kiss. The longing in Ethan's heart threatened to smother out all other thought. He pulled her closer, held her tighter. *I don't want this to ever end,* he thought.

Ashley gave herself completely—deepening their kiss, wrapping her arms tightly around his neck. Ethan had never known such joy and peace. He finally pulled back just a bit and saw the tears that streamed down her face. The sight shocked him, and he let go of her rather abruptly.

"You're crying."

She opened her eyes and smiled. "For the joy of this moment. For the way I still feel when you touch me. For the promise of our new future together."

He gently touched her wet cheek. "I've never known happiness until this moment. The past no longer seems important."

"I was reading something in the Bible. It was in the forty-third chapter of Isaiah. It said, 'Remember ye not the former things, neither consider the things of old. Behold, I will do a new thing; now it shall spring forth; shall ye not know it? I will even make a way in the wilderness, and rivers in the desert.' This is God's 'new thing,'" Ashley said softly. "I see that now. We don't need to remember the former things. They're gone. We can't reclaim the years we've lost or make my mother take back her words that so damaged us both. But we can look to the new thing God is doing."

Ethan murmured her words. "A river in the desert. How appropriate that seems."

"I thought so too. Ethan, I'm not the same girl you married in 1918. Just as your appearance is altered, so is mine. And just as the nightmares and scars of the past have damaged and wounded your heart, so my heart has suffered as well.

"We aren't children anymore. We can't be wild and impetuous. We can't run away from the world and hope it will never find us. I'm willing, however, to risk my heart with you. I want to move forward and trust God for His new creation in our lives. I will court you and I will remarry you, for I have no intention of ever letting anything come between us again. Not people or wars or time."

Ethan hugged her close and knew she could probably hear the wild beating of his heart. It didn't matter. They were together. They were home.

Ethan heard the back door open and close but remained where he was. Natalie came back into the room, pausing momentarily by the door. Ethan looked over Ashley's shoulder at his daughter, wondering if he'd see resentment on her face.

"Do I get a hug too?" she asked, looking as though she felt left out.

Ethan grinned. "You can have as many hugs as you want." He opened his arms to her and Natalie rushed to join them. She giggled as Ethan pulled her tight, smashing her between him and her mother.

Ethan knew the time had come to press his question. "Natalie, will you let me be your new daddy?"

She pulled back and shook her head. "No."

Ethan felt stricken, her stern expression forever frozen in his memory. He looked at Ashley, who appeared just as surprised as he was.

"I don't need a new daddy," Natalie said. "I've already got a real good one." She smiled and added, "I just want you for my forever daddy."

Ethan felt the tears come to his eyes, but he didn't try to hide them. "I'd like that too, Natalie." He buried his face against her neck and let the tears come. He felt Ashley and Natalie both tighten their hold on him. They were his again. As they had always been.

God had made rivers in the desert—streams of joy running through his dry and weary heart.

EPILOGUE
May 15, 1930

*A*shley allowed Ethan to conduct her on a private tour of the newest of Fred Harvey's resort hotels. La Posada—the resting place—was a marvel of Spanish and Mediterranean flavoring. Surrounded by orchards and gardens, it rose up to look as though it truly had been there for years and years. Ashley almost expected to see some grand Spanish don stroll across the stone walkway to introduce himself and welcome them to his home.

"This wishing well," Ethan explained, taking her to an ornate wrought-iron creation, "was brought from Mexico."

"It's lovely," she said, completely impressed with the well and the expanse of lawn that surrounded it.

Ethan handed her a penny. "Make a wish."

She fingered the coin for a moment, then pressed it back into his hand. "I don't need to. They've all come true."

He held her gaze for a moment, then nodded and slipped the penny back into his pocket. "Guess we won't make too many walks back here."

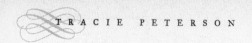

She laughed. "Well, at least not for a while."

They pressed on, strolling the grounds as though this were their own private hacienda.

"Miss Colter tells me she received an amusing telegram this morning," Ethan said as they moved at a leisurely pace toward the doors. "It came from one of the railway officials. It offered congratulations, then stated that they hoped the income exceeds the estimates as much as the building costs did."

Ashley laughed. "They certainly went lavish and lovely for this resort. I can just imagine the people who will come here and the happiness they'll find in such a setting. It's truly more than I could have ever imagined."

"You don't know the half of it," Ethan replied. "I'm just glad it's completed. I've never been involved in such an ambitious affair, but I wouldn't have traded the experience for all the world. Miss Colter does remarkable work. Her visions are most incredible. When she first brought me here and showed me this sunken piece of land, I couldn't begin to imagine her dream. Then she started hauling in dirt and the construction company came in to work, and before I knew it the walls were up and the stucco was spread and all the rooms were finished."

He led her inside and they toured the lobby before going upstairs to the ballroom. "It's over two thousand square feet," Ethan told her.

The blend of Spanish and colonial furnishings impressed Ashley. "I can just imagine the grand dances that will be given here." She turned and grinned. "The movie stars will come and bring their rich friends and throw elaborate parties. At least that's what Glenda told me. I only hope that it's successful, for the sake of the Harvey Company."

"I pray it is as well," Ethan replied. "Over a million dollars has gone into this creation. They need to find a way to make back that money." He frowned. "But given fears for the economy, I'm not entirely sure it's sensible to believe they'll ever see a profit."

"Is it really that bad, Ethan? You aren't worried, are you?" She looked into his eyes. "We still have the money Grandpa left me—and the house, of course."

"There's really no way to determine at this point how bad things will get. I know just in talking with the railroad officials there are a good many railroads that will probably die out because of the crash. Some officials say they were anticipating something like this, although I don't know how a person could ever predict a situation where certain stocks plunge from over a thousand dollars a share to less than ten dollars a share."

"All those dreams and hopes," Ashley said, shaking her head. "I think of people like my mother, who have lived in luxury all their lives and now face poverty."

"The very wealthy probably aren't facing poverty," Ethan said. "It's probably more a matter of degree. The degree of wealth they enjoy is less. But I would be willing to believe they're still enjoying wealth, nevertheless."

"And the poor get poorer," Ashley murmured.

"Exactly."

"Mama!" Natalie came running at breakneck speed. "Grandma—I mean Grandmother Murphy—is here."

Ashley looked at Ethan and felt her entire body tense. Swallowing hard, she couldn't think of a single thing to say. Ethan stepped in for her. "Tell your grand-mother we're on our way."

Natalie whirled around, the skirt of her lilac-colored dress ballooning out as always. "I'll tell her." She hurried from the ballroom and down the stairs—her shiny black shoes clattering all the way.

Ashley looked at the floor. She'd been expecting her mother's arrival, but now that the time had come, she felt like running in the opposite direction. "I hope she's changed. Her letters sound as though she's sincere in trying to be a better person. She still pries about my financial situation and about the sensibility of remaining in Winslow, but she doesn't badger and demean me."

"Then we must give her the benefit of the doubt, no?"

Ashley knew Ethan was right. Still, she had worked so hard to move away from the resentments of the past. Seeing her mother again might just force all those emotions to the foreground. "I don't want to become the woman I used to be," Ashley murmured. All around them people in various stages of animated conversation drifted past. "I didn't care about the hardness of my heart. It suited me well and kept me safe."

Ethan nodded. "I know. I used to feel the same way. But we aren't those people anymore. Just like we're not the kids we were when we first married. God's helped to bring healing to our family, and healing started with forgiveness. You forgave your mother for the past. You can't go taking it back now."

She smiled. "No, I don't suppose that would be right."

"Well, we certainly wouldn't want to have God doing

the same to us." He grinned and put his arm around her waist. "Now, come on. We'll go greet Mother Murphy and see what news there is of your brothers."

Ashley knew he was right and walked along in silence, praying for the strength to deal in kindness and love. She thought of the few letters she'd shared with her mother over the last months. Her mother's financial state had been weakened by the crash, but there had remained enough money to begin laying new foundations. No one knew what the future would bring. There were both threats of depression and promises of prosperity. Only God knew the truth, and that suited Ashley just fine.

Ethan led her to the main lobby, where solid walnut swing-back benches set a regal stage with their embroidered Moorish cushions. It was here that Ashley found her mother. Sitting in a rather queenly pose, with Natalie standing before her, Leticia looked for all the world like a ruling monarch. Natalie chattered away and surprisingly enough, it appeared that Leticia was actually listening.

When her mother glanced up, Ashley managed a smile. *Help me not to be afraid, Lord. Help me not to say the wrong thing.* Their new relationship was so fragile—like one of the beautiful blue-and-white Chinese Chippendale jars that stood just to her right. One wrong move could send everything crashing to the ground.

Her mother stood as they approached. Ashley grasped Natalie's shoulders, more to steady herself than to keep Natalie from going elsewhere. "Hello, Mother. Did you have a nice trip?"

"Indeed, I did. It was far more pleasant than the last

trip I made to Arizona. I was able to secure a private car. It seems one of your father's acquaintances holds a high position with the Santa Fe. Once he learned I was to make this trip, he offered his car to me."

"Grandmother said the room had velvet on the walls and that there were brocade chairs and very comfortable sofas," Natalie declared. "And she had all her meals right there at a beautiful oak table with candles and everything." It was clear to Ashley that Natalie was quite enthralled.

"Oh, and I met the most marvelous gentleman, and he tells me he knows you both," Leticia stated.

Ashley looked at Ethan then back at her mother. "Who is this man?"

"Marcus Greeley. Apparently his new book is well in the works. He's come here to interview Ethan at length. He was quite enthusiastic about it. Apparently your Ethan is quite the celebrity—a true hero of the Great War. Mr. Greeley said his story and your subsequent separation will make a . . . let's see, how did he put it? 'A feast of words.' "

"Truly?" Ashley looked at her husband. "Did you know about this?"

Ethan's face reddened. "I'd . . . ah . . . hoped he'd just forget about me." He gave a short, nervous laugh. "I'd just as soon be left to my own devices."

"But, Daddy, you're a hero and Mr. Greeley just wants to let everybody know." Natalie reached out and took hold of her father's hand. "I want everybody to know too."

Natalie's words meant a great deal to Ashley. Over the months since Natalie had first learned the truth about Ethan, she had grown closer to him and more trusting of their relationship. Now they were back to being the good friends they'd been when Ethan had first come to Winslow.

"I do hope you won't have to give this man all the details of your . . . ah . . . separation," Leticia Murphy said, looking to Ashley as if to convey her thoughts with a glance.

Ashley knew her mother was worried about her involvement—the lies she'd told Ethan about Ashley's death during the influenza epidemic. "I'm certain Ethan can think of a delicate way in which to relate the story."

Her mother grew notably more relaxed. "I'd appreciate that."

Ashley smiled, and to her surprise, her mother offered her a hint of one in return. Her face seemed softened somehow, yet she continued to bear herself in an elusive manner. Ashley thought her still the height of fashion in her two-piece dove-colored suit. The hat of matching color gave her a finishing touch of elegance.

"And what news have you brought of my brothers and their families?" Ashley asked, trying to sound light-hearted. In the months since her mother had returned to Baltimore, Ashley had received and written several letters to her brothers. They were all happy to be reunited, chiding her for letting them worry and for letting so many years pass without knowing of her whereabouts.

Her mother frowned. "They're struggling," she said matter-of-factly. "The bank isn't faring well at all. Mathias fears they might well close their doors. His wife, Victoria, is quite beside herself. Parker and Richard find that their legal services are more in demand than ever, but people haven't the financial means to pay. It's a difficult time, to be sure."

Ashley nodded. "We haven't felt the effects as much as you have back East, I'm sure. Ethan even tells me that the Santa Fe was on top of the situation and actually has come out of it in a fairly stable manner."

"It will take time," Leticia stated, sounding far less desperate than she had when she'd first learned of the crash. "But most things worth having are that way."

Ashley wondered if her mother meant to include their relationship in that statement. How strange it seemed that a mother and daughter should struggle so much to share their lives. Ashley could only pray and ask God to ease the tension between them.

"It was kind of you to let me stay at the house," Leticia said. "I arranged for someone to take my luggage there. I hope you don't mind."

Ashley smiled. "Not at all. I'm really glad you were able to come."

Leticia looked at her for a moment, then transferred her studying gaze to Ethan. "And when is this wedding to take place?"

"Sunday!" Natalie declared before either her mother or father could speak. "I get to be in the wedding with them. Isn't that wonderful, Grandmother? I have a new dress and even new shoes."

Leticia peered down her nose at the child momentarily, then offered a smile. "I imagine you'll be the prettiest girl in the room."

Natalie shook her head. "No, Mama will be. She has a new dress too, and she looks really pretty in it."

"Mother, I would imagine you're tired," Ashley interrupted, embarrassed by her daughter's comments. "Would you like me to take you back to the house? We have a car now."

"Gracious, no. I intend to tour this lovely facility. If Natalie would do the honors, I would like that very much."

Ashley was surprised that her mother was so openly friendly toward her granddaughter, but nevertheless she was glad to see it. "Natalie, would you like to show Grandmother around La Posada?"

"Sure." She went to her grandmother's side and took hold of her arm. "Come on, I'll show you my favorite room. It's the lunchroom and it has the most wonderful tiles for decoration. And there's a big hutch where they display beautiful plates. You'll really like it, Grandma."

Ashley was surprised her mother didn't correct Natalie's use of "Grandma." Instead, her mother seemed quite content to let Natalie lead the way, chattering about the contents of the room and why it was the best in the resort.

Just then, Mary Colter and Marcus Greeley walked into the room. There were several men with them—men whom Ashley didn't recognize. No doubt they were either reporters or railroad officials. Either way, the party looked very important.

"Mr. Reynolds," Mary declared as she approached them, "I don't suppose I shall ever get used to calling you that." She smiled and nodded at Ashley. "Mrs. Reynolds."

"Miss Colter, it's good to see you again. La Posada is

magnificent. I'm truly amazed at what you've done here."

"Not bad for a piece of ground that used to house the roundhouse, eh?" She smiled. "Now, my boy," she said, looking at Ethan, "will you be joining us at the Grand Canyon? We're making plans for an additional hotel, and I'd love to have you working on the project."

Ashley noted that everyone seemed eager for Ethan's answer. He put his arm around Ashley and finally spoke. "I'm quite content to remain here in Winslow. There's a great deal I wish to accomplish right here, but I thank you for the offer."

"Well, the good ones—the ones who give you little trouble and do as they're told," Mary said, looking at the men beside her, "those are the ones you always lose first."

"Ashley and I are being remarried on Sunday. We'd love for you to join us," he told the group.

"I'm sure we wouldn't miss it," Mary said. Then spying someone across the room, she took her entourage, minus Marcus Greeley, and moved off in pursuit.

"So I suppose you know why I'm here," Marcus said with a grin.

"I do. I'd rather hoped you'd forgotten me," Ethan replied.

"Are you kidding? Your story is going to be the selling feature of my book. Even women will want to read a copy of *Those Who Fought*. They'll be swooning with excitement over your reunion with your wife and child."

"*Those Who Fought*. Is that the title?" Ashley questioned, hoping to take the focus off of Ethan. She knew her husband was embarrassed at the prospect of his life being poured out onto the pages of a book.

"Yes, the publisher liked the sound of it and so did I. People are quite willing to hear the tales now. And, in spite of our growing isolationist mentality, I believe the general public desires to honor those who gave so much on the battlefield."

"I'm sure you're right," Ashley replied, looking at Ethan. "If you don't mind, however, Ethan and I need to see to my mother's luggage. She was having it delivered to the house, and I don't wish to leave it sitting on the street."

"Of course," Greeley answered. "I'll look forward to seeing you for the interview tomorrow."

Ethan nodded, even as Ashley pulled him away. "I thought perhaps you'd like a reprieve," she whispered as they walked from La Posada and crossed the street on their way home.

"Thank you. I still fail to see why he needs my story. There are so many others that need telling."

"Yes, but you have to admit, our story has so many twists and turns. There probably isn't another like it. You came back from the dead. How many men can lay claim to that?"

They paused and turned back to look at the hubbub surrounding the grand resort hotel. The grounds were full of people, and a general atmosphere of festivity lent a spirit of delight to those who attended. Even if their financial world had fallen apart, the partiers seemed quite good at masking their situation. From what Ashley could tell, these beautiful people were quite content.

To her surprise, Ethan took her into his arms right there on the side of Second Street. "Ethan!" Ashley declared. "What do you think you're doing?"

"I'm going to kiss my wife," he said softly.

"But it's broad daylight and we're standing in the middle of everything. Someone might see you."

Ethan chuckled. "Let them watch. I'm not ashamed. Are you?"

Ashley looked past his gold-rimmed glasses to the dark brown eyes that studied her so intently. "I will never be ashamed of you. I still can't believe you're really here. Sometimes when I wake up in the morning, I struggle to believe that everything that has happened isn't just some sort of dream."

"Well, soon you'll have the proof beside you in your bed."

Ashley felt her face grow hot and looked past Ethan to the hotel. "We'll have to stay there someday. You know, to just be spoiled and pampered. I happen to know that the Harvey Company takes very good care of you."

Ethan laughed. "I know that to be true as well. In fact, I'm entitled to a free stay. Part of the bonus for working on the project. We could spend our honeymoon there. You know, give the house over to your mother and Natalie and have some time just to ourselves." He pulled her closer to him.

"I think I'd like that," Ashley murmured, looking back at her husband. "Oh, Ethan, I'm so very happy. Please promise me we'll always be this happy."

Ethan frowned. "You know I can't do that. There will likely be hard times—we have to accept that. To do otherwise would be unrealistic and set up expectations that would only serve to disappoint us in the future."

"I know what you say is true," Ashley replied, "and I know God will be with us no matter what. But I wish I could have some guarantees."

Ethan laughed again. "Life doesn't come with guarantees, but it does come with choices. And I choose you, now and for all time. All I want from this point forward is to enjoy the years to come with you at my side."

He kissed her tenderly, leaving Ashley breathless. How could it be that after so many years of marriage, separation, and the belief that he was dead, Ashley could still find herself so quickly stirred by his touch?

They began walking up the street, heading for home. "By the way," Ethan said, reaching out to take hold of Ashley's hand, "how do you feel about having more children?"

Ashley was taken aback for only a moment. "I suppose," she said, "we shall need to buy more ponies."

Ethan stopped abruptly before laughing out loud and pulling her close. "And build a bigger house."

"Oh, we could get by for a time," she replied. "After all, it takes several months to bring a child into the world." She flushed and looked away. Having another baby was her secret desire. How funny that he should have brought up the matter.

"So you don't mind the idea of giving Natalie a brother or sister?" he asked seriously.

Ashley looked up and saw the longing in his expression. Perhaps he had feared she'd refuse such an idea. She immediately felt sad for the time he'd missed with Natalie. *No,* she thought, *I can't live in regret. I can't keep thinking, "if only."*

Ashley reached up and gently touched Ethan's

bearded cheek. "I would like very much to create new life in our new life together. I think it would be marvelous to have a whole houseful of children."

"So long as they're your children," Ethan whispered.

"So long as they're ours," Ashley corrected. "So long as they're ours."

––––––––

The remarriage of Ethan and Ashley Reynolds was a quiet and simple affair in spite of the large number of people who turned out at Faith Mission Church that Sunday. Natalie, again everyone's darling, did a combination of sliding and hopping down the aisle in her animated fashion. Her cream-colored gown gave her a rather angelic appearance, Ethan thought.

Then Ashley came forward in her salmon-colored dress that looked quite similar to the one she'd worn the first time they'd married. Ethan's breath caught deep in his throat. A radiant glow shone from her face. *How can it be that she's mine? How is it that I should be so blessed?*

The ceremony lasted only a few minutes. They exchanged their vows; then Ethan took up the wedding ring he'd first given Ashley so many years ago and replaced it on her finger with a pledge of all that was his. His worldly goods, his heart, his very life.

And then the affair was over and they were laughing and sharing well-wishes from all their friends and family. Ashley looked rather tired by the time they were ready to put the party behind them, but Natalie seemed as fresh as ever. She came to them, her eleven-year-old gangly frame seeming almost half a foot taller than when Ethan had first met her.

Natalie wrapped her arms around them both and laughed. "Now we're really a family and nothing will ever change that."

Ethan rubbed her curls. "But we've always been a family," he said, knowing a deeper joy than he'd ever thought possible.

Natalie looked up at him and then at Ashley. "Grandpa said that family was a matter of heart. That sometimes total strangers ended up being as close as family. You were a stranger at first, but I always liked you. Guess my heart knew you were my daddy."

Ethan felt his eyes mist ever so slightly. He looked at his wife and saw the tears in her eyes. "And my heart must have known you as well," he said in a voice barely audible. "But then, how could it not? For you are my heart." He looked back at Natalie, adding, "You are both my heart, and no matter the future . . . we are family."

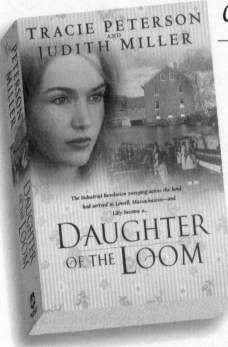
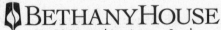